Also by Richard Slotkin

Abe

Richard Slotkin

A JOHN MACRAE / OWL BOOK

HENRY HOLT AND COMPANY

NEW YORK

Abe

A Novel

Henry Holt and Company, LLC
Publishers since 1866
115 West 18th Street
New York, New York 10011

Henry Holt® is a registered trademark of
Henry Holt and Company, LLC.

Library of Congress Cataloging-in-Publication Data
Slotkin, Richard, 1942–
Abe : a novel / Richard Slotkin.
          p.   cm.
ISBN 0-8050-6639-X
1. Lincoln, Abraham, 1809–1865—Childhood and youth Fiction.
I. Title.
PS3569.L695A64 2000   99-33514
813'.54—dc21   CIP

Henry Holt books are available for special
promotions and premiums. For details contact:
Director, Special Markets.

First published in hardcover in 2000
by Henry Holt and Company

First Owl Books Edition 2001

A John Macrae / Owl Book

Designed by Paula Russell Szafranski

Printed in the United States of America

3   5   7   9   10   8   6   4

For Iris, with love

Meanness of politics, low filibusterism, dog-men that have not shed their canine teeth; 'tis the work of the River, this Mississippi River that warps the men, warps the nations, they must all obey it, chop down its wood, kill the alligator, eat the deer, shoot the wolf, "follow the river," mind the boat, plant the Missouri-corn, cure, and save, and send down stream the wild foison harvest and tilth and wealth of the huge mud trough of the 2000 miles or 10 000 miles of river. How can they be high? How can they have a day's leisure for anything but the work of the river? . . . How can they be literary or grammatical?

—Ralph Waldo Emerson, *Journal* 1853

Acknowledgments

I want to thank Jack Macrae for his careful, tough, and intelligent editing, and Carl Brandt for his faith in my projects and skill in finding them friends. And many thanks to Iris for her sympathy and support, her patience in listening to long disquisitions on flatboats, log cabins, and the Tariff of Abominations—and her keen eye for literary and historical excess.

Contents

Abe

BOOK I:

My Home Is over Jordan

Chapter 1: "In Adam's Fall . . ."

Nolin Creek, Kentucky, December 1810

Mam leaned forward and he wriggled his small needful body into the bony curve of her. It was dark all over home except where the fire made orange tongues, and flickered the log walls. Mam opened her Book, lifted her knees to rest it—and her lap rose under him so Abe fell softly into her.

His mother's hand moved on the face of the page. *It was coming, very soon now.* Her long fingers, big-knuckled with flattened tips like tongues, moved on the face of the page, and the spots and whirls and flashes, black on white, flowed out of them (*very soon now*), black spots and squibbets, and just as it always, always happened the flow of spots made her voice come: the telling voice, reading voice, the voice he loved more than anything: the voice only for him, in the dark, licked all over with orange tongues, flowing . . .

. . . So his Mam, she put him in his leetl basket, that she made out o' bull-rushes. An' his warm swaddlin' all round him jest as he liked it. An' she set him to float down the river, down to where that princess was waitin' . . .

He already knew what came after but needed to hear her speak it, tell how Moses would grow up tall, and whup the man that whupped the children, change the serpents to sticks and break the sea so the children could get over, and home to their milk and honey . . .

Abe leaned back in the warm swaddling, the bony curve of Mam's body home-solid behind him, the river flowing under them all, dark, and him drifting with it, yearning towards a dim shore that almost had a shape.

Summer 1811

Abe and Mam sat on Two-Shoes, their mare.

Pap came out of the cabin with the rifle from over the fireplace. Never looked back. Never closed the door. Leftside the door was an empty hole, Pap had took the cabin's eye out. Pap's mouth was clinched. All their clothes and blankets, their food, Pap's long box of tools, Mam's cooking irons, the ax and plow-blade were piled in a two-wheeled cart Old Sam was hitched to. Pap said "Hup," and Sam started down the trail, moving off under the black trees with Sary running beside. Jack the Dog sprung up and padded quickstep after.

As the mare lurched to follow, Abe saw how black empty had come in through the open door and dead eye—inside where there was still the fireplace and Mam's chair and the table where they ate and her bed. But Pap never closed the door, so the dark got in, the empty. Now they'd never go home again, and nobody come ever to close the door against the dark, nor make the fire speak in tongues.

Sun splintered in the branches, they thumped on and on down the slot, black trees rising curling up and over him and falling away. Mam sang to him:

> "I'm jest a pore, way-farin' stranger
> A trav'lin' through this world of woe . . ."

But his home was gone behind them and the dark coming in through the door Pap never closed. *Pap should have broke the table, like Moses. Then if the dark got in, it couldn't stay.*

His body jerked as he fell in dreams—Mam gripped him, and there he was again. It was night. Overhead a black river of sky ran between banks of trees, stars sparking on riffles of cloud. Pap stood in the door of a cabin holding the buckskin curtain aside so Sary could scoot in. She lit a rush dip, the empty window lit alongside the door. But this one was on the wrong side.

"Home, Abe," his Mam said.

It was the first time ever he knew her wrong. He twisted himself, trying to see her face.

She put her hand under his chin and he pressed his whole face down into her palm, and felt the flat warm smooth power of that hand closing over him eyes nose and mouth. He breathed her. Even if this wasn't home, at least she was.

Knob Creek, Kentucky, April 1815

They were plowing the south field. Pap *geed* and *hawed* Old Sam round the stumps, leaning on the plow-handles to drive the blade down the furrow. The earth broke and curled away to either side, loose dirt like dry water between Abe's toes, and a little brown smoke of dust drifted away. Jack the Dog trotted after Abe—a stumpy fice, haired over wild as a porky-pine, pink tongue lolling.

At the top of the field was a steep brushy bank, broken by ravines that cut back into rising ground. There were higher hills back of that, with rocky bald patches, which Pap called "the Knobs." Broad snake-tracks ran down out of the breaks and into the unplowed half of the field.

Clouds kept blowing by overhead, moving towards the Knobs, grumbling. Pap's face was knuckled, he kept looking up at the clouds blowing over towards the hills.

Then Jack said "Uf!" His ears pricked. He shot off sudden, pulled up short, and begun barking into the gap in the bank. Abe ran to the break and looked in. The cleft slanted back between high rough walls. The bottom was raw and full of round stones.

"Abe!" Pap's voice cracked, Abe's heart bolted and snubbed— Jack shut up barking, dropped his tail and turned his head. They both looked down the slope to where Pap had checked the horse. "Abe! You stay out them gullies now!"

Abe ran back down the slope, "What's gullies, Pap?"

"You stay *out* them gullies. There's painters and wolves. Mind now."

The high clouds blew by overhead, towards the gullies and over past them, up towards the high Knobs beyond. Muttering.

Pap looked up at the clouds, ugly, and said to the horse: "Blowin' right over my land. Drop ever' last bit o' rain up in the hills."

"Pap? Is it the rain makes them gullies?"

Pap looked down at him. He worked his mouth a little and Abe asked himself, *What was goin' to come out?* But nothing did. Pap just shook his head, like Abe was too many for him.

Up in the loft under the roof-tree Abe and Sary wrassled their blankets around to get well covered, dry shucks and leaves rustling in the ticks. This early in planting season night chill seeped through the shakes.

Down below Mam was banking the fire, Pap shuttering the window. Mam said: "They have built a school on Cumberland Road. I want Abe and Sary to go."

In the loft Sary put her warm lips in Abe's ear and whispered, *They will larn us books and cipherin'!*

Shhh, if Pap lets us.

Pap slammed the bar down across the door. "We got a crop to put in the ground—sech as it is! If could get my rights . . ."

Mam said softly, "Maybe your brother Mordecai will see his way—" Pap's hard look must have stopped her.

Pap snorted, "I like the idea of a *Hanks* tellin' *me* what kin owes kin."

Then Mam had her quiet. Abe and Sary waited, wondering what she would get for it.

Finally: "I am goin' to read the children their *good*-night," she said. Pap said *Um.* Abe and Sary rustled themselves closer into their blankets so as not to be caught listening.

Mam came up the loft. Abe made room for her, dry leaves crunched in his bed-tick. First thing she said was, "Now you tell me 'bout them gullies you saw, Abe. What do *you* think made them gullies?" When he told her about the rain in the hills she said My, that was a smart thing for him to figure out. He couldn't see, but he knew she was smiling at him; could see clear as dreaming her long face, the clear straight-looking eyes a little drooped at the corners, deep-set under strong black brows, the sad planes of her face running down from sharp cheekbones—and how when she smiled at him the sad lines broke and lifted and her whole face shined.

"I think I'll read you Joseph tonight," she said. "Joseph was a right smart little boy, jest like you, Abe."

It was too close under the roof for her to hold him on her lap, too dark for him to see the black dots and whirls spinning out under her fingers. But it was no matter, Abe could picture her just as clear as soon as she opened the Book and begun to read.

She read him how Joseph was the best-loved son of Jacob, who was one of the Fathers of the Children of Isril. The other Children was Joseph's twelve brothers, and the brothers was angry 'cause their Pappy liked Joseph best. *So they took an' throwed him in a pit—a pit like you dig to trap a critter in. An' some nigger-traders come by, an' his brothers—they sold Joseph down into Egypt . . .*

"Mammy," said Abe, "what's niggers?"

"Niggers is slaves, honey," she said.

Slaves means whupping.

"They sold their brother to slave for a stranger down in the land of Egypt. Where he'd jest live a no-account life, never have nothin' to hisself—where they'd never have to set eyes on him again."

Abe couldn't see in the dark. He put out his hand and touched her. Couldn't hardly talk. "Why was they so mean to him, Mammy?"

She wasn't looking at the Book. "I don't know. I don't know what makes a man . . . what makes folks as mean as they *can* be. If you got somethin' they want . . . But sometimes the meanest folks can *be* is ag'in them that ain't got a thing."

"They sent him where nobody'd ever see him no more!" Abe remembered the door swinging open, the dark at home now where

Mam used to hold him reading among the orange tongues, *then the empty come inside the cabin and et it up.*

Mam reached over and patted his head. "Shhh," she said. "Now don't you know? Book says, there can't a sparrow fall but the Lord will see it. Mean as folks can be, there's a power to make things right. The Lord, he give Joseph that power. That's why the Lord made him so *smart*, don't you see? Now you hesh, and let me tell you what happened to that Joseph . . ."

. . . who become a servant in the house of Fayro. And one night a dream come to Joseph—a providence dream, sent by the Lord for a warning. So next morning Joseph rose up and went to Fayro . . .

Suddenly, as sharp and clear as a dream, Abe saw *exactly* what Joseph would have seen—the gullies, the snake-tracks running into the unplowed ground—and he knew what Joseph would have told Fayro: "He told him the rain was comin'," Abe whispered, "down from the hills and through them gullies, and it's a-goin' to wash his corn right out the ground."

Then his throat closed. He knew he ought to warn Pap, like Joseph warned Fayro. But Pap was a hard man to tell things to, he was more like the Fayro Moses had to deal with, you didn't want to tell *him* anything without a good big stick in your hand.

November 1815

The schoolroom was not much bigger than the cabin, and had only one window. A dozen children were ranged along three plank benches, Abe the youngest, on up to the Simms boy, who was fifteen—his linsey shirt splotched orange from tobacco-spit. Sary the biggest girl of three, all sitting on the front bench and no boys next to.

Abe felt lucky to be there. Mam had had to work on Pap from planting through harvest before he gave his word they could go. He had a grudge on book-learning.

Schoolmaster Riney sat behind a pinewood table. Stacked on it were small piles of books—Mr. Riney's precious *Preceptors*, his His-

tories and Geographies, his Spellers and Arithmetickers. Pegged to
the log wall behind him were a pair of broad planks, planed smooth
and painted black, and hung between them a bag of gypsum rocks
to write with.

Mr. Riney had wrote things on the right-hand board, neat figures
of curves and sharp angles, lined up regular: a big one next to a
small. The schoolmaster was a little man, with sandy hair sprouting
all which ways, a standing collar, boiled shirt, and black frock coat.
He took a pointing stick in his hand and tapped it on the first row of
figures drawn on the board. "We will have our alphabet! All at once,
each letter as I point to it!" He tapped the first figure, and almost
everybody said:

"Ay!" Then: "Bee!" Then "Cee," and "Dee," and on down the figures, tap, tap, tap and Abe never saw how they knew what to say. So
he begun to puzzle the figures: they were all different and every one
a different sound. He was puzzling so hard he missed what, suddenly, everyone was tee-heeing about, till the Master said, "The new
boy—Abraham."

Abe looked up and met his eyes: sharp black points like iron nail-
heads they were.

"Abraham, can you say your letters?"

"No sir." He paused. "Don't know which of 'em is mine."

The tee-heeing and haw-hawing just about buried him.

The Master rapped hard for silence and got it. He smiled at Abe.
Now he heard the boy speak, he realized the lad was no more than
six or seven—from the size of him, the long wrists and ankles showing beyond shirt and trouser cuffs, he had guessed him to be ten or
eleven. So he gentled his voice: "They are all of them yours, Abraham. But shall I show you the ones that are yours *particularly*?"

The boy's white-blue eyes widened and he leaned forward in a
way that was almost wolflike; his hands rose and the fingers spread
a little as if some energy were filling and lifting him. It almost
seemed as if he would spring and snatch the proffered gift from the
Master's mouth.

Mr. Riney turned to the left-hand board. "Abe," he said. Then he
said "Ay, Bee, Ee," and as he said each wrote the figure on the board.

He turned and fixed his eyes on the boy—"*Abe*"—then tapped and carefully sounded the letters in turn, "Ayyy-b-' " with a wee breath-stop when he touched the "E."

The Master made a gesture with his left hand, for Abe to stand, and as the Master pointed again to each letter Abe said: "Ayyy-b-uh . . . Ayyy-b-uh."

"And the letters?"

"Ay," said Abe, "Bee. Ee. But how come it don't make Aybee?"

Tee-hee and haw-haw didn't bother him. It might have been him and the Master alone.

The Master smiled. "Some of the letters are special—the vowels. You've got two in your name." He tapped the board: "Ay can sound 'ay' as in *Abe*, or 'ah' as in *ax*," and he turned and wrote on the board AX. "Ay. Ecks." Then he tapped the E. "It's this 'E' that's the dandy: because sometimes she sounds 'ee,' like in *cheese*, and sometimes she sounds 'eh' like in *set*—set *down* there Andrew Simms! And sometimes"—he grinned around at them—"sometimes she has no sound at all. And when she does *that*," he said triumphantly, "when she is silent, she changes the sound of A from 'ah' "—he tapped AX—"to"—tapping ABE—" 'ay'! Do you see?" He slapped his pointer on each word in turn, and as he did Abe answered, louder every time: "Abe! Ax! Abe! Ax! Abe! . . ."

. . . He sang them all the way home through the woods, *Abe! Ax! Abe! Ax!* over and over, like the echo-bang of Pap's ax-work off in the trees. Those were *his* letters, that showed him the read of *his* name.

Out in the schoolyard at recess, Abe was writing his letters in the ground with a stick—ABE AX—when it come to him: he needed three letters to make "Abe." When Mam signed *her* name, she only needed one. He'd seen her do it when she signed him up for the school. He scratched her mark in the ground and said, "How come she only writes X?"

Andrew Simms, fifteen years old, was sitting nearby peeling a stick with his knife: "You talkin' to me?"

Well he hadn't been, but Abe wouldn't answer up if he took that tone.

Simms got up, walked over, and looked down at what Abe had written in the ground. "I heared you. You said, 'How come she only writes X?' " He poked his chin at Abe daring him to answer.

Abe had to keep his eyes on Simms, but he felt the schoolyard gather around them. Suddenly Sary was pulling at his arm. She wasn't any higher than his chest but was two years older, Mam and Pap told her to take care of her "little" brother. "You leave Abe be," she told Simms, "he ain't a-botherin' you."

"Well what's he doin' then?"

Don't say! But Sary was a girl and a girl must answer—as if *explaining* could make a thing right. "He's puzzlin' his letters is all!" Her apple cheeks were flushed. There was a chance she might start blubbering!

Simms sneered, "Oh yes? Well what's so all-mighty *puzzlin'*?" Inside he was all a-glee. Now Abe had to keep shet or else back his sister: if he did the one Simms could call him pucker-ass, and if the other Simms would whup him.

And Abe knew it. He ought to have *gone for* Simms right off, because there wasn't but one way such a thing could end. But his sister hanging on his arm distracted him—so he found himself doing the worst thing of all: explaining how he was just trying to figure how come his Mam only needed the one letter X to write her name.

Simms bugged out his eyes. "Lincoln, if you ain't a prize eejit! Your Mam signs an X 'cause she can't read!"

Abe ripped his arm out of Sary's grip and balled his fist at Simms. "You swaller that or I'll make you!" Simms turned his head and grinned victoriously at the boys ganged up behind him . . .

. . . and quicker than thinking Abe went for him, head down arms swinging, caught Simms flush and knocked him sprawling and pounced on him flailing with his long bony arms and knuckly fists. Simms was down before he knew it was a fight, breath gone and no time to catch it. They rolled in the dust, everyone yelling, Abe wanted to pound Simms's face but couldn't get at it.

For Simms it was like fighting a giant spider or clawing out of bramble-vines. Abe wasn't half his age and was built like a bean-pole but he also was only half a head shorter and his arms longer. Simms couldn't get loose, he was on his back and a black wave of terror and shame told him he was whupped by a seven-year brat . . .

While Abe was plunged headfirst in blood and fire, his eyes burning, his body a-swim in it, every part of him alive, punching grappling kicking, never-ever had he felt so much power in himself, clawing and grappling with arms and legs like a dog tearing into a shoat . . .

A blast of sudden ice-wet paralyzed him—a bucket of water, and Master Riney's hand jerking him up by the scruff of his shirt. The water drenched the red fire and strength out of his arms and legs but the last of it still burned in his head and he yelled, "She can too read!"

He got willow-switched on his rump and spent that afternoon sitting sore-butt in the corner with his back to the lesson. But no *shame* in that. Even Master Riney knew you *had* to fight, though you weren't supposed to. And he had to switch you for it regardless: that was the rules. *At least I whupped Simms.* He'd heard the boys talking after: *That Lincoln, he sure is a wildcat!* But at the same time he *wasn't* sure he'd whupped. What Simms said about his Mam stayed said.

But afterwards Mr. Riney told Abe, quiet so no one else heard: "So your Ma can read. If you'll mind *me*, I'll teach *you* how: then you can read to *her*, if you like."

Well, he made a go of it. Found pieces he knew she'd like, Bible pieces, and read them to her. But somehow his reading was always *small* next to hers. He'd puzzle out some little piece of Joseph or Moses, hauling the words in slow, and straining to lay them out one after another the right way, and when he was done he'd only *just* got Moses born or Joseph sold. Whereas when Mam read those stories they just run and flowed and spread out, they were as much about you and your doings as they were about Moses and Joseph and the rest.

So he picked out things to read that would get *her* started, Bible pieces from the *Preceptor* at first, then new things from the other books Mr. Riney let him read in. This was how he came to learn about Adam and the apple tree.

It started with a verse from his Speller that he didn't understand: "In Adam's fall, we sinn'd all." Adam was Bible, so it was odd in the first place to find him in the Speller. And there was no making out how Adam's falling was *Abe's* fault. To Abe's surprise, Mam was upset by his question. "Maybe I *have* give you the Gospel too easy a way!"

Then she told him: How Adam was the first man God made, and put him in the Garden with all good things, and a wife, only he must not eat the fruit of a certain tree, for it would give him knowledge. And how the serpent tempted Eve and made her eat the apple; and she liked it and give Adam some (which showed she warn't *close*), and Adam et, and *he* liked it. Then how the Lord come down angry, burnt out the Garden, drove the two out into the woods, nekkid and punished, the man to earn bread by his sweat, the woman to bear children in pains, and all of them now and again to get bit by serpents.

Well what was it to do with him?

Mam took a breath, and explained: How all people born was children of the children of Adam, blood of his blood. And the curse come down on them too, in their blood, same as if it was them et the apple that was forbid: sweat, and pain, and bit by serpents.

Abe puzzled that over. It didn't set right. It was all right for Mr. Riney to punish him for fighting Simms: whupping gets whupping. But if he'd birched Abe *afore* he done it—or birched Sary just for being Abe's sister . . .

But when Abe said that Mam got scared. Not angry, which would have been bad enough, but afraid. "Shush now, honey! Don't say another word." Then: "I know," she said soft, "I know it seems hard. But we're in the hands o' the Lord. It's His world. There can't *anything* come that ain't accordin' to His will."

So he didn't ask her any more. But if the Lord didn't want his tree bothered with, why didn't he just give Adam a different spirit? or a different wife? Why not just keep the serpents out of it? How can you blame someone when you yourself have fixed it so he is bound to do a wrong thing? It seemed like meanness.

February 1816

On a cold day in deep winter, as he was starting for school, Mam gave him a dried apple out of their store. "Sister Cam'ell 'minded me, Abe—last week was your birthday!" Her eyes were a little sad, though she still smiled for him. "I lost track o' days since we don't go to Meetin' . . ."

They'd stopped on account of Pap getting into an argument with the Preacher about niggers. Pap said the way he larned Bible, a man was to earn his bread in the sweat of his *own* brow not some nigger's, and the Preacher said . . . but it didn't matter what the Preacher said. Pap's own father had quit Virginny on account it was pizened with the Thing, and Pap was danged if he'd put up with It in Knob Crick. Abe didn't mind not going to Meeting, but it made Mam sorrowful.

At school Mr. Riney asked them whose birthday did they think it was. The taste of dried apple was in his mouth, so without thinking he said, "Mine!"—and got tee-heed and haw-hawed to a fare-thee-well, which made him mad so he said, "It is *too*—last week, anyways!" Mr. Riney made him hush.

Whose birthday it *was*, was George Washington's. "In Virginia," said Mr. Riney, "this day is a holiday, with the day of our nation's independence and the day of our Lord's birth." Then he told them about the Great Washington: there was a lot of it, some read out of a book and some Mr. Riney had got by heart. How when he wasn't but a boy Washington was marked for great things, by his good character and how he told the truth. How one time, in his father's garden, he cut down a kind of tree that was forbid to him, even to eat of its fruit.

But Washington—the Great Washington—wasn't blamed for it

like Adam, and all the rest of us after him! *No, because he didn't eat no fruit, but cut the thing down with his ax and stood up bold as . . .*

But now the story was changing again, Washington was growing tall and strong, and he went out like Moses to burn the bushes of the wilderness—when suddenly Britishers come across the ocean, "to take away our liberties and make us slaves . . ."

. . . which is niggers: Britishers making us niggers like the brothers done Joseph and the Egypts done the Children of Isril, so if anyone was Moses this time it was . . .

"Washington took command of the American armies, fought the Britishers and . . ."

Washington! Washington swinging his ax two-handed, driving the Britishers and their chariots into the ocean and breaking the sea on them . . .

"But his work was not finished. It was Washington, and the Founding Fathers, who gave us our Constitution, our Republican Form of Government . . ."

. . . which was the Ten Commandments! and brung them down the burning mountain to the people—only this time they wasn't Isril they was

". . . the United States of America!"

. . . And if that was so, they were in the Promised Land right now! Right here in Knob Crick Kentucky the United States America the World! And if that was so, then . . .

But after Washington United the States there come trouble amongst the people: some wanted to bust up the nation and leave on account of . . .

Abe, figuring furiously, nodded as he squared this difficulty with Moses's Gold Calf troubles.

But no! The Americans' trouble was *still* slavery: somehow the Americans hadn't left their slavery behind in Egypt or wherever, but had took it along with them—or anyway *half* of them did. So the half that was free said to let 'em all go, but the first lot said well we'll just break the Meeting if we can't get our rights . . .

"Abraham," said Mr. Riney, "do you have a question?"

Abe discovered he had stood up out of his place. But Mr. Riney looked friendly so he spoke: "I thought they come . . . I thought he brung them to Promise Land to git shet of slav'ry. Wasn't that why he drownded the Britishers?" He never heard the tee-hee and haw-haw, his eyes fixed hard on Mr. Riney's face.

Who got the heart of the question, although there was something mixed up about the asking Riney couldn't see how to untangle. But that was no never-mind: this was the hard question, the one you couldn't ever get away from in this country, no matter that better and wiser men had done their best to put it where it could do no harm.

So he told Abe the difference lay in the *nature* of the people involved. That what the Britishers wanted for slaves was freeborn people like ourselves, that had the right to *be* free by the *nature* of what the Lord made them. But the slaves that were owned by the people of the United States—owned by Washington himself!—they were of the Ethiopian race, "This people among them, of strange blood, with whom it was forbidden to mingle . . ."

"Niggers!" yelled Simms. "You mean they's jest niggers!"

"Simms!" Mr. Riney rapped. "I won't have you talking low in this school!"

Abe caught, on the fly, the useful information that it was low to say *niggers*.

Mr. Riney said the slaves of the United States, which it *wasn't* wrong to hold, was Eth'opians, children of "that unfortunate race of Ham," condemned forever to be hewers of wood and drawers of water, servants to their brothers . . .

But there was that same problem again, about Adam and his children. For if the "Unfortunate Race" never done it, then why should they be punished for it by becoming niggers? And how could a thing that was wrong for one man to do be right when another man done it?

Well, Mr. Riney says because some is born to it: which was like what Mam said about Adam's fall. Yet Abe and Sary, and Pap and Mam too, done their share and more of chopping wood and hauling water—did that make them niggers? did they catch the curse of Ham on top of Adam's?

The more he thought the more tangled it become. Now he understood why Pap was down on niggers: for soon as That Unfortunate Race showed up everything turned backside front, Washington and the Americans start acting like Egyptians—and doing it in the Promise Land where they themselves run to get free, so if it warn't for the honey and milk you probably after a while couldn't have told it from Egypt the Old World or even Virg . . .

"Abe?"

Master Riney was asking him a question. Abe was embarrassed. Somehow his too-fast thinking had stood him up out of his place again.

"Abe," said Mr. Riney, "did you want to tell us what Washington did—when he saw the factions were set on breaking up the Union of the States?"

Abe searched back in his mind: all the while he had been thinking so hard about Moses and Washington and the Unfortunate Race, Mr. Riney had gone on talking, so now Abe reached back to try and find what it was he'd been saying, but it kept slipping through like water between his fingers: so he reached back more and thought about what *kind* of man Washington was, and what he *would* do—

"*He took the law in his hands, and broke the tables on their heads!*"

Spring 1816

Well, it wasn't all *that* funny, not as funny as Simms and the rest made out. Bible and history weren't all that different, no more so than father and son. If Washington wasn't *exactly* Moses, they were like enough that it ought to *signify* something. But before Abe could work that notion up to a question the season turned, and Pap took him out of school to help with planting. All the time they were plowing and dropping seed, Abe's head was pestered with questions that swarmed like skeeters and itched him frantic—and nothing to scratch himself on but Pap, which was always risky.

He waited till Pap got seed in the ground, and so was in a peaceful mood. Then, one afternoon when he'd helped Pap split oak billets for a barrel, he asked him: "Pap, if it was Moses discovered Isril, and Columbus discovered America, and Dan'l Boone discovered Kentuck, then was it you discovered Knob Crick?"

Pap snorted in a kind of laughing way and said, "Well I sure run the lines of this claim."

"Then how come we ain't wrote down in the book that way?"

"It's wrote down at the Land Office. That's all the writin' down it wants." He squinted at Abe: "What book is it you're worryin' at?"

No way round it now! "The one at school."

Pap squinted. "I reckon there's a lot ain't in that book." He was satisfied to be displeased. "There was Lincolns come over the mountains *with* Dan'l Boone. Your Grandpa Abraham, that you're named after, he come."

"Did he discover Kentuck too?"

"Well, if he didn't *discover* it, he come jest after. Sold out a seven-hunderd-acre farm in Virginny and follered Boone and Harrod over the mountains."

"Why'd he sell out?"

"Cause it's better land in Kentuck. And easy terms. Back then she warn't so crowded up with Virginians, lawyers, and niggers that a man must go to law to hold his claim."

"Pap! Did *you* come along with Dan'l Boone and them . . . ?"

"No," said Pap. "I was born this side the mountains. Never been in Virginny in my life." He spat against the stack of barrel-staves. "Never goin', neither. But your Uncles Mordecai and Josiah come with him. Josiah jest a baby when they first come, and Mordecai warn't no older'n what you be." He looked at Abe thoughtfully. "You even favor him some around the eyes." Pap looked far off, his eyes searching although his voice kept the practiced singsong of this story he had told often enough at the tavern: "Yep: sold out and come to Kentuck—ever'thing they owned in two wagons. Pa cleared the land, Mordecai helpin'. Claimed three big farms—six hunderd acres, and four hunderd and two hunderd." Something *turned* in Pap, he looked like he had bit something bitter. "Prob'ly meant to give one to each son. But he was killed afore he got the chance."

"Who was it killed him, Pap? The lawyers, the niggers, or the Injuns?"

Pap blinked and looked at Abe, then threw back his head and

laughed fit to bust. Abe didn't see what was funny, though he was glad for Pap's good mood. Pap rumpled Abe's bristly black hair: "Injuns, niggers, or lawyers! I will remember *that*!" He would tell it next time he was to Elizabethtown, at Bush's Ordinary. He looked at his son, happy and a little grateful. He begun to tell his tale a little showy, like it was to please the men at the tavern.

"I warn't even your age," he said. "I was out front o' the cabin, jest a baby playin' with some truck or other my Ma give me, watchin' Pa split rails—when all a sudden, *pow!* goes a musket-shot, then a sound like an ax chunkin' in soft wood. I look up, don't see my Pappy. Don't see nothin', tall grass in my face. So I git up on my legs, go over where Pappy is lyin' lookin' up out the grass, nothin' in his eyes but the shine of the sky. There was a red gush down the front of his shirt, I never knowed it was his blood—never knowed to be scairt, but set down next to him to figger what happened.

"Then I hear somethin' snakin' through the grass, rustlin' closer and closer.

"All a sudden—a face pops out not ten feet from me! I near jumped out my skin, never see sech a face in my life: black painted to the eyes and blood-red above, top of his head peeled except a roach of gummed-up hair. Big silver medal on a chain 'round his neck. Britishers, up at Detroit, they used to give Injuns medals for Kentucky scalps.

"And then he seen me!

"His eyes, they kind o' *bulged*. He showed his *teeth*. Then he crouched up, knife in his right hand musket in his left, he come for me with a rush. I was froze, my eyes jest froze to that big silver medal swingin' 'cross the middle of his chest, and jest then *CRACK!*" Abe jumped as Pap banged his hands together.

Pap grinned: "Injun stands up stark—like he run into a wall—then topples like cut timber, *bang*, right in front of me. Knife in his hand warn't no further than I am from you."

Pap was pleased with his effect: Abe was spellbound, mouth open. "What done it, Pap?"

"Well—it was your Uncle Mordecai." Pap made a wry face. "He ain't much of a brother and never was, but he's a cool hand with a rifle. He warn't but sixteen then, in the cabin when he heared the shot. Quicker'n you could think he snatched Pa's long rifle and took his stand inside the door. Here come the Injun, crawlin' out the woods. But where Mordecai stands he can't get a bead on him. Knows he won't get but one shot, so he waits. Then the Injun makes his rush, Mordecai catches the swing of that silver bangle, and fast as lookin' he pulls the trigger—*crack!* Drills the Injun clean through the heart."

Abe could *see* it: *Uncle Mordecai kilt that Injun dead. And Pap says I got his eye.* He raised his dream rifle and popped that Injun plumb through his big silver medal. The rifle smoke drifted over the grass. The echo of the gunshot faded.

Chapter 2: **Uncle Mordecai**

Summer 1816

The ears were cut and they were stripping the husks. Later they would plane the kernels for Mam to pound to meal in the samp-mortar, or steep in ash-water for hominy. Husks and cobs for the hogs.

Two men rode into the clearing, trotting their dark chestnut horses right up to the front of the cabin. The sun was low behind them so you had to shade your eyes to see. Mam stood up slow, the corn-ears falling from her lap. Sary hid behind her. Pap stood in the cabin door, his right hand out of sight—resting (Abe knew) on the long rifle.

The first man sat up tall looking down at the Lincolns. He wore a dove-gray swallowtail coat, boiled shirt with black necktie, and gleaming black boots.

The second man was the same chestnut color as his horse.

"I suppose you are Thomas Lincoln," said the man.

Pap said nothing.

"My name is Prescott Oakes," said gray-coat. "I reside at

Elizabethtown, and have the honor to serve as attorney at law to the Middleton heirs, of Philadelphia, Pennsylvania."

Pap cleared his throat. His eyes flicked to the horse-colored man and back. "Well, I am Thomas Lincoln."

"I see there is to be none of your famous Kentucky hospitality," said Oakes. He reached inside his coat and brought out a hand of papers. He gestured them towards Pap.

Pap stood rooted in the door.

The horse-colored man studied on the back of Oakes's gray coat. He had a short bell-mouth gun handy in a holster slung from his saddle.

"You boy!" snapped Oakes. The horse-colored man stiffened and Abe startled—saw the gray sleeve extended, a black skin-tight glove holding out the hand of papers. "Give these to your pappy."

Everyone stayed froze. It was too still to breathe. Abe couldn't stand it: he ran up, snatched the papers, and ran to Pap. Pap looked down at him—something was twisting his face from the inside. He whispered harshly, "Did *I* tell you to take them papers?"

Abe stood clutching the papers. He had done an awful thing.

"Read them or not," said Oakes, "or get someone to read them to you. They are a notice of ejectment in due form, signed by the Honorable Judge Herron of the Circuit Court."

Pap's eyes showed whites, just a flash, then he grimmed up again. "Paper?" he said bitterly. "Think some *paper* can put me off my land?"

The gray man puffed air through his nose—a kind of silent laugh. "You bought this place of a man that showed you paper. Paper giveth, and paper taketh away." He straightened. "If you wish to go to law, we will meet at Elizabethtown Circuit in a month's time."

"Wait!" said Pap. His voice was fierce but there was a crack in it. "Jest hold up there," he said pleading. "Haygood showed me registered title when I bought of him. I marked the bounds myself, and registered at the Land Office. I got *good* terms—and I *been* payin'."

The lawyer (for Abe realized that was what he was, and by the sound of him a Virginian too, which meant that the horse-colored man must be . . .) the lawyer checked his horse and looked down at them from his high seat. "I'll argue the case here, Lincoln, if it will spare us the day in court. Haygood could have sold for a dollar and still diddled you. The property wasn't his to sell. All this land around here—ten thousand acres—the State of Virginia gave it in grant to the Middletons for services rendered, back when Kentucky was Virginia's western counties. Haygoods and What-nots squatted on the land, and those government boobies didn't know better than to register their claims for pre-emption."

The lawyer's lips twisted into a kind of grin. "But even if Haygood had a show of title—when you registered, you let them write you down *Linkhorn*."

"I ain't to blame for how another man writes me down."

The lawyer looked false pity at him. "Next time learn to do it yourself." He flipped his hand in good-bye, wheeled his horse, and kneed it to a spanking trot, and the horse-colored man turned and followed after.

"Lawyers," said Pap, confirming that the worst had come to them now, *lawyers Virginians and niggers* all three at once.

Mam and Pap wrangled till dark, Pap angry, Mam persuading. "Can't let 'em take me to law," said Pap—he kept coming back to that, but never said why. Maybe at law the Virginians lawyers and niggers would swarm Pap and scalp him. The strange awfulness of the lawyer's visit was wearing them out, they couldn't stop talking about it. Somehow that piece of paper was going to drive them out of their home. *If only he hadn't run up and took it!* But just like with Simms and George Washington, he jumped without thinking first.

Mam said, "Ask your brother for advice. He will spare us that. If we can't figure a way, they will drive us off."

Pap's shoulders slumped. "There's nobody I trust to write him a letter."

Mam gestured towards Abe—who looked up from the papers to find them both looking at him silently. She smiled at him, real happy: "Tell Abe what you want to say, and he will spell it out good as anyone."

Mordickie Lincoln
Lexing Town, Kentucke

Dere Bruther,
I rite in hopes you air well. I am in sum trubles abowt
my tittles for land, and . . .

at the end of which Pap scratched *Thos Lincoln.*

They let Abe read the letter from Uncle Mordecai when it came three weeks later, telling his "Dear Brother Thomas" that he would be in Elizabethtown on the first of September and pleased to meet with him at Bush's Ordinary. It was only right Abe should go along, said Mam, for hadn't he wrote down the letter? Even Pap had to say that was so.

So Abe was to meet at last his Uncle Mordecai, who was famous in history with Boone and Washington. Pap said he had the same eyes as his Uncle—what would his own eyes look like on a man famous in history?

Elizabethtown, September 1816

Bush's Ordinary was a big two-story tavern built of thick maple logs, with smaller log and clapboard structures slapped onto its back and sides. The whole first floor was an open great-room, a big stone fireplace at one end. The kitchen was out back, and smells of frying meat, burnt bread, and coffee drifted in amongst the room's own rank smell of raw whiskey, mildew, the sweated unwashed bodies of thirty men, tobacco burnt and spat.

Supper was greens, corn dodger, and fat-meat fried together in lard, and a good deal of salt in it. They had small-beer to drink, for Pap would not touch whiskey, nor suffer Abe to touch it. Yet the other men drunk a-plenty—drovers and wagoners and such, they came in and went out at all times while the eating was going on.

A long, bony man came in, squinted at them, then grinned and came over. He was sallow-complected with lank hair hanging about his face, which was deeply lined and had five-day bristles on it.

(Pap had clean-shaved for town.) His grin had an eye-tooth missing. He stuck out his hand and said, "Tom Lincoln!"

Pap hesitated, then stuck out his hand and said, "Uncle Thomas,"
and the man sat down across the board.

"I'm Abe," said Abe and Pap cuffed the back of his head.

"*Hesh* till you're spoke to."

The older man gave Abe his gap-tooth grin. "Why Abe, I'm your
Mam's Uncle Tom Sparrow."

Pap and Uncle Sparrow talked some: Uncle real friendly, smiling
and shaking his head, even slapping the table if Pap come near saying a good thing—which Pap didn't hardly rise to, but talked small,
his mouth pursed up like giving words was losing money. Maybe
Pap didn't like Uncle drinking whiskey, which give him a kind of
sick-sweet smell. And he'd drib some out the side of his mouth
when he talked, eating.

How was his good niece Nance, Uncle Sparrow wanted to know,
and how was the farmin' in the hills? Things warn't too prosperous
back in the Knobs. A sad look come over his face. "Thinkin' I'll have
to pull stakes. I'm lookin' over to Indiana. Good land, terms is *easy*."
He offered a smile: "Two of us together, Lincoln—we could prove
up smart."

Pap lifted his lip. "I seen your fields, Tom. I've pulled a wild
coocumber-vine and shook ever' stalk o' corn you had."

Uncle Sparrow grinned, kind of sheepish. "Well, the jimsons an'
cock-burrs does git the start of me, I'll allow."

"Hey Tom Lincoln!" called a man from over by the fireplace. A
dozen men sat at ease on the benches, smoking and chawing, spitting into the fire. They hollered for Pap to join them. Tom Lincoln
was a favorite and they knew Uncle Sparrow too. They asked was
Abe Tom's son, that had said that *good thing*? Pap said he was, sat
down grinning, and chucked Abe in the shoulder which meant *keep
shet*. So Abe folded up Injun-fashion on the floor by his knee.

Two of the men were Virginians, just over the mountains. They
hadn't heard the *good thing*, and the rest wanted Pap to tell it again.
"Go on, Lincoln. These fellers are minded to buy land over west, but
are concerned about Injuns."

The Virginians allowed that was so. They wore broadcloth coats, their boots were clean, and their possibles kept in carpet-bags tucked behind their knees. They twitched their boots whenever one of the Kentuckians rolled up his cheeks and spat a loop of tobacco juice towards the hearth-fire.

"No," said Pap, "ain't been war parties in Kentuck since Gin'ral Harrison whupped the Shawnese in the year eleven. Nearest *bad* Injuns is out *El*anoy-way, by the Big River. But in the old days, when my pappy come into the terr'tory . . ."

. . . so Pap spun the yarn, "jest like I was tellin' my young'un here," right down to the part where "The boy here looks up at me and says, 'Which was it kilt him, Pappy? Was it the lawyers, the niggers, or the Injuns?' " Well they all went *haw-haw* at that, Kentuckians louder than Virginians. Maybe one was a lawyer—had that kind of boots.

"That brother o' yours," said one of the Kentucky men, "he that same Mord Lincoln was out with the Mounted Rifles in 'thirteen?" The man loosed the whole of his quid into the fireplace. "My pappy was with him when they rubbed out Tecumsee. Said he never *see* sech a man for Injuns."

A second Kentuckian, an older man, said he could testify *personal* that it was so. He minded one time in Lexington, back in the year eight, right after the treaty was signed that the Injuns had to get out of the state. He was setting with a bunch of fellers, and old Mord Lincoln, on the porch of a tavern on the North Road. "Along come half a dozen of the raggediest Injuns you ever see—old men, squaws an' brats, mebbe half a dozen—ask which way to Salt Fork. I jest spit: ain't a-goin' to do my Christian by a redskin with Old Mordecai lookin' on. But he says, 'Tell 'em.'

"Well I'm wonderin' is he gone soft in his age, but when Mord Lincoln says do a thing, you *do* it. Mordecai sets a while lookin' after 'em, noddin' his head. Then—like *that*—snatches his rifle leanin' by the wall, two jumps he's on his horse and lopin' off into the trees with that rifle in his hand." The storyteller spat in the fire. "Two days later he come back: six scalps looped to the saddle-bow."

There was a murmur of admiration. "He was a hard case all right. But a good man for a new terr'tory."

"Old-timers had to be that way."

"I reckon—but Mordecai Lincoln: he's somethin' *particular*. Tom, you remember what he used to say? *Said* it was Bible, but I allow he 'terpeted some. 'Now go and smite Amalek, an' spare not man nor woman, nor infant nor suckling, nor his camel nor his ass.' "

Haw-haw, *his ass!* haw haw haw. "Didn't know Injuns had camels." "No, but I kin swear he killed their asses," said Uncle Sparrow and they haw-hawed some more. "Oh yes. You *might* call him a *hard case*, but you'd better not let Old Mordecai hear you say so."

A tall figure stepped into the circle—sudden as if he had popped out of the floor. The laughter choked. The man's face was shadowed by a big-brimmed slouch hat. "Don't let him hear what?" he said softly, and took off his hat.

As he done so, the men in the circle raised up slow to their feet— even the two Virginia men.

The man was uncommon lean, tall and stooping, high-set shoulders like a wolf's, wearing a buckskin hunting-shirt with two horse-pistols and a skinning knife stuck in the sash, and broadcloth pants tucked into well-made riding boots. A shock of iron-gray hair stood stiff as a brush over a broad brow. Black eyebrows overhung the ledge of his forehead, and white-gray eyes like slices of mica glinted from under. His face was bony and hollow-cheeked, a lipless S scored the shape of his mouth above the bony knob of his chin. His skin was sallow brown like an old leather poke, and tight over the bone-edges. He grinned them a double line of too many perfect small white teeth.

The circle mumbled good day, Uncle Sparrow added "Mr. Lincoln," but the man just crooked a long bony finger at Pap and said, "You Tom," and pointed his chin to the corner.

Pap took his hat in both hands and stepped out of the circle, Abe following, awe-struck. This must be his Uncle Mordecai Lincoln. And that was what happened when a man stepped right out of history into a roomful of folks: a hush more awful than prayer, growed men standing up to give respect—afraid, too, though they mustn't show out.

They sat in a corner, Abe next to Pap on one bench and Uncle

Mordecai on a rush-bottom chair. Pap said he was glad Uncle Mordecai had come.

"I had business."

Pap wet his lips and said, "I need advice."

"Advice?" said Mordecai, and his face split to show his small neat teeth. "Ain't but three ways for a man in your situation: kill the man, take him to law, or pack up your plunder and run. I suppose killin' is out of it—times is against it, even if you had the stomach. So take him to law."

Pap was shaking his head, his eyes everywhere but Mordecai. "No good goin' to law."

"Why not?" Mordecai snapped. "Every other man does. Can't cut wood or kill your own nigger in Kentucky without some son of a bitch takes you to law."

"Ever' time I had to do with lawyers I got skinned," said Pap miserably.

"Because you are ignorant, and you got no gumption," said Mordecai. "Who was it wrote that letter for you? Who read you your papers? Wasn't that wife o' yours I don't reckon. It's all she can do to make her X."

Uncle Mordecai counted off points against Pap, one finger at a time, to prove he was ignorant and had no gumption: "You had that Mill Creek farm, two hunderd forty acres—lost it 'cause you recorded your survey wrong. So you come to me for money to buy that place in Nolin—then let a man law you out the land, and your improvements in the bargain."

"You never give me that loan," said Pap.

Mordecai ignored him and put up a third finger. "Now it's Knob Crick and the same story again."

Pap went red in the face, his words strangled. "It was my own money lost. You never give me *none*."

Mordecai shook the three fingers in Pap's face. "Would have been money throwed away. I know you: *shiftless*."

"Shiftless? Everything I got is my own workin'. You never give me a thing, Brother," said Pap. "I had my rights in Pa's land, but you took it all, you and Josiah—took it and sold me like a nigger." He pointed his finger like a pistol and said, "You'd have cheated Josiah too, if he hadn't been old enough to shoot you or take you to law."

"Old enough?" Mordecai sat up straight in his seat. "You mean man enough." He snorted and curled his no-lips. "Take me to law if you like. Kentucky law is Virginia law: oldest son inherits of the father, the rest must look to *him*." He leaned forward. "As to selling my own flesh like a nigger? I 'prenticed you to carpenting. Ain't my fault you made no more of it than you did." The mica-glints under his brows sparked and he showed his long rows of little white teeth. "*I* contracted you your learning of old Hanks, and that set of tools— the rest was *your* foolishness."

"What *rest*?"

Mordecai's eyes blazed up, and he poked his bony face right at Pap: "I mean marrying his niece's woods-colt! I mean letting him palm off his Hanks bastard get . . ."

Pap half-rose—then froze, shaking with the full-up hate that couldn't get out of his skin.

Uncle Mordecai leaned back again, the line of his mouth set. After a moment he said, "No—you ain't up to it."

Pap dropped back to the bench.

It was like Uncle Mordecai had cut Pap down, just talking words. Abe had always thought of Pap as the strongest man, and he was sure a thicker man than Uncle Mordecai. But Uncle Mordecai was like a steel-head ax and Pap like a block of wood. Was that what they were all of them like—the men from history, Moses and Boone and Washington?

But now Uncle Mordecai made his voice go softer. "I won't give you money, Thomas. I won't argue for you to take them to law. I ain't one for lawyers. Kentucky is full up with lawyers. It wasn't like this in the old days." He barked, which was his laugh: "Mebbe I made a mistake killing off the Injuns, at least they kept the *lawyers* out." He looked at Pap, calculating coldly. "So I am selling off, taking my people and moving to the Elanoy—out by the Big River. It's prime land, Thomas. We get the Injuns killed off, a man could have himself a nice plantation. You could carpenter for me."

"I farm my own land," Pap snapped.

"Well"—Mordecai waved his hand—"farm it in Elanoy."

"I got no taste for killin' Injuns," said Pap.

Mordecai spread his lipless grin: "No man gets vurry far in this life if he can't kill a man when he needs to."

Then, for the first time, Uncle Mordecai looked at Abe: his white eyes just a glint in the deep sockets, bony face and jutting chin yellowed by the candlelight. "This your boy Abe?" He looked over at Pap. "Looks like a *Hanks* to me: spindle-shanked and shiftless as niggers. 'Prentice him to a trade or he'll wind up scratchin' dirt the rest of his born days."

Fall 1816

Pap's word was final: "Kentuck ain't no more a white man's country. We're gittin' out." He cooked most of their corn crop down to whiskey, stilling it through an old gun-barrel. Abe set gluts to help him split whiteoak staves, and helped him bind the kegs. Pap took his ax down to Rolling Fork and cut logs for a wagon-size flatboat, large enough to hold his whiskey and small enough for one man to manage. Then he chucked cured meat and salt in his blanket-roll, knotted all their cash money in a rag-cloth. "I'll be back afore the moon goes round," he said. He pushed off into the run of Rolling Fork, steered round the bend, and was gone.

The rest of that day was uneasy. Pap was the kind of man always *there* when he was around, and lately he'd been there with *spurs* on. They kept expecting him to pop out from behind something. So when they heard the horse-clops coming they startled: but when they looked out, it was only Mr. Riney, sitting his bony old gray in the yard, his hat in his hand.

He made his bow to Mam. She said Mr. Lincoln was not to home, but would Mr. Riney like to light? He said no thank you, ma'am. Was bound off for Memphis, his brother come into a plantation there. Heard the Lincolns were pulling out as well. "I was right sorry, Missus Lincoln, when Abe stopped school."

Mam couldn't answer without disrespect to Pap.

Mr. Riney opened his saddle-bag and took out a wrapped parcel; leaned down and gave it to Mam. "This here's for Abe," he said. "It's a book of stories. *The Fables of Aesop.* Decent, moral stories, collected by a Gospel minister."

Mam held the book carefully in her hands, like to warm it. Then she smiled, and said her thanks (and for Abe to say the same). Then she gave it into Abe's hands, and he felt the dry hard square weight of it—pages and pages for sure, give into his hand for his own. Oh: it was just the most beautiful.

From the other side of the world he heard Mr. Riney say, "I hope he will . . ." then stop.

"Missus Lincoln," he said at last, "Abe is the smartest boy I ever had the teaching of."

"Thank you," said Mam. "I know. I am most keerful of it."

Mr. Riney nodded, then he turned and clopped off into the trees, and the three of them were alone.

Pap was gone. They stayed around the cabin and did home chores. But as night came on their comfort chilled. "Mammy?" said Sary. "I wish you'd read us Ruth and Nomiah."

But Mam looked sickly and shook her head. "I can't . . . I can't read but what the spirit *give* me to read." She bowed her head over the Book and closed her eyes, but the letters must have burned through the lids because she read out the words as clear as ever she done:

"And the Lord said: Behold, I will cast ye out of the place of your abiding. And if thou say, why have these things come upon me I will answer: Can the Eth'opian change his skin, or the leper his spots? For the whoredom of thy mother and of thy people, therefore will I scatter ye, as the chaff that passeth away by the wind in the wilderness."

It was hard words, the hardest Abe ever knew Mam to speak. They crumpled Sary up like dried corn-shucks. "Oh honey." Mam hugged Sary close. "Honey honey—the Lord's a merciful Lord: nothin' can't happen unless He makes it so!" She showed Abe her sad pleading eyes, and reached out to bring him into her comfort too—

But it was strange—a piece of Abe stood off from her arms and outside the strong smell of her he used to love to just bury his head in.

He went off by himself with Mr. Riney's book. At first he had to spell his way into it slow, but after a couple of days the words broke loose like crick-ice letting go in a thaw and started to run together: then he was off to Aesop-country inside his head, and lived there the better part of a month.

There was one story in particular he kept going back to, "The Wolf and the Lamb." It was almost as if there was a spirit hiding in it, calling to him to come find it out. It was a cruel story, it made his stomach suck and drop—but still it drew him. A Lamb went to the stream to get a drink, and suddenly there's a Wolf there, that come down out of the hills. Wolf says he's going to eat the Lamb for punishment, because Lamb's been muddying the water so's a Wolf can't drink it. But Lamb says it can't be his fault, since the stream ran *down* from the hills. It was plain Lamb had the best of that argument: for water don't run but the one way. Well then, says Wolf, you been scandalizing of me these three years, and I'll eat you on that account. "Upon my Word," says the Lamb, "that was before I was born!"—so you see the Lamb was right again. But being right made no difference: "Sirrah," said the Wolf, "if it was not you, it was your Father, and that's all One." So he seiz'd the poor innocent helpless thing, tore it to pieces, and made a meal of it.

The story wouldn't let Abe alone, no more than the Wolf would let the Lamb alone. There was a *meaning* hidden in it. Abe lay in his tick at night, stared into the dark, and tried to puzzle out what it was. He thought about the Wolf showing his rows of long sharp teeth as he chomped into the Lamb—and then it come to him: Uncle Mordecai was a Wolf. There wasn't a thing you could say, right or wrong, that could stop him grinning his long bony too-many-teeth grin, or tearing you to pieces with his words or his skinning knife.

Suddenly he felt his blood pound in his ears: he had just read a book-story the way Mam read Bible! His first notion was to go right to Mam and show her. But his thoughts ran on, too fast as usual, minding and reminding him: Mam's notion of the Lord was sort of Wolfish too, wasn't it? Punish you even if it wasn't you done it, but your Pap or your Mam. Here they were throwed out of Kentuck and blowed over the river and into the woods. But *they* weren't a rebellious house, were they?

He must see if there was anything he'd missed in the book. He snatched it out of its nest in his tick—then froze with the book in his hand, torn between the precious gift and Mam. He wanted her so bad right then, he almost wished he never saw the Aesop book. But it was full of discoveries, he felt taller the more he read it, he couldn't give it up. He opened the book . . . but it was too black to see anything more than the pallid glow of the pages. He couldn't make out a single letter.

He felt something *swish* through the middle of his spirit—and he knew something with one part of his mind which he must not let the rest of him know: something secret.

But it was no use to deny it: *Once you know a thing, you can't unknow it. That was Adam's problem right there, why he couldn't get shut of the original sin.* Mam, reading with her eyes closed—not being able to read but what her spirit give her. It meant what Simms and Uncle Mordecai said about Mam's X was true:

Mam couldn't read, not really. Not like he could himself.

And Pap couldn't either, not hardly: couldn't set out the letters of his own name the same way two times running.

But if Abe was the only one could read, then some day, maybe soon, everything was going to depend on him: Bible, schoolbooks, papers with the law wrote down on it that you must get off your land *like stubble in the wind* and if Abe didn't read things right, what would happen to them all?

The lonesomeness of it was so wide and deep he felt like falling. The ghostly ax swished and split his spirit in two:

One part was afraid, the other wasn't. The part that wasn't grinned like a Wolf.

The next day Pap came back.

November 1816

He'd gone more than a hundred miles out and the same back: down the Rolling Fork to the Salt, into the Ohio, and across to the Indiana side. Flatboat run on a snag and sunk to the gunn'ls, he lost four-five kegs, but chopped her loose with the ax, bailed her out. This was near a settlement called Troy. Pap sold his whiskey and the boat timbers to the tavern-keeper. He met a man there, Reuben Grigsby, strange old cuss, just starting for a hunt in Injun country. Grigsby had marked out some prime claims twenty mile or so back from the river, in the hills along the upper waters of Little Pigeon Creek.

No: there warn't no Injuns there.

Big woods though: not what you'd call bottom, it was *gladly* land, hilly but with good soil. It was gov'ment terms, which meant *easy*, and so was the survey gov'ment, which meant *sure*. Pap walked in, blazed the trees, and stacked brush in the four corners of a claim, built them a half-face camp to winter in. Old Grigsby had a still-house. Pap contracted to make barrels for cash money: with what he got for his own whiskey there might be almost enough to pay their first installment.

"A half-face camp to winter in?" said Mam.

"We're goin' to Pigeon Crick," he said. "Kentuck ain't no more a white man's country."

That was Pap's word, and the end on it. The next day Pap went into the woods, and the *bang! bang!* of his long-helved cutting ax told them he had begun to chop them loose of Kentucky, root trunk and branch. He split out planks for a wagon and staves for barrels while Mam and Sary scraped the last of their corn and pounded it to meal in the samp. Then Pap went for the pigs with his broad-ax: chopped the head off a shoat and throwed it in the pen, and while the stumpy bristle-haired hogs went at the head he snatched six piggies one at a time by the hind trotters (leaving only the sow and boar to drive) and lammed their heads on the gatepost—then hung 'em, split 'em, let their guts out lolloping into a bucket, and set 'em to smoke.

They gutted the cabin slick as Pap done the hogs: emptied hauled and filled till all the cabin innards was in the two-wheeled cart. Then Pap pried out the cabin window and tied it atop the load, shouldered his rifle, horn, and pouch, said *Gee-up!* The horses leaned into the traces and the cart rolled ahead, Pap and Mam touching up the team with the goad, Sary and Abe with Pap's old ironwood staff driving the two hogs, Jack nipping them along from the rear.

The cabin door swung loose and the empty air blew all through it as they went into the trees.

Five days later towards evening they came to the river. The trees opened out, there was a winter sky blue as crick-ice and an early moon rising with a glow like ripe punkin. There was the river, a great wide open sweep of moving water spangled with bits of moon, racing yet always in place.

The cart rumbled and boomed aboard the ferry, the ferryman shoved the big platform clear, and they felt the current lift and take her. The river swept down from out of sight, one heavy solid incessant force, whole and unbroken, rushing beneath their feet and past them and away.

He felt Mam's hand on his shoulder.

> "I'm goin' there to see my mother,
>   I'm goin' there, no more to roam.
>   I'm jest a-goin' over Jordan . . ."

The raft moved steadily across the current as the raftsmen thrust hard on their giant sweep-oars. Abe looked back: on the Kentuck side low bluffs and the lights of the landing. No Egyptians in chariots. No Virginians lawyers or niggers to caper and cuss and get themselves drownded coming after.

He turned and looked ahead. A black wall of trees rose towards the darkening sky.

BOOK II:

The War Against the Trees

Chapter 3: The Clearing

Little Pigeon Creek, December 1816

A muddy trace ran north and west from the Ohio River settlement of Troy Landing. The big woods closed behind them like a door, shutting them off from the river. Their eyesight died in massed trunks and webs of branches that walled the trace. The cart groaned and cracked its wheels over projecting roots, pitched and rolled in the trail-ruts. Abe's feet were sore and wet, his winter moccasins were not much better than a decent way to go barefoot among the roots and rocks. That night the boar and sow ran off—Pap cussing as he woke to hear them snouting off into the brush. Jack ran barking after them, and near got lost himself.

At last Pap stopped the cart beside a blazed elm tree. There in a small clearing was the half-face camp: a lean-to of small logs roofed with poles and brush, wide enough for four to sleep if nobody rolled over, just high enough in front for Pap to sit erect. A big oak was felled across the front, its inner face marked with char. A fire built against it would shine warm into the camp.

All around the clearing the trees stood stiff, whispering a little.

They laid a hide on the ground, then bed-ticks and blankets. Abe fetched a bucket of water from a spring off in the brush. Mam boiled them some corn-mush. "I will come at my cookin' irons tomorrow, and make us some dodger." As they were snugging in Sary whispered, "Mammy, I'm skeery. It's jest too lonesome."

"Don't be afeared," Mam whispered back. "There can't a sparrow fall but the Lord will see it."

Some time during the night a wind came up, and Abe woke and heard it. It was like no sound of wind he ever heard before: not Kentucky wind blowing broad across the fields, but a wind with nothing to blow through but trees, trees for thousands of miles in every direction, a dense intricate network of trunks limbs branches and tiny naked little twigs and stems all laced and interlaced, more than you could think to count, more even than there were stars—and the cold wind breathing through them, whispering, whining a little, hissing, the whole forest hissing all over out in every direction as far and farther than you could think.

Next morning they started clearing the trees off their land.

Chill woke them in gray half-light. Mam built up the fire and warmed the mush from last night. Pap took up a long-helved cutting ax, Abe a shorter one. They marched into the brush, Pap trampling the way with his heavy boots. Abe wore Pap's old boots filled out with rags and hair.

It was an old forest. Stands of poplar and hickory stood among legions of saplings and slender dogwood. Mixed tribes of elms, chestnuts, sweetgums, and black walnuts surrounded little towns of sugar-maples and smooth gray beeches. Great heavy old whiteoaks and blackoaks, their hides wrinkled and carbuncled, wearing red-brown leaves like rags on a scarecrow, stood ambushed among the understory tangle of sassafras and scraggy hawthorn.

Pap notched a tree on the side he meant it to fall; then stood off and swung his ax, a beautiful swing up from the sway of braced legs, hips pivoting, arms following, wrists snapping the head in hard so the ax bit deep *bang!* but just then gave the blade the tiniest flirt to pop out the chip and free the head. He took a waist-thick oak down crackling and popping, then a slim beech, the ax slicing wounds in the gray skin-smooth bark.

Pap nodded for Abe to try it. He swung as he had seen Pap do, but the ax-head weight pulled him off balance, he just scratched the tree's face. Again. And again. Slowly it came to him, legs and hips learning the brace that would base the swing, until at last it was all there, as natural as breathing: his eye locked onto the notch like Uncle Mordecai plugging that Injun through his silver bangle; what the eye saw went to the foot like water to roots, foot to leg to hips, shoulders arms-wrists-hands *bang!* The beech's backbone snapped, its heartwood crackled, and it leaned slowly back, then down with a rush, its arms and sky-high head smashing through the limbs and branches of the neighbor trees *whump* to the forest floor.

And another and another, the next day and the next day and the next, until the number of days from the start got lost in Abe's head-thickets somewhere. Ash and oak they cut right down, smashing through the canopy to the forest floor. The bigger walnuts, hickories, and beeches they girdled: chopped a trench around the trunk right down to the brightwood, left them to die standing. Or if it was elm or maple they'd stack dry brush and set fire roaring against the trunk, the resin sizzling and popping in its veins then lighting off with a screech as the bark cracked.

Sometimes they'd come to a huge old hickory, elm, or beech: "Creation trees," Pap called them, Bible says "there were giants in the earth in those days." They'd bang away most of a morning, ax and ax till they split the heartwood and brought him smashing down breaking the arms and backs of lesser trees. They lit fires and burned these fallen monsters into sections a team could haul away—"niggering off," Pap called it, a lazy way to do the job.

Maybe Pap and him weren't up to killing Injuns like Uncle

Mordecai. But they could kill the biggest trees God ever made, chop-down girdle and burn, the fired sap screaming in the trunk-cracks. Call that *shiftless*? Well, *I* guess not! *Bang! Bang! Bang!* Another and another and another.

They'd come back to camp smelling of sweat and woods-fire, like as not carrying fresh meat, hungry enough to eat a wolf with the hair on. Mam and Sary would raise up to watch him and Pap march in, axes hupped to the shoulder like muskets, back from the war against the trees.

Eating or lying down to sleep, he always felt the ghostly shape and weight of the ax in his hand, as if it branched out of his spirit and was part of his body.

He'd fall asleep like a man falling out of a tree, sudden swift and hard. No time for Mam or reading. In the moment between putting his head down and dropping over the edge he would think about trees, cut falling burning . . .

Screaming . . . Abe was awake in the dark and there was screaming—a crazy high-pitched squeal from where the horses were tied. They were all sitting up in their blankets, Mam hugging Sary, Pap kneeling at the fire-log with the long rifle cocked. Abe groped forward to the ax that leaned against the fire-log. Jack had scooted out of the lean-to but jerked up short, planted himself, and began barking, short sharp ear-splitting yaps that made his small sturdy body bounce in place. But he wasn't going after It, whatever It was.

Then there come a snuffling sound like the biggest hog you *ever* . . . The horses shrilled and stomped furiously—

"Bear," said Pap. "Horses broke tether and run."

"Did it get 'em, Pap?" asked Abe.

"Not yet." He looked off in the dark, calculating. "Won't get but one anyway."

Abe tried to see how it might be, but all that come was Old Sam's long face and quiet eyes, his jaw turning as he chewed a tater Abe gave him. "I hope it ain't Old Sam."

Pap snorted. "Jest my luck if it takes the mare and leaves us that old plug."

That seemed hard. But that's how Pap *would* look at it. That's how Uncle Mordecai, or any man would. As worst as ever you wanted a thing, that's just how much you had to *not* count on getting it.

Sary said, "I wish the Lord would take keer and save 'em both."

Pap and Abe were up at first light. Light mist, low to the ground. Pap took the rifle and Abe the heavy militia musket and they went after the horses. Jack run ahead quickstep on his short stiff legs. The raveled tail of the broken tether lay on the snowy ground. One set of horse-tracks went off to the northwest, Two-Shoes the mare by their size. Old Sam's big splay hoof-marks ran due south.

Jack skittered to a gap in the brush and began yapping like last night: fierce and frightened at once. Pap said, "Hush!" and stung his rump with an acorn. Twenty feet in they found the bear track: like a man's foot, but bigger and broader, and claws on the toes. The tracks started south, then turned back on themselves and run north.

"Reckon he couldn't figger which he wanted," said Pap. He considered, then told Abe, "You track south after Old Sam. It's safe enough—Sam won't run far, and I reckon this bear went northaway. But look sharp! If you see the bear, stand still as death. If he comes at you, yell like the devil and wave your arms. Don't run nor climb no tree—bear can outrun a horse, climb like a squ'rl. And don't try to shoot him with a musket. It'll jest make him mad."

Old Sam's tracks were easy to follow, black through the light coat of snow. But Abe stalked along slow and watchful, freezing to listen for trouble. Abe wasn't just Abe but also Uncle Mordecai, with his long rifle and dead-shot eye. Jack wasn't just a little old fice-dog but a bear-hound. And they weren't just hunting up Old Sam but stalking the bear Itself. But Jack would nip his pants-leg and he'd have to get on.

They worked south, following the folds between low forested hills. It was cold, Abe's breath came in smoke, and mist drifted among the tree trunks. The tracks cut uphill through a fire-cleared swath into a copse of trees. Old Sam was standing in the trees, just at the top of the hill—his trailing rope tangled in deadfall.

Abe ran up to him, rubbed his velvet muzzle, and patted his cheek. "Hey Old Sam!" He took a piece of corn pone out of his pocket and gave the horse a nibble. Then he sat down on a log and had some himself. Suddenly the air turned yellow—the sun sucked up the last of the mist, and just like that a whole hidden world uncovered below their hillside.

Below him was a broad up-sloping plain of white snow cut into three big squares, Z-edged by split-rail worm fences. The top of the white rise was marked with bare black trees set out in even rows as if trees were crops—and beyond these a cluster of log buildings, chimneys blowing smoke.

Down in the nearest field creatures were moving.

One of them was a bear.

Abe's muscles seized up between running away and standing still as death.

One of them was a bear and the other *wasn't* . . . was a dark woman, or a man with long hair loose down his back, sitting just as calm, right up close to the bear. But the bear never went for the man-or-woman, only raised up stooping on his hind legs, swinging his heavy body left and right, left and right: then shuffled forwards two steps, and two steps, and two steps—and then swayed again, right side left side. It seemed like the dark man was nodding in time as the bear moved, maybe he was singing to the bear, not any words but just a sound like *ay-a hey-a, ay-a hey-a.*

And so Abe saw it was a bear and an Injun, the Injun singing to the bear, making the bear dance, making him do whatever he wants, *he probably sent that bear to get our horses,* and the next thing Abe knew he had dropped to one knee behind the deadfall tree: leveled the musket on the back of the bear's head and cocked the hammer back with a soft *snick. Just like Uncle Mordecai would do!* Heat flushed into his chest arms and head, he felt wonderful, he felt . . .

Then he remembered Pap saying *You can't kill no bear with no musket.* So he shifted and drew a bead on the Injun. The long barrel of the musket touched the shape of the Injun. The rifle grew out of Abe's own body, his trigger finger was the root, and it fed power into the iron finger that was merely the frozen extended beam of his own Mordecai-sharp eye. Pap had said *No* but Pap wasn't here, and Abe knew if he could just think *so* he could do it. He felt himself begin swelling up with the power of doing it *and Uncle Mordecai wouldn't say* don't shoot *Uncle Mordecai would say now go and slay and spare not his camel nor his* . . . Abe's vision flew down the line of the barrel like a bullet.

But he had forgot Jack, who just then bolted out into the field, yapping and running his small fast legs so the snow fairly boiled out behind him. The Injun stood up, the bear stopped dancing and turned around . . .

The bear turned around and took off his head.

The bear took off his head and inside there was a white-haired old white man's head with a red face. He opened his mouth and yelled, "Hey!" The Injun paid the dog no mind but stood up and pointed to where Abe was ambushed.

Abe was up on his feet, the musket still cocked in his hands but pointed up. He yelled "Jack! Jack!" crack-voiced, pulled the trigger and shot a good lead ball at the late morning sun—and Jack never stopped running but turned so sudden fast and short it seemed like he sucked himself in at the muzzle and blowed himself out his own asshole, and come smoking back up the hill towards Abe.

Meantime below, the "bear" had thrown his head down on the ground and was yelling "Hey! Hey you up there!"

But Abe wasn't staying to see any more. If the bear and the Injun belonged to that house on the hill they were friendly, and it was foolish and shameful to have drawn a bead on them. On the other hand it didn't seem good sense to get too close to a strange Injun and a white man dressed up like a bear dancing in the snow.

Back at camp Mam gave Pap a hard look for sending Abe alone to track a bear, and didn't care when Pap explained it was the horse not the bear Abe went for—because he knew right well (or ought to) that it *could* have been a bear when Abe found it. Which was righter than she knew.

When Abe told about the old white man and the Injun, Pap said,

"That's jest old Reuben Grizby and his tame Injun. They say he is queer in the head."

Mam said, "I don't like no crazy man for neighbors."

"He may be tetched, but he's the richest man in these parts. He's the man I contracted to make kags for. Cash money. Me and Abe will go over there tomorrow or next day."

"Why's he got a tame Injun, Pap?"

"I don't care if he does," said Pap, "*or* if he's *tetched*, 'long as I get paid for those kags."

It was hard not getting any better answer than that, but Abe couldn't complain. He'd got away with less than half the George Washington truth of what happened, and he hadn't shot Reuben Grigsby nor his tame Injun. Which he might have done, if he hadn't been just a little less *Mordecai* than he figured.

. . . Pap never found the mare till a January thaw, then smelt her out. Two-Shoes was no more than bones, most of them cracked and disconnected, with rags of hide and hair. Only her head was still in one piece, but the bones showed where her face-skin was torn away, and she had a dead grin.

Grigsby's house was built around a big old double-cabin, the dog-trot that joined the two improved into an entry-hall, capped with a clapboarded second story under a shingle roof.

Pap knocked at the double doors of the entryway, and Reuben Grigsby Jr. opened—lean and tall, he had on a boiled shirt and broadcloth trousers in the middle of the day. He stood in the door instead of inviting them in, which Pap let on not to notice. Reuben Senior was over at the still-house. "Aaron!" Junior yelled, and a boy came running from back in the house: five or six years older than Abe and about the same height. He wore wool pants and lace-up leather boots. Junior told Aaron to take these folks over to the still-house, and Aaron pushed his lips out to show he'd rather not but was afraid to say so. He picked his way through the mud to save his boots.

Old Reuben stood in the still-house door and waved them in. He was a lean old man with tousled white hair and little sharp blue eyes. "Jest in time the both of ye!" he shouted.

In the center of the cabin was a fire-pit, over which two kettles of mash were cooking, the smoke rising out a smoke-hole in the roof. A stocky tow-headed boy, maybe two years older than Abe, was tending the fires. He gave the Lincolns a look and said "Hunh!" instead of Howdy. He bugged his eyes at his brother: "Hey Aaron, think she'll let you back in the house with the whiskey-stink on you?" The air was rich and various: wood-smoke, rotten fruit, yeast, burnt grain, a slash of raw alcohol through it all.

A dark squat figure rose out of a pile of furs in the corner of the room. The tame Injun. He made some howdyish noises—his eye lit on Abe and might have flickered.

Grigsby introduced his son William (the tow-head) and his old friend Johnny Konkapot, which was the Injun. He said for them all to set. Aaron said he wouldn't—had to get back to the house. "Got his knittin' to mind," sneered William. Aaron turned red: "I'll lam you for that!" "Or get someone else to do it," said William, and shut the door on him. Their father paid them no mind, but made himself comfortable.

Old Reuben tipped his jug and filled five cups. "I know ye don't drink whiskey, Lincoln," he said, "but this is brandy-wine. Good Book says, 'Drink ye no water, but a little *wine* for thy stomach's sake.' "

Reuben, Pap, and Konkapot dropped their heads back all three at once and threw their brandy down. William supped his quick and blinked. Abe tipped a little onto his tongue—it burnt and froze at the same time. Just the little taste and his tongue went numb, then a sweet taste, then his cheeks and eyes froze up. The men grinned; Konkapot's teeth were most of them missing.

"This yere's the best whiskey-house in the terr'tory," Grigsby said. "We jest set out here, me an' Konkapot, smell the whiskey cookin', smoke a pipe when I want to, talk when I feel like it, ain't that right, Johnny?"

Konkapot nodded and grinned. "*Don't* talk too."

Abe looked around the room. On the wall above the fireplace

were rows and rows of small dark objects: chopped-off wolf-paws, tied in bunches of four and hung from pegs in the wall. There were enough to almost cover the wall. Abe's head was full of smoke. "Ain't you got no bear-skins?"

Old Reuben gave Abe a quick sharp look. "No son," he said hard-throated, "no bear this season."

Konkapot said, "Hunh!" and gave Abe a teeth-gone grin. He put up his hands like a man holding a rifle and squinted along the imaginary barrel. He laughed with no sound coming out. Abe grinned back at Konkapot, the brandy smoked in his head, happy he didn't kill Konkapot until he got to know him better.

Reuben talked kegs with Pap—how many, how soon, how much he was prepared to pay. Pap nodded like his head was tied on loose. Old Reuben's little eyes were sharp on the target. He stuck out his hand, Pap shook it, the deal was struck. Then they must seal it with another shot of the brandy-wine.

Abe wobbled out the door, following Pap. After the whiskey-room the air was clean and sharp as a knife, the point of it stuck in Abe's forehead right between his eyes: ouch. Will Grigsby said, "You ain't no man for drinkin', are you?" It might have been friendly meant. Abe smiled in response, and to show friendly himself asked, "How come you let that Konkapot live with you?"

Without warning William shoved Abe hard, so that he stumbled forwards and almost fell. His face was red with fury and shame. "You say that again, and I'll *whup* you!" he cried.

Late February 1817

James Gentry was the second-richest man in Little Pigeon settlement. He owned the store and tavern where the roads crossed. It was dark in the store even in daytime, but lit by tallow-lamps. Mam whispered that a body might as well burn money to see by. She and Sary wandered up and down looking at iron pots and folded piles of woven cloth, touching them a little, shyly. Abe and Pap went over to the bar to trade for gunpowder, their own having got wet.

Gentry was a small neat man, smooth-shaved and his hair parted in the middle, a linen shirt buttoned to the neck. The boy with him looked to be fourteen, the same face only smaller. Gentry said, "Lincoln." But before Pap could say "Gentry," Abe saw up on a shelf behind Mr. Gentry a row of books, all different colors and sizes, enough to start a school with almost, so he yipped, "Pap, jest look—!"

Pap's iron hand clamped his shoulder hard, wrung it, and shook him. Pap swooped his face right down into Abe's, his slab-lips tight: "Don't say a *word* till your Pappy has spoke!" Pap spun Abe's whole body around and shoved him away. "Go with the women till you larn manners."

Abe slunk over to where Mam and Sary were looking at the cloth. Behind him he heard Mr. Gentry say, "This here is my eldest. Say how do to Mr. Lincoln, Allen." Allen said, "How do Mr. Lincoln," just like he was told.

"What'd you do, Abe?" whispered Sary, but he shook his head. She was just a girl, it warn't shame for *her* to be over here with the calico and pewter while the men were talking at the bar!

He wandered outside. There was a boy in the yard about his own age, throwing his knife into the bare ground. He jumped up as Abe came over. He had a rooster-comb of red hair on top, his face was freckled as a toad's back, and he had the bluest eyes Abe had ever seen. He grinned gap-toothed. Then, quick as a flash, flicked the knife into the ground by Abe's moccasined foot. He stuck out his tongue and said, "Want to fight me?" Then he laughed—short sharp hard laughs like a woodpecker's drumming.

Abe stepped forwards quick so the knife in the ground was behind him. Then he scratched a line in the dirt with his toe. But he didn't say anything. If this boy was bound to fight, let him spit over the line.

Freckle-face grinned again, then stuck out his hand. "I'm Matt Gentry, this here is my Pappy's store." Abe said who he was but Matt already knew all about Lincolns: "We're Kentuck an' so are you. Heared my Pappy say so."

Abe nodded but couldn't say anything. *Kentuck!* It seemed like the other side of the river was as far away as the moon and they'd been lost in the trees forever.

"You homesick?" asked Matt. "This place ain't shucks to Kentucky. We had niggers to work our land in Kentucky. Here *I* got to do *everything*. You ever have any niggers?"

"No," said Abe. "Pap was ag'in 'em."

"Well, I thought they was purty good to have, mostly. Couldn't take 'em over the river though. We're a Free State." The red-head's face lit up: "Want to listen what they're a-talkin'?"

Matt ran around to the other side of the store. Here the ground fell away and left a crawl-space under the sill. Matt wriggled in, Abe after. Puncheon boards creaked overhead as Pap and Mr. Gentry shifted in their boots. Mr. Gentry was saying, ". . . to raise your cabin. I can sell you a keg on tick, but like as not Old Reuben will bring one. He can be unaccountable free when he takes a notion." His voice dropped lower. "Comes of his being born white, but raised Injun."

"I heared about that," said Pap.

"White blood give him his eye for the dollar. But then he'll give away a keg of prime whiskey if there's anything to celebrate. That's the Injun coming out." Gentry's voice dropped a tone. "He was took younger than your boy there. Kickapoose raided their settlement. Father and growed sons went down fighting, scalps took. Baby sister wasn't fit to travel, they swung her by the feet and busted her head on the door-post. Mother couldn't keep up so they kilt her two days after—burnt or tommy-hawked, I don't recollect which. But they took Reuben for their own—he'll show you their marks cut into his arms. Eight, nine years he run with 'em."

Abe, in the dark under the floor, tried to picture Old Reuben Grigsby young, his own age—then Injuns leaping out of the trees to shoot his pappy and chop his mam and bust his baby sister's head the way Pap done the piggies when they left Kentuck, and carry him off away alone deeper and deeper into the dark maze of trees.

Above Matt and Abe the men were briefly silent. Pap said, "He's bought his luck hard."

In the dark under the floor Matt put his mouth in Abe's ear and said, "Ain't this great?" He was shaking and giggling, and Abe got afraid he would get them caught. He pulled on Matt's arm and crawled back out. When they were outside he said, "Your Pappy whup you if he ketches you listenin'?"

"O' course he would." Matt was indignant. "Did you think he wouldn't? Wouldn't your Pappy?" But his anger passed in a blink. "Course I heared about Old Reuben afore. But you got to anyway." He started to fidget and his eyes raced around. "Most o' what you want to know they keep secret. You got to sneak 'em if you want to find out. Listen under the floor-boards. Or night-times? When they think you're sleepin' you listen." He grinned. "Hear 'em rustlin' in the bed-tick, he a-buckin' and she a-groanin', *hee-hee-hee!* Don't you love that?"

Abe didn't know what Matt was talking about, and it showed.

"You ain't got a notion of it, do you?" Matt looked shrewd. "Say—how old are you, Lincoln?"

He had to think—the birthday he remembered was the George Washington–dried-apple time, he was seven then. "Well," he said, "seven—or no, maybe eight . . ." because it come to him that his and George Washington's birthday must have got lost while they were fighting the war against the trees.

"Huh," said Matt, "I figgered you older. I'm eleven and ain't any taller'n you." Then he grinned and let that go. "Well? Don't you know any secrets?"

"I used to know some," Abe said, "but I can't remember 'em jest now." He wanted to ask more about "buckin' and groanin'," but was ashamed to as it seemed to be something he ought to know. He told himself he would listen some night and learn what it was.

Pap was in a good mood as they walked back to the camp. Abe wanted to walk with him, but was afraid he was still mad, so he walked a *little* behind—yet to Mam and Sary following, it would *look* like he was walking with Pap. The trick worked so well he nearly forgot it *was* a trick, and almost asked Pap to tell some more about Reuben Grigsby and the Injuns, but remembered just in time he wasn't supposed to know the little he already knew. It come to him that the trouble with Matt Gentry's way of sneaking out growed folks' secrets was, you got the knowledge but couldn't use it.

April 1817

In early April the whole district turned out to raise their cabin. After the long winter of nothing but cold and silence and trees there came this great explosion of people in their clearing—men and women jabbering and shouting *Howdy*, half-growed boys sniffing each other like stranger dogs, and half-growed girls letting on not to see the boys, and the shirt-tail young rolling and tussling on the ground like pups. Besides red-haired Matt Gentry, there were a number of boys near enough Abe's age: the Casebier boys lived on the next claim, Aaron and Will Grigsby, the Carters and Henry Brooner. For vittles they had venison and roast hog in plenty, and rabbit and quail, and corn bread and pone and pies. The Gentrys and Grigsbys tried to out-do each other: Reuben brought a keg of his best whiskey, Gentry matched it; their wives wore go-to-Meeting clothes and managed not to say a word to each other.

Mam took to Henry Brooner's Ma right off. She was from Kentuck same as Mam, the two of them sang that good news to each other, and began right off calling each other "Sister." The Whitmans rode in, young Miz Whitman with a belly swelled out most remarkable: the women gathered to her and set her in the shade like a queen. The men showed the same honor to Old Tom Turnham: a lean old man in a faded blue army coat, his white hair tied in a club with black ribbon. Old Tom had served under General George Washington himself, and been spoke to by him. They set him down in the shade with care, not that he was feeble at eighty, but to show respect. Abe froze up solid with reverence, couldn't hardly say *Howdy* when Pap introduced him—questions sprouting in his head like weeds, but before he could muster courage to ask even one, Old Turnham held out his wrung-up claw and smiled a toothless pink-gummed smile that scared the liver and lights right out of him.

The men laughed and jabbered and et and drunk. Then they

turned to and fairly swarmed the cabin up in a single afternoon: the skilled broad-ax-men like Pap notching and saddling the ends, trimming and squaring the logs, shaving long slices of beech and sugarwood with short swift precise swings, so the logs would lie "belly to belly, like man and wife," as Old Reuben joked . . .

Oh, it was the best day Abe had seen yet. When the last of the people rode off into the trees, the silence rang in his ears.

May–June 1817

Spring came on, and they set fire in the woods. All the men in the settlement and their horses teamed up for log-rolling, moving from farm to farm, hauling out all the timber cut and niggered off over the last year, setting it in great piles to burn it away. It went on all spring: the air was full of smoke, the whole country smelt like a smokehouse, it made your eyes sting and throat close up it got so thick sometimes, and wafts of ash like gray snow on the leaves and the windows and the doorsills.

Then with summer rising they had to get their crop in the ground, and only Old Sam to draw the plow. It wasn't like Kentucky, a four-square acre to be plowed in lines like printing in a book. Their cleared patches snaked among girdled trees and standing stumps. Less than half as much open ground among all their clearings as there had been in the field Abe remembered plowing back in Knob Creek.

The first day, Abe learned that the war against the trees wasn't done. Cut 'em down all you liked, girdle 'em till they rotted standing, or burn 'em like Injuns at the stake, but the trees kept coming at you from underneath. Below the leaf-mold the ground was webbed through with roots—pale slick ropes and vines and hard knotty cords, and little fine tough threads all twined and twisted in amongst each other like a net. If you tried to cut deep they'd trip the plow-blade, drive the colter down like a stake, and jerk Old Sam up short. If you ran your furrow too shallow the blade would bounce along and hardly cut at all. It worked best with Abe standing atop the blade for weight, Pap leaning on the handles to keep the plow leveled as Old Sam plodded forwards and the blade went tearing through the nets with a ripping uneven popping sound—and it would catch anyway and pitch Abe off. Then they had to roust out shovels and dig the dirt away around some great old rock-hard root, and go at it with axes.

Even the walls of their cabin began to bleed sap as the season rose, and put out fingers of twig and new leaf here and there along the walls, inside as well as out.

Across the Troy road from their front gate was a good-sized wild blackcherry tree. Mam's eyes lit when she saw it, she had Abe clear the brush to help it breathe. She said it was to be her "cheerry-pie tree," she hadn't had a taste of cheerry-pie since she was a girl over the mountains. There wasn't anything better, they would see—some sweet to go with the salt sweat of their brows. In the shank of the day Abe would sit on their rail fence and watch his cheerry-pie a-growing—first white flowers, then the fruit-buds a-pipping, a tiny blood-spot at each tip.

As the ground hardened, the roads up from the river prospered with new traffic. Most of it came up the wagon-road north from Rockport, or the Buckhorn road that ran north-west from the ferry-landing opposite Lewisport, Kentucky, past Grigsby's to the cross-roads. But enough used the old trace the Lincolns had followed from Troy that they wore it into a road. People came into the territory every day, from every different part of the country, driving two-wheeled ox-carts and sway-backed Conestogas, women and babies riding atop the load, men and boys driving the team and herding the hogs or cattle. Abe would sing out howdy, ask where they was from and where going, tell them who he was, and his Pap and Mam, and this was their land here, Pigeon Crick.

Early Summer 1817

Summer wasn't older than one turn of the moon when a spavined Conestoga pulled up to their gate. A man and a woman sat up on the box, the woman . . . she might almost have been Mam, the same long face bones, broad forehead, and wide thin-lipped mouth, only her face was cracked about the eyes. The man's face was hid by a big slouch hat. He swept it off sudden and showed a long head, stringy dark hair shot with gray, and a snag-toothed smile: "Boy don't you remember me? I am your Uncle Tom Sparrow! This here is your Mammy's Aunt Betsey." Aunt Betsey hollered, "You be Abraham, ain't you?" and spread him a smile that had lost any number of teeth: it gave Abe a queer feeling, like seeing Mam suddenly old.

A tall almost-growed boy ambled around from the back of the wagon where he'd been droving hogs (the hogs trotting like pups right along with him). He had a long bony face, a little like Mam's, only one cheek was bulged out—till he spat a wad of tobacco-spit *spunk* on the back of the boss hog. "Howdy," he said, and his mouth slowly spread a tobacco-stained grin, "I'm your cousin Denny Hanks."

Mam must have seen them from the house, for here she came running, and Sary with her, crying and calling out it was her Aunt Betsey. Abe was flummoxed by the noise, then by Aunt Betsey hugging him like to break his neck. Meanwhile Tom Sparrow was telling Mam, "This here is our nephew Dennis, your *Aunt* Nancy Hanks's boy—say howdy, Dennis, to your cousin Nance." Pap came up slow behind Mam. Howdied Tom Sparrow, a little more proper than friendly. But Tom went on a-jabbering, running through the names again, Aunt Betsey and their nephew Dennis Hanks, that was the orphan son of Miz Lincoln's *Aunt* Nancy Hanks, "her that your own good wife was named after—that was married to Levi Hall and lived over by . . ."

"Dennis *Hanks*," said Pap.

"Well now, yes," said Tom, and a little blood came into his cheeks. "By her *first* husband, afore Mr. Hall. They parted ways *early*, so she jest called the boy 'Hanks' . . ."

Something wasn't right in this, for everybody suddenly got a little offish-looking. Abe looked at Denny lounging against the gate. He met Abe's look and winked. "Let them mind the relations. All I got to mind is the pork." He had run the pigs into Pap's yard, and they were scouring over the cleared ground snuffing for grain.

Mam cried and smiled again, and said they must come up the

house, so they did, while Abe helped Denny drive the hogs into the pen. The pen wanted a good deal of being tight, so Abe explained they hadn't been in no rush to finish on account the pigs all run off when we come up the trace, but some day Abe and Jack were going to hunt them up and put them in this pen.

Denny said, "You lost 'em cause you ain't got the trick of drivin' 'em." He picked up a pebble and stung one of the pigs so it jinked and bolted towards the pen. Another little porker tried to dodge, but Denny nailed it plumb between the eyes with a bolt of tobacco-spit. The pig shook its head, sneezed, and scurried into the pen. Denny grinned.

After supper, the women gave over their happy chattering. Pap had business on his mind. The Sparrows could squat in the old half-camp till they raised a cabin. But they couldn't raise sooner'n fall: the wood to be cut and seasoned, then the crop to harvest. "You come too late to break ground for *your* crop," Pap grudged. "Ain't no joke breakin' *this* ground."

Tom Sparrow smiled plaintively. "Well now, Nephew Lincoln, be it bad luck or prov'dence, I could not sell my place in time to help you clear."

Mam looked unhappily from Pap to Uncle Sparrow and back. But Denny's eyes were glittery: "Got to be prov'dence," he said. "Can't call it bad luck if you're late to plowin' an' early to supper."

Denny grinned, Pap glowered, Mam's face looked stretched. Things had got tight, Abe felt he had to cut them loose somehow. "I reckon," he piped (and they looked down at him), "I reckon His eye *is* on the Sparrows."

They all stood there like they couldn't catch up with what they'd heard, then Denny give a loud *haw-haw-haw!*, Tom Sparrow snorted, Mam giggled, Aunt Betsey and Sary joined, finally even Pap had to smile.

So things got easy for a while.

Chapter 4: The Pigeon Massacre

Summer 1817

The summer came on, hot yellow sun pouring down into the clearings and the air under the big trees thick with heat. The crop was in the ground, and Pap nor any of the other men (Reuben Grigsby apart) saw need for weeding or cultivating. The men went out every day with long rifles or bird guns, a horse to pack the meat and hides on. Away from the settlement there was plenty to shoot, and they shot all of it: possum, rabbit, wild pig, squirrel, beaver and badger for fur, turkeys brants ducks pheasant, and deer deer deer deer.

For Abe and the younger boys it was an easy time. There was a swimming hole a mile north of the Lincoln claim, where Little Pigeon Creek dropped into a basin in which cool amber-tinted water slowly turned. The only one lived out there was Old Konkapot, kicked out at last by Mrs. Grigsby; he squatted in the woods upstream. So the boys could swim naked or play at Injun-fighting or wrassling or run races.

When Denny was around everything was perfectly easy. He was

the biggest, the best at scuffling, shooting, and knife-throwing. If the Grigsbys got fractious, or Allen Gentry got chested out and started bullying the smaller boys, Denny'd just cock an eye at them: "If the crick ain't big enough, try the river." Denny was a prize wrassler, but never a bully: if he whupped you he'd offer you his hand up. He said he'd larn Abe some of his secret holts that he wouldn't show anybody else. There wasn't *anything* mean about Denny.

They'd swim awhile then just laze, listen to the older boys tell stories. These were amazingly funny, especially the ones Denny and Sam Casebier told, so your head and sides hurt from laughing. Some, when you thought about them later, there was no sense in them—it was the way they were told that almost killed you laughing. Like the one about the nigger stealing watermelons, that wasn't any funnier than a Kentuckian stealing apples, except for the faces Denny made and the mouthy, drawling way he talked.

Abe tried telling the Aesop story of the Fox and the Grapes, but it wasn't neither *secret* nor *funny*, and Denny didn't agree with the morals of it: he said, maybe the Fox was *right*—maybe the grapes *was* sour. Couldn't tell 'less you got a taste, could you? And if you couldn't, wasn't it better to think they was sour than stay up nights wishing you had some? You could learn a lot from Denny.

In the shank of the day, like as not, they'd go upstream to visit Konkapot—even the Gentrys, for all their sneering at Old Reuben. They'd come in a bunch, brazen and shy at once, and there he'd be: cross-legged by his bark shelter, maybe cleaning his old rifle, maybe stitching a hide shirt with gut-thread, his lank hair long as a woman's swaying forwards.

After the first few visits Abe saw that Konkapot knew when they were coming: they never surprised him taking a piss or sleeping off a drunk or even with his back turned—always awake, letting on to be fussing at his old shirt or gun. They'd bring him fish or some useless truck from home. Their idea was to trade him stuff so he would tell them Injun secrets. Did he ever kill any white people? take their scalps? But somehow when they were actually sitting with him— him smiling his no-teeth smile, nodding, thanking them for the fish, telling them where they could catch plenty more, his small black eyes as impassive as beads but full of watching—they could never do it. So they'd ask how he was, how was fishing or hunting, never the main thing, the ones asking getting poked in the back by those afraid to ask but warn't satisfied with the questions. (Dang it, then ask him yourself!) Yet it was exciting to *almost* have asked him, and all the way back they'd jabber about what Konkapot might have said "if *you* had the gumption to ask him."

Abe let Denny or Sam or Allen do the talking and the others the poking: he'd just watch the old man's face, as if the answer would just show out there one day. Now and again Konkapot would catch him looking, and pinch his glance with a wink.

Once Abe was slow to rise out of his gazing—the other boys had hoisted their tails and were jabbering good-bye—and Konkapot looked him straight in the face. "You Tom Lincoln boy," he said.

Abe got shamefaced: "Yessir, Mister Konk . . ." but did you *Mister* an Injun? "My name is Abe."

"Ahh," Konkapot flashed his teeth-gone grin, and aimed an invisible rifle with his hands: "You dhat boy, hunted *b'ar* one time."

The memory of that near mistake made Abe even worse embarrassed. But none of the other boys were paying attention. Konkapot had spoke so softly only Abe had heard him. Abe decided he liked Johnny Konkapot, and wished he wasn't too strange to get to know.

The summer turned. They harvested their first crop of corn. It was a small crop and with Lincolns and Sparrows working together took no time to pick, strip, scrape, and pound to hominy and meal. Then Pap went off to carpenter Miz Grigsby a cherry cabinet for cash money, and Tom Sparrow and Dennis Hanks went to cut timber for their cabin. There was mostly women's work around the cabin and three women to do it.

He went back to the swimming-hole, but the fun of it had gone off. With Denny gone there was no one to keep Allen Gentry and the Grigsbys from spoiling the fun with their bickering and bullying. The joking got mean sometimes, and the stories warn't funny like Denny used to tell, but having to do with shameful secret things like *nekkids* or what Matt called (hee-hee!) *buckin'-and-groanin'*. You had to let on to know what they was about, and enjoy them, or get laughed at yourself.

Abe wandered off upstream on his own, pretending he was tracking game. On a small mud beach he saw the track of a moccasin. He dropped down, as his Uncle Mordecai would have done, for Injun sign. Then he moved off, swift and silent—well, silent according to the playing of the game. He came through a screen of brush to the back of Konkapot's camp. It was empty. Good. He was about to start creeping down to the brush shelter when suddenly the branch over his head began to shake all by itself. His heart bumped, he turned—and there was Konkapot. He gestured for Abe to come on in and set.

The two of them sat, Injun fashion, at Konkapot's fire-pit. Konkapot stroked the ashes with a stick and a little orange flame lifted like the head of a pet snake. Konkapot looked at Abe. "You come *talk* Kongupah."

"Talk," Abe agreed, then remembering the first time he'd met Johnny at Grigsby's still-house added: "Or don't talk."

Konkapot considered that. Then he grinned and shook all over like he had the chills. Abe reckoned he was probably laughing, but without letting breath out. Konkapot took up a short-stemmed pipe, then a pinch of crumbled brown leaf. Lit a twist of grass in his fire, set it to the pipe, breathed up some smoke and let it out. He made like to offer it round a whole circle of people, but wasn't anyone else there. Then he offered the pipe to Abe. Abe sucked a little into his mouth—it bit his tongue, he spit it back out. That seemed somehow not good manners, so he smiled, the smoke got up his nose and made him cough. It left a taste in his mouth that was sweet and bitter by turns.

They sat there, not-talking, while Konkapot smoked the pipe out, his lips making little popping noises when he puffed. From a distance, the smoke had a spicy smell. Konkapot's not-talking went on past the time Abe expected he'd start again.

Then Abe noticed Konkapot was looking at him. Not like he usually looked at the boys, his eyes touch-and-go like a bird afraid to light. He was looking at Abe *measuringly*, nodding to himself. Then he said: "You' pappy gone to make meat. Don' take you."

"I ain't old enough," said Abe. "I ain't so old as Matt. Jest a little *tall*."

"Nah," said Konkapot. "You hunt: *plenny* good. Good t'ing you *not* shoot b'ar *dhat* time!" Konkapot did his silent laugh again.

"I ain't no hunter," said Abe. "Never shot *at* nothin' bigger'n squ'rl, and never hit one yet."

Konkapot took the point seriously. "Not ready yet, make *meat*," he allowed, "but you can larn *hunt*." He leaned forward: "*Dhese* men," he said, and waved his hand around as if the trees were a bunch of the most *pitiful* people he ever heard of, "*dhese* men make meat." Spits. "Easy make meat, dhese time here. Plenny deers. Plenny squ'rl. *Dhese* year, plenny."

Abe had never heard Konkapot say that much all at one time before. It was astonishing. And it seemed to exhaust the old man too, for he stopped talking and sat there so quiet it seemed like he'd stopped breathing. Then he whispered—like his breath was wore out—"You got *listen*. You want deers-meat, got to *listen* deers."

They sat quiet again, Konkapot looking at Abe, mild and friendly, but real clear. Abe thought Konkapot might talk some more, but he didn't.

After a while Abe stopped expecting him to talk.

Then he noticed the light had gone orange, the sun was dropping, he'd best get back to home.

Konkapot nodded his head, yes, as if something was agreed. "You come back, *I* show you *listen*. *I* show you *hunt*."

So as summer slid into fall, and Pap and Denny roved out farther afield hunting deer (for the woods near the settlement seemed to be hunted out), Abe slipped off into the brush with Konkapot, and the old Indian taught him the woods. It was a different learning from Pap's. Pap could put his eyes on an oak, tell you right off how many puncheons or staves or shakes a man could split himself out of it. He could use up a tree just looking at it. Konkapot looked at a tree and told you what kind of critters lived in it or fed on it, or what kind of "givin's" it offered you. That's a bee-tree. This one, make rope from strings under his bark. Blackoak, bark keeps your asshole tight. Burning-bush berries, eat him you can shit plenty too much, all you want. This small tree, all twisted back on himself? He'll find you water: just dig—he knows how to *listen* water.

He showed Abe where sang-roots like to grow, how to spot their wiry stems and berry-buds in a tangle of weeds. *Man-roots,* he called them: when you dug them up they were crotched like men, and also—Konkapot made a fist to show the unbelievable hardness of cock a man could get by eating that root. If you was weak or tired, chaw on it and your spirit come back to you. The skin of the earth was a thin dress laid on riches and powers. *Listen* her and she lifts her dress, she shows you—everything.

This is what roots are teaching.

Listening was Konkapot's secret of hunting. If you wanted the good of critters, you had to learn to listen how they think, what makes them scared, when are they hungry and what do they like to eat and where would they look first to get it, when did they want ... and Konkapot would put his trigger-finger through a thumb-forefinger hole, by which Abe figured he meant the same as buckin' and groanin'. Now was getting to be the time for *that* in particular. So now you were to take doe-sign for a promise of buck, vixen for fox, sow-bear for the boar, and so on.

How can a man know what a critter thinks? A man can't even tell what another man *is thinking.*

Konkapot brushed the words off like dust. Men and critters got the same breath: hungry, they got to eat; scared, they go hide; cock stands up, they want the woman. Get old, get shot—they die, both the same. *Listen.*

Mam at the supper table: "Where you been all day, Abe? You been down to the swimmin'?"

"No'm."

Silence.

Sary looked at him. "Aaron says you been talkin' to that ol' Konkapot."

Pap looked up from his vittles. "Konkapot," he said.

"He's teachin' me how to track like an Injun," said Abe. "You always said, Injuns is best for trackin'."

Pap nodded. He *had* said that, and he was right. Still, "I don't want you spendin' all your time with an Injun. I can show you trackin' myself when the time come. And there's plenty to do 'round here."

But in truth there *wasn't* much to do, and Pap off hunting was not around to see.

Konkapot's salt lick was the other side of a patch of swamp. There was an old beaver-dam, long time ago there'd been a pond, but it since bogged up. Hunters from the settlement went round it, but Konkapot knew how to pick his way across mostly dry-shod, and on the other side, where a spring fed the swamp, there was a little salt-seep.

Deer came down to it in the early morning: their coats a reddish-brown softened over with a breath of gray. Look how shy they step, how careful. Their little pointed feet and long legs, like walking tip-toe. Look how their ears turn, this way that way, listening. How when they need to listen, they become still: wasn't for the shine of their eyes, you'd think it was mist among gray branches. Nothing listens good as deer.

It was three does, and a young fawn born just that spring: the ghosts of his baby-spots mottled the soft leaf-tones of his hide. The deer stepped mincingly out of the trees, their ears swivel-ing. They came down to the lick. When two dropped their heads to nuzzle the lick, there was always one with her head up, ears swivel-ing. Deer are worried. Scared all the time. That's how they *live.* Good to be frightened *some* time.

That's what deers larn you.

Konkapot gave Abe the rifle. He winked and pointed. That meant for Abe to aim the rifle at the deer.

The two of them were stretched out behind a downed oak. Abe

checked the rifle's flint and priming: good. He carefully poked the gun over the log, slowly, thinking he must point the rifle as silently and delicately as the deer moved. He rested the long barrel on the log and sighted on the deer that was standing, head erect, watching while the others took salt. His eyesight ran the length of the barrel out to the deer: the animal littled by distance, but somehow enlarged in the notch of the rifle sight.

Abe pressed the hammer back slow and steady with his thumb, willing that the sound of the hammer cocking be no more to the deer than the tick of a water drop, not even as loud as a twig-snap for that was danger to a deer, frightened all the time, listening listening, nothing in the world can listen to everything the way a deer can listen ... the doe's head turning, bright liquid eyes watchful, black wet nostrils flexing and flaring, tasting the air, the ears turning to the *drip* as the hammer went to half-, *drop*, and full-cock ... the doe worried about it, a second doe raised her head, the deer afraid of him and she didn't even know who or where or what he was. This was how Uncle Mordecai felt with that Injun in his sights. *Shoot now shoot now shoot now or they'll spook and run away shoot shoot shoot.*

The deer raised their four heads all at once and stood there, frozen, all four pairs of ears swiveled in his direction, then away, then back again: the silence of their listening seemed to fill the air out to the end of all space.

I can't shoot them while they're listening.

Abe's thumb eased the hammer back, releasing the cocked spring, eased it down with tense care and delicacy so that not the least sound should frighten the deer. He looked down at the ground, ashamed to look at Konkapot.

But he couldn't do that forever. When he looked up, Konkapot was watching him, and nodding his head in approval.

Back at Konkapot's camp they sat quiet. Then Konkapot said, "One time: *Sperits* make *dhis* place. People live under groun'. *Long* time. Plenny cold. Plenny *dark*. Hungry? All *dhat* time." He thought a moment, then said again, "Hungry."

But there was a young man, he said, a good hunter. He understood, knew how to listen what those animals were thinking. He
would go out and hunt, always trying to make meat to feed the
people waiting for him, hungry. He killed, killed a lot. But always,
you know, he felt inside—because he could understand how they
thought, those animals down there, he knew what they were feeling
when he was killing them, he understood, and so he was always
sorry. And one time he said it, right out loud, he killed a deer and
said he was sorry, it was the only way his people could live themselves and not die, yet he was sad about it: inside.

Then out there in the dark in the underground he saw two lights
shining—like deer's eyes when they come to your fire at night, curious as any damn squirrel. Only tall . . . this deer was very tall.
Looked at him a certain way: with her eyes. Then she run off. And
so he tracked her—he could tell it was a doe, she didn't drag her feet
the way a buck will but stepped very light, but still it was a big doe,
very big, very tall. And he thought how the meat of that doe would
feed the people, such sweet good meat, and so much. But then, the
more he tracked this doe the more he was also sorry to have to kill
her, for she was so tall, the tallest doe he ever heard of, her steps so
beautiful to follow, and her smell on the ground.

And then: he come upon her, sudden. He don't catch her: she's
waiting for him, listening for him to come and waiting for his arrow
like a gift, like she makes herself a present to him. And that hunter,
that young man: he saw how she been listening *him* that whole time,
just like he listened *her*, smelled him just like he smelled her. He
picked up his bow. He set his arrow. He was going to shoot. He took
aim at her: and that time, going to shoot, he looked in her eyes.

"Not deer's eyes." Konkapot nodded his head, looking far away.
"*Woman* eyes."

The hunter dropped his arrow to the ground.

Then it wasn't a deer, but a tall woman. She was the color of a
deer, only with a woman's skin, and her legs very long but only two
of them. And she had a dark brush like a woman, not a white one
like a deer. "So *she* took him—dhat *hunter*—*she* showin' him: a certain *place* she got, a certain hole: and other side *dhat* hole . . ." He

raised his hands and arms, his head, and swiveled his body side to side, indicating everything around them: trees, late sunlight coming through them, the brush, sounds of birds, the smell of a cookfire. Konkapot smiled. "So dhen: good t'ing you don' *shoot*, some time."

It was like an Aesop story, to tell Abe a man didn't have to pull trigger just because he had the drop. There was a time to kill, and a time to let be.

So then: that was Konkapot's learning.

October 1817

It was early fall, the sun gone ripe. Pap and Denny had hung the smokehouse full of deer carcasses. Reuben Grigsby paid most of what he owed for the kegs. And for sign (Aunt Betsey said) their works found favor in the eyes o' the Lord, here come their hogs back that had run off, returning like the Prodigal. Or better, said Mam, for the Prodigal come lean, but these were fatted on the mast they snouted off the forest floor—beechnuts, acorns, butternuts, mulberries. Now winter was in the air they hankered for husks and scraps.

Pap poured out their cash money on the table. Mam looked over his shoulder, Abe and Sary stood to her side; Denny and Aunt Betsey peeped over Tom Sparrow's shoulder at the pile of coins and paper. Pap counted it out. If he warn't out of reckoning, he had to allow they had enough to go to Vincennes and pay the first installments on *both* claims. Might even be some extra—if there was, Pap had a mind to a cow.

"The Lord been good to us this year," said Pap, and rapped his knuckles on the board, and everybody said Amen. "Pra-aise Him!" said Aunt Betsey, like it was Meeting.

That night Mam came up to Abe and Sary and read them Moses in the desert, and manna from the heavens.

Next afternoon when Abe went out to the sinks, there come an unaccountable *hush* over everything. Air still, not a breath in the leaves. No bird. Only, high up in the cloudless blue above the trees, he could see turkey-buzzards circling and drifting north and east. Abe judged they were watching the woods past Whitman's, up towards the headwaters of Little Pigeon. Then he heard a sound rising behind the northward trees, a low rushing sound like a wind. But the air was still, not leaf budged, not insect clicked, not.

A huge black cloud glided sudden up out of the trees, moving by itself swift and steady but still no wind, its edge no sooner seen than its full dark body rising after it, lifting and stretching and stretching out, the trees bowing and clashing their leaves in the down-draft.

"*Mam!*" Abe yelled as the cloud came up and up and he saw its edges were fraying out in winged flying scraps—not a cloud but a cloud of birds, a million million of them, the air full of their whooing, and the wind of their wings made the air shudder as if flat hands were pounding over the mouths of his ears. The sky blacked out as the birds piled up over the cabin and their shit fell like rain, pelting Abe as he ran for the cabin, shit splattering like a downpour on the roof-shakes.

It stopped suddenly. Pap threw the door open and they stepped outside. There was the clearing again, the sun pouring hot through the still air, everything splotched with bird-shit. The bird-cloud wheeled northeastward towards the headwaters of Little Pigeon, circling down now, like a black whirlpool with its root in the woods north of Whitman's.

"A pigeon-roost," said Pap, his voice hushed, Meeting-like. "Ain't seen the like since I was a boy." Then Pap noticed Abe, grabbed his shirt, and shook him almost like he was mad, only he was happy, fierce-happy. "Get Uncle Sparrow. Tell him it's a pigeon-roost—he'll know what to bring!" Then he ran for the horse-shed, hollering for Nancy to get some salt made, *plenty* salt . . .

They broke through the brush into a patch of open woods. Beyond was a thicket of old trees, black branches thick and rough with leaves—until you looked again and saw every one of the limbs crowded with hundreds of birds, ranged along the branches like mourners seated on the witness-bench, or clumped together thick as maggots in a carcass wriggling for room. From back in the grove came the sound of tree-limbs snapping, crashing down, a sudden lift in the constant all-encompassing bubbling of the birds, the pattering incessant bird-shit rain.

Old Reuben was first on the ground, stalking round and round his campfire like a tethered wolf. When he saw them he hollered, "Hi-yi! You damned tenderfeet! I been a-waitin' here since I seen them buzzards! Can't fool a buzzard, and you can't fool Reuben Grigsby! We can *smell* a killin' on the way!"

"Dang it, Grizby!" Tom Sparrow yelled. "Git out the way and let a man make some meat!"

As each family arrived they built bonfires and unpacked their gear. The men grabbed poles or ax-helves and went among the trees. Abe hung back. It was full dark, the bonfires washed the outer pillars of the grove with orange tongues of light. The fire gleamed in the million eyes of the birds so that it looked like the branches were full of fire-flies. *Listen birds,* Abe tried to tell himself, but it was too many to listen, and what was happening in the trees was no more hunting than swatting flies. From behind the fire-lit pillars he heard the thumping of the poles and the crash of branches, men yelling, the sudden intense up-bubbling of sound among the pervading coo and rumble of the pigeons.

Matt popped up alongside Abe, his face soot-smutched, grinning, his eyes brilliant blue in the fire-light. "C'mon Abe!" he yelled, his hoarse tight voice already rasped raw and the night just starting. "C'mon with me! We gonna kill us a goddamn mess o' these goddamn birds!"

Something bound Abe to the spot. *If you can't listen a thing you ain't got the right to kill it.*

Matt jerked on Abe's arm; then his eyes sharpened: "What's the matter? Ain't you 'lowed?"

That broke the tether. Of course he was allowed, he warn't no girl nor baby! A bolt of terror and also a kind of joy shot through him, he grabbed an ax-helve and pelted on Matt's heels into the grove.

Limbs were crashing and thumping, a million birds cooing and hooing and oodling all around and overhead, birds whirring at your eyes like giant moths. Abe started swatting with his ax-helve, bashing birds out of the air like a man batting flies. Men with poles were thumping the tree-limbs and the birds' bodies would drop like ripe fruit, or sometimes a whack would crack the limb and the weight of the birds do the rest, the men ducking from under as the limb fell— then club and club the live whirring that slapped at your knees, Abe swinging the ax-helve blind into the flutter and squirming around his shins like a man beating down swarms of bird-sized bugs, swat, splatter, thump. Abe's bare feet churned in a muck of birds. Shit rained down, splat on his head, stinging an eye. "Next time wear a hat!" Denny hollered. Now the men were bringing in kettles of burning smutch, greenwood fed with hog fat, and the greasy smoke dropped more birds out of the upper branches. Everybody was swaying and running and roaring and singing and laughing, faces blacked with smutch-smoke and blood and bird-shit, hooting and hallooing like they gone crazy, clubbing everything that moved.

Smoke still drifted among the trunks when they started gathering the bird-harvest by morning light. They scooped the feathered beak-thorned lumps into sacking or hide bags, or strung 'em in dozens on thongs to sling from saddle and pack-frame bows. They tromped half the dead into the mud—more than half. No need to take bruised fruit with so much prime lying all over the ground. The mud itself was more than half bird-shit.

Pap showed teeth in the filthy mask of his face: "That's what I call a pigeon hunt!"

Aunt Betsey said it was the same as the manna from heaven. They emptied the sacks of dead pigeons, plucked split and gutted the bodies, strung and spitted them to smoke or laid them in salt, all of it in a frenzy of haste to be done before the dead birds rotted or went fly-blown.

Whether it was *manna* or just *good luck*, Abe finally couldn't stand any more of it, and sneaked off for a bathe in the creek. There was a thicket of young cottonwoods above the swimming hole, and as Abe came up to it he heard Matt Gentry's hoarse whisper: "Git down!"

Matt was crouched in the thicket, blue eyes flashed in his dirty freckled face, his hair was a matted red tangle. He kept grinning and sticking out his tongue, "Look! Look!" he rasped and jerked Abe close. Through the screen of leaves Abe saw pink and white shapes moving by the water—

"I got 'em!" Matt rasped. "Waited for 'em to go wash an' I *snuck* 'em, an' now I *got* 'em!"

All Abe saw was the flash of it and couldn't hardly remember exactly after because he had no names for what he was seeing, only women/girl *shapes*, six seven eight of them curved and bending, splashing and chattering in high birdlike voices, the doubled bulges of their chests with eyes in them, buttock splits and black bush-tails at the groins . . .

Matt's mouth kept running like he couldn't stop it anymore "I seen 'em, I seen all of 'em, I seen their nekkids, I—!"

Abe *screamed* at Matt and grabbed him by the shirt and shook him. Fury whipped through him, red as blood and fire like when he tried to kill Andy Simms, and he threw Matt away—then went for him furious like a swimmer thrashing across the pool. Matt was crying and yelling, "You crazy son of a bitch!"

Something snatched Abe and threw him sideways in the brush. He lit and rolled, ready to come again—

But there was Denny holding Matt by the arms, Matt yelling, "Lemme go! Lemme kill him! He's ruined everything!"

"Ease up there, hoss," said Denny. "The game has got away." There was no sound from the pool. The women and girls must have heard them and run off.

"I'm goin' to drop you," Denny said to Matt. "When I do, you git on home."

He let Matt go. Tears had cut runnels in the dirt of Matt's face, washing some of the freckles clean. His blue eyes were full of righteous outrage and his mouth was twisted with it. "He's *crazy*!" He took a breath. "Hangin' 'round that old Injun." He was panting. "Goddamned Injun-lover!"

Denny grabbed Matt and shook him: he was more than twice

Matt's size. "I said that's enough now. You *git!*" Denny dropped him, and Matt scooted into the brush.

Denny looked seriously at Abe. He shook his head. "*You* got to larn to take things *easier*," he said. "Wasn't any of *our* womenfolks got see'd."

Tossing and turning on the shucks all night: why *didn't* he take things easier? Nobody cared a hang how the pigeons come or how they killed 'em. Nobody but whoever was kin to those women cared if Matt and Denny had see'd their nekkids.

Dawn-light in the chinks. He crept down from the loft. Mam was asleep in the pole-bed with Aunt Betsey: Pap off to Vincennes, all the luck of their year in a leather pouch. Pap took his luck as it come. So did Denny.

He eased out the cabin door.

On the far side of the clearing something moved: brown against brown tree-trunks, color wouldn't show what it was but his eye caught the movement.

The cabin door was ajar. He reached in and to the right, where Pap's long rifle always leaned ready to hand, just where it had been that day when the lawyer and the nigger rode onto their land in Knob Creek, just where Grandpappy's rifle must have been leaning the day Uncle Mordecai plugged the Injun. The cool barrel in the palm of his hand. He lifted it, eased it round the door-post careful not to knock it. Then he had it, right hand on the curving neck where the stock flowed into the body of the piece. He looked to the priming: primed.

He would need a rest for the long barrel. Woodpile off to his right. He moved that way, glidingly. Lowered himself behind the woodpile and took his rest. All the time his eyes were open as Konkapot taught him, not probing the edge of the woods like a finger poking something—taking in everything in general not one thing in particular, letting all the light around you into your eyes, all the little movements . . .

There: brown against the brown. Now it was becoming something, moving stiffly, jerkily this way, that way. Now it is this: a wild cock-turkey, stepping point-toe into the yard, pecking grains and bits of offal off the ground. He's got long legs, longer than a chicken's, and a body like a big brown melon. There he spreads his fan. There he lifts his head: a shiny knobby red-and-blue cock-head lifting on his long scraggy neck. A bright eye—head profiled left, the wattles swagging off the nose like a bull's balls. Head profiled right . . .

Abe eased the rifle forward on its rest: soundless. Eased the hammer back, his hand muffling the snick as it came to full cock. *Come on,* Abe thought as if his spirit was talking to the bird's, *come here come closer so I can kill you. I want to kill you, I want you to come closer so I can kill you.*

Listen him, Konkapot said. *Listen what he is how he think.*

The turkey stopped. Wasn't sure. Profile left. Did he hear something? Turkey thinks: *Hungry. Lots corn-seed. Bits of dead pigeon. It's easy. I sure as God am one lucky turkey!* Profile right. Profile left. The eye bright with greed.

In the flash before the barrel-smoke blanked it out Abe saw the cock-head explode.

"I got him!" Abe yelled.

He crouched by the turkey. It flopped, its scaly legs jerked, and its wings flared and quivered. Its red naked neck ended in rags of skin and a small spout of blood scrawled signatures in the dirt. He remembered the warty head, the wattles looped over the beak, the beady eye, left right, hungry, frightened. Gone.

Then he was sorry.

Then Mam was there, and Aunt Betsey behind her, both in their shifts, Denny with one gallus holding up his trousers. "Whoo-ee," said Denny, "plugged the head at forty paces. There's a lucky shot!"

Abe wheeled on him hot: "It ain't luck!" he yelled and realized he was crying.

Mam paid them no mind. She looked into Abe's eyes and he looked back. It had been so long, an age of the world since last she saw him so, and he saw her: how her deep eyes were so blue, night-blue not gray-blue like his own, and the smooth dome of her fore-

head, the narrow tapering planes of her cheeks, and her wide thin-
lipped mouth smiling at him real gentle. She said, "Mebbe if you
give thanks for this turkey, Abe, it'll set better with you."

". . . though what we'll do with *more* bird-meat I'm sure *I* can't
tell," he heard Aunt Betsey mutter.

So he sighed, closed his eyes, and said the words inside. *Thank
you thank you, I'm sorry I killed you for nothing.* He wasn't sure was he
saying it to God the turkey or Konkapot. Behind his closed eyes he
kept seeing the bright eye of the bird in its red-blue gnarled and
warty head. *Boom!*

That night Abe dreamed:

They were battling the trees with axes—Abe and Pap and Denny,
Old Reuben dancing from stump to stump, all the men were there,
their axes made the trees ring and shake and crack. Branches
dropped all around them, loaded with birds, the clearing was crawling with birds plucked naked as worms, the men were clubbing
them. When Abe looked down the pigeons were looking up at him
with hundreds of fire-fly-bright eyes.

Their eyes were the eyes of baby girls. Abe said to himself *It is
Old Reuben Grigsby's baby sisters.*

The men were painted like Injuns and they were massacring the
baby girls with their axes, Old Reuben was doing it too, dressed up
like a black bear, whooping and yipping. Abe couldn't stand it, he
looked away . . .

Konkapot was sitting in a tree, watching them.

Konkapot had a silver medal around his neck.

On the far side of the clearing a man with a long Kentucky rifle
was taking aim at Konkapot. In the dream Abe said *Don't shoot him
don't shoot the Injun the Injun is the only one that ain't an Injun*—but no
sound, and then he knew there was no way the man with the long
rifle would heed him.

The man with the rifle was Uncle Mordecai, his pale eyes bright
and sharp as the barbs of fish-hooks. Abe looked in those eyes, felt
the hooks stick him.

Then he was himself looking down the long barrel of the gun: he could see a round silver medal on a thong hung from Konkapot's neck. *Swinging right, left, right.* He leveled on it. Patience. Hold steady. The medal swings *left* through the notch of the gunsight *when it swings right again I will shoot out his heart.*

He woke in the dark. He'd escaped the dream, but it wasn't gone. It was lurking in the black corners of the loft, waiting for him to sleep again.

He crept downstairs, the pegs hard on his bare feet. He heard Mam and Aunt Betsey snoring in the bed. He hesitated.

"What's the trouble, honey?" Mam got out of bed, the tick crackling, and stood tall and pale in her shift. Next he knew he had his face in her chest, her great long-fingered soft hands were stroking his bristle of hair, he was drenched in the salt-sweaty smokey grassy smell of Mam. He couldn't speak the dream to her, he was ashamed and afraid of it, he just cried, "Mam I don't want to have to kill nobody."

Her hand stopped for one heartbeat in its petting of him, as if *that* fear had power to stop even her love. But then she give his head a little squeeze, and hugged him closer. "You ain't got to kill nothin' you don't want to, Abe."

He felt the hard bone in the middle of her breast against his forehead. In the old days when she hugged him like this it was to the soft of her belly.

Mam took her Bible off the shelf. She guided him across the room and they sat on the fire-step where the banked hearth could warm them. It was too dark for Abe to read, but Mam never needed no light but what was in herself. She opened the book on her knees. "Did I ever read you David and Solyamun?"

They was Kings of Isril, in the Promised Land of Milk and Honey. David, when he warn't but a boy tending his Pappy's stock, used to sing to keep 'em all in a bunch. Yet when a wolf come to kill the lambs David warn't afraid, but outs with his slungshot and whaps that wolf right in the eye, kilt him dead and skinned him out *slick*. And later he kilt Go-liar, the champion wrassler of the Philsatines (which was a kind of Injuns the Isrils had), cut his head right off. He had two gifts, Mam said: the warrior's gift, and the singer's, to sing *and* tell stories such that they changed people in their hearts. Book tells how once he drove the blue devils out of Old King Saul. They say he wrote the Psalms we sing at Meeting.

"Mam? Did they make David King on account of singing?"

"No," she said. "It was for the other gift: the gift of a man of war."

A man who could kill a wolf and a giant. And scalp 'em.

"But it come at a price," said Mam. "For when David asked the Lord could he build a church for him—the House for the Lord in the Holy City Jerusalem—the Lord said no he couldn't, because he was a Man of *Blood*."

"Well, there ain't no other way for a king to be." There wasn't but two choices: learn to kill and like it like a man, or stay home with the women.

Mam smiled. "Well now, David, he hadn't no choice but to shed blood. The wolf was after his sheep. The giant was a-goin' to kill his people. It was David's providence to have to clear the woods. But David had a son after him . . ."

And that was Solyamun, who had his father's gift for song and larning. Mam stroked the open pages of the Book. "His words is in these pages. Where anyone can read them, anytime. Proverbs which is wisdom, and Solyamun's Song which is his joyful book, and his sad book which is 'Clesiasties." She began to read and the words run soothing through him: "To ever'thing there's a season, and a time to every purpose under heaven. A time to be born and a time to die. A time to reap and a time to sow. A time to kill . . ."

Yes, he thought, *I know. You can't un-know what you know.*

". . . and a time to heal, a time to gather up . . ."

So you could *be King if you weren't a Man of Blood, if your Pap and Uncle Mordecai done the work of blood on your account. Only—was it* right *to get the thing on such easy terms, without having to dirty his hand one single . . . ?*

". . . and a time to cast away, a time of peace . . ." *A time, a time, a time . . .*

. . .

He woke again to morning light in the window. His head was in Mam's lap. She was asleep with her back to the rough stones of the fireplace. It was a hard place, but she looked like she was smiling to be there.

Chapter 5: **The Bear**

Fall–Winter 1817–1818

They had a week of bright sun burning through crisp frost: and it was like the forest had took fire of itself, the yellow orange and red blowing up in it all of a sudden. When you walked under the beeches and maples the high-domed roof blazed gold with sun, and slices of gold leaf peeled off and floated down the air and paved the ground under your moccasins.

The men came back from Vincennes, Tom Sparrow riding the jackass mule and Pap leading on a rope a slab-sided brown-and-white cow. The cow's heavy belly swagged from her bony haunches like a hide swung from two pair of tent-poles. "Here we come," cried Tom Sparrow. "Git out the honey, children, *we* brung the milk!" All that fall and into the first of winter they had corn bread made with milk and a touch of soured dough, and hoecake with butter and honey.

Pap and Uncle Sparrow also brought back the talk of Vincennes to spice their meals. Harry Clay was the coming man for President.

He was pushing for his "American System": tariffs to keep the British out our hair and make money for "internal improvements"—roads canals steamboats and such, so a man could get his crop to market. Uncle Sparrow misdoubted Clay was "sound on the nigger," but Pap wouldn't hear him: Clay wanted the niggers off the white man's back—was head of a new Colonizer Association, free the niggers and send them back to Africa where they belong. "I bet Henry Clay is smart as Solyamun," Abe said, and was proud when Pap agreed.

Mam didn't care for politics. Her heart was set on a new Meeting, a House to have it in, and a Preacher. "The Lord been prosperous to *us*. We got to do as well by *Him*." That fall she visited cabin to cabin, talking up the Meeting. She got Grigsby to donate the land, so that Gentry felt obliged to say they might cut the timber on his land and use his teams to horse it to the site.

Abe began to like Mam's notion of "providence" better than the "luck" Pap was so happy about. When a thing came by providence, God meant for you to have it. True, you couldn't always be sure *why* He meant you to have it—since, in Mam's way of thinking, God was unaccountable: one day return good for good you done, then like as not lay an ejectment on you, or a massacre. Yet with providence there was *something* back of the give and take. Whereas with luck, things just come or didn't, no reason at all to it, not even unaccountable ones. In Abe's estimation the pigeons were luck: whether the good of eating them or the bad of the stink, they were no-one's deserving. But the cow? She was providence. They'd fought the trees a whole year to earn that cow.

Fall went out storming and winter came in the same. They were bound to the cabin more than usual. To Abe it seemed like reward for how hard they worked all year. Nights Mam would read to them, David and Solyamun, Moses and Adam and all. Then one night she turned to him: "Why don't you read us something, Abe? Out of that book Mister Riney give you?"

Everybody looked at him, except Denny, who was stretched out on his back in front of the fire trying to get the hang of a Jew's-harp he won from Allen Gentry on a fishing bet. Every now and then he'd give out a buzzing nosey twang.

"It's too dark to read, Mam," he said.

"Speak it how you larned it, Abe. That's all I ever do."

"Which one should I tell?"

She smiled, and winked. "Jest look around you, and say whichever come to mind."

Denny gave the Jew's-harp another *twoingy boingk*, then tucked it in his pocket. "I think I'm gittin' the hang of it."

That put Abe in mind of the story of the Fox, and the Crow up the tree with the cheese in its beak. He looked into the corner so as not to see them all watching him, and told how the Fox flattered the Crow it could sing so beautiful, till the fool bird give out a scrawk and lost the cheese. When he was done he looked at Mam again— she was smiling proud, and Pap gave Denny and Tom Sparrow a satisfied look. Denny had even sat up to pay heed. Sary was the most excited, and asked him to say another. The Crow in the tree reminded him of George Washington's cherry tree, so he told that one.

The women and Sary all said that was a good one too. Denny said, "I don't reckon I'd let on if I busted *my* pappy's best tree on purpose."

Mam said: "That's why *you* ain't goin' to be George Washington when you grow up."

Denny smiled to be laughed at. "Shucks," he said, "it's hard enough work bein' Dennis Hanks."

Later that night it come to Abe that Mam had given him her secret, how she worked her reading so as to make it *tell* people something—tell them *sideways*, not bossy like Pap. Maybe . . . maybe she was trying to show him a way to become King or George Washington without having to be a Man of Blood like Uncle Mordecai.

Rain and sleet in the shank of the year. There were wolves about the settlement, *hooling* and *yowling* off in the woods behind the patter of sleet on dead leaves. Pap brought word Matt Gentry was poorly.

That gave Abe a twinge. He and Matt had been fast friends, then come the *nekkids* and Abe got crazy mad and threw him down. He remembered the frantic fevered look on Matt's face. So when Mam went to Gentry's store to trade for blanket-cloth Abe went with her.

Matt had a little room to himself on the second floor of the house built onto the back of the store. He lay in bed staring at the roof. He didn't look peaked or feverish, just dull and sad, eyes bleak, mouth slack. "Abe," he said, like it made no difference.

"Matt. What's wrong with you?"

A bright line of tear showed along Matt's eyelids. He gathered himself to speak like he was lifting a weight. "I don't know," he said. "Winter come in. I looked out the winder—it felt like the sky jest closed down on me."

"I'm sorry I cussed at you!"

Matt shrugged; *that* made no difference either. "I jest feel . . . feel *low*. Like it ain't worth the trouble to breathe." He looked up. "Sometimes so sad I want to howl like a bitch wolf and never quit."

Abe didn't know what to do to help. He remembered how David had drove off the King's blue devils by singing. Abe's singing would probably do more harm than good. But—"Say Matt, I read a story in a book. Want me to tell you?"

So he told him the one about the Fox that tricked the Crow to drop the cheese, being reminded by "singing," and because it was one of the cheerier Aesops—the Crow didn't have to die for the sake of the moral. Abe reckoned Matt would think *he* was the Fox, red hair and all.

He was right. Matt perked up. "You got that out of a book, did you, Abe?" His eyes sharpened, he seemed to have a touch of his old energy. "Can you read *any* book?"

Abe allowed he could, in reason.

Now Matt was grinning again: "All right! Next time you come, I'll git a surprise for you!"

. . . "My," said Mam on their way home, "Miz Gentry says you was better for Matt than *doctors*." She beamed at him. "I knowed you had that kind of gifts, Abe."

· · ·

The very next week Mrs. Gentry invited Abe specially to come over and set with Matt. They were like pie to him, even Allen looked at him respectful—or at least, like he needed to stand off and calculate on Abe some more.

Matt's surprise was a book from his Pa's shelf down in the store, which he had smouched for Abe to read to him. It was called *The Arabian Nights Entertainments, Consisting of One Thousand and One Stories Told by the Sultaness of the Indies, to Divert the Sultan.* Abe read out the title to Matt to show he could do it, and Matt said, "A thousand and one," kind of awed. A thousand and one different stories: it was like they had found a treasure mine.

Treasure mine it was: for just about every story in it was about some poor boy striking it rich in the most gorgeous way—palaces covered with gold and jewels, heaps of coins and rings, delicious food to eat, and almost always beautiful princesses. Matt perked up when princesses come in sight, but Abe said no *buckin'* talk if he was going to read. Matt said all right, but you could almost hear him *buckin'* away inside his head.

These stories were somewhat like Aesop, only the morals weren't the same. Abe liked the Sinbad stories, which told how you could get rich by working at it, if you didn't mind sufferings monsters and shipwrecks along the way—and was good to the poor. On the other hand, anyone could have found that Ali Baba lamp and got the lamp-nigger to fetch him those jewels and palaces.

Abe was fondest of Shebazade the Sultaness, because she was the one *made up* all the stories. She reminded him of that black Queen of Sheba in the Solyamun Song, who was tall as towers and sweet as grapes, and also concerned with the building of wonderful palaces of gold, costly jewels, hewed stones, and pomegranates. Abe speculated the two women might be the same, Sheba being a pet-name for Shebazade. Could be she met Solyamun, and after he passed hooked up with the Sultan. Or t'other way round.

But Matt didn't care if Shebazade was Solyamun's granny, or Henry Clay was George Washington's left-hand son. What Matt cared about were the virgin princesses, with "the grace of the Arabian the morals of the French and the ardor of the Eth'opian"—the *spots* of the Eth'opian, Abe said, and Matt said no, you jackass, it's *lepers* got the *spots*, and they laughed till their sides hurt.

Winter, Spring, Summer 1818

The weather cleared. Then, just like last winter, Abe and Pap went out again to fight the war against the trees. Same war as last year: cut girdle and burn. Winter slid out, spring slid in: the dead trees heaped and burned in huge piles, the air spoilt with smoke. Then plowing, Abe standing on the blade so it would cut, ripping and tripping through ground shot through and through with root-webs, gee-hawing round the standing stumps and girdled dead trees. Then the crop in the ground. A time to clear brush and a time to nigger off, a time to girdle and a time to burn, a time to plow and a time to plant—same as last year . . .

. . . and summer after that, the same. On the Fourth the Little Pigeon militia drilled in the heat and re-elected Old Reuben Captain, to Jim Gentry's disappointment.

The summer swole and ripened, maybe hotter than last year. They'd get rain but the storms didn't blow the heat away, and the thick air held the wet in the ground. The bogs along the branch spread out, there was standing water in the gullies, white-flowered snakeweed sprung sudden and lush all through the woods. The skeeters were fierce and plenty too much, as Konkapot would say. The first corn came in musty, with worms in the tops. Abe wondered if the dead birds poisoned the ground. Konkapot wouldn't say.

Folks got snappish. Talk of starting a Meeting hung fire. Gentrys and Grigsbys weren't on speaking terms, not even to give each other the snoot. Carter was going to law on Whitman. Pap started worrying the cash payment for next year's installment on their claim. But when he went to Gentry to collect his carpenting money, "standin' at his door like a nigger with my hat in my hand," Gentry

said he was cash-poor this season. Cash-poor? The man was speculating claims with Pap's owed wages, "and the son of a bitch says
why don't I collect from Grizby if I'm that *hard* up."

But Grigsby was short too, so he said. Gentry wasn't buying his
whiskey, he had to flatboat it downriver "and don't make but a
penny profit on a keg." But here—he'd hire Pap to float his goods to
Shawneetown: six dollars a week wages, Pap to build the flat. "I
ain't his hired hand," Pap yelled at Mam. He slammed his carpenter
box down in the corner. Then he kicked it. "I always hated the
damned trade! Wage workin' ain't man's work!"

The hard looks Pap couldn't afford to give Gentry and Grigsby
he passed down to Tom Sparrow and Denny Hanks—and Mam and
Abe and Sary too when they didn't walk smaller than small. It was
Tom Sparrow's notion to settle in Indiana, warn't it? Little credit to
him, and less to Pap for taking Tom Sparrow's word on anything.
Should have listened to his brother: Mord Lincoln was a *man* anyway, if he *was* a mean son of a bitch. If anyone practiced on *him* the
way Old Hanks done Pap . . .

August. September. Damp heat clung. Sloughs that had formed
along the creek-beds got stale. Skeeters whined and stung, hovered
in drifts above the water. They had dumb ager shaking ager chill
ager and buck ager. People left off tending their stock, cows were let
roam the woods and feed themselves on thistle and fat-stemmed
snakeweed.

Then Tom Whitman came to say his cow had got the trembles
and fell down paralyzed. By the time Pap got there the cow was
dead. When Pap came back he said it was probably nothing but jim-
son weeds or snake-bite. But his face was pale, his eyes ran all over
the place like they were afraid to settle and look at one thing. Next
day Mister Brooner came by and spent an hour jawing angrily with
Pap down at the gate. Some of Old Reuben's stock had got the trembles and died, in this heat his cows were always grazing off his
pasture into the woods on Brooner's section. When Brooner told
Reuben he ought to kill the sick ones and pen the rest the old man

grabbed his rifle and ordered him off the place: said Brooner was a damned fool, didn't he know Milk-sick a-comin' when he see'd it? Brooner was in a rage: "I won't have my own stock ketch sick off his! If that old renegade won't kill them cows, some man will sure as hell do it for him!"

The day after that young Miz Whitman got the pukes and was dead before Tom could get help. Whatever it was killed her, her baby took it in suck and died too. Pap said it must be buck ager, this was the time for buck ager and Miz Whitman had had the pukes.

Mam said: "You know it is Milk-sick."

"Hush," said Pap. "Talk like that can git a man burnt out of his claim."

There was a crowd in front of Gentry's store. Jessie, one of Matt's little sisters—the Milk-sick had got her one day and killed her the next. A healthy little Christian child.

Abe found Matt in his secret place under the floor. He was sitting with his head bent over and his knees hugged tight to hide his face. Abe felt it was the time to not-talk. He sat with Matt, listening the way Konkapot taught him. It seemed he could hear words running fast inside Matt's head, words that didn't make any sense. Matt lifted his face runneled with tear-marks. "I never never," he said, "I never never looked at her, I lied about it I never never really done it."

"Ain't your fault, jest her bad luck." But that wasn't much better than lying: who could say it *wasn't* providence?

Next day Something came down on Matt Grigsby in his own bed. Sister Casebier told Mam they heard him groaning at first light, went in and he's on the floor crouched into hisself like a dog, father and brother standing off, afeared. His Ma come in to him—meaning nothing but kindness—and he, he *sprung* at her, went for her throat biting and groppling so they had to twist his fingers off her one by one.

Mam started off right away, taking Abe along, thinking maybe Abe could talk Matt round like he done before. But before they came in sight of Gentry's they heard Matt howling, a hoarse full-throated howling like he had turned into a wolf, and a mad wolf too—only just that hoarse note left in his howl to remind you who he used to be.

Abe knew what happened. Matt had gone to sleep grieving, his guard was down, and the black miseries come back and took him for good, turned Abe's best friend in the world into a howling dog. Mam was walking next to him. He reached out and grabbed her by the hand. She looked at him. His eyes were almost level with hers, but he felt small and wished he was smaller. "Mam," he said, "don't make me go look at him." He couldn't explain. They had tied him to a stump in the yard like he was a dog, so he couldn't hurt nobody, and left him there to howl. *If I see Matt like that he won't ever be Matt for me again. Once you know a thing, you can't ever un-know it.* "I'm terrible afeared of him that way. Mam, I'm *terrible* afeared."

She turned back, still holding his hand. "Then it ain't needful you should go. If your heart's ag'in it, it ain't needful." But she was disappointed. And he came down inside himself: he wasn't up to what *she* was for kindness any more than he was up to Uncle Mordecai for killing. He'd been judged by experience, and found wanting.

Next week the Milk-sick killed the youngest Turnham boy, and after that Miz Brooner, Mam's good "Sister Lizbeth," though Mam herself nursed and prayed over her.

Milk-sick Milk-sick, if I knew what it was I could tell it stories and make it go to sleep, I could cuss and scare it off, I could listen *it like deers I could track it and shoot it and bust its head on a post and skin it and nail its scalp its paws its ears to the wall—or even if it was a million million things, if I knew what they was I could smash them out of the trees with poles, I could choke them with smutch I could burn the whole goddamned forest down to finish them off . . .*

But nobody knows what Milk-sick is, whether it is catching by touch like spot-fever or hoof-and-mouth, or by breathing paludals like the ager, or by poison in the snakeweed their cattle et—

Or maybe it is no *sickness* at all, maybe it is *judgment*.

But what fault could it be, if the punishment takes young girls like Matt's sister and little babies like Miz Whitman's and leaves old rips like Reuben Grigsby safe? The fault couldn't just be one thing, but something tangled and mixed up with everything they were and done, like the weave of roots and rootlets and runners that webbed the earth—the plow ripping stumblingly through it, tripped and catched in the web-work, or busted on some big buried root-monster that had to be chopped out with mattocks—and even when you cleared a field, next year there'd be saplings shooting up, and always the web of roots working and spreading. Just that way, something in him and in everyone he knew and loved, some fault or darkness was working itself to the surface, and judgment coming down on himself and all of them on account of it, coming down sure and steady and merciless as the growth of trees or the turn of seasons.

October 1818

Abe heard the sound in his sleep, the deep hoarse hooting roar, and he clawed his way awake the way he climbed cold water from the bottom of the swimming hole to reach air. Pale bits of predawn sparked in the chinking. Downstairs Jack was crazy, yarfing and scuffling at the door. Pap hollered.

As Abe scrambled down the ladder he heard again that hoarse mournful roaring honk, wood splitting, the shrill *Yeeee!* of the hogs in terror. Pap had thrown on a hunting-shirt that hung to his knees. He had the rifle in his hands, looked to the priming. "Keep a-holt o' that dog," he told Abe. Then he opened the door and stepped out into the gray air.

Through the frame of the door and past Pap standing bare-shanked Abe saw a black shapeless mound suddenly rise itself into a great slope-shouldered black bear, man-tall, whitish muzzle with

a great loop of tongue hanging out the side. The hog-pen rails were
thrown down, the smokehouse smashed to flinders, and the smoke
of its banked fire wasting in the air.

Pap shot. The bullet punched the bear in the nose, Abe saw a
brief explosion of blood, the bear swatting at his nose like a man
swatting flies—

Then the bear came for Pap, scooting at him sudden on all fours,
Pap turning slow as a man in a dream and wading towards the door
like the yard was swamp, the bear monstrous fast and close . . . Till
just in the nick Pap heaved himself through the door throwing Abe
backwards hard to the floor—so he heard but couldn't see Pap slam
the door and drop the bar just as the bear rammed into the door
from outside, and Abe remembered the smashed timbers of the
smokehouse.

But the door held. The bear gave another hooting roar with a
screeching edge to it, *Pap must have shot his nose off.* Pap was jerkily
reloading the rifle, ramming patch and ball down on the powder.
He glared down at Abe, his eyes lit with insane rage. "You son of a
bitch!" he screamed. "You like to kill us all!"

"Tom!" cried Mam. She was sitting up, her cover throwed back,
her hair a tangled nest.

Pap wasn't listening. He had lifted out the window and was
leaning through the hole. He fired, the whipcrack sound of the rifle
loud in the closed cabin, the sharp bitter nose-bite of powdersmoke.

"Scairt him off," said Pap. He was shaken. "What bear will go for
a smokehouse with the fire lit?"

They found out next day when Old Reuben rode by to tell Pap the
men were meeting at Gentry's. The bear had gone a rampage
through the settlement, killed the twenty-dollar bullcalf Grigsby
bought for breeding, mauled one of Gentry's cows, and carried off
its calf. Pap pointed to his busted smokehouse and hog-pen: if
Reuben wanted to see real harm, let him look. "It's a b'ar has lost his
fear of human men," said Reuben. "We got to hunt him down while
his track is fresh."

Abe went to the meeting with Pap and Denny, expecting one long wrangle. Instead there was the most amazing good and friendly spirit among the men, more than any time since the Milk-sick begun. Even the men that hadn't lost by the bear were willing to go "to protect the settlement." Gentry and Old Reuben treated each other like Christians after a soul-refreshing. As if going into the woods after a wounded hungry mean smart angry bear was more fun than cabin-raising.

Abe was desperate to be let go along. He had showed yaller with that turkey he shot, and with Matt. This bear was luck, maybe even providence, a chance to show that the turkey business wasn't the end of him.

Pap said no, of course. A boy couldn't keep up with men nor hunt bear no more than a fice-dog could run with hounds.

But he was big as a man, almost. He could run with any man or boy in the county. And there wasn't anything for him to do around here.

Pap said if so he could sure find something.

But Abe could hold the horses if they had to go into the brush after the bear. "Besides," Abe cried, "it ain't hardly no more danger-ous than stayin' home with Milk-sick!" Instantly he was sorry and ashamed he'd said it: asking to be let to run off and play, and leave Mam to face the *worst thing* all by herself. He threw Denny a look that begged for rescue.

But it was Mam that come instead. "I reckon visitin' the sick ain't boy's work," she said.

He felt a pang. He looked at her. Was she a little sad? He'd do whatever she said, stay or go.

She said, "A boy has got to go be a man *some* time, Tom."

Uncle Sparrow said, "I sure don't want him under *my* feet while you-all 're gone."

Denny said, "If he holds the horses, you an' me kin *both* git our shots on that bear."

Jack protested all next morning, jerking at the rope that clinched him to his post while Abe Denny and Pap mounted up. The air held some of summer's damp weight, but a fall cold had got into it. Mist clung and chilled Abe's body through his deerskin hunting-shirt. The green in the trees had started to go ripe. Nervous riffles ran through Abe's belly muscles sharp and helpless as squitters.

Abe was on Uncle Sparrow's mare, she danced her feet ready to start. Pap rode Old Sam and Denny the jackass mule, both slow but they wouldn't spook at a gunshot. Mam smiled up at him and said "Honey." Her light eyes shone under the black of her brows. Sary stepped up close. "Git the bear, Abe," she said, "but don't let the bear git you." Then she stood next to Mam. It surprised Abe how tall she'd got, almost to Mam's shoulders. *Two of a kind* run the thought in his head. While the men were gone after bear the two of them would hold *everything* safe.

"Git up," said Pap, and they followed him clip-clop out the gate. Jack began argufying to be let go.

They hadn't gone a mile when here came Jack lickety-split, his short stiff legs spanking the dust out behind him. Abe leaned off the saddle and gathered him in the crook of his arm. Jack settled down in Abe's lap and rested his chin on Abe's forearm. It felt *real* good to have that dog with him.

The hunters gathered in Gentry's yard. Reuben Jr. and the next-oldest brother Charlie were there, Casebier and Whitman, Jim Gentry and Allen. Reuben Jr. held the leashes on three of Grigsby's long-legged sad-faced hounds. Jack yapped at them, but the hounds kept their dignity. Old Reuben had brought Konkapot to track for them. When Konkapot saw Abe he showed his no-teeth smile. Then he led the way to the blood-spoor the bear had left when he dragged the calf into the brush.

Konkapot read the ground slow and careful. Tarry spots of blood glued to twigs and weed-stems—Konkapot picked them delicately, like lice, and popped them in his fingers leaving little red smears on the palps. Where branches were broken he licked to test the fresh-ness of the sap. *Listening* that bear, Abe thought. What's he hear?

Konkapot sighed and said something to Grigsby. Whatever he had *listened*, it didn't make him happy.

. . .

They tracked the bear two days, getting closer: the scat showed it, wetter, more stink. The dogs knew it, they were restless, whining with eagerness. Found a deer carcass, pretty ripe—dead when the bear found it, he was hungry enough to gorge on the rotten innards and ragged black flesh.

The men began to argue which should ride up front, where a man had the best chance at the bear. Man that killed would get the hide—they could share out the meat, but what was the use of half a hide? They'd got to agree on some *rules*. "Way it is now," said Casebier, "it's three o' you Grizbys git a shot afore any us git our chance."

"It's my hounds," said Old Reuben. "Konkapot is my tracker. It was my bull got et."

"We've all lost by that animal, Grigsby," said Gentry.

Pap said: "I git my shot at him that bear is mine."

Konkapot spat on the ground. "B'ar belong b'ar: 'less some time *you* kill him."

They grumbled, but agreed to take turns, one rifle from each family at the head of the file. "Whoever's got the luck to bay the critter, let him fire an' the rest hold. I don't want no son a bitch shoot me in the back when I'm a-drawin' bead on that animal." They set out with Reuben, Pap, and Tom Whitman at the head behind Konkapot, Reuben Jr. with the dogs right behind, then Denny and the boys Allen and Abe (Jack curled across Abe's lap, too short in the legs to run with the hounds). Behind them as rear guard came Charlie Grigsby, James Gentry, and Casebier.

They rode upslope. Rocky bones poked through the hide of leaves on the forest floor. Then the hounds begun to whine and scrabble their paws scooting out leaf-trash and dust. Old Reuben hollered to cut 'em loose, Reuben Jr. unleashed, and the hounds shot off the trail sideways into the brush, hooling and howling they smelt the blood hot. Old Reuben and Pap and Whitman turned their mounts and busted into the brush after them, Reuben Jr. right behind.

Konkapot watched them go. Then he sat down on a deadfall log and began stuffing tobacco in his pipe. His work was done. He wasn't allowed to kill no more than the boys.

Denny kicked the jackass mule to start it down the slot. Then with a whoop the rest of the hunters came bulling past them, the pack-horses whinnied and reared—Abe nearly lost his seat. Jack jumped off flop into the leaves, righted himself and tore off down the slot yarfing furious.

Denny sat the jackass while Abe and Allen got control of the frightened horses. "Well," he said, "there goes your rules." Then he led the way in. The slot twisted and dodged, Abe plunged on regardless hoping Denny knew where he was going. Behind him he heard the whuff of Allen's horse and Allen cussing.

Then he heard the hounds baying again—doubling back this way, crashing through the brush to the side of the trail. Abe wondered where Jack had got to, poor little dog lost in the trees. Denny hauled the mule's head around and yelled, "Git up!" then broke brush sideways off the slot, rifle in his hand, hot after the bear.

Stay there and wait or follow Denny?

"Come on," Abe hollered to Allen and led the pack-horse in, trying not to lose sight of Denny as he shunted the mule among the trees, ducking the lower tree-limbs, losing his hat.

Then Abe heard the loud frantic barking of the hounds not far ahead, and that unmistakable long hoarse moaning roar that told Abe they had bayed the bear.

He broke into a clearing, a wall of rock closed the far end. At the foot of the wall the hounds had cornered the bear—three of them crouched back on their haunches, yelling and slashing their fangs at the bear but staying well out of reach: the bear, lifted on his hind legs and chested out, waving his clawed front feet, showing his long yellow tusks. Instead of a nose he had a blackened blood-mushroom on the top of his snout, and fresh blood running from it.

Halfway between the woods and the bear, and a little to the right, Denny had jumped off the jackass mule. Abe saw him look quick to his priming and take his stand.

Abe whoa'd his own horse, jerked the pack-horse to a stop—but had to fight to hold it, got turned around, saw Allen Gentry fighting to hold his animals the same. He missed seeing Denny's shot but heard the crack of the rifle and a blunt sound like Mam beating dust out of a blanket that he guessed was bullet hitting bear. He got the horses controlled, and turned expecting to see the bear dead and Denny kilt him.

It wasn't dead, only brushing at its head with its left paw like it had got a skeeter whining in its ear. Then it dropped to all fours and lurched at Denny—the dogs jumped back sudden like they were jerked on one string yet never stopped facing the bear and yelling at him, threatening what they'd do if they got their teeth in him.

Just then Pap and Old Reuben came pelting out of the woods behind Denny, Old Reuben yelling something so they both reined in. They jumped down, left the reins fly and their horses run off. Pap stung the bear with a shot that sent a pop of dust out of his hide, and the bear reared up and backed towards the wall again. Reuben was holding on with his rifle, waiting for his shot . . .

. . . when three more a-horseback come busting out of the trees further to the right, Jim Gentry, Casebier, and Reuben Jr.—who reined his mount to a stand—but the other two never stopped only raced in and let fly with their rifles, *So much for first man takes the shot.* Dust spit twice off the rock-face above the bear, which was bad enough, but not as bad as Reuben Jr.'s shot: who reined his horse but couldn't still its jitters—but he fired from the saddle regardless and plunked the jackass mule in the rump so it kicked Denny in the guts and knocked him down—and then Junior's own horse reared and threw him ass over topknot to the ground.

Denny was rolling on the ground holding his gut, nothing between him and the bear but dogs, and the dogs were bluffing. Casebier and Gentry were hollering and cussing, trying to load their rifles and keep their saddles while their horses buck-jumped and tried to bolt away from the bear- and blood-smell. Reuben Jr. was picking himself up and looking to see where his piece had fallen. Lucky that Old Reuben was there and a cool head, still holding his shot till the bear made to drop down and take another run at Denny. Reuben stood him up again with a shot that made him swat his left cheek, by which time Pap was reloaded—taking his aim at the standing bear—

—only just then another district was heard from, a shot banging out of the trees off left blew a spout of dust off the bear's breast. Charlie Grigsby had finally caught up.

Abe saw Pap's aim break, he had to keep shifting to meet the bear's movements, then the others started banging away one after another and all together as fast as they could reload, *bang spang bam spat*, ringing shots off the rock-face and taking little dusty bites out of the bear's hide—only Pap and Old Reuben trying for steady aim and a careful killing shot. Both seemed to find it at once: both rifles leveled steadied and fired, Reuben maybe a hair before. Abe thought he saw a red flash by the bear's eye. Then it dropped to all fours, rocking. Then it curled itself carefully down onto the ground. Slumped. Then it didn't move anymore.

The dogs ran at it, making out to worry it. Their rejoicing was a little cagey. Maybe the dead bear would get up and eat them. Denny picked himself up, rubbing his stomach, looking poorly. Only Reuben stayed where he was for the moment, carefully reloading and priming his piece as the others walked past him, to stand looking down at the hairy mound. Abe and Allen eased closer and peered over the men from the height of their saddles.

Abe heard a sigh at his back. Konkapot. He must have walked straight to the spot somehow, while they were all dashing here and there in the woods getting lost. The old Indian sat himself down on a log at the edge of the clearing, with a look of puzzlement on his face as if dead bears were somehow *curious*.

The bear lay on his right side. There was a raw hole where his left eye should have been, and a welling of black blood to the brim of it. The bear's nose was a horrible mess, Pap's bullet had smashed what it hadn't shot off, and it must have started putrifying for it was all black and stunk awful. Under the stink of rot was the sharp rank odor of the bear's own body. The thick black fur waved and rippled, it was fairly jumping with fleas. Reuben Jr. snubbed the dogs to a deadfall. The hounds kept jumping and whining—now that they couldn't get at the bear, they sure wanted a piece of him.

"Who won the hide?" Charlie Grigsby wanted to know. He wouldn't mind toasting the winner with a sip of whiskey from the skin on his pappy's saddle-bow.

James Gentry pointed: "That was my shot took out his eye."

Pap grounded his stock and leaned on the rifle. "Gentry, you nor ary man here can set a-horseback and shoot the eye out of a live bear."

"Not 'less he's Dan'l Boone," said Casebier.

Denny spoke raspingly, holding his sore gut-muscles: "Which Dan-Boone shot me in the jackass?"

Gentry said, in a tone of polite inquiry, "You ain't claiming you killed that bear, are you, Lincoln?" He waved his hand. "Because there wasn't a man here didn't take his shots, and make the most part of them. That's how I see it."

That gathered them back of Gentry. Wasn't anyone thinking, let alone willing to say, he had *missed* the most of his shots. How did he know it *wasn't* his shot done the work? Things was fast and furious there for a while.

"Well then, who gits the hide?"

"Split it fair and square," said Tom Whitman.

Old Reuben spat on the ground. "What good is one part in seven out o' one mangy hide?"

Not much they thought, each separately and all at once.

"Hold on," said Gentry, "how do you figure seven parts?"

"Seven growed men with rifles," Reuben answered.

"Three of which is you and your sons," Casebier noted.

Pap had been ciphering on his fingers. "I make it eight," he said. "Dennis Hanks makes it eight."

"He was tendin' the horses," said Reuben Jr.

"I put the first bullet in that bear." Denny spoke up, tetchy. Abe said, "I saw him do it. Me and Allen did." Allen didn't say anything, watching his daddy.

"Grigsby," said Gentry, "if you get a share for two extra sons, why not a share for my Allen . . . Lincoln's boy too." He looked around, winning them over. "They worked hard and took their risks with the rest of us."

Tom Whitman's face took an angry set as the blood roused by the fight began to drop. "Shit and dam-nation," he snapped. "What do I need of another bear-skin?" Abe remembered: Whitman's young wife and baby dead of the Milk-sick, Whitman sitting alone in his farmyard, letting the yard run to weed and his clearings to cock-burr and saplings.

"Dang it." Old Reuben was exasperated. "I still say what's the use to splittin' the hide small. Let some take the meat, one quarter to a fam'ly; someone else git the hide, someone bones an' tallow . . ."

Just then here came Jack smoking through the leaves and flying over deadfall, yip-yapping with rage, his porkypine hair bristled out and his sharp fice teeth showing fierce, his eyes nailed to the bear like he had had him in his sights a year and now he was by God going to make *meat*—bolted between the horses' legs and shot into that bear headfirst like an arrow from the bow. He took a-holt with both jaws among the fur and fleas and began twisting and wrench-ing out a chunk of meat for himself.

That's when the dead bear woke up: raised up his shot-to-pieces head, opened the one eye he had left, rolled over and onto his feet.

Jack jumped straight back as if the bear had throwed him, and lit yapping.

The men froze, Tom Whitman not a horse's length from the bear, not a rifle reloaded except Old Reuben's and he too shocked to raise the piece.

The hounds went crazy, the horses screamed and reared and jerked back, the ones that were drop-reined turned and bolted. Abe and Allen were the only ones mounted, their horses kept turning to run and they'd turn them back, so they pivoted round and round in circles. Jack was yapping so high and piercing it was almost screeching.

The bear huffed and they were close enough to smell the rank stench of his breath. Then he sneezed, shook himself, turned, and loped off round the rock wall and into the woods, rolling and sham-bling somehow faster than a horse could run. Jack never stopped his high frenzied yapping: but waited till the bear's rear end disap-peared round the rocks then *went for* him—only as far as the edge of the rocks—and told him off for good and all. *Whuff!* He shook himself all over. That was one bear you'd never hear from again! Then he trotted back to Abe on his stiff jaunty little legs.

The men still stood where and how death in the shape of a come-alive dead bear had left them: Reuben in the act of lifting his piece, Pap raising his with the horrible sudden realization he hadn't reloaded, the others beginning to turn away or crouch down or shut their eyes.

"Well *I'm* damned," said Casebier.

Tom Whitman stood there blinking like a man waking up from a dream. He had been nearest. If the bear had gone for one of them, he'd have been easy meat. He touched the skin of his face with a kind of tenderness. It was like a wind out of that bear had blowed the grief rage and deathliness right out of him. He smiled.

Denny spat on the ground, just to show he could do it. "Next time kill the bear afore you divvy up."

Konkapot was shaking all over. You might have thought he was scared, but Abe knew it was just the silent trembles of the laughing he was too Injun to let fly.

The other men gradually came down from wondering relief to a sense of grievance. They had that bear *killed*. Then suddenly it was the bear had *them* killed—but let them off. It was like they'd been joked, but who was it joked them?

The horror hiding in the joke showed out when they settled in camp that night: they'd gone after the bear because it was easier to kill than Milk-sick. If they couldn't even kill the bear . . .

Chapter 6: **Milk-Sick**

October 1818

As they came back through the yellow woods it began to drizzle.
They passed by a burnt-over grove—it was where they had massacred the pigeons and their fires had got loose among the trees. The
livid green leaves of the snakeweed were lush over the ground. A
large pale shape was moving among the blackened trunks.

The cow stumbled out into the trail. It spread its legs to brace
itself and stood there with the great bag of its belly swinging from
the four-post rack of its haunches. Its head dropped like it was too
heavy to hold up. Its muzzle was slobbered with snot, dust-dirty, that
hung down in strings. It rolled its eyes and made a strangled moo.
Trembles ran under the hide along its slabby sides. The braced legs
wavered like the bones had gone soft, then locked at the knees—the
cow stretched its neck and tried to lift its head and the effort made it
break at the foreleg knees and drop its chest and belly to the ground.
It bellered and rolled its eyes in terror and fell hard on its side.

The cow lay there, still alive in its eyes that it couldn't even roll—

its last breath was staling and dying in its lungs—and then the eyes went out.

It was their own cow. Abe couldn't think why they'd meet their own cow all the way out here, with Mam and Sary and the Sparrows to keep watch on it.

Then something happened to Abe inside. It was like an ax, a spirit-ax, split him *swish* through the middle of his brain right down through his heart and his guts.

On one side of the split he was Abe riding home from his first bear hunt, cradling his dog Jack on his lap, the hunt was a bust but lots to tell Mam when he got home. Mam would cook them a good hot supper, hog meat and corn pone made with real milk, and honey or tree-sugar to sweeten it with. He could see it clear and solid, a story he had read a thousand and one times and got by heart. *Mam. Mam was the one sure right strong safe good thing you could count on always for anything, come Pap or storm or fear or bear or sickness or God, Mam.*

But the part of him on the far side of the spirit-ax-split was cold and numb as ice-frozen fingers. He was Stupid on that side, couldn't think, didn't know anything, only . . .

Only that the cow was out here where it hadn't no right to be, and it was dead of something, something that killed cows, froze them from the inside and killed them. And if that could be true nothing was sure, all his knowing wasn't worth spit wasn't worth one small piece of mangy bear hide from a bear that could have killed them all but ran away.

The Sparrows' cabin. The door hung awry, a black gap in the cabin-front like a missing tooth. Pap had told Uncle the leather would rot, he must make a wooden hinge and Uncle Sparrow said he reckoned he'd get around to it. Denny didn't touch the door, only peeped into the gap.

Came back and said, "Ain't there," and they rode on home.

They must have made Abe wait by the gate while Pap and Denny went in. Because next thing he remembered was coming inside—

He saw Pap and Denny standing by the pole-bed, two people were in it: he recognized Uncle Sparrow's stringy-muscled arm covered with black hairs.

Then she was there. Mam. She staggered out from the corner where she'd been sitting on a stool wrapped head to toe in blankets. He couldn't see her face but he recognized the height of her and her long-fingered big-veined hands. Then he saw her face and felt the spirit-ax swish through him again as cold and sharp as an ice-wind.

It was Mam *wasn't Mam*. He didn't know. *He knew.*

Her skin had gone yellow and her deep eye-sockets were lined with soot. Her hair was long, matted, dull as Konkapot's. She came to him and put her hand on his face. He closed his eyes. Mam.

"He can't stay here"—a croak using her voice. Talking like he wasn't there. He was not crying, only his heart whaling away inside his chest like Pap in a thicket furious chopping his way out.

Then he *wasn't* there.

Or didn't remember.

He didn't remember how when they got to Gentry's he found Sary alive. Later, when Denny said he was sorry for throwing Abe down to stop him running home and Abe had cussed him, he didn't know what Denny was talking about. Denny looked at him a little frightened. "You said you was goin', and I wasn't to sneak up behind you and look at your Mam."

He couldn't forgive Denny or not forgive. As far as he knew none of it happened.

Yet he must have stayed somewhere those first nights, for he remembered that when they buried Aunt Betsey and Uncle Tom Sparrow he and Sary had to ride over there with Denny.

The burying done in a patch of land across the Troy road from the Sparrows' cabin: *a haunt can't cross a highway.*

. . .

"Four times you run away," Denny told him, later. "Mister Gentry or me brung you back. Then we give up."

Across the yard the door swung open and they came out. Mam's tall shape, *was it Mam?* leaned against Pap, wobble-walking, Pap was walking her out to the jakes, limpsy stumbling. She dropped to her knees and before Stupid could shut him he cried out "Mam!" But she had dropped to hands and knees and swayed like the sick cow and Pap knelt down and then she snapped her body like a mourning sinner with the jerks and the sound come out of her, that sound, the hoarse strangled barking sound like an animal was try-ing to claw out of her, and then she blew puke out all over the ground. Then she snapped her body and blew puke all over the ground. Then she fell on her side and her body snapped like a whip and she barked and strangled and blew puke out all over— and he was there, he'd run right through the *No* he was looking down at her yelling.

But couldn't remember what it was he was yelling.

But remembered Pap grabbed him and shook him and him paying Pap no mind but crying to Mam he was sorry he was sorry he come and looked at her and he wouldn't ever do it again.

Pap brought her out to the jakes two more times. Each time he did she changed, as if the sound coming out of the closed-down cabin was the noise of some kind of horrible carpenting, scraping and cut-ting and chopping on her till she wasn't Mam anymore but some-thing else. You could still see Mam's shape in It, the line of her bones the flash of her eyes the set of her head and then she would lose hold and It would rise in her and make her change, take away her body and her face and her eyes and leave a horrible wooden sick thing— the pukes would take her and crack her around and it was like something ugly was coming out in her, eating its way out, like she was turning into an animal from the inside—

Only she wouldn't she kept fighting it, she kept swallowing it back down.

And after a bad spell she'd tell Pap to let them come in, Abe and Sary, and they'd have to look at her.

Stupid couldn't remember what she looked like. Smart knew: she looked like Milk-sick.

He remembered he was sitting on a stump by the cow-shed where he slept nights, or didn't sleep. Oh yes: and smoothed out a patch of ground, took his knife and begun to scratch out in the ground a list of all the things he would do and not do if the Lord got Mam out of Milk-sick. If only she'd get over it. If only Milk-sick wouldn't kill her. There were things he would do. There were things he would never do again, never even wish for again. If the Lord was listening, if the Lord really did listen to sparrows and such, he would never talk bad the way he did when he was with the boys. No more gold palaces, no more nekkid Shebazade princesses, no more telling Aesops to people so they'd say how smart he was, no more figuring and adding up different stories but take the Word as it was give, no more reading even *never again if that is what You want if that is what You will take all right then I'm done with all of it, I give it up I swear.*

And never kill nor even hurt a thing ever again, pigeon nor turkey nor bear let alone an Injun or other person. If that meant he wasn't up to Moses Washington and Uncle Mordecai, then so be it, he was willing to let that go too.

Only when he was just started on the list Stupid grabbed the muscles of his shoulder and arm and all he could do was stab the knife into the ground, punching it again and again till the blade snapped, then took Pap's broad-ax and slammed it into what he had written until it was chopped to nothing.

• • •

Pap said they might come in, Abe and Sary.

Mam was lying in the bed.

Pap said, "Nance, I brung the children."

She made a croak. Then Mam croaked, "I'm hurtin' inside," like she hadn't heard what Pap said or didn't care.

Pap didn't say anything. He fisted his hands.

Her voice scraped and tore: "Oh hurts," she said.

Pap said, "Nance. I brung the children."

"Abe-Sary?" she said and Pap motioned for them.

It wasn't really Mam. It was and wasn't. The Milk-sick had eat her up, it wasn't Mam's face anymore—skin a yellow mask stiff and dull and stretched hard over wedges and curves of bone, scored with lines like knife-rakes in a board of yellow beechwood. Dry cracks and skin-flakes instead of soft lips, lips bruise-color. Eyes sunk out of sight in blackened sockets like skull-holes.

And she stunk. She stunk of the pukes and every time she breathed out she stunk, a stink like she was rotting inside, like she had eaten a mess of them dead-rot pigeons—horrible yellow shit-rot stench with a sharp line of acid through it.

Then she looked at him and she was Mam. Only her face was ruined. She said "Abe."

Closed her eyes. Put out tongue, milky-brown slick animal tongue, licked lips. "Thsty," It said.

Mam opened her eyes. Found Sary. She moved her lips a little. "Sary," Mam said, ". . . care?"

Then she looked at him again. She said: "Abe."

Then she went away.

Then? *He doesn't remember.*

People came in Gentry's wagon—Mrs. Gentry, Mrs. Barrett—Mr. Gentry driving and Tom Barrett with him. Peter Brooner rode behind on his horse. Pap made mouth-sounds meant for thanks and greeting. The women came over to Abe and Sary and said comfort things, Bible things, *sorry, trouble, Lord's will, prayers*. Abe didn't pay any attention to the women, he wasn't interested in what they had to say.

His whole body hurt. There was an animal inside him trying to get out, twisting, a wolf frenzied by the smell of blood, it wanted to jump out his mouth it wanted to bark it wanted to howl it wanted to tear flesh with its teeth. He bit it back. He swallowed and clenched his teeth to keep it down. He hiccupped. He must never let it out. If he let this animal out he might never be human again, no more than Matt Gentry tied up howling in the yard.

On the other side of the Troy road three men were swinging pick-axes to break up the soil, shoveling earth up out of the hole: black loam on the top, then yellow clay from underneath.

A haunt can't cross a highway.

Above the hole stood the old blackcherry tree. Its pointed leaves were mostly fallen, *Cheerry-pie! You'll see! Ain't nothin' tastes . . .*

They stood outside the cabin and watched Peter Brooner and Pap carry It out the cabin door, wrapped in old blankets head to toe and tied around with thongs the way you bundle meat. They lowered It carefully down into the plank box set in front of the door. The foot-end, Mr. Brooner's end, bumped the side of the box. *Bonk.*

Abe heard the sound of a bird: *chee-up? chee-lee?* It was perched on the roof-tree.

They carried the box across the road and lowered it in the hole under the blackcherry. Then they stood around the hole, Pap at the cherry-tree end, Abe and Sary on either side of him. The women had tears on their faces. The men's faces were clinched. Nobody said.

Then Mrs. Gentry said, "I wish we had a preacher."

People looked furtively at Pap, then dropped their eyes. If there wasn't any preacher, the man should say the Words. *All them nights Her reading Bible, he don't know what to say? Maybe he knows and won't say.*

Mr. Gentry cleared his throat. Someone had to say the Words, and he was the most important man there. "The Lord giveth, the

Lord taketh away. His judgments are true and righteous altogether. Blessed be the name of the Lord."

They all murmered *Praise him* and *Jesus* and *Yes Lord* and Pap said: "Amen." As if that was all the Word there was to say on Mam dead of Milk-sick.

Winter 1818–1819

. . . For a long time they scarcely left the cabin and never went further than the jakes. Food the neighbors had brought, they et of it when they got hungry, left it sit where it was till next time. The air inside the cabin went sour with their own bodies' smell, and the table-food spoiling. Pap fingered the lock of his rifle. *Should he hunt? What was the use of meat?* Denny slept and slept and slept.

Abe sat in the corner—waiting. There was a hush in everything, the world froze to a stop. If he didn't look out the window he could believe it was a blizzard outside, everything white and still and silent: waiting.

The spoiling food didn't freeze, though. It got riper. Sary looked at it like it was snakes. She wanted Pap to kill them for her. Then one day she got up and started clearing the table. Pap and Denny stared at her like they'd never seen such, their shoulders slumped with tiredness though they hadn't done a thing since that would wear a body out. Abe's heart began to pound, frightened, couldn't say for what. Sary stirred the fire and the air sweetened. She measured corn-meal into a wooden bowl. *No wait,* he wanted to cry out, but it would be terrible to break the silence. And Sary wouldn't have heard, it was taking all her mind to measure the corn-meal and mix in the water and lard.

Pap stood at the door hefting the rifle. Then he reached his hat off the peg and went out.

Denny held true longer, laying on his tick most of the time, his eyes filmed like the iced-over ponds. Only he was using whiskey to help. Pap smelt it on him, booted him to his feet and bullied him out the door to hunt or cut brush or round up some hogs. So Denny did that dawn to dusk, came back so worn out his eyes were almost as dead as whiskey eyes.

And Pap's eyes the same from working steady on the carpenting jobs the neighbors gave them—a shiffrobe for Miz Gentry, more barrels for Old Reuben—the saw rasping and wheezing all day except when Pap was splitting planks with his maul. Make enough noise you don't have to listen for what you ain't never going to hear again.

Winter set in with a cold snap that stopped the sap in the trees, but there was no wind. The trees were almost silent. Nothing moved, nothing grew, nothing changed. Waiting.

Sary, though: she burnt the pone and made it and burnt it again and made it again. The men et like pigs, if a gnawed bone or rind dropped to the floor they left it lie. Sary took it to heart that Pap Denny and Abe didn't care how she was trying to care for them: but kept at it regardless.

Abe could hardly stand to look at her. He knew he ought to be good to her, Mam would expect it of him. But how?

If Mam was here she'd have read them some Bible. She'd have seen their trouble, and something would have come to her out of the Book—but how did she know where to turn in it?

He remembered the rules she told him: she'd put her mind to what the trouble was, and let it remind her of something in the Book—and whatever Bible come to mind then, *that* was what she went for. She'd never argue it to be some other thing: she accepted the Bible these *particular* troubles put her in mind of, and looked into it, and read it out.

Pap's saw rasped from the woodpile. Denny was off hunting. Sary hunkered on the hearthstone watching the mush-kettle—hadn't learned yet how long and hot to cook it so she stared at it all the time like it was a caged wolf, poking it with the wooden stir-spoon.

Mam's Bible was on a shelf by the bedstead. Sary was his concern, and Ruth was Sary's book, so that was what he turned to first.

He found the Ruth part in the Contents, and the book opened read-ily to the right page, as if a trace had been worn in the binding through all the many times Mam must have turned to it. There was a little smutch in the margin of one page and it took his eye (he must let it happen as it would). Of course it was Sary's favorite: *Entreat me not to leave thee, or to return from following after thee.*

Entreat me not to leave thee. The story was about *not* leaving behind the people you love, and never coming back. His heart jumped—*It works!*—jumped so that he knew he must warn himself not to get too het up, not to run afore his horse, not to be prideful or assured because then God might take these words back just to teach him a lesson.

His eyes returned to the page, the smutch in the margin at the head of the verse, *Entreat me not to leave thee.*

Mam's finger-mark.

The blood was pounding in his ears, deafening him the way the thundering wings of the pigeons had months before.

The Book fell open to those pages she'd worn a trail to in her reading. Places she touched, reading, they'd show her marks. So he could track her through her Book the way Konkapot and him tracked deer through the trees: let it open gently, as it would, to one of her pages; let the eye find the smutch-marks on the page that showed just where her eye went, what words her mind took in. Then it would almost be like she was reading to him again, just the way she always had as far back into the dark as memory could go, *an' so his Mam she put him in his leetl basket an' set him floatin' down that river . . .*

January. He stalked her patiently through the fall-open of pages and tracks of finger-marks, taking the reading as it come: Chronicles. Exodus. Adam and the apple tree. Moses changing the serpents. To everything there is a season—but the frozen clods on Mam's grave were still rock hard, sharp-edged as when the shovels first cut them. The blackcherry still stood naked watch, twigs and bud-tips cased in ice. The seasons were waiting on him. If he could find the right words she would . . .

He mustn't say.
February. March.

It was night and he was alone in the cabin: sitting at the table. The only light came from the fireplace, orange tongues licking the dark log walls. Jack was curled at his feet. Then the dog bounced up and bristled at the door. Something outside? Abe got up and went to the door and opened it. Outside it was complete night. A pale blue line marked the road, the heavy black wall of trees rose on the far side.

She lifted the gate carefully, closed it behind her. She was simply walking towards him across the yard as if no *terrible thing* had ever happened. Why ever did he think it had? A wave ran through him from his knees through his belly into his head—cold terror then hot joy then somehow both at once.

Something was a dream. Was it this?

The wood of the door-frame was rough to his hand.

It was really her. Mam. She was simply *there* in front of him. Mam looked at him, her eyes crinkled, she was smiling kind of puzzled: what was troubling him?

He was paralyzed. He couldn't breathe.

So of course she had to touch him:

And he felt it.

He felt it so it was true.

So true he gave up unbelieving in one complete out-breathing and didn't hold back but let her wrap him around and press his face into her belly, and right there he smelled the sweet wood-smokey salt-sweaty smell of her. Mam.

Oh Mam, he told her, *Oh Mam I missed you so*

She was going to speak, she was opening her mouth—

Then the dog began to howl, *aa-oooo . . .*

He was awake, sitting up in his blankets.

Cold. In the loft.

She was here and then she wasn't.

Jack howled again, out in the yard. Whined, complaining, then stilled. Abe felt the *dog* start to come up in him, the empty midnight howling dog, he knew if he let it out now he'd never stop, the light in his head would go out and he'd be Matt Gentry chained up moaning in the yard. From below he heard Pap snoring deep slow and raspy, like a man dull and uncaring sawing away on a plank of wood.

Abe caught himself. He mustn't be distracted by anger. *She was there and then she wasn't.* What did it mean?

She started to speak and then the dog howled . . .

That was when he knew. He didn't want to know it, but he knew. The thought came to him, and he couldn't deny it. *Whatever thought come to you, that was the one you had to act on, you couldn't pick and choose or the power would go right out of your reading.* He wrassled it down, but it wasn't any use. You can't un-know a thing you know. Then he wished he hadn't thought it. Maybe if he hadn't thought it it wouldn't have been true. But he had thought it, and so it was true, and in the morning he'd have to go down and find the words and make the truth final.

They would be in Ecclesiastes, Solomon's *sad* book: the page opened easy, and the smutch pointed him unerringly:

A living dog is better than a dead lion. For the living know that they shall die: but the dead know not any thing, neither have they any more a reward; for the memory of them is forgotten. Also their love, and their hatred, and their envy, is now perished; neither have they any more a portion forever in any thing that is done under the sun.

He lifted his eyes from the page. What was that sound? *Pink pink.* Meltwater dripping from the roof-shakes. The season was beginning to turn.

Spring 1819

Early in the morning, before anyone else was awake, he slipped out of bed, picked up his ax, slid out through the barely opened door, and stalked across the yard to the gate, the road, Mam's grave. Cold moist spring morning air. He moved through a soft light fog that blurred all things.

He stood looking down at where she was hid under the ground. The headboard sagged sideways and a thin crack ran its length. The shovel-cut clods had melted. Long coarse grass like hair had grown over her. Under the skin of ground the grass was running its threads through Mam and the little worming roots were knitting her into the dirt.

The hard-set buds of the blackcherry had begun to flex and open a little, a spot of blood at the tip of every bud. He hefted the ax and stepped up to the tree. He swayed his body back on his hips following the backswing of the ax, then whipped ax wrists arms body slamming the ax-head deep into the cherry tree. He felt his blow shiver through the tree's body and limbs, felt how it would feel to the tree, the quiver in the twig-ends the dull throb in the heartwood spreading down towards the roots . . .

But the roots weren't shaken, they went down too far, were locked too hard and deep in the black earth. *Down there where Mam has gone.* But she had gone deeper than tree-roots. Where she had gone was as far away from here as Heaven is from the earth— *further, maybe, because you can still see the stars from here. But where Mam has gone to there's no light comes back.*

He said out loud: "Mam." But he knew she wouldn't answer. Mam was dead. Dead Mam did not know anything, not any, not even their love, neither did she have anymore a portion forever, neither food nor talking nor reading to him. Did not even remember herself *for the memory of them is forgotten.* Nothing was what she remembered. He remembered—but he would die too, and memory with him. "You don't need to tell me about *dead,*" he said aloud. "I know what it is."

Nor about the Lord neither. Mam said there couldn't a sparrow fall, she judged the Lord by her own lights. If she was in charge there *wouldn't* no sparrow fall—or if one fell she'd grieve him. *But the Lord ain't Mam. If He's like anyone in my family, it's Uncle Mordecai. He don't care if pigeons is falling like rain, and human people dying like pigeons. Sparrows ain't in it. It don't seem to me the Lord can keep His mind on anything smaller than the Children of Isril or the United States of America.*

He pried the ax-head out of the tree. Touched the wound. Sap was already rising in it. What's the Book say? A time and a season to every thing. Sun comes up and goes down. There's rain or there ain't. A time to chop down and girdle, a time to nigger off; a time to scratch ground and a time to kill meat. But no use to any of it, none at all.

"I ain't a-goin' to kill you," he told the blackcherry. *Maybe if I was George Washington it would be some use, but I ain't George Washington.*

The War Against the Trees was over.

BOOK III:

The Kingdom of Pap

Chapter 7: **Sarah Bush Johnston Lincoln**

Elizabethtown and Little Pigeon Creek, 1818–1820

Sally Johnston was the widow of the jailer of Elizabethtown, Kentucky: a spare woman of middling height, quick and accurate as a bird in her movements. Her bright sharp eyes saw each thing for what it was. Mayors and postmasters came and went, ministers were called and re-called, but in fifteen years there hadn't been but one jailer in Elizabethtown, Kentucky, and she was his wife.

Then Johnston went into the ground, and she wasn't the jailer's wife anymore, only a widow-woman renting a cabin from her husband's relations. Her in-laws stooped under the weight of public expectation they'd "take care of Johnston's widow," which expectation they had not the least notion of meeting. She was twelve dollars in debt, had three children to raise—pretty Betsey was thirteen, Mattilda was eight, John D. only two.

Then, like a particular providence, here came Thomas Lincoln back to Elizabethtown from north of the river: a big man with his hair slicked back and his go-to-Meetings on. He smiled in a way that was sociable and sorrowful both. He'd lost his wife, his Nance, a year back. Had heard of *her* trouble. Hard to believe his old friend Dan Johnston . . .

Her late husband thought Tom Lincoln a piddler: "Always a-doin', nothin' *done*." Yet he seemed to done well over the river. She had enjoyed talking with the man when he used to come to town, and Johnston would tell how Tom Lincoln kept the company at Bush's laughing with his stories and "good things." Sally Johnston did like a *sociable* man.

But she would have things plain between them. He could have a wife in her, but she was no house nigger. If he paid her debt she was grateful, but she wasn't in despair to pay it herself. He wasn't to expect she'd bear him children: it was hard on her innards birthing John D. and she didn't mean to risk worse. She knew the shape of her moon and could tell when her blood was falling: if he couldn't abide that he might look elsewhere. He shrugged, never expected anything else.

So Lincoln paid off her debts, a Preacher married them, Johnston's kin bought them a horse and wagon to haul herself off in, and they took the road north to the Ohio crossing.

Sally Johnston (she still called herself that to herself) believed she had done as well as might be for her children and herself. Tom Lincoln was a man of property and prospects: they'd grow with the territory. She could bring some of her housekeeping with her: the cherry bureau worth forty dollars cash; her and her children's clothing; a clean new-made featherbed for herself and Mr. Lincoln, one for each of her children, and two more for Tom Lincoln's orphans; and a trunk of "treasures" she could draw on when she needed to turn a sorry day around.

Then they crossed the Ohio, and the woods closed down over the road to Pigeon Creek. Alone with his new wife and children Tom Lincoln didn't hardly have a word to say. Wasn't surly—only dull like he was thinking about something: harness, maybe, or smoking a ham. The children stilled. Sally Johnston thought it was because they were unused to the woods. Then it come to her there was probably other things to get used to she hadn't been quite smart enough to see a-coming.

The cabin (when they got to it) was smaller by a good deal than she expected. It might be "middlin'" for Indiana, but Kentucky "middlin'" was more generous. She couldn't see how she was going to fit herself and three children (let alone a forty-dollar bureau!) in there along with Tom Lincoln and the three young people who stood in line to make them welcome—

That overgrown boy-man with the silly grin was cousin Dennis Hanks. The plump girl with tear-marks on her cheeks would be Sary. And Abe—she remembered him from one time Mr. Lincoln brought him to town, a thoughty talky little thing that noticed everything and had a word for it. He wasn't more than ten or eleven now, but had done some *remarkable* growing.

Tom Lincoln said, "Here is your new family." Then he named all their names and said, "I expect you'll show Miz Lincoln your duty." The man was Dan Webster in a tavern but his notions of family talk weren't much better than *gee* and *haw*. She could guess what the inside of his cabin would be after a year with no woman, Sary a child, and Tom Lincoln and Dennis Hanks for menfolk: just look how they kept *theirself* when they weren't going to town to honeyfuggle silly widows into marrying them! Hanks was rank as a bear, Sary's dress all patches. Abe was thin as a rake, all bony angles and a mop of hair that probably hadn't been combed since his ma died—full of creepers too, unless she missed her guess.

One good look and she had seen everything exactly as it was: the cabin wouldn't do. Past a certain point, neither would Tom Lincoln. Dennis Hanks was good-natured and careless, and when he looked at pretty Betsey there was nothing on *his* mind but *cootin'*. Keep him off he might make a decent husband; let him sleep in the same house with Betsey and the two of them would make nothing but scandal. Little Sary didn't know if she was woman of the house pushed out by an intruder, or a little girl that wanted mothering bad: treat her like a little woman and she'd take all the mothering a body'd have to give her. And Abe? Probably wanted mothering more than any of them. He just wasn't going to stand for any, not just yet.

She managed Tom Lincoln well enough. Her three girls got along fine: Sary was a loving child, and grateful for all these women in the house after a year alone with Pap, Denny, and Abe. John D. was happy as a pup at first. Growed-up men in the house was a wonder to him. He tried cozying up to Tom Lincoln, but Mr. Lincoln wasn't the cozying kind. He'd have had better luck with Denny Hanks, but Denny had to move back to Sparrow's on account of Betsey. That left Abe: he couldn't fire thunderbolts like Tom Lincoln; was the kind of God you might get next to. So he took to following Abe everywhere, gazing up at him with a silly hankering look.

But Abe paid the little boy no mind. Wasn't mean—just didn't *rise* to him. Nothing against John D., he was that way with all of them. If you did something nice for him he'd nod, like to say he appreciated the kindness—wasn't *your* fault it done him no good. His heart was broke, and that was that.

It was spring, they were out in the yard, the girls boiling their winter clothes in a big iron kettle set in the fire-pit, taking turns throwing things in and stirring them with a wooden paddle and passing them to Sally to hang out on a line Tom Lincoln had rigged. A few feet away Abe squatted cross-legged mending broken harness. Sally Johnston Lincoln was strong in her ways, but she was almost ready to throw this'n up as a job too many. John D. was yearning up at her, he had given up on these Lincoln menfolk. She gave him a smile. Her hands were full, so she begun to sing, John D. liked that.

> "I gave my love a cheerry, it had no stone,
> I gave my love a chicken, it had no bone,
> I gave my love a ring, it had no end—
> I gave my love a baby, an' no cry-in'."

She gave Abe just a little smile. "Well," she said, "can you riddle me these riddles?"

"I know it, Mama," Betsey called.

"Give Abe a chance," she answered.

He thought about it, then shook his head—"Can't do it"—but smiled, like just trying to think it out made him happy.

She sang again in her clear reedy voice:
"A cheerry when it's bloomin' ain't got no stone . . ."
Abe's face lit like tinder taking fire.
"A chicken when it's pippin' ain't got no bone."
He shook his head, *of course!*

> "A ring when she's rollin' ain't got no end—
> A baby when he's sleepin' got no cry-in'."

Abe rolled his eyes, he should have guessed that one. Then he blinked in surprise—he had got to his feet and come over where she was standing, and hadn't minded he was doing it.

Sally wasn't about to let him go. "Want to try another?" It was up to him now. He paused. Something passed in his eyes like a, like a *cloud* she thought, the way you can see the wish to go to sleep pass through a child's eyes. But he didn't go to sleep this time. He said, "*Yes* ma'am."

"All right then." She took a wet skirt from Betsey, wrung it and turned to hang it on the line, and as she did so sang:

> "I give my love an apple, without no core.
> I give my love a cabin, without no door.
> I give my love a palace, where she might be,
> That she might unlock it, without no key."

The girls were laughing and Abe was grinning "like an eejit," rolling his eyes up, wrinkling his brow, clowning out his thinking while she ran through the questions again, how *can* there be an apple without no core, a cabin without no door? and what kind of palace can you unlock without no key? "I'm hanged if I can tell," said Abe.

The girls were laughing by the wash-kettle, John D. laughing on the ground at her feet. She saw something twist suddenly through Abe's face, as if it was a fist he clenched to hold something in. He looked at her and she saw he was as near crying as a man could go and she must save him from it. She spoke mock-sharp, "Abraham you have *not* guessed my riddles. For that, you must fetch me a cut o' ham out the smokehouse."

He looked his thanks, turned, and went off, and she was afraid she'd somehow lost him again. Something in that riddle song had poked a sore spot.

But she hadn't lost him. He came to her next day when everyone else was out, and asked would she sing that riddle-song for him again, he wasn't sure he'd got all of it. He called her *ma'am*, but still . . . So she give him the song again, and he nodded for each line like a man biting coins and finding each one true. When she was done he said: "I read one time about a magic door a man unlocked without no key. He had to say magic words. There was palaces in the story . . ."

"That sounds fine," she said. "What was the words?"

"It was foreign words. 'Open See-same.' It was an *Arabian* story book, about a princess that used to tell a king stories so he wouldn't chop her head off."

It sounded heathen and outlandish to Sally. But it was like a man to find *some* way to keep his woman slaving away night after night. "I hope she never run out."

"She never did. He changed his mind afore she ran dry."

So did you, she said to herself, *and only just*. But here he was, and she meant for him to "open see-same" as of now. "I reckon you like to read things." She beckoned him over to the corner of the cabin where she had her treasure chest. She knelt, opened the lid, and lifted out the little drawer of medicaments that covered the top. Underneath were some wrapped parcels, and amongst them a small stack of books. Abe hunkered alongside her. She took the books out and gave them one after another into his out-size awkward hands. He took them with a caressing touch. His eyes were bright and fierce looking at the books, turning them to see the marks on their spines.

She said, "These come to me last year, from my Sister that's crossed over. I figger if anyone would know how to read 'em, you'd be the one."

He looked at her, this time like a child and not a sad little man.

"My Mam used to read to me and Sary. She had a *way* of readin' . . . couldn't write none, but she used to read."

"Your Mam was *fine*, Abe," she said. "I can't read *nor* write. Never larned." If he refused her on that account . . .

"Shucks," he said. Then he made a smile: "Well Ma, I reckon *I'll* have to read to *you.*"

He put the pile down, then picked up each book in turn and named it for her. "This here's *Columbian Orator.*" He cracked it open and peeked inside. "It's readin' and speakin' pieces, like the old *Preceptor* I used to have in Kentuck. This'n's *Scott's Elocution,* looks like more pieces and harder ones, and we got *Defoe Robinson Crusoe,* looks like stories—*Bunyan The Pilgrim's Progress,* more stories—*Bible* kind." He paused, looked at the last spine, then opened the book and looked inside. "And this here: this here is *The History of the United States, from the Discovery of the New World Until the Battle of New Orleans,* by William Grimshaw." He moved his hand softly over the face of the page, reading aloud, *"Comprising, Every Important Political Event, to the Present Time; with a Progressive View of the Aborigines; Population; Religion; Agriculture, and Commerce; of the Arts, Sciences, and Literature; Occasional Biographies of the Most Remarkable Colonists, Writers and Philosophers, Warriors and Statesmen; an Appendix Containing the Complete Texts of the Declaration of Independence and Constitution of the United States; and a Copious Alphabetical Index."* He looked up at her, his pale eyes wide with the wonder of it. "Ma," he said, "I reckon ever'thing I ever wanted to know is in these here."

And so she found Abe's key after all, just like she'd found a way to win Tom and Dennis Hanks and Sary. It took her a while before she recognized Abe had found *her* key as well.

For the next few years Sally Bush Johnston Lincoln was satisfied with her management of things. With herself and three girls to keep house the cabin was generally in apple-pie, go-to-Meeting order. Abe said when the four of them were at it, it sounded like a houseful of birds. She got Tom Lincoln to largen the cabin with a cook-shed out back, and if she couldn't make him a neat man at least she got him to stop throwing his table scraps on the floor.

Dennis Hanks come hankering around Betsey, hat in hand and manners just so. She'd have liked to keep Betsey out of his bed till the girl came sixteen, but it was nip and tuck between Sally Lincoln's 'druthers and the itch between Betsey's legs. Sally was smart enough to draw rein before the itch won out. She gave Denny her say-so the day Betsey turned fifteen, and added she hoped he knew better than to ride a unbroke filly as hard as a old gray mare. Denny blushed and said *Yessum*. She missed Betsey some after the wedding: it wasn't that the *wife* didn't come round, it was that the *child* was gone. Yet she was glad she had got her daughter off to a decent start.

As for herself, she wasn't going to complain. Tom Lincoln was a good-enough husband. He just wasn't a man to take pains. He'd hunt enough to keep meat on the table. He'd plow and plant, but as long as the corn could force its way through the thistle bindweed and burdock he wouldn't bother himself to cultivate. If the need for it come and knocked on the door he'd go out and make them some cash money, carpenting. But he wouldn't go out of his way to make a dollar. They lived respectable, but weren't ever going to live no better. Her town days were done with, no use pining for parlors, women in nice dresses visiting to talk over the doings of the town. Out here in the woods she did miss the sociable life.

That was where Abe was a comfort and a pleasure. He'd come up to table with his stomach empty and his head full, and while he was loading up the one he would unload the other. How a body could eat that much and talk so much at the same time was a wonder and a caution. He'd take his spoon and pack away a mess of grits and greens and fat-pork and pone like a man shoveling his way to China, all the while expounding and explaining stars and planets, Christopher Columbus, *Pilgrim's Progress*, *Robinson Crusoe*, and Jumpin' Jehosaphat—the girls a-teasing him to tell more, John D. yipping out a "How come?" or a "Why's that?" whenever Abe run dry, and Tom Lincoln mostly staring at his plate half-asleep:

Till he'd snap to, like a man who suddenly recognizes that

danged fly has been buzzing his ear for nigh on an *hour*, and squinch at Abe: then rap his spoon on the table and say, "Can't we have no peace with our vittles?"

A man had his rights in his own house: if Mr. Lincoln wanted peace at his table, Sally Lincoln would see he had it. But with Abe it was talk or bust. So she set aside time after supper for Abe to read to them.

Even a mother had to admit he wasn't exactly pretty to look at, with his long bony face, wide slab-lipped mouth, big poky nose, eyes deep-sunk in the skull, and a harum-scarum head of black hair as coarse as grass. When he was in one of his glooms there wasn't a dead man in the state looked more solemn. But then something would turn his mood, he'd spread out a smile that would just tear his face up and start over—and when he laughed he'd wrinkle up his big nose and curl his upper lip to show teeth and gums like an old horse, *haw! haw! haw!* you laughed twice as hard just to see him.

In her memory, those were mostly sunny days—her first two years at Pigeon Creek. No clouds at all, unless it was one no bigger than a man's hand . . .

Troy Landing, Summer 1821

He called her *Ma*, which was just short of *Mam*. Her eyes were sharp where Mam's had been soft, but they had the same careful see-everything won't-let-you-go look. She could handle Pap too—maybe better than Mam did. After she'd been with them two turns of the seasons he began to believe she brought a turn in their luck—maybe even a turn of providence.

The fire that lit him up again was in those books she gave him. Each one had special powers. Put 'em together and they were like a set of tools, better than Pap's carpenter tools he got from Mam's Uncle. Grimshaw told him at last how you got from Moses to Washington, and took the story right on down to yes-by-God Henry Clay and his American System. But the *Orator* and the *Elocution*, they were the keys: for their teaching was how a man should speak when he rises an equal among the citizens of the republic—how he should stand, how he should say words, how he should *reason*, and with plenty of pictures and examples in case you didn't take the idea right off. "We live in a republic, the orator's natal soil; we enjoy as much liberty, as is consistent with the nature of man; we possess as a nation all the advantages which climate, soil, and situation can bestow; and nothing but real merit is here required as a qualification for the most dignified offices of the state. Never had eloquence more ample scope." All a boy had to do was learn to speak like a republican man, and there wasn't anything he couldn't be or do.

So when Pap told Abe he would take him to Troy, Abe received it as something pretty near a providence. Ma and her books had come just in time to prepare him to set among the men at the landing, and talk over the Missouri Troubles. Even in Pigeon Creek men and boys had been wrangling over Missouri for weeks. Abe would go to Troy loaded for bear: he read up his Grimshaw, and "Dialogue Between a Master and a Slave" from the *Orator*, and what Henry Clay said about it in Mr. Gentry's *Western Sun*.

They rode out from under the trees, and the whole high sky opened out overhead, quick as a man could take off his hat. The next trees ahead were a dark line far across the wide gleaming sliding mass of the river. He had forgot how big the river was, how high and wide and open.

The town of Troy sprawled along the Ohio for a mile or more. To the northwest the Anderson River came down out of the trees—a stream big enough in spate for back-country farmers to raft produce down to market. Taylor's Tavern, right at the landing, was a bee-hive swarming with busyness, buzzing with talk. There were keelboatmen and flatboatmen bound downriver, town folks in frock coats, farmers from back in the woods, planters come over from Kentucky to trade. In the space of ten minutes Abe saw more money change hands than he reckoned he had seen in a year in Pigeon Creek.

If Abe had his will he'd have had the news of the whole Ohio Valley before supper, but he couldn't let that dog bark. He followed Pap everywhere, heeling a step or two behind. Pap seemed to approve—it was hard to tell since Abe was mostly behind him when he'd tell a man, "This here's my boy Abe" and start swapping news.

Everyone turned out to see Captain Donaldson come across the river on the ferry. Pulleys had been rigged upstream from the landings on each side of the river. The ferrymen would haul the raft upstream, steer her across the current with long sweeps, then drift her in to the opposite landing. The machinery of it was splendid to see. *The man that invented pulleys must be smart as Columbus.*

They dropped a ramp so Captain Donaldson could drive his wagon-load of niggers onto the shore. Abe remembered how, when he was just a pup, he had decided to call them *Eth'opians* or *The Unfortunate Race.* But that was book-words. *Niggers* was what men called them, so niggers it would be: two rows of round heads, ten of them, covered with a kind of woolly hair, sitting on the bed of the wagon. One of them turned to look: white eyes bright in a face the color of cherry-wood.

Then Abe heard Pap say his name—but not *to* him. Pap was talking to Mr. Taylor, who answered that his boy Eph and Abe were a fair match for size, but his boy was older. Pap went on talking about Abe like he wasn't there. "Well," Pap said, "there ain't a boy his size in Pigeon Crick can throw Abe more'n one in three."

"Troy Landing ain't Pigeon Crick," said Mr. Taylor. "I'd lay five against four."

"Hunh," said Pap, "I'd a' thought you'd set your boy a *leetl* higher. He's got age on my Abe, and heft."

Taylor came back, "Your Abe has got the heighth and reach." He held out his hand: "Make it five against three?"

Pap said, "Two falls of three?" Taylor nodded and they struck hands: this afternoon after vittles have set. Taylor walked off and Pap stood looking after him, rubbing his hands together and smiling.

Abe said, "You want me to wrassle Eph Taylor?"

"You'll whup him," said Pap. "You'd better whup when I've laid three to five."

The idea of wrassling somebody he didn't know was discomfortable. The way Pap done things didn't set right. He ought to asked Abe did he want to.

But Abe let it go, because Pap seemed pretty well pleased with him: let Abe sit by him after their nooning in the tavern, when business was either done or put off and the men were warming to their talk. This was what Abe had come for, and he listened to them, waiting his chance.

There were a dozen men in the great-room of the tavern—Mr. Taylor and Pap of course, and Captain Donaldson; McCandless the miller, and a farmer named Calloway. The most impressive man there was Lawyer John Pitcher: a big man wearing frock coat, vest, and necktie in the middle of the day.

"That's why I quit Kentucky," said Pap. "White man can't git by in Kentucky without niggers." Abe saw McCandless nod: they might argue this one through together.

Captain Donaldson reared back: "I don't see anything wrong with Kentucky," he said, daring any man to say different.

"Now now," said Mr. Taylor. "No one said anything against Kentucky. If a man can get along with the *institution* . . ."

Captain Donaldson didn't understand a man that *couldn't* live with it. Said slavery was law *and* Scripture, and every great man from Moses and Joshua to George Washington, Thomas Jefferson, and yes-by-God *Henry Clay* owned niggers . . .

And said right out slavery was wrong, McCandless snapped back. "Contrary to our free institutions," he quoted. Maybe we were stuck with it for now, but *the Fathers* were bound we should do away with it "in the fullness of time."

"Henry Clay says the same," said Pap. "He wants the nigger out of the white man's way."

Calloway showed his teeth. " 'Henry Clay says the same'? Well, he has a mighty strange way of sayin' it! Where's Henry Clay stand on Missouri?"

Pap squinted, spied an ambush. But he set his jaw and looked Calloway eye for eye: "Wherever it is, Calloway, you can bet he won't let nobody bust up the Union over Missouri."

Calloway looked smug: "He's for Missouri in the Union—*with niggers.*"

Now Abe leaned in. Pap was bound to call Calloway's bluff: Henry Clay was for keeping niggers out of the free territories. But Pap just blinked and looked stubborn.

Mr. Taylor cleared his throat. "Well now, Calloway, he ain't *for* the Thing—not *as sech*. He's against it *as sech*. What he says is, since you've already got the Thing *there*, let it be; an' bring Maine in a Free State—swap-even, an' let's hear no more about it."

Pap gave Taylor a fierce grateful look. But Calloway looked sly. "Well Taylor," he said, "I guess I ain't as smart a man as Henry Clay. It's hard enough for me to understand how a man can be against slavery *as sech*, and *for* the institution where he finds it. I let that pass. But I'll be hanged if I can tell how letting the Thing spread to Missouri brings the 'fullness of time' any closer!"

That brought Abe up short. *He* couldn't see no way around that one either. He looked to Pap, Pap knew Henry Clay inside out, he could put them straight. But Pap looked uncomfortable. Calloway had set him back. Abe tried to think how Pap could reason it out, but the books were no help. Abe was stumped.

"Any man wants to cut *my* niggers loose," said Captain Donaldson, "he better come loaded for bear."

"Well now," said Mr. Taylor, "now just hold on there." He had picked up a *Western Sun* and was rummaging its pages for something. Pap jumped in with, "Let Taylor read us a piece." He was holding their ground till Taylor come up with something, but he looked uneasy. It was a close place.

"Now here's what Henry *Clay* told them," said Taylor. He cleared his throat and sat up tall, which meant he was speaking for Henry Clay. " 'Slavery hangs over the South like a black cloud. If the cloud pours down all its waters in one place, the result is ruination. But if the winds of heaven disperse the cloud, so that it diffuses itself over the whole land—then the result is a good harvest for each and all.' "

Taylor looked round the company like a man well satisfied, and folded up the paper as if to say that *that* argufication was wrapped up and ready for the post.

"Well that's so," said McCandless.

Abe tried to picture it in his head, how slavery was a cloud, *a black cloud, a big jumbled black cloud like . . .*

Pap looked relieved, nodded judicious approval. "We're all neighbors in the Union. I don't mind sharin' the rain."

"Lincoln," Captain Donaldson averred, "you say right. Let Missouri in, and let everybody get some rain."

. . . a cloud like black flocks of pigeons spreading everywhere, dropping shit and bodies all over everything, millions and millions . . .

They had settled the Missouri Troubles and felt fine. "Ain't nothin' wrong with a little rain!" chortled Mr. Taylor.

"Lessen it's rainin' niggers!" a sharp voice peeped out.

There was a thunderclap of silence and every last man turned to look at Abe. He felt his eyes bulge in his head: what had he done? He never planned it—all the studying he'd done, all the things he'd been getting ready to say, and then this has to pop out of his mouth!

Pap glared at him.

Then Taylor said, "Haw haw," McCandless started laughing, *hee hee hee,* and every man in the room was slapping each other on the back and laughing, even Donaldson and Calloway, "Haw haw haw, raining niggers, haw haw haw!"

Abe's face was full of blood. They were laughing at him and it wasn't fair, he could have got up some good things to say if they'd give him a chance. Mr. Taylor tousled his hair and said, "A little child shall lead them . . ."

"Well Mr. Taylor," he said, "I could say . . ."

Pap's hand bit his shoulder. "I reckon you said enough for now. Time to let the men talk." He gave him a little push towards the door. Pap turned to Mr. Taylor and said, "Women, children, and chickens—they never git enough."

Donaldson agreed: "Women, children, chickens—and niggers," he said, and the laugh went up as big as before.

Abe wandered down to the landing. Captain Donaldson told his niggers to set there on the wooden platform Taylor had built for a steamboat dock, and there they sot—with Taylor's hired man keeping an eye on them. It was like they were in a pen with invisible rails.

Raining niggers. Abe was sorry he said it. It had got him laughed at, when what he wanted was to say something the men would listen to. He looked at the niggers and felt a grudge against them. His spirit chilled. He'd never seen so many all at one time together—just the one that come into the yard with that Virginia lawyer back in Knob Creek, and a scatter of dark faces in Elizabethtown. His mind made a picture of them suddenly lifting off like a flock of blackbirds and it reminded him of the pigeons, the whole huge wave of them rising to cover the sky, the bodies smashed with shot plopping out of the sky like rain, the ground covered and the air rotten with dead birds and bird-shit. His heart began to tick-tick, he was almost afraid.

Up close they looked like people, if people was turned the color of horses and smoked wood. It was hard to look at any one of them too close—there was something chancy about it. If Abe had stared at any man as long and steady as he'd been doing with these, he'd been in a fight directly: you didn't just put your eyes on a man, not unless you were a shirt-tail brat that hadn't learned better. Yet it didn't seem to rile these *niggers*—a glance at him, a flash of white eyes, then they'd turn away.

There's something wrong with them and they know it. They had the wrong kind of hair, like a sheep. Their faces were queer: noses molded smooth to the face, slab-lips thicker than Pap's or his: then sudden pink tongues *the wrong color—Milk-sick* flashed in his head, that painted Mam's tongue brown and her face yellow thick-skinned and lip-swole. Rage flashed in him—then he was afeared, and a little sick at his stomach.

A rustle ran through the black people on the landing, one man got up and the rest rose in response. The hired man got alert. They were moving around their invisible-barred pen, their feet clopped like horse-hooves on the boards—some were wearing wooden clogs.

There was a burst of talk and laughing from the tavern—the men were coming out to take the air and finish the day's business. Abe remembered he was part of that, wrassling Eph Taylor at five against three.

The niggers were talking quietly, laughing, glancing over at the white men, nodding to each other. "You den," said a deep voice— Abe as stunned as if a horse had spoke, the first actual words any nigger ever spoke in his hearing. The speaker was a big man, broad-chested and black as if he'd had himself dipped in tar. He snatched the cap off the head of one of the other men and set it down on its crown at the edge of the platform. Then he nodded and began to clap his hands softly together. Abe saw that the palms of his hands were pink, as if he'd worn the color off them. One of the others, a short skinny boy, stepped out, stamped his clog down once—then begun stamping his feet, an irregular rhythm, *rappatappa tum, tappa tum,* faster and faster.

The tavern crowd whooped and bustled down to see. Then the thin boy stepped back and the cherry-wood-color man jumped in the middle. Everything the first had done, he did faster. The white men whooped and tossed coins in the hat, or cuts of chewing tobacco. Abe felt in his pocket—nothing but a piece of dried sang-root he was saving to chaw before wrassling. Now Captain Donaldson was *bragging* on his stock. "Can't beat a nigger for dancing, and ain't no niggers in Kentucky can out-dance mine!"

The second man stepped back, and now the big black man came forwards. He didn't stamp: just stood there and looked round the circle of white men—putting his eyes on all of them, just a flick and pass on. The men stilled for one heartbeat, but before anyone could think *Was that nigger looking at me?* he had leapt in the air as high as a man's shoulders kicking both legs out to one side banging the clogs together in mid-air . . .

He come down sudden and lit a-stamping, bangaratta *bang* ratta-batta *bang-bang!* and more than that—high-kicks left and right and front, sometimes clapping his heels sometimes scissoring his legs past each other with a silent beat that was stronger in the ear than an actual heel-bang. Abe snatched the sang-root out of his pocket and threw it in the hat—and if it hadn't been impossible he'd have sworn the black man give him a wink for it as he hung in mid-kick in the middle of the air.

"Jumpin' Jehosaphat!" hollered Taylor. "That nigger sure can dance!"

The dancing niggers got the men primed for fun and they started hollering for the wrassle to begin. Mr. Calloway scratched a circle in the bare ground with a stick, then sketched a line in the center. Pap took Abe's moccasins and blanket-coat. Across the circle Eph Taylor was pawing the ground with his feet like a bull. Pap looked fierce. *Three ag'in five.* Pap would be mad if he lost.

Abe turned to face Eph Taylor. Taylor was a few years older, thicker through the body, shorter in arms and legs. His face was rashed on the cheeks, but it didn't seem to bother him none. He grinned at his neighbors and shook his two hands over his head. Mr. Calloway beckoned the boys up to the line in the dirt. "Now toe the mark," he said, and they each stepped their left foot up to the line. "Take a-holt," said Calloway, and they gripped each other, right hand to the other's right forearm. Eph Taylor's arm was thick, but Abe's big hand went a fair way round it. Eph looked up at Abe and grinned.

Then Calloway yelled, "Go!" and before Abe could set himself Eph Taylor rammed himself forwards slamming Abe in the chest, Abe tilted back and Eph bull-rushed him sprawling back (the sky whizzed) flat on his back, *wham!*

"That's one!" Eph crowed and his neighbors let out a bellow, there was a clamor of voices betting on the next fall. "Best wrassler in Pigeon Crick?" Taylor hollered. "I guess there ain't much wrasslin' in Pigeon Crick!"

Pap picked Abe up from behind. "Abe," he said, "git in there and whup him."

He remembered what Denny had taught him. To keep easy in himself. First fall don't matter: you got to larn the other man's way o' wrasslin'. Konkapot would say: first fall *listen* him. Second fall, *make meat.* He toed the mark again. This time when Eph tried his bull-rush Abe was ready, his long legs bracing him, his long lean body twisting aside to throw his hip into Eph and break his balance—then left hand on the scruff to push and right on Eph's belt to finish the hip-throw—and Eph Taylor belly-flopped as free and flat in the dirt as if the ring was a swimming hole.

"Whoo-*hoop!*" yelled someone. "Go it Pigeon Crick!" Abe's heart was banging and bounding inside him. The crowd was hundreds of eyes, bright and cold and laughing: they wanted to see a whuppin' and would just as soon it was *his*. Even the niggers were watching from the landing stage, which was built a little higher than the ground so they overlooked the crowd of white men. Abe saw the big black man take something in his mouth and bite it: it might be Abe's sang-root. As if the nigger chewing it could do Abe any good.

Children women chickens and niggers. Suddenly he was fed up being joked on. His mad rose in him, he felt stronger. All that time he had spent puzzling his books, and nobody here gave a hang who he was or what he thought. Even Pap—if Pap was *for* him it was only in the measure of three against five. Well he'd show 'em who he was. He'd wipe the laugh out of their eyes if he died for it.

He swung his eyes around the circle, not too slow and not too fast—just slow enough so a man knew he'd been *looked* at before Abe's eyes moved on. Then he showed his teeth and said, "There *ain't* no better wrasslin' than Pigeon Crick. And I'm the best *in* Pigeon Crick."

That fetched them. That got 'em a-whooping. Now the ones that bet on Eph were mad and *hot* to see Abe whupped. The ones that bet on Abe were excited enough to double their bets—so if he lost they'd be on him like fleas on a cur. Ma says Brag is a good dog but Holdfast is better. *So here comes Holdfast. Women and niggers and chickens and children never git enough, no sir, and we want meat!* Abe's heart was banging but in his head he was calm and cold. Eph Taylor was his meat.

Eph batted the dirt off his chest and come back grinning and shaking his head. But what sense was there in a smile on a slab of dead meat? Abe felt his eyes were beaming waves of blue cold, like an iced-over pond.

This time when they grappled at the mark there were no bull-rushes or trick throws, just four-square wrasslin'. They leaned into each other gripping hard, shifting grip quick, straining with their legs—pushing, then suddenly letting back, *chance a fall to make a fall*, then striving in again, strength against strength. Abe could feel the heavier, harder weight of the older boy pressing on him. Eph Taylor ducked his head and bored into Abe's chest. Abe dug his bare feet in the ground, toes and feet like taproots, solid bottom for the powerful leverage of his long body and long arms winding and wedging themselves in every crack. He wormed his left up under Eph's chin and pushed, pushed up from the roots, bent Eph's head up, got Eph's neck and shoulders leaning back. He felt a cold happiness rising in him, filling his chest, beaming out his eyes. Every word he bit back on Pap's account, every small he walked to keep Pap's favor, was rising in him like puke, only this was a pizen-puke, if he spoke it they would all drop dead. Eph Taylor's bad luck he was the one, he was dead meat, and his camel and his ass. He wished Uncle Mordecai was there.

Fast as a snake-strike Abe whipped his left leg between Eph's legs, snagged him behind the knee, and throwed him *whump!* on his back in the dirt.

. . . He remembered, later, how the men cheered, slapped him on the back. How Eph Taylor picked himself up, shook his head—a little shamefaced—then stepped up shook Abe's hand, "Well, you *can* wrassle." It was like pricking a bubble, *pop!* the brag and icy hate went out of Abe like that. He felt ashamed glorying on Eph Taylor, and Eph noways proud or mean. Coins chinked as men paid off their bets with Pap, "Jee-hosaphat, Lincoln, that boy o' yours sure can wrassle."

All that book-larning, and he hadn't got no better praise than they give a dancing nigger.

Chapter 8: **Hiring Out**

Little Pigeon Creek, 1821–1823

Sally Lincoln saw trouble coming and did what she could to keep it off. Men-children were bound to out-do their pappy or get out from under soon as might be. But Abe was different: he had that old head, and that sweetness in his nature. If Tom Lincoln hadn't been mule-stubborn, and small in his concerns, maybe the boy would have come round to him in time.

The truth was (though Tom Lincoln wouldn't see it), Abe worked as hard at books as some men she could name worked at farming—harder, or anyway more to the point. He didn't just run the words through his eyes, he studied over them, puzzling till he got clear to the bottom. Was there Jews still or did they die off at the end of the Bible? George Washington says there is "a inseparable connexion between duty and advantage"—did that mean if a body done good, good *had* to come of it? If you was alone on a desart island, and could have things any way you wanted, what way would you have them? It got to where he even wore her out, and she told him he must let her finish her chores unless he wanted raw mush-rat for supper.

She found him one day hunkered behind the shed, scratching with a stick in the bare ground, a book open to one side and a planed oak board on the other with a knife stuck in it. He would scratch in the ground, then wipe it smooth, then scratch some more, so intent he never knew she was there till her shadow fell over his shoulder. When she asked he said:

"There's too many things to know. I can't keep track unless I set them down on the board." The plank was marked halfway down its length with rows of knife-cut hen-tracks and zig-zags, darkened with rubbed-in ash and grease. "I got to work it out on the ground afore I cut it in. Can't cut fast enough to keep up with thinkin'. And it don't take long to run out o' board—then I got to plane her off and start again. So I work it on the ground till I get it *set* in my mind, then mark the board."

She couldn't go to Tom Lincoln, so she tried Dennis Hanks. He was sitting on his porch holding his own new baby in the crook of his arm and letting it suck on his little finger for want of the tit. That baby come just near enough nine months after the wedding for Dennis Hanks to keep his standing with Sally as a man of his word. Dennis said he thought he could make some paper and ink for Abe to use instead of a knife and board.

For a wonder, Dennis did it right off—it was a mark of how Abe stood with him. The ink was easy: blackberry juice, briar-root boiled and pounded, and a little copperas dug out of the bank by the deer-lick. Then a pen from a turkey-buzzard's wing feather. Paper was harder: Denny pounded up a mess of grass and birch-bark and such and spread it on flat rocks to dry in the sun. Sally hadn't ever seen Dennis Hanks do a job of work so careful. But what come out wasn't any easier to write on than a corn-meal pancake. They had better luck mashing old newspapers in water to wash the ink out, then pressing and drying the glop. That worked tolerable, except the copperas in the ink et through the paper in a day or so.

In the end she had to set money aside and buy him a bottle of ink and a book of papers. When Tom Lincoln give her a look she told him it was her own money and she'd use it as she liked. Well, she got her rights of him—and paid for it with a week of sulls.

> Abraham Lincoln
> his hand and pen
> he will be good but
> god knows When

When the settlement worked itself up to fee a schoolmaster, she made sure Abe and Sary and Mattilda and even little John D. went there. Mr. Dorsey run a blab school—pass by any hour and you'd hear the children at it, "Zaccheus *he*, did climb a *tree*, his Lord to *see*"—and taught Abe to cipher to the Rule of Three (two times three is six, three times three is nine). Sally thought a day of blab would satisfy Abe, but it just give his appetite an edge.

> Time What an empty vaper
> tis and days how swift they are   swift as an
> indian arrow   fly on like a shooting star   the
> presant moment Just is here then slides away in
> haste that we can never say theyre ours
> but only say theyre past

One day he came home with his face burning. They'd been blab-reading and when Abe's turn came he had lost the place. The master switched him for stupid, and when he told the master ("He told him *sharp*!" Sary said, by way of explanation) he wasn't stupid, just read too faster than the rest and got ahead, the master switched him again for sass.

Sally was soothing, but told Abe he ought to kept a civil tongue. When Abe said he wasn't going back she reminded him pride was a fault. But he didn't go back.

For once Abe's and Tom Lincoln's 'druthers ran the same way. It was fine with him if Abe *didn't* go back—nor none of them, for that matter. At fourteen the boy could read and write as well as a growed man needed to, and his ciphering not far behind. And what did a *girl* need schooling for? There were things around the place needed doing, and when those were done Abe was big enough to hire out. Tom Lincoln could use some cash money—had not made much on his crop or his carpenting this year. Could see where he might not make the next installment. Maybe he ought to pull up stakes and move to Illinois? There was good land to be had, people said, and the terms was easy.

Sally didn't think much of pulling stakes. But Tom Lincoln wasn't wrong about needing money, so when he came back from Gentry's and told her he'd hired Abe to Gunterman she had to allow he was right. Abe looked glum as he rolled his blankets and set out. But the boy had to come to it some time: it was Adam's curse, that was all there was to say about it.

He came back day after next with forty cents in his pocket. Tom Lincoln was splitting fire-wood on a tree-stump in the yard. Abe walked past him towards the cabin. Tom Lincoln *hunked* his ax into the stump and hollered: "You Abe!"

Abe stopped, hesitated just a tick, then (Sally saw) turned and walked slow to his Pappy. There was something wrong with the set of his shoulders, she hoped Abe hadn't hurt himself. Tom put his hand out. Again there was just that brief pause, then Abe took out the money and put it in his father's hand. Tom Lincoln looked at his son as if there was something he didn't like. "When you bring wages, you bring 'em right to your father." He gave the coins a little toss and stuck them in the pocket of his jeans.

She stood at the door to let Abe in. His face had its dull look, but he give her a smile regardless. She asked had those people give him his breakfast and he said, "Didn't want none." He grinned. "Not *then*."

He hadn't hurt himself. Gunterman hadn't treated him noways mean. But he had took something wrong, and took it to heart. Well, she wouldn't coddle him. But Abe wasn't afraid of work *as such*. It was almost the first unreasonable thing she saw in him, and it puzzled her.

Summer 1823

He didn't love the work itself, but he didn't hate it. It was the way Pap hired him out that graveled him. They were jawing with the men on Gentry's porch, Abe glad to be with them even if they paid him no mind. Gunterman, a new settler, complained he couldn't keep his hogs penned. Pap said, "My Abe can split rails with any man in the settlement."

The other men turned and looked at Abe as if he just then appeared amongst them, and rumbled agreement with Pap's boast. Abe was shamefaced to be looked at, a little proud to be thought well of.

Gunterman ran his eyes appraisingly up and down the length of Abe. It made Abe edgy. "Can he put up a rail fence in two days?"

Pap smiled an *extra* smile and rubbed his hands together. "Horse-high, bull-strong, and hog-tight!"

Gunterman considered Abe's possibilities. What he saw made him skeptical. "Can't pay but fifteen cents a day."

Pap scratched his chin. "Well, that don't seem fair."

Gunterman's eyes dropped Abe and went for Pap. "Twenty then?" He held his hand out palm up. Pap spit to seal the bargain and slapped his hand down on Gunterman's. "Done!"

Like a man selling a horse.

Splitting rails for Gunterman was no worse than splitting rails for Pap. But it was hard when Pap hired him to people like Gentry or Casebier whose sons had been his swimming-hole friends. He'd been a guest in those houses: seated at table, given the choice slice of meat for his plate, plenty of corn bread, greens, and pie. To feed a guest well does honor to the house. But when he showed up as a hired hand, what was he?

The worst was working for Reuben Grigsby. Here it wasn't a case of hiring out where he'd been friends. In the eternal Gentry/ Grigsby wars, Pap tended to the Grigsby side, where the keg-money was, but Abe had friended Matt against Will Grigsby. But now "in the fullness of time" (to quote Henry Clay) the meaning of Aaron Grigsby hanging about the Lincoln cabin became clear: Aaron was courting Sary.

Sary turned red as apples and went all over fluttery when he came mooning by. Even Ma was taken in. She looked on Aaron as a likely husband, he could read and write, he'd have property of his father when he come of age. She judged he had the right feelings for Sary—couldn't hardly say two words when he was with her.

And Pap? who never got past Miz Grigsby's door-sill? Pap was eager as an orphan pup to call the Grigsbys kin, and didn't have sense or pride enough to keep dark about it. He'd go up to them after Meeting (for they had a Meeting now, a House built with Gentry timber on Grigsby land), smiling and ducking his head, taking all the *bretherening* and *sisterening* for a sight more than the Christian politeness it merely was, *yessing* every one of Old Reuben's or his sons' damn-fool opinions. *What are the Grigsbys going to think of Sary if her own father thinks he has to wheedle her way in their door?*

And then he had to go wheedle Abe a job of work. If it was discomfortable working for Gentrys that were supposed to be friends, it was misery to work for Grigsbys—that were supposed to be just-about kin but treated Abe like help, and their help like trash.

Old Reuben didn't put on airs like his wife and oldest son. He'd slap you on the back and call you Old Hoss or some such. But he didn't care a hang for man or boy (his sons apart), and aimed to skin you as close as you could stand it. The older brothers, Reuben Jr. and Charlie, put on decent airs to suit their mother. No one more respectable polite at Meeting, but they'd do dirt to anyone not a Grigsby that couldn't fight back. They were used to having things their way. They'd whipsaw you in a trade. As for brawling, Willie would weasel up the fight and Reuben Jr. and Charlie gang up to do the whuppin'.

Abe slept in the loft of the horse-barn with four other hands Grigsby took on for plowing. There was also a permanent hired man, Zeb Franklin—an old lean whiskey-wrecked man from back in the Kentucky hills who lived in a raggedy lean-to against the wall of the cow-barn. He had a daughter, Hepzibah: a rack of bones and grimy skin, a hank of hair with no more brains or sense under it than would keep her from feeding herself to the hogs. When she smiled it was like a whipped dog's smile on a human person's face—it made Abe's skin crawl.

Abe went off into the woods one day to sneak a quiet read for himself. He had *Crusoe* with him: lately he found it pleasant to dream about living alone on a desart island. He stepped into his secret clearing—it wasn't empty.

It wasn't Man Friday either. It was Zeb Franklin's Hepzibah. She was leaning against a rock with her bare soiled legs splayed in front of her, dress hiked to her belly, between her legs she was all black hair and her both-hands fingers working in her slit. Her eyes bugged at him. She smiled her whipped-puppy smile but kept her fingers working in the hair between her legs. "I thought you was them," she said. "It's all right if you want to if they say so."

So afraid he couldn't feel no fear at all, only knew he'd feel it later: but now he backed off silent, turned, and scooted away through the brush. No secret who *they* was. Reuben Jr. and Charlie had worked that poor dummy of a Hepzibah to where she'd let 'em buck and groan her whenever they got the itch. But Abe reckoned the pleasure they got of her was nothing to the pleasure Reuben Jr. got of doing it first or Charlie got of doing it more times than Reuben Jr.

When plowing was done Abe went home: three dollars for a month's wages, Old Reuben held back a dollar for his vittles. "Your Pappy never told me you ate like three growed men and only worked like part of one." When he got home Abe gave Pap the money. Ma made a fuss over him. John D. was real happy to see him and up in the sleeping loft made Abe tell stories till Mattie and Sary hissed from the other side of the blanket to shush and go to sleep. *There was a boy in Isfahan named Aladdin that found a magic lamp . . .*

When he went to cut timber in the northwest corner of the claim, John D. asked would Abe larn him how to clear off. Abe said he would—John D. being the same age Abe was when Pap showed *him*. John D. crippled some brush with his ax, then sat down to watch Abe work, which is what he meant by *larning* a thing. "Abe? If we had us one of them lamps with niggers in 'em, an' the nigger give us three wishes?"

Bang! "If we did I'd tell him cut more and talk less."

"If we did, *I'd* never do another *lick* of work!"

Considering how little John D. was doing, Abe didn't see that he'd gain by the exchange. Besides, "Who would you get to rub the lamp for you?" Abe rested on his ax. "It's a *story*, John D. You'd best not count on lamps. Or niggers either." He marked a big old beech for girdling, set himself, and began to work his way around the trunk. The work came naturally to him now. His body could take care of it while his mind ran on other things.

No, he was thinking, *you couldn't expect to find a lamp with a spirit-nigger inside. You can't get to Baghdad from Pigeon Creek. But the republic of the United States—that is just up the road or down the river. Where a man who knows things can become anything he wants. As long as he larns how a man's supposed to talk when he speaks out in public . . .*

John D. said something from very far away.

Abe found he was staring at the tree. It was like he had woke up sudden from a deep deep dream.

John D. was saying something—had maybe been saying it some little time. "Abe? What's the matter with that tree?"

Abe looked down. "Nothing wrong with it."

"Then why you been a-starin' at it all this time?"

Abe shook his head. "I jest drifted off, thinkin'." He looked down at the boy. "John D., do you know that any man that larns to make *sense* when he talks can go as far as he likes in this country?"

"Well *I* reckon," said John D., confidently. If Abe said it it was bound to be true even if it didn't make no sense.

"But do you know *why* that is?" John D. didn't, but was willing to hear. "Because this is a republic. And a republic is jest the only *reasonable* form of gov'ment there is. So if a body larns to speech and reason . . ."

"Then he can go as far as he likes!" John D. answered. Abe had played this kind of game with him before.

Abe nodded a sharp *yes* and went back to girdling the tree with new energy.

John D. thought awhile, then said: "Abe? How far off you think you want to go?"

Pap hired Abe out to Mr. Howell, whose claim was up past Konkapot's old clearing. Abe hadn't been to visit Johnny in years, but he reckoned John D. would be excited to meet a live Injun. He told him they must let on to stalk up on Konkapot, like Crusoe snuck up on the cannibals and discovered Friday.

"What's cannibals?"

"Injuns that eats people—especially little boys."

They snuck up from downwind, the way Konkapot taught him. Then there was a foul tang in the breeze, a yellow stink. Abe signed for John D. to stay. He went ahead and peered through the screen of brush that had grown up around the clearing.

There was Konkapot's broken bark shelter. Two bare legs, splayed apart, stuck out of the gaping entry-hole.

Abe stepped into the clearing. A high humming sound came from the shelter, the stink got worse the closer he got. The humming was swarms of shiny black flies drinking where the eyes and ears opened and the lips parted. Konkapot. What used to be Konkapot.

He sent John D. home and went cross-lots to Grigsby's. Abe was crying as he trotted through the woods. But what was the good of missing Konkapot now, when he hadn't give him more than half a thought these two years. Now he was dead, forgetting and forgot. *Larn you hunt.*

Reuben was in the still-house with his jug. "Konkapot's dead, Mr. Grigsby." The old man's eyes were about half full of whiskey. "Well well well," he said. "Old Johnny Konkapot." He shook his head. "I best send Franklin to put him under."

Abe looked down at the drunk old man. "I'll see him buried."

Grigsby gave Abe a shrewd look: "I ain't payin' to bury Johnny Konkapot."

"Don't want any pay," Abe said. Old Reuben was mean, and judged every other man by himself. "Ain't you comin' yourself to see him under?"

Reuben shook his head and let his eyes wander around the still-house—the mash barrels, the wall covered with nailed-up wolf-paws. "Naw," he said, "naw, I ain't goin'."

"You ain't goin'," Abe said. "Wasn't he your friend?"

Grigsby shrugged the word away.

He knew Old Reuben now: he wasn't worth anything *but* money. Abe felt his anger rise and prickle. Sometimes Abe was afraid that what grieving had done to Matt Gentry, anger was going to do to him. He brought his wolf to heel. "I thought what to put on his marker."

"Ain't goin' to be no marker," the old man said. *Afraid his wife would see it, or those boys of hers.*

"I'll write it out and put it in with him then."

Grigsby waved his hand, *do as you please, let me be.* He took a pull on the jug.

Abe went out the door and turned for home. It was full dark but he'd been larned to find his way in the woods.

Abe and John D. stopped by the clearing next morning on their way to Howell's. Abe pulled the wigwam apart and put flint and steel to the old wood. The smoke settled the stink some. Abe dug a narrow trench beside the body and rolled Konkapot in the hole so he was almost flat on his back. Then he threw the blanket in over him.

Abe took a fold of hide out of his shirt and dropped it in on the body. "What's in it?" John D. wanted to know.

"I wrote some words for him," Abe said.

"Say 'em."

> "Here lies Johnny Konkapod,
>   Have mercy on his spirit, God—
>   As he would have if he was God
>   And you were Johnny Konkapod."

 Abe   *139*

John D. was impressed. "Did you write that yourself?"

"I got it out of the Vincennes newspaper, and fixed it up some to suit him. It 'minded me of a thing he larned me." *A man can listen deers and bears and even wolves, because he is a critter like them. But God? A man can't listen God, because they ain't noways alike.*

John D. nodded, serious: "If we got to be jedged like the Book says, I reckon it'd go softer if the Lord see things the way a man does."

Abe said, "It would depend what kind of man it was."

Two days after, John D. came home with a black eye. "It was Will Grizby done it," he told Sally. "He said Abe was a Injun-lover, I said no sech an' anyways Konkapot was a *good* Injun. He laughed like *that*"—John D. curled his mouth in a sneer—"an' said, 'I reckon he is *now*.' So I hit him an' he knocked me down. If I was big like Abe I'd've . . ."

Little Pigeon Creek, 1823–1825

Sally Lincoln did her best to keep peace in the house. The two of them, Tom and Abe, were like a pair of dogs forced to share a yard: bristling, uneasy.

Abe was determined to pay his Pap as little mind as was possible with all of them living in the same cabin, just the one eighteen- by nine-foot room and the loft. After supper, as long as there was light in the windows, Abe would sit at the table and read: his eyes locked into the pages in front of him, his body twisting a little this way and that as he read, his lips moving a little sometimes but no sound come out. Then when there was no more light in the window he'd shift to the hearth and read there as long as the embers lasted—even if it was no more light than foxfire—now lying stretched out on his stomach, now rolling on his back, now twisted up with his back in the angle of the hearth, now with his long legs propped straight up against the wall. But whichever way he wrung or twisted himself his eyes were always nailed hard to the book, nothing else going in nothing else coming out.

It graveled Tom Lincoln just to look at him, graveled him so he couldn't attend to his own doings—whetting his ax or cleaning the rifle. Sally would look up from her mending and see him glaring at Abe, grinding his teeth together till he couldn't stand it no more. "Boy! Ain't you got somethin' better you ought to be doin'?"

Abe would lower the book and look over it at his father, slow. "Nothin' *better* I ought to be doin'."

Then if Pap told him do this or that he'd do it: but with that look in his eye that gave his father no satisfaction of his obedience.

Sally saw what was coming and took measures to head it off. She bearded her husband at his carpenting. "Mister Lincoln," she said, "I know you for a just man."

He put down his draw-knife and looked at her uneasily. "What if I am?"

"Abe's a good son. Does his chores. Brings in wages."

"What if he does?"

"If there ain't no other call on him, let him have his own time to read."

Her husband looked at her but said nothing. Mule-stubborn. He knew she was right but would he say so?

She said: "I won't have you nagging at him when he's readin' of a night. He ain't got school nor other means to better hisself. Let him use the means he's got."

Tom Lincoln said nothing. He took a stroke with his draw-knife. Without looking at her he said, "If he does what else he's supposed to."

She won a kind of truce. Tom would glare at Abe doing his nightly, silent, solitary, flat-on-his-back book-dance all around the cabin floor, and never say a word: only look. She had done her best. She couldn't stop it eating on him.

And Abe? For once he didn't seem to notice a difference, didn't think to wonder why Pap stopped interrupting his book-larning. It wasn't that Sally missed credit due to her: what bothered her was how *careless* he was of the peace she worked so hard to make.

"Abe? Whyn't you read us that Vincennes newspaper?"

Abe picked up the paper and begun to read: THE BALDWIN TARIFF BILL, Senator Clay's Address. THE AFRICAN EXPERIMENT, Report of the American Colonization Society.

Tom Lincoln warmed to that. "It's my notion exactly. Ship ever' last nigger back where he come from. Henry Clay says the same. Reuben Grigsby does too."

Abe's face was too calm by half. "I thought you and Henry Clay wanted to spread the niggers around over Missouri."

Tom Lincoln gave his son a sharp look—but watchful, unsure of himself. "It comes to the same thing. Long as they ain't where I am at."

Abe looked him eye for eye. "It ain't the same thing at all. Not if you think about it."

"I don't need to think about it," Tom snapped. "I don't need to think about somethin' I already know."

Abe looked at him calm, you'd never guess what he was thinking in a hundred years. Only he showed the ghost of a smile. "No," he said, "I reckon you don't."

Tom Lincoln shot Sally a look and for the first time since she knowed him she felt sorry for Tom Lincoln. He didn't know if he'd been sassed or agreed with. And neither did she.

But if she hadn't known Abe better she would have said, whatever the words, there was meanness in the spirit of them.

Chapter 9: **Tom Lincoln's Boy**

Troy Landing, Winter 1825

The next time Abe saw the landing, Pap took him there to help with a wagon-load of salt Gentry had contracted for. The settlement's own lick was used up on account of all the new settlers and their stock.

The landing had grown as well. Taylor had built himself a good-size hog-slaughtering establishment near the Anderson River ferry (which he also owned and operated). The stink was ripe. If it wasn't for the breeze off the Ohio that tended to blow it into the woods, you couldn't have lived in Troy without bungs up your nose. But the town itself was bustling. There was a regular steamboat dock now: the water was too shallow for the big packets, but smaller boats stopped regular.

Mr. Taylor also owned a salt-works that he leased to Captain Donaldson, who brought his niggers over the river to make salt—which made the business profitable and scandalous both. The scandal was it was against the law to work slaves in Indiana, against county ordinance for a nigger even to spend the night. But white men wouldn't work salt, it was muck-work in swampy ground where the air was skeeters and the water full of pizen snakes. So the good people of Troy had to put up with the outrageous sight of a gang of niggers marching down the road with spades, throwing up shanties to live in, stretching out upon the sacred soil of the state as if they were the whitest men in creation. They even had a woman to keep camp for them, a small wiry woman named Dilly, with a face like a dried fruit and a rattlesnake disposition. She bossed the camp; and if townsfolk wandered by curious to see how those people were when they were at home, she'd catch them by the eye and make them scat.

Now and again someone would cry up a mob to burn 'em out. Yet it never quite came to pass. Everyone needed the salt, more than one made money by its being worked in Troy. The salt itself was poor stuff, full of bittern to start with, and the lime and tallow they used to cut the grain weakened it. Its brine soured easy, gave pork an off-taste that Mr. Taylor tried to cover with saltpeter, molasses, and tree-sugar. But he let on to be proud of it.

Taylor gave them good greeting. He remembered Abe had whupped his Eph fair and square, and not only held no grudge but made out there was something famous about it—another thing, like the salt-works, slaughterhouse, ferry, and steamboat dock, that made his establishment special. He was sorry, though. The wagons from the works were due tomorrow. What salt they had in hand Taylor needed for a big pork contract. He cocked an eye at Abe: while they were waiting, he could use another hand at the slaughtering.

"What's wages?" Pap asked, and with no more notice of Abe than if he was a post the bargain was struck.

Pig killing was the ugliest work in the world. There was a great squirming mass of pigs in the slaughterhouse pens. You singled out a big old porker and run around the slops to drive him into the killing pen; lammed him in the head with the backside of an ax; triced him up by the hind legs, heisted him, and slashed his throat, his stubby trotters kicking quickquick while the blood pumped out of him; then slit him from asshole to tongue, dropped his guts in a bucket, skinned him, and sawed him up in sections.

Abe and two men worked the slaughter. Kenton was a rawboned Kentuckian from back in the hills, Deetsel a Dutchman out of Pennsylvaney. By noon they "smelt worse'n the Devil's asshole," as Kenton put it. Neither Abe nor Deetsel saw fit to argue the point. Abe went round to the pump to get himself a drink, turned a corner—and nearly ran spang into the colored woman camp-keeper. She was no higher than Abe's chest, starvation lean, a face dark and wrinkled as jerked meat, but the look of pure outrage and disgust in her small black eyes brought him up short. He gawked at her: the first colored woman he recollected to have seen in his life.

"What *you* lookin' at, you long-eared jackass?" she snapped. He backed away to let her pass, as much in fear as courtesy—she looked like she'd have walked right through him if he hadn't. That was Dilly. She sure lived up to the talk about her.

Abe worked in the pens most of the day. In the late afternoon they heard the rumble of the salt-wagons and came out of the pen to watch. Deetsel took a plug of tobacco, wrapped in a clean cloth, from inside his leather shirt. He bit off a chaw, offered it to Abe (no thanks) then Kenton. They worked their cuds and leaned against the fence. Dilly came out of the warehouse behind Eph Taylor, and the two stood waiting for the salt-makers.

Captain Donaldson sat next to the driver of the first wagon. The planter had put on flesh since Abe saw him back during the Missouri Troubles. His cheeks had a slack puffy look, nose hen-tracked with broken veins. The big black man who had danced so splendidly that day drove the second wagon. He had on a blanket-coat Abe envied, and a pair of winter moccasins that covered his legs to the knee.

Eph Taylor was in charge at his daddy's slaughterhouse. Abe heard him tell the Captain about Pap waiting at the landing for the load Mr. Gentry had contracted. Donaldson blinked and muttered something. Eph gave him a disgusted look. Then he called out, "Sephus—let's get these unloaded. Leave two barrels for the gentleman in town."

Sephus was the big black man in the blanket coat. He called out for his men to "git on it," and they piled down off the wagons, dropped the tail-gates, and commenced unloading. They were dressed in this and that, clothes made of stitched-up scraps—not much to look at, but at least they appeared like clothes. To look at the three hog-butchers, you couldn't say were they wearing clothes like men or only slathered head to foot with a plaster of gray-brown hog-shit mud. Kenton squirted a loop of tobacco-spit to one side and made a face at Deetsel. "Jesus Gawd," he said, "we stink worse'n them."

"Ya," said Deetsel, "and our color ain't mudge better."

Captain Donaldson left the unloading to Sephus and went to talk with Eph by the loading-stage. The blacks lifted the salt-barrels down, tipped them on edge, rolled them across the yard to the warehouse. Dilly spoke to each of them as they passed her, muttered words that made them laugh or growl back at her. The black men weren't as strange to Abe this time, but he still found it hard to see their faces as faces. Black skin seemed somehow like a mask put on to hide the real skin underneath. There wasn't but the least flick of an eye to show they noticed the three butchers watching them—though they'd have had to been dead themselves, and three days ripe, not to notice how the white men stunk.

But not-noticing didn't do them any good with Kenton. The more he looked at the niggers the madder he got, working his cud quicker and quicker as if he had to chew harder to keep something inside from springing out. Then, suddenly, he unloaded the quid entirely into the mud and stomped straight over to the warehouse where Sephus stood supervising the stacking of the salt-barrels.

One of the other blacks saw Kenton coming—didn't say anything, just stood straight and stared, and you could see from the set of Sephus's shoulders he knew something was coming at him from behind. He turned deliberate. Kenton stopped sudden, just out of reach, and glared at him. Kenton said, "Nigger? Nigger, you got the notion you're better'n me?"

Sephus said nothing. Abe saw his face: it seemed calm, no tension in the line of the mouth or look of the eyes, which were round and mild-looking. Dilly's wizened face popped out of the ware-house door. "Cap'n!" she hollered.

"I want that coat," said Kenton. "I ain't a-goin' to stand for you in that coat."

The black man just looked at him.

Abe saw Kenton's arm whip back to snatch his butcher-knife out of the scabbard that swung at his right hip, Abe's heart went *bang!*—

The black man still stood there, looking very calm and mild: only now he was holding a long sharp broad-blade knife, point up, in front of his face—holding it like he had just took it out to have a look at how sharp it was. Then he lowered it just a little, as if he was offering to let Kenton have a look too.

Kenton made no move at all, only stood there. Abe felt a hand grip his arm—Deetsel. Without thinking Abe had started over to where the fight was.

Then Captain Donaldson came storming over with Eph Taylor behind him, little Dilly shadowing them a step behind. "Sephus, goddamn it!" he yelled at the black man, then shot a finger at the Kentuckian and said, "You Kenton!"

Kenton broke his stare at Sephus to glance at Donaldson. He held his ground, but the settle of his shoulders told Abe he wasn't going to fight. "Sephus," Kenton sneered. "Well if that ain't a swell name for a nigger."

Eph Taylor was red in the face. "Kenton, go on back there and git to work."

Kenton stood still a moment. Then he shook his head. "No," he said. "No I ain't. I ain't a-goin' to stand for it." He slid his butcher-knife back in the scabbard with elaborate slowness. "Give me my time," he said.

Abe thought he heard Dilly say something about *trash*. Eph reached a poke out of his shirt, counted out coins, dropped them into Kenton's upturned palm. The Kentuckian kept staring at Sephus even then. Then he closed his fist on the money, turned, and stalked off to get his things from the bunk-shed back of the warehouse.

Sephus never moved—except at some point, without Abe

noticing, he had put his knife away. Abe saw the handle, later, sticking out the top of his knee-high winter moccasins.

Miz Taylor made it plain Abe was to wash the pig off before he came near supper, if he had to chop a hole in the ice to do it. He did throw off the buckskin killing clothes Taylor lent him, and plunged naked into the frigid water of the Anderson. But he reckoned he'd have to been boiled in lye-soap to get all the pig out. He got in late and snatched dinner in the kitchen. Pap wasn't in the great-room, probably gone to tend the horses. Abe slid into a corner to listen to the men jawing. He'd earned a listen, without Pap to spoil it.

The talk of the tavern was how Kenton almost carved up Captain Donaldson's prize nigger. That wasn't how Abe saw it, but he kept dark. He suspected it wouldn't do Sephus any good if it was known he'd pulled a knife on a white man.

"Donaldson would never let anything happen to that nigger. Worth more to him than ary *white* man." The Captain was not popular with most of farmers and hands in Troy.

"What's there to him more'n any other nigger?"

The man who had spoken first, a farmer named Rudabaugh, looked contemptuous of the question. "How d'you reckon Donaldson can work niggers in a Free State, and never a one run off? It ain't *him* standin' guard *I* can tell you: curls up with a jug an' lets Sephus make salt."

"Well why don't that Sephus run off, he's so smart?"

"Wife and children over Kentucky. Donaldson told Sephus he'd pay him wages this side the river, so he can buy hisself out an' his fam'ly to boot." Rudabaugh nodded consideringly. "He might make Donaldson's price, too—if he lives to be a hunderd." He lifted his lip: "That Sephus is a smart nigger, but he ain't smart enough."

"You Abe!" Pap been looking all over for him. Where in blazes was the wage-money Taylor give him?

The barrels were loaded on their wagon early next morning. But there was a steamboat coming in, and Pap halted the wagon to watch. Steamboats landing in Troy were still a novelty, even little one-stack boats like the thirty-ton *Decatur*. Everybody came down to watch her chuff and whistle and mill-wheel up to the dock. Then the gangway dropped and Donaldson's niggers and the boat's own stevedores trundled barrels of pork up the ramps. Passengers gathered on the hurricane deck to watch.

As soon as they were done with their part of the business, Captain Donaldson's boys formed their circle on the landing stage. It was just as Abe remembered it from four years before. One of them put on the wooden clogs and commenced that stamping kicking dance, while the rest clapped and stamped and slapped their chests and thighs to make a rhythm for him. Sephus put the hat down. The passengers clapped too, and the ones who had come ashore gathered in close and threw money into Sephus's hat. The local men lifted a lip at the fools throwing cash at a bunch of niggers. They'd got used to the show. Wasn't anything so all-fired *particular* in a bunch of dancing niggers.

The second dancer out-stamped the first, the third out-did the second, and so on down to Sephus: and he came forward and out-did all of them together. There was nobody could stamp the clogs faster or more complicated, or kick higher when you least expected. To see him smile you'd never guess he had that big hog-sticker in his moccasin-top, and the gall to pull it on a white man. The boat hooted for departure.

Pap poked Abe in the ribs. "Let's git a-goin'." He looked satisfied with the show—with everything. He hefted the little poke of money with Abe's wages in it: put that with what Gentry would pay for fetching the salt-kegs and he'd have a nice piece o' money. "I reckon we done business this trip."

We done business? Red fire in Abe's head then blue ice. *We done . . . ? You swapping lies in the tavern and me working like a nigger up to my eyes in pig shit—*

The devil jumped inside him and he stood up in the wagonbox. *Treat me like a nigger I might as well dance like one.* He shook himself all over like a dog coming out of the river and hollered "Whoo-hoo!"

Pap froze with his whipstock in hand. The men on the landing turned to look.

Abe stuck his tongue out at Eph Taylor, jumped off the wagon, and landed on the hard ground. He hollered *Whoo-hoo!* again, jumped up and slapped his feet together, lit and jumped and did it again. Someone said "Haw haw," and Abe felt the crowd pull back to clear space around him, while from the margins more faces crowded in. Eph Taylor begun to clap, clap, clap, grinning at him. Old Reuben's bear-dance come into his head so he roared and shuffled and stomped. Then the turkey came to mind whose head he blew to flinders with Pap's rifle, and he commenced to strut the circle, poking his head this way and that on his long scrawny neck and flapping his arms like the world's tallest skin-and-boniest turkey.

The whole town was laughing and hooting, the passengers watching from the hurricane deck too, yelling, *Go it Longshanks! Show them how!* and such. The steamboat gave one farewell hoot, Abe kicked one leg up high enough to comb his hair with his toes, then lit grinning. The men and boys stormed in around him. It seemed he was a hero of sorts. He liked it.

Mr. Taylor slapped Rudabaugh on the back: "That boy can dance as good as ary nigger!"

Little Pigeon Creek, Summer 1826

It was reading kept him steady. If he wasn't hauled off to chores, if he had light enough to see by, he would open the book and his spirit would fall out of his eyes and into the page. There were places folded in the pages like clearings in the woods: Baghdad, the split of the Red Sea, Crusoe's fort, Washington's cherry orchard, the open-sesame cave, Bunker Hill, the gate Pilgrim lit out of heading for the Heavenly City—and the "American republic" as *Orator* called it, most perfect form of government in history, "and nothing but real merit is here required as a qualification for the most dignified offices of the state." All a boy had to do was learn to speak like a republican man, and there wasn't anything he couldn't be or do.

Well, what did he want to be and do? He wanted to not be anymore the one that rules and orders was laid on by everyone else, especially Pap. He wanted to make his own rules for his own self. There were men did that, and more: men that made the rules their people lived by ever after. Moses made 'em for Israel. Washington and the Fathers made 'em for the United States, "our republican form of government," the most perfect that ever was.

If you wanted to be a man like those men, you had to know what they knew, you had to understand the reason at the bottom of all their doings. You had to get at the *fundament* of things. The first republican law of all was the Declaration of Independence: no mystery about it, no open see-same, no seven seals to be broke or seven vials to pour out. Grimshaw give you the whole of the Declaration, word by word, in the "Appendix." So if you could read, it was laid out plain: the root and beginning of the American republic.

He puzzled it over. Many of the words were hard, the sentences long and with lots of pieces, some of them quite sharp and beautiful. If he read them silent he'd lose the thread that held the parts together. So he took the book off into the woods (ducking out on John D.), and when he was sure he was alone tried reading it out loud, as if he was telling it to someone else that didn't understand it. Speaking it over like that—stopping when the marks said to hold up a bit, trying to listen to himself while he was saying it over—he begun to get the hang of it. There was a *necessity* to the way it come out: the early parts leading on the next ones as natural and reasonable as water run downhill.

Listen: When one people finds it necessary to break up the bonds that have tied them to another, "a decent respect to the opinions of mankind requires that they should declare the causes." Now that is reasonable twice over: decent respect for people's opinions is reasonable, and you show respect by explaining your reasons why you do a thing instead of just doing it. Pap could take a lesson by that.

And then the reasons: that all men are created equal; that they are endowed by their Creator with rights; that the rights are life, liberty, and to pursue happiness.

Reasonable? That was better than reasonable. That was all a body could wish. To be equal to any and every other man? To have a right to be happy? You couldn't ask a lamp-nigger for better than that. In Abe's experience, equality was hard to come by and happiness seldom and not to be expected. But if this was the right of it, then he'd been fooled somehow, or the truth kept from him. If the republic was what it was supposed to be, what it been wrote down to be, he had a lot more coming to him than he ever expected to see in Pigeon Creek.

But the piece didn't stop there. It went further: that the only reason to have gov'ment is so you can have your rights; and when a gov'ment gets in the way of those rights, you have *another* right to "alter or abolish" the old gov'ment *and start a new one*, arranged any way that keeps you safe and makes you happy. So the Constitution and all the legislature that happened since—the debt relief, the internal improvements, even the Missouri Troubles—was all of it just the working-out of what was already laid down right here in the Declaration.

There was a *system* to it as natural as the Rule of Three: three twice is six, three three times is nine, and so on. Once the first rule was proved and set, everything that followed come sure and certain—no one could *rightly* stand against it nor *rightly* take it away. Anything that didn't square with those first rules, you wasn't bound by it. You could change it or throw it out, or even make you another gov'ment to your liking—as long as *it* stood by those first rules.

Well that was all right with Abe Lincoln! That suited *his* notion of fair play and justice. He didn't want any better set of rules than what was laid out right there. Only—you had to be a man to get the good of the republic. A boy didn't have no more show than a nigger or a woman.

Abe and John D. were hoeing Grigsby's corn, churning the soil and chopping out the burr-weed and thistle. August leaned over on them, hot and dry—Grigsby wanted *two* crops out of his fields.

John D. said, "I wish we wasn't here all the time. Wish we could go afar off an' live in them Araby palaces."

"It's too far off, John D., and a long time ago—Bible times. Things worked different then."

"Well," said John D., "but if you was to go far off as you liked, where would you go? Would you go for Araby palaces or an island to yourself? If it was me, I'd go for palaces."

Abe leaned on his hoe. "If it was an island, wouldn't have to work no harder than to keep yourself. Nobody's say-so but your own. That wouldn't be bad."

"Is that where you'd go, Abe? If you could do it?"

Abe gave John D. his joking straight-face: "Naw," he said, "if I had my will, I'd run off to the American republic."

Even with the help of Abe's serious-joke look, John D. had to hunt for a reply to this one. He came up empty. "Abe? Ain't we already there? Ain't this here the United States republic of America?"

"Naw," Abe said. "This here is the Kingdom of Pap."

From the far side of the field a call—"You-ou!" It was Old Reuben, son William next to him sitting astride the fence. "I ain't payin' wages for you to stand there a-jawin'!"

Sally cornered Abe by the cow-shed. "I don't like the way you are with Aaron Grigsby. I see you and John D. makin' eyes behind his back. When he talks you ain't far from rude. Your sister means to marry Aaron, and I don't see no wrong in it. If you've a thing to say, Abe, I want to hear it now." She had took him by surprise. His eyes went a little wild. She couldn't tell was he angry or scairt or both.

"Is it her wanting or *his*?" he snapped, meaning his father of course. But then he looked hang-dog.

So it wasn't Aaron that graveled Abe, but Tom Lincoln's marrying Sary off as a way to borrow Old Reuben's money without security. But that was nothing to do with Sary. "Aaron is her choosing—always been! Your Pappy may have his notions of the how and why of it, but that don't signify." She would have things perfectly plain: "I mean her to be happy in her marriage. She can't be that if her own brother won't treat kin like kin."

His eyes ran all over the county looking for what to say, as if he was afraid of plain truth. When he met her look there was defiance in his eye. "You reckon we're kin to Grigsbys?"

"Ain't a question of *if*, only *when*." Her eyes narrowed. "They treatin' you mean over there, when you hire out?"

"No meaner'n the rest of the help."

He was proud, she knew. Maybe unreasonable proud. Maybe Grigsby didn't treat Abe the way you ought to treat kin, or almost-kin. But on the other hand, if you were working for a man, how *should* he treat you but as one of the help?

He saw she didn't understand him. "Pap hires me out to Old Reuben. Then *he* hires me out to someone else."

She was puzzled. "Ain't the wages the same?"

They were.

"Well then," she said.

His eyes were hot. "I ain't *his* to hire out. I ain't his horse. I ain't his nigger. Nor I ain't his son, neither."

It was too many for her. Was Abe mad on account of Grigsby *not* treating him like family, or mad because he was? Whichever, it wasn't reasonable.

Abe give her a yearning look. "They don't think we're up to them—not any of us."

Well: Mrs. Grigsby *was* house-proud . . . But Sally girded up. Things was never all they should be. You had to see them as they was and take them as they come. "Sary ain't marryin' the whole family, jest Aaron. He ain't the bull o' the lick, but he's got a good heart."

Abe shook his head. "It ain't enough."

Jim Gentry was Reader at Meeting that Sunday, and read out Sarah Lincoln and Aaron Grigsby as agreed to be married. Tom Lincoln was full-belly proud to be so associated with the two biggest men in the settlement. After Meeting the Grigsbys and Lincolns stood to either side of their couple. There were things for Sally Lincoln to take pleasure in. Sary's round face was apple-red with pleasure, and Sally rated a woman's chance of joy in a man according to how hard she blushed on his account. Other pleasures had a little edge to them: watching Mrs. Grigsby's Baptist side fight off her Virginia

side so she could stand with the Lincolns as even Christian, her
small mouth cinched like a purse.

Old Reuben was grinning and gabbling and slapping men on the
shoulder, same manners for Meeting as for the tavern. He had laid a
feast on wooden tables in front of the Meeting-House. Roasted pig
and venison, heaps of hominy and bowls of pease, all manner and
sorts of pie—and of course barrels of brandy-wine, mentioned in
Scripture as a thing to be took for your stomach's sake. For music
there was a hired fiddler, and Reuben had actually laid a floor
of raw planks to dance on. Pigeon Creek Meeting was against dancing frivulous, but if it was for a Christian purpose, then: One two
three *four*—

> Higher up the cherry tree
> Sweeter grows the cherry
> The more you hug an' kiss a gal
> Quicker she will marry!

They formed fours and eights, men and women, boys and girls,
and skipped around the boards. Reuben Jr. swung red-haired
Jemimah Hardin around, and threw his brother Charlie a look that
told him to eat his heart out.

> Charlie he's a fine young man
> Charlie he's a dandy
> Loves to hug an' kiss the girls
> Feed 'em on sweet candy!

Then Reuben Jr. went off to wet his whistle and Charlie grabbed
Jemimah and hauled her onto the floor again—Reuben Jr. squinted
to let him know he'd pay for his fun.

> Take her by the lilywhite hand
> Lead her like a pigeon
> Make her dance to 'Weevilly Wheat'
> An' scatter her religion!

There was a decent chance Charlie and Junior might come to some sort of ruction. They dogged poor Jemimah, edging each other out to be nigh her when the next dance was called.

Sally didn't like the turn of things. It should have been Sary's day to shine.

The fiddler called "Turkey in the Straw," the couples sorted out. Sam Casebier had Jemimah Hardin almost to the floor when Will Grigsby "fell" under his legs and tripped him, and Charlie snatched her arm and squired her to the boards grinning victory. Then here came Reuben Jr., handing his mother up onto the floor. Didn't Charlie like that! Well it was a Grigsby show, sure enough . . .

Only just then a great long lanky shape jumped spraddle-legged over the fiddler's back and landed with a *bang* on the puncheons! It was Tom Lincoln's Abe, with a skunk-skin cap on his ugly raw-boned head, wrists and ankles hanging out the ends of his patched-up go-to-Meetings, and a pair of wooden clogs on his out-size feet. He threw the skunk-skin hat so Reuben Jr. had to drop his Ma's hand and catch it, then he gave a *whoop!* and jumped five feet straight in the air . . .

Treat me like a nigger I might's well dance like one.

. . . and lit a-stamping and a-pounding and a-banging those wooden clogs so the planks rang with it, *rappa-batta bangabatta rappa-batta bang!* side-kicking and clapping his heels, sky-kicking so high the boys hollered and the women screamed, the men egging him on, clapping and hoo-hawing and ki-yipping, *by Ned I never see the like . . .*

Abe Lincoln kicking up his heels, grinning like a jackass, dancing like a nigger right in Reuben Grigsby's face, and his wife and his sons—

"Dang you Lincoln!" Reuben Jr. hollered, dropped his Ma and went for Abe, Charlie behind him. Abe squared to meet them still grinning—but Dennis Hanks bulled past the fiddler, grabbed Abe by his belt, and swung him around to stop him trying to whup both Grigsbys at once—then Peter Brooner jumped between Abe and the Grigsbys, and Jim Gentry and Tom Barrett: "Back off boys, this ain't the place or time . . ." "No but don't you doubt some time it's gonna—!"

Mr. Brooner's hand was firm, easing Abe away from his fight and back to the family. "Abe," he murmured, "I'm sorry to see this."

Abe wished he could say he was sorry, but he wasn't—only a little bit for Sary's sake, not near enough for Pap, who came rolling down like a thunderhead: "Git in the wagon! Git in it now, or . . ." But Abe didn't care if Pap rained on him or out on the hills somewhere. It was bound to come. If it was today, that was all right with him.

They rode home in a thundering silence. For once in her life Sally didn't know *what* she thought, or what she needed to *do* about it. Abe was in the wrong, fighting—and in church to boot. And on Sary's own day! It was mean in him, and careless. Mister Lincoln was in his rights to be angry, and spare not the rod—in reason. But one look at the two men and she saw they were both past caring about *rights* or *reason*.

Tom Lincoln got down from the wagon slow and deliberate, as if his bones were sore. Abe climbed off and stood waiting for him, Sary and Mattie holding John D. off out of the line of fire. Pap stopped ten feet from his son and stared at him hot-eyed, working his jaws. He had a stiffened length of knotted rawhide in his hand— used it to goad the horses. He was trying to keep a-hold of himself and it wasn't easy.

Abe didn't flinch, just stood looking at Pap like there wasn't anything out of the usual to be seen. She despaired, *He must whip the boy just to get a rise out of him . . .*

But instead of striking out Tom Lincoln started working his mouth: "Well you showed out," Tom said. "I been waitin' for it and you finally done it."

Sally's mind was like a millrace: What was holding Tom Lincoln back? It was as if there was an invisible line between the man and his son, and the man afraid to cross it.

Instead he turned on her—shook the goad, his eyes raging, "He can fool some folks, but I see plain—plain enough him standin' there"—the words and rage boiling up so hard he choked, wheeling back to face Abe—"stubborn and *sot* and . . . and think you are better, better'n everyone—better'n your own father"—his voice cracked—"and got no more shame in you than dance like a nigger in front of the neighbors, and our new kin!"

Abe just stood there, his face gave nothing away, nor was it angry scairt or sorry, no more than if it was made of wood.

John D. cried out, "It warn't his fault, Pappy! Them Grizbys was gonna jump him!"

Tom Lincoln never heard. His face was swole up like to burst. He moved in on Abe, hunched forwards, the limber goad springing in his hand. Then he stopped again. "Right in church," he said, "an' sech a day! What could they done to make you act the nigger an' start a fight?"

Tom was giving Abe an out. Sally couldn't think why he would, but the boy was too smart not to see it. Now he could say *Will Grigsby said this* or *Reuben Jr. done that*, and Pap would say *That warn't enough to justify*, and Abe would say and Tom would say and she would say and the whole thing pass off with no more than maybe a little hiding—

But if Abe saw that way out, he didn't want it. He just stood steady and still watching Pap lowering at him, not like he was afeared, not like he was setting himself to take a whipping and not cry out. Like he was . . . considering.

She thought: *He won't let his father whip him. He will fight Tom and that will be the end, no fixing it he'll be gone, gone for good and ever in this life.*

The two men stood facing each other, eye to eye, a bull against a bean-pole. Only—the bull was shaking, like some terrible thing was trying to get out of him.

Sally thought: *No, of course not! Abe won't fight, he won't raise his hand against his own father, not her Abe he wouldn't never*, and for just one beat of the heart she felt it still warn't but ordinary bad.

Then Abe: smiled.

Tom Lincoln swung his arm and knocked Abe sideways and down to the ground. He rocked back on his heels, cocked the rawhide goad in his hand, and stumbled towards Abe like a man wading through a bog. Sary and Mattie were yelling, *Pap! Abe! Ma!* John D. was fighting the girls to get loose . . .

Somehow—she didn't know how—Sally got to Tom Lincoln and grabbed his arm. Tom shook her off, but now he was facing her. Behind him she saw Abe, sitting on the ground, lift the back of his hand to touch a bleeding lip.

"I won't have him sass me!" he said. It was terrible how he said it—the anger was bad, but there was something worse, like Tom Lincoln was afraid of something, like he might break out weeping. *That would be too awful,* she thought, *the man would never live through it.* She reached up two hands and pressed them hard against his bristly cheeks. "You give him his lickin', Tom," she said. "He won't sass you no more."

Tom Lincoln's eyes were wild. She couldn't bear to look in them. "You give him his lickin'," she told him again, "you done enough now." He give her a look—it started grateful, it shifted mad, then slipped into something bleak and empty. "I mean for him to go back there," Tom cried, "back there and say he's sorry, or I'll—!" He pushed her aside and rounded on Abe again, flexing the rawhide goad in his fist.

The girls had run to Abe on instinct, softness for his hurt, and softness to keep off more. If he stayed down . . . but he wouldn't stay down. *He's too proud.* Abe eased his sisters away, got up slow. Sally marked the boy's look: not angry nor in defiance but something worse—he looked at his father like Tom Lincoln was trash, and better than this warn't expected of him.

She wouldn't have it! No by God, not if she died for it! Quick as snap your fingers she jumped between them, no bigger than a child and each of *them* larger than an ordinary man, Tom thick and jowly as an old bull and Abe lean as a whipstock and hard as an oak rail. She set into Tom Lincoln like a fice-dog at a bear: "You Tom!" she snapped and he blinked. She started walking at him and cut her jaws loose. "I won't have it! I won't have you whup him! Jest you look at your son one time! Can't you tell he ain't no boy to be whupped? It don't matter what he done it's *his* doin' and *he* must bide it, and it ain't for you to say no more!"

Tom blenched and stepped backwards as she came on. "Well now Sally, a father has got to . . ."

"Don't you 'father' me, Tom Lincoln! A father ain't got no more whuppin' rights than a son will stand for, and *he* won't stand no more! He'd *stop* you doin' it, only he's too good-hearted a boy to raise a hand ag'in his own Pappy, and *you* know it—and you dasn't—you dasn't—I won't *stand* to see a creatur' whupped when he can't or won't help hisself!"

"Well now, Mother," Tom said, "if that's how you . . ."

But she spun away from Tom Lincoln as soon as she saw he hadn't strength to say no to her, and rounded back on Abe. "And you, you great stretched-out—!"

. . . She was right up under his chin glaring up at him, he would remember the bright fierceness of her eyes and that her words came in a hissing whisper like steam from a boiler:

"I won't have no more o' this! I won't stand for it! All the men in this country grow up keerless or mean, and I don't intend for you to be neither one. Your Mam raised you kindly, and I won't have her doin's spoilt! Not by your Pappy—not by you neither!"

That winter, after harvest, Tom and Abe drove a passel of Grigsby's hogs down to Troy. Mr. Taylor said business was booming, he could use a boy regular now—six dollars a month and found. Abe said he was willing. Pap said he was agreeable.

When they told Sally Lincoln she said she wouldn't have it no other way. She thought Abe looked hurt when she said it, but it wasn't the time to be soft with him. Nor herself, who when it come to his actual leaving would be sadder of his going than he would. Good as he was, he wasn't getting no nourishment of his family: what was meat and drink to her just seemed to turn pizen in him. That was sad, but you had to see things as they were. And act according.

BOOK IV:

The Landing

Chapter 10: **The Ark of Philanthropy**

Troy, Summer 1828

The small sternwheeler's single stack dashed a black scrawl on the overcast. Her paddlewheel ceased flogging the water and *Cresap* coasted towards the shore. The stiff breeze whipped up steep short waves that banged and burst against the port quarter. Out on the hurricane deck Denton Offutt took his first look at Troy: a scattering of log houses in an elbow-crook of the Ohio. The small crowd at the landing was Denton Offutt's welcoming committee, if they but knew it.

Offutt was a city gent, middling as to size, scanty as to hair. He could oar a boat and swing an ax if need be, but favored the look of softness: if a man wanted to *become* prosperous, he had to *look* prosperous. He wore a black frock coat (shiny with wear) over a suit of impressive yellow plaid, and a boiled shirt. Amongst the buckskin and homespun he'd pass for well dressed.

Inshore of the steamer a big raft-ferry, a two-horse freight-wagon aboard, was being hauled upstream on pulley-ropes. The ferry suggested *possibilities* in Troy. If a man wanted to get rich in this country, what he wanted was location: a navigable river in front and a growing inland trade behind. The water here *might* be deep enough to dock steamboats . . .

But then, as if to check Offutt's enthusiasm, *Cresap* dropped anchors. The captain stepped out of the pilot-house, tugging the peak of his blue cap in deference either to the wind's bluster or Mr. Offutt. He bellowed politely into the blow: "I regret our pilot thinks it unsafe . . ." The river was low and *Cresap* couldn't risk running aground, so they'd row him ashore in the skiff: round-bottomed, cranky, and filthy. Denton Offutt *might* make it through wind and wave undrowned, but for his coat the trip was certain death. The creature was too frail to stand cleaning, and just now he lacked ready money for a replacement.

"Look there," said the captain. A tall figure stood erect in the stern of a flat-bottomed scow, bending to a seven-foot oar as he bucked the scow slantingly out to *Cresap*, evading the brunt of the wind and the teeth of the chop. The ferrymen hollered and shook fists at the boy as he passed. The tall boatman paid them no mind, but swung his scow broadside into the lee of the steamer.

Offutt ran down to the main deck. A pair of crewmen held the scow to the steamer's side with boathooks. The negro porter passed over Offutt's satchel and trunk, and stepped aside with a flourish far too grand for *Cresap*. Offutt hopped into the scow and they pushed off.

Denton Offutt knew boats—had sailed his father's brig out of New London, first as chantey-boy and fiddler and later as mate, and he'd made one voyage to Canton. The boatman was no more than a boy, but he was *phenomenally* tall, six feet and more and lean as his oar. And he knew his craft, maneuvered the big scow with deft shifts of the steering oar using the powerful leverage of long arms and legs and the skill and strength of his out-size hands. His ragged trousers had given up trying to cover his blue and bony shanks. A scrawny rooster-neck stuck out of his shirt, and on top of that a head too large for the neck. The domed forehead was (physiognomically speaking) a sign of intellect, but the face was about as ugly as a face could get: the skin a sallow half-breed yellow-brown starved tight to the skull; mole on the right cheek; wide slash of mouth, slab-lipped, under a big fleshy nose that looked like it was stuck on for a joke; gray-blue eyes deep-sunk in the skull under a ledge of black eyebrow as thick and coarse as the thatch of head hair.

"I'm Abe," said the boatman. "Thomas Lincoln's boy."

"Offutt, Denton T. Your pa own this ferry?"

"No—Pap hires me to Mister Taylor." He pointed his bony jaw at the log-and-clapboard construction that rambled up the slope from the landing. "His landing, his hotel. My folks live at Pigeon Creek, back in the trees."

Hotel, the thought flickered brightly—but Offutt blew it out. From the look of Taylor's town and Taylor's boy, he had a notion what was meant by *hotel.* Idlers were drifting towards the landing, a gang of negroes stood in a bunch, watching. *Steamboat must be Fourth of July to these people.* "She don't look much," said the boy, as if he'd read Offutt's mind, "but we've got the packin' house, Mister Taylor has. Make our own salt. Mister Taylor leases the lick to Cap'n Donaldson, that's his niggers works it."

"I wondered why so many negroes north of the river."

Abe gave him a sharp look, then nodded. "Negroes," he said, "right." Then he went into his pitch again, probably picked it up from his Mister Taylor, who sounded like a man of speculative capacities—in a small way. "They make all the salt *we* can use, ship the rest downriver. Mr. Taylor says Troy is the *entrypote* of the deestrick."

"Entrypote?" said Offutt.

"That's a Frenchy word," said Abe. "Means the place the goods come in."

"French?" said Offutt.

"O' course," Abe answered. "Frenchies used to *own* this terr'tory. Plenty still over by *Vin*cennes."

"Hmmm," said Offutt. French or not, the *entrypote* idea deserved consideration. He recalculated Troy's steamboat possibilities. Perhaps with dredging? If Mr. Clay carried the election the government would subsidize internal improvements . . .

"Yes sir, you couldn't do better'n settle in Troy. Why General Lafayette himself said, when his boat was . . ."

Offutt threw back his head and laughed. "Son, there isn't a wood-lot between Pittsburgh and Memphis that doesn't claim Lafayette went aground on their *personal* sand-bar, and said they had the up and comingest town he ever saw!"

The boy wasn't embarrassed. "Well, it *was* afore my time. I sure *wish* I'd seen him, though." He gave Offutt a sad smile and confided, "Ain't many famous people stop in Troy. And when a *chance* come—like with this 'Ark' everyone is talking about?—there's people say they won't let her land."

Offutt clucked sympathetically, though he had no idea what "Ark" the boy was talking about. But the sympathy provoked further complaint, as it was supposed to do.

"There's a duke on board of her, s'pose to be, and a passel of educated folk, perfessers and philosophers. But the preachers and boiled shirts are afraid to let her land—they say it's on account of the infidelity, but everyone knows it's because of *the Woman*."

"Well, a preacher would take that view of it," said Offutt. This "Ark" was most likely a keelboat of women for the river trade: there were "gunboats" tied up near most towns on the western rivers. The lad must have misunderstood the honorific *duchess* and *perfesser*, which denoted the mistress of the brothel and the piano or squeeze-box player. But it was natural the boy should hanker after a cargo of women prime for poling at two bits a toss.

That reminded Offutt. "What's the fare?"

"Shucks!" said Abe. "I forgot to say afore you come aboard." His face flushed, and he gave more attention to steering than the scow seemed to need.

It was plain the boy liked running the boat so well he didn't much care if he got paid for it or not. But the man who owned the boat might feel differently. Besides, if Abe hadn't liked boat-work enough to bring that scow out through wind and waves, Offutt wouldn't have got ashore without damage. "What's the usual rate?"

"Depends if there's weather or sech. Two bits?"

Offutt smiled. "Two bits it is. And a penny for the pilot." There

was a tin cup nailed to the steersman's bench. Offutt flipped two silver coin-snips into the cup, and laid a copper penny-piece next to it.
The boatman hesitated, then picked the penny up with long fingery
toes like a monkey's, transferred it to hand and then a leather pouch
slung round his neck. He looked happy, maybe a little embarrassed.

The scow bumped the landing and a small boy held her for
Offutt to step ashore. A tall plump florid man reached down to hand
Offutt up. "Welcome to Troy," said Mr. Taylor.

"A pleasure sir," said Offutt. "I have heard much about the *entrypote* of southern Indiana . . ."

Troy and Little Pigeon Creek, 1826–1828

It was Abe's third year at Troy. At the start he just butchered
Taylor's hogs, cut his wood, waited table in the tavern when a
steamboat brought a sudden crush of guests. But the more Taylor
hired of Abe, the more he was pleased with him. Abe had a ten-
dency to wool-gathering, would pick himself the oddest corners to
go off and read where King Solomon himself wouldn't ever thought
to look for him. But he was a good influence on Taylor's sons Eph
and George, and taught Green (his youngest) his letters slick as any
schoolteacher. And when he was working, he *worked*. He was worth
any three men with an ax in his hands. He had a name worth money
for splitting rails and setting fence, "horse-high, bull-strong, and
hog-tight." He was wide-awake when he wanted to be: if he could
improve a thing he'd generally do it. He cut firewood on his own
account and sold it to passing steamboats. Had the knack of sang-
hunting in any season, sold cuts of dried root or scraped some in
whiskey for patrons at the tavern. The boat service was his idea.

He had other advantages. If some man or boy passed through
who fancied he could wrassle, a little bragging on "our Abe" would
bring on a wager, a match, a crowd—all of it money in Taylor's till.
It became a regular routine for Abe: kill hogs morning and afternoon, throw a stranger on his ass before supper. Or if Donaldson's
negroes were at hand, and set out the hat for clogging, someone

was sure to remember how Abe "showed that sassy nigger how to dance." Then he had to put his grin on and do his jokey, long-legged, sky-kicking, eejit-grinning mockery of the niggers' clog-dance.

Sometimes of a winter evening, if things got dull in the tavern's great-room, Taylor would tell Abe, "Go on and speak us a piece." He'd stand up, solemn as a cat so a body would just about kill himself laughing only to look at him: sort of bounce and balance on his knees and shoot out his arms, first one side then t'other, and orate you a "Give me liberty," or a "Now is the winter of our discontent," or that one about how the Jews have eyes that would set the crowd banging their mugs on the table and roaring him on to do another one—Taylor beaming with pride, "That's my hired boy Abe! He could make a dead cow laugh."

One old farmer told Taylor he ought to pay Abe wages just to sit in the bar and talk. Well, he wouldn't go *that* far. But went the nearest thing to it: talked Tom Lincoln into letting Abe work through to planting, and come back soon as might be in summer.

For his part, Abe was satisfied. So long as he did his chores Taylor left him free to follow whichever way his nose pointed; and if Taylor took his share of Abe's speculations, he let Abe enjoy some of the fruits. But more than money, living by the river was as good as schooling. When Abe was done working his time was his own to read as much and as late as he liked. (There were rushes in plenty for lights, and God knows enough hog-tallow to dip them in.) Mr. Taylor had books as well: a *Pilgrim's Progress* with pictures, a *Complete Works of Shakespeare*, a *Life of Washington*, Ben Franklin's *Autobiography* wrote by himself, *Famous Pirates*, a Methodist hymnal full of poetry, and a beat-up copy of *Joe Miller's Jokes*. Also there were the Vincennes and Louisville papers Mr. Taylor subscribed to, plus odd copies from every state in the Union left by steamboat travelers.

Then come plowing time Pap would show up, Mr. Taylor would give him Abe's wages for the year, Pap would pretend to count it and nod like it matched *his* calculation. Then Pap and Abe would start back and when they were under the trees Pap would say, "What about that ferryin' money," and Abe would give him whatever he hadn't spent on clothes or paper and ink. There was no question but Pap had the right to that money too. Only, when Abe put it in Pap's hand he felt a chill in his heart. Every year the chill bit a little deeper.

Abe stood a *little* higher now with the old boys from his swimming-hole days. They greeted him with a whoop when he returned from the landing, the way they used to for Dennis Hanks—primed to laugh and poke each other over the jokes and stories and scandals he brought back. And just as they had looked to Denny for gov'ment when they were young . . .

They told Abe how Will Grigsby snuck up on Matt Gentry tied up out in the yard—for the miseries got him same as before—and spat him with a pea-shooter to make him yowl.

Abe laid for Will back of the Meeting. "This here's church," Will cried, "you dasn't in church!"

"Church or not," Abe said, "if I hear you bothered Matt again I will kick you till you spit blood." His eyes were blue ice.

"My brothers'll git you if you do!"

"Maybe they will. But you know *them*, and you know *me*. You can count on *me*."

But none of that amounted to a *difference*. In Pigeon Creek he'd never be anything but Tom Lincoln's Abe, joker and bully-boy: "Do the old man a good turn, and hire the son to split you some rails . . ."

Little Pigeon Creek, May 20, 1828

. . . or make Reuben Grigsby some more whiskey kegs. That's where he was bound that morning when, passing Aaron and Sary's cabin, he heard his sister mewing like a cat and trying so hard to scream the baby out that was caught inside her—and he stopped at her gate wondering should he ought to maybe go on in there and do something? But he was afraid. It didn't sound like Sary crying, which was always a high sweet awful sound—this was throaty and hoarse and

ripping. He remembered how in the Milk-sick he had listened outside the cabin and heard Mam barking and moaning . . . *It's for the
women to take care of* he told himself, and went on down the road to
split Old Reuben's barrel-staves for two bits.

Then just at noon he saw Old Reuben coming and knew by the
hunch in his shoulders and how he wouldn't look Abe in the eye.
"You better come along down to Aaron's." Yet Abe never asked was
the baby come. Let himself go Stupid. Plunked the broad-ax softly
into the head of the oak block and followed Old Reuben back to her
and Aaron's cabin. Grigsbys were standing around Sary's bed—

Mebbe we let her lay a mite too long.

—awkward, shuffling their feet, that look on their faces part stupid, part ashamed, and also just fussed and bothered on account
of the

the dead woman in the bed.

Dead Sary. Laid out flat as an empty sack. They had wrapped
what come out of her in swaddlins and laid it alongside her.

*Two days ago when he pushed in to see her she was ripe and full as a
pumpkin, hid her apple face under her quilt for shame of her brother seeing
her condition.*

"Reckon we *did* let her lay a mite too long."

Aaron slumped in the corner looking poleaxed. Ma wasn't there.
Nor Mrs. Greathouse the midwife. Nor Betsey Hanks. So Sary was
croaking and screaming like that and nobody with her but Grigsbys:
bothered to be there and all the *fuss* their white-trash daughter-in-
law was a-makin', and should they ride over and get her Maw or
Miz Greathouse? *Naw* says Reuben *let's wait awhile, I got to go see how
that shiftless sprout of a Lincoln is makin' out with my whiskey-kags* . . .

But the shame of it was on him, on Abe Lincoln, who let his own
Mam puke herself to death who left his sister screaming and mewing with pain, dying and dying while Grigsbys stood around and
watched her do it.

Troy, Summer 1828

He went back to the landing right after Sary went into the ground. People said it was cold in him. But the dead don't care. At the landing people were alive, there were *chances* to be took a-hold of if you were wide-awake.

Then word came that Robert Owen's "Ark" was coming downriver. Owen was a rich Scotsman who bought and sold townships the way another man might trade hogs. But he was also a *philanthropist*, which meant he used his money to do good for others. Right now he was projecting his own colony, organized on the most scientific and democratic principles—and a school in it, to bring the highest sort of learning right out amongst the people in the new western country. He had built a keelboat in Pittsburgh, filled it with scientists and philosophers for his school, and set sail for his holdings at New Harmony on the Wabash, just south of Vincennes—and two days' ride from Troy.

If he'd been satisfied to stop at philosophers, the Hoosiers would have been content to laugh at Owen and let him go. But Owen had made a scandal and an outrage by taking unto himself— as second, as presiding genius, as God-knew-what—Miss Frances Wright: *that Woman*, called by the Christian papers "the Red Harlot of Infidelity," a woman of reading and breeding, fearless, shameless to speak in public before audiences of men, advocating free negroes, free thought . . . free love. That was enough for the good men and women of Troy: they vowed to send her packing with stripes and shame if ever she should appear in their midst. Captain Donaldson said if she came a-nigh *his* niggers he'd see her strung up for it, if she *was* a woman.

Abe read everything he could find on Owen and Frances Wright in the Vincennes and Cincinnati sheets, ransacked old New York Washington Philadelphia papers, read every word of the *New Harmony Gazette* and a fugitive copy of *The Genius of Universal Emancipation* that had a whole article in it by Frances Wright. She was planning to start a model plantation on land she owned just outside of Memphis: buy negroes and train them up to freedom, same as if they were white. Negroes were men, weren't they? "And Man is above all a reasoning creature," she had written. "Once launch the animal man on the road of inquiry, and he shall—he must—hold a forward career. To hold him still he must be chained. Snap the chain and he springs forward. He may be sometimes checked, but his master movement is always in advance."

Improvement: that was *his* game too. *The animal man, the road of inquiry* . . . What would it be like to go to school with the smartest, book-learnedest men—and women!—of the age? Maybe Owen was the Devil's left-hand son, and Frances Wright a cross between the Queen of Sheba and the Whore upon the Waters. But a man had to take chances to get ahead in life.

Abe kept his eye peeled for her keelboat—though how he would come aboard and how he would get himself enlisted for the school was more than he could figure out. Abe didn't have a tithe of the cash required to go to school at New Harmony, and what he had was owed first of all to Pap.

Then Denton Offutt came to town.

Abe had an eye of Denton Offutt. Thought he was sharp and knowing. A gentleman, too: look at his clothes! And the way he spoke: "negro" instead of nigger, that was . . . *genteel*, and easier in the mouth than Eth'opians or Unfortunate Race. People might take it as chested-out for Tom Lincoln's boy to say *negro*, but he meant to work up to it: in the meantime using "niggro" to split the difference. Offutt had some scheme in hand, and from the look of him there was money in it. Make himself useful to such a man, and some of that money might come Abe's way. But useful *how*? He had to be patient, *listen* Offutt till he got his drift.

For his part, Offutt had an eye of Abe. The merchant had in hand a small speculation in woolens and ironmongery, which required men of means and *imagination*—men who could see the profit in merchandise which was itself invisible to the naked eye. If anyone could help Offutt find such men in Troy, it would be Abe. The boy kept his eyes open, his work took him all over town. Then there were those roots Abe sold—herb cures were an excellent side-line to any traveling enterprise, portable, popular, cheap to manufacture. In new country like this, it was good to have several strings to one's bow.

Offutt, feigning a casual stroll along the waterfront, "happened upon" Abe splitting billets at his wood-pile for sale to the next steamboat. After an exchange of courtesies, and some talk of the wood and ferrying business, Offutt remarked that Abe had a head on his shoulders.

Abe shrugged: "Who don't?"

"Well Captain Donaldson for one. He doesn't seem a heady sort of man to me."

"Well, he holds himself smarter than that ... that *niggro* he's got." Abe blushed: *negro* or *niggro* just didn't come as natural to his tongue as *nigger*.

But Offutt took Abe's compromise as polite enough. He tipped Abe a wink: "What do you think?"

Abe decided to trust Offutt with his true opinion: "Don't take *brains* for a man to cheat his property."

Offutt made an effort to seem casual in his interest. "What was that root you shaved in his whiskey last night?"

One of those smiles came over Abe, rearranging his solemn coarse features into a picture of happiness. He knew there was money in sang-roots. Old Konkapot might have been a drunk no-account Injun, but the longer Abe lived the more it seemed he was righter than he was wrong. Abe reached a piece of root out of his jeans. Offutt rubbed the cut face with his thumb, then nipped a piece, frowning at its bite.

"Not much for taste," said Offutt handing the plug back. "Where do you dig that kind of roots?"

"There's plenty around here—if you know where to look." He smiled pleasantly at Mr. Offutt. "There was three-four other fellers used to hunt sang afore *me*." He shook his head sorrowfully. "They give it up and gone to Texas."

Offutt held his poker-face. "Well, it might be plenty hereabouts, but I've seen better quality. They're kind of puny—and the taste is off."

Abe just smiled the bigger. "Mr. Offutt," he said, "there ain't but one way sang tastes, and that is jest awful. And unless I been honeyfuggled, sang-roots half as long as your arm is purty near *Creation* sang-roots."

Offutt, a good sport, laughed at having the tables turned. He always said you can't joke a joker, nor out-smart a smart man—on his home ground. But what did Abe get for his roots?

"Penny or so for a hand-span cut."

Offutt flinched: "My boy! My boy! A *penny*? Why son, don't you know the good of sang-root?"

"Of course!" Abe was indignant. "When you're tired and have a job of work, or to lie out in a deer-blind all night." He blushed. "Konkapot—the Injun who taught me to find it—said it was a help to a man in . . . in case of a woman."

"Well I'm not surprised an Injun didn't know any more than that. And you are young yet to have an appreciation of . . . of those cases of women. You *should* get thirty cents a pound around here, same as a gallon of whiskey, and five cents a cut same as a drink. But if *I* had such roots? I'd ship 'em East, or down to Orleans—where they'd fetch six or seven *dollars* the pound."

Abe was impressed. Offutt pushed his advantage. "And do you know who wants sang-roots that bad they'll pay seven dollars the pound? *China merchants*, that's who!" Offutt warmed to it, rubbing his hands like a man contemplating dinner. "In China they call it the *Gin* Sang. Means the man-root." Offutt winked. "Those heathens have got about five or six wives apiece. They want the *Gin* Sang because it'll stand a man's pecker up regardless." Offutt leered. "Three or four hundred million Chinamen, and every blessed one as lost without his sang-root as a baby without mother's milk. Why son, China merchants will load up a ship with seven-dollar sang-roots and sell 'em in Can-ton for *thirty or forty dollars the pound*. Four hundred *million* Chinamen! And you selling for a penny!"

All Abe could think was to say he was sorry, but it didn't hardly cover the case.

Offutt beckoned him closer. "There's more to it yet," he confided. "You want the dried root for shipping. She packs easy and won't spoil. But the taste is nasty, and your Chinaman doesn't like it any more than a white man. But they *know* the root: they have got a way of leaching out the bitter without hurting its virtue." Offutt had seen the finished product—tasted of it in Can-ton itself. He believed if he put his mind to it he could figure out the receipt for himself. He was sure there was spirit in it (whiskey would do), and gunpowder, and maybe saleratus to leach the bitter. The only thing kept him from finding the right formula? Time! His other affairs had him on the hop so he never had leisure to work out the formula. And—truth to tell now!—he'd never had enough root in hand to permit experimentation. Not before this.

What was the formula worth? "Why son—!" He spread his arms grandly, helplessly. "If they pay thirty dollars a pound for the dried article in Can-*ton*, what do you think a man could get for the *finished* product? Do you pay more for wool or blankets? And what do you guess folks *this* side the ocean would pay for a taste? Not some bitter root to chew on or scrape in your whiskey, but the genuine sweet-as-milk Chinese Gin Sang? Does a white United States Christian American care less about his pecker standing up than a heathen Chinaman? By God, Abe! If a man could get the right of it—!"

It was a tight place. Abe's current stock of roots was enough to last him the season. If he risked them on Mr. Offutt's experiment . . . But if he took the chance, maybe he'd make enough to buy himself out of Pigeon Creek and into the New Harmony school. Mr. Offutt was looking at him consideringly. Was Tom Lincoln's boy up to the chances of being partner to Denton Offutt? "I've got roots a-plenty," Abe said. "If you tell me what to do, I can brew up a batch however you like, as many as you want till you get it right."

Offutt looked serious. "My boy," he said, "I will let you in with me on this tonic experiment. If we find the formula, I will leave whatever product we jointly make for you to sell on your own account." He considered further. "I *might* be interested in the Gin Sang trade after I finish my present business. Now *if* I was to get into the Gin Sang line—*if* I was to come through here next season—and

if you were to have a great lot of that sang-root put by and dried
out . . . Why, I'd buy all you had, ship it to Orleans, and split the proceeds with you." He stuck his hand out. "What do you say?"

All it took was one shake and Tom Lincoln's boy was partners
with Mr. Denton Offutt. There wasn't, as of that moment, another
man in Troy that could say as much!

Denton Offutt was not an ordinary man. He only looked ordinary, like an old battered lamp with a genie inside. Instead of rubbing him you just asked him a question and got his Yankee mouth
a-going, and the words come rolling out like genie-smoke, full
of wishes and magic. A road appeared under your feet, flowing
away like a golden river, the first passages plain as a day's chores
but the further you went the more Arabian-Nightsish things got—
merchants, Orleans, the China trade, Can-*ton* market paying thirty
dollars a pound in spices and gold coin. The look of things changed.
Troy wasn't just a no-account landing peeking out of the trees at the
river running by. It was the place the journey begun, the gate you
went out of when you started for the Golden City.

Once the sang-root experiment was well launched, Offutt left
Abe to tend it. He was working on another "notion" that he kept
dark about. It wasn't the wool thing—he'd already got Mr. Taylor,
Lawyer Pitcher, and McCandless to go in with him on that. No, now
he was huddled up with Captain Donaldson at supper in Taylor's
great-room. There was a larger crowd than usual, passengers from a
steamboat laying over while the boat's crew repaired the paddlewheel a snag had took a chaw of. There was a table full of rather fine
looking gentlemen, and ladies with them as well—you didn't see
women in the great-room after supper as a general thing, but you
couldn't expect strangers to know that.

Abe couldn't hear what Offutt was saying, but it was good as a
circus to watch the two men's expressions change—Donaldson
hang-dog and Offutt tender-eyed, Donaldson rousing himself and
Offutt blowing hale and hearty, Donaldson agreeing dimly and
Offutt clinching the thing (whatever it was) with a shake of the
hand. McCandless came over and joined them, and they began lift-

ing glasses to each other and congratulating themselves on their good sense.

Abe reckoned whatever deal Offutt was angling for with Donaldson, he had made satisfactory. Abe carried them a platter of ham and biscuits, and lingered to hear what he could. They were talking about what everyone was talking about, the Ark and the Harlot. It was Miss Wright's views on nigger . . . niggro equality they were worrying—but for some reason, Donaldson now seemed *happy* she was coming to the district. That was odd, even with allowance for his being so drunk his cheeks were paralyzed and his eyes loose in his head. "She can have 'em," he said a little too loud, "she can have 'em for all *me*. I be glad to get shut of 'em, eat me out of house and . . . Only: I won't stand her '*malgamating* 'em!"

Offutt made a hushing motion with his hand, smiling. "Never fear, there's no chance of that I promise you, Miz Wright is a *lady* whatever people may . . ."

"I won't have it!" Donaldson slammed his cup on the table and stilled the room. "You can fuck 'em all you like, as long as it ain't 'malgamate!"

There was an angry stir among the steamboat gents and ladies. "That's all right now," said Offutt, "only talk more quiet won't you?"

McCandless gave Abe a mean little smile, to draw him in, then tipped more whiskey into Donaldson's cup. "I don't get your drift, Donaldson. I don't see the diff'rence."

"Don't see—!" Donaldson blinked as if the heat of his red cheeks was blowing steam in his eyes. He pistoled a finger at Offutt's nose. "Listen: you 'malgamate a nigger-woman its *her* gets the 'vantage of *you*. But if it's a fuck . . ."

Donaldson stopped and looked up. One of the steamboat gentry was standing over him, working his jaws. "Your speech, suh"—he had a soft Carolina drawl—"your speech is offensive to the *ladies*."

Donaldson blinked as if he'd never heard of ladies. Then scrouched up his face, danged if he'd be bullied on his own ground. "Ladies? They don't like it, let 'em go on an' git. Why's there ladies anyways, where a man's drinkin' whiskey?"

Carolina smiled wanly. His eyes were cold. He was clean-shaved with sidebars, wore a fine coat of blue broadcloth, and his linen showed spotless at neck and cuffs. "If you were a gentleman, I should resent your rude, drunken, ignorant bellering. But as you are not, I will see you answer for it by means more suitable to your condition."

Mr. Taylor, smelling trouble, hurried over—began fussing, mollifying the Carolina gent, putting his body between him and Donaldson, meantime giving Abe the eye. Offutt took the hint too. They hoisted Donaldson to his feet, staggered with him through the kitchen. They heard Green Taylor holler "Sephus!" out the back door.

They got Donaldson to the door but stuck in the frame three abreast. The Captain was dead weight—passed out. Before they could untangle themselves the black man materialized out of the darkness in front of them. If he thought anything about Donaldson's condition, you couldn't tell from his face what it was. "I'll take him," he said. They let Donaldson slump and the negro caught him. Donaldson's face was buried sideways in the black man's chest. The planter snorked and snored, open-mouthed. A pretty sight.

"Keep him out of the way till he gets his legs under him," said Offutt. "There's a gentleman off the steamboat may come looking for the good Captain with a horse-whip."

Sephus gave Offutt a level look and nodded. "Might's well kill de man as shame him dat way to his people. I'll put him in de salt-wagon an' set watch on him." He drew Donaldson's arm over his neck and the two staggered off into the dark.

Offutt watched them go with a look of concern. "Was that the *smart* negro they all talk about? Sephus?" Abe nodded.

"He seems *ready* enough," said Offutt uneasily. "I never had to trust one to take care of an investment before this."

Abe didn't like the idea of sharing Offutt with Donaldson's Sephus. "Ready? He ought to be. He has to do that every time Donaldson comes to town."

Early next morning, Abe was walking out to the pens where a dozen hogs were waiting to be knocked in the head. A low mist made the river a carpet of smoke. A keelboat, black with the low sunrise behind her, cleared the point and turned into the reach that passed along the waterfront of Troy. The early sun lit the flags that flew from her masthead. The one on top was the Stars and Stripes—a specially big and bold one. Under that was a blue flag with a picture of a beehive on it and words written in a circle around the hive. The boat's name was painted in red on her side, *Philanthropy*. The "Ark" was more than wish or rumor: it was as solid as oak timber could make it. And here it was riding by him on the river.

A black stove-pipe jutted out of the cabin roof forward of the mast, a curl of smoke said the philosophers scientists and philanthropists inside were tucking into their coffee and bacon—and She was there, Frances Wright Herself, what words was she speaking *right now* while Tom Lincoln's Abe stood dumb as a post, watching her drift down the reach?

The steersman leaned into the tiller and the keelboat turned her back on Abe as she entered the downstream bend.

On top of the morning's disappointment, that afternoon Denton Offutt told Abe he was leaving: wanted Abe to ferry him out to the steamboat *City of Vincennes*, which was just entering the reach. Eph and a hired man were already stacking Offutt's baggage in the well of the scow.

Abe looked stricken. "I reckon it is all up with our experiment."

Offutt felt a touch of guilt. It must seem he was dropping Abe like a one-bite apple. "All up?" said Offutt heartily. "Not at all." He leaned to whisper confidentially as Abe walked him down to the landing. "I have business in Vincennes. But I'll likely come back this way."

Abe picked up that *likely*, and nodded grimly. Offutt felt a touch of remorse: he *had* led the boy on. "In the meantime, you just keep working on that Gin Sang formula till it comes up to where *you're* satisfied. Sell as much as you've a mind to. Never mind my share— you're doing the work, you take the profit." He winked. "That square now?"

"I reckon," said Abe. Offutt was leaving him behind. Abe handed Offutt into the scow. Men hollered good-bye to Offutt, and see you again right soon I hope. Offutt waved back.

The *City of Vincennes* backed water, huffing, waiting for her passenger. Abe leaned into the oars. The river was running stiff and the pilot had laid the steamer slantwise to the current, which tended to drift her out towards the middle of the stream. Abe pulled into the current, gauging his distance to the drifting steamboat. "If you was to come through here another time, when do you reckon it would be?"

Offutt got a little wary. "Not before next season." Abe looked sadder still. "Well," said Offutt by way of justifying himself, "I have a lot of business to take care of, my wool and ironmongery." Then he grinned: "You know, I have also a commission from our friend Donaldson."

Abe perked up at that.

"Yessir," said Offutt, rubbing his hands together. "The Captain is over a barrel in respect of cash money, and no collateral but negroes. I have agreed to lease some of them to your Miz Wright, for her model plantation. He won't part with that Sephus, but there's a woman he owns will do for managing hands. What d'you think?"

Abe's first thought was, *It's Aunt Dilly, that lucky black so-and-so, going to work for Frances Wright, even a nigger has more luck than me.* His second thought was: *If Offutt would do that much for Donaldson . . .* He glanced back and forth between Offutt and the side of the drifting *Vincennes.* "Mr. Offutt," he cried, "will you do me a favor? Will you find out how I could get into that school of theirs? Mr. Owen's school?"

Denton Offutt was watching how the mate of the *Vincennes* set himself to snag the scow with a pole-hook. He looked at Abe in surprise. "Why sure, son. I can't promise anything, but I can inquire . . ."

The tall boy grinned, that pulled-out-a-plum grin again. "I'll see you when you come through in fall!" he said.

The grin made Denton Offutt feel a tad guilty: he wouldn't come back to Troy unless he had nowhere else in the world to go. So he threw the boy a bone: "Keep at it, Abe, and I expect by then you'll be the biggest man in Pigeon Creek!"

It was a mistake: instead of smiling gratefully, the boy's face fell. But it was too late to make it up. They were right at the side of the *City of Vincennes*. The mate's pole-hook snagged the scow and drew her to the companion gate. Offutt sprang aboard. Abe passed his trunk and portmanteau up to the black porters who reached for them.

Offutt turned to look as Abe's boat drifted backwards. The leeway of the *Vincennes* had carried them out nearly to the middle of the river. The *Vincennes'* steam-whistle shrieked to signal their departure—

Then Offutt saw a four-oared skiff shoot around the bow of the steamboat, and recognized the Kentucky brothers who ran the Ohio ferry, one at the tiller, the other standing in the bow with a boathook and four negro men pulling the oars. The skiff dashed past Abe's slow-moving scow, cutting him off from the Indiana shore. They were well out in the river, there was no way Abe could buck the current and out-run the skiff. He stood straight, holding his oar like a quarter-staff, waiting. But the skiff never came near enough for him to swat. The brother in the bow reached out with his boathook and grappled the scow. The brothers yelled things Offutt couldn't make out. The negro oarsmen grinned.

The *Vincennes* began to chug and churn its way forwards. The grappled boats bobbed on the steamboat's wake. Offutt ran sternwards along the deck, calling out "Abe!" The boy waved at him, then sat down on a thwart and folded his arms. The skiff began towing him over to the Kentucky shore. "Dang it," said Offutt, "they got him on the Kentucky side of the river." Would they whip him? Take him to law? Most likely both.

"Dang it!" Offutt said again. It was on his account, too. He hadn't meant to do the boy actual hurt, and up to right then would have said he hadn't done any. Now, even if it wasn't his intending, he'd put the boy in harm's way.

The two boats dwindled and shrank. The *Vincennes* rounded the downstream bend and he lost sight of them behind the wooded point.

Chapter 11: **The Judge**

Pate's Landing, Kentucky, Summer 1828

The brothers who ran the ferry were named Dill. Lin was the older and did the talking—". . . see how you like the law we got *this* side . . ."—while John Dill just showed his long yellow teeth, and bullied Abe up the road to Squire Pate's plantation. A stand of trees shut like a door between Abe and the river.

They turned into a lane marked by a white-washed gate. A pebbled path ran between low shrubs to a fine two-story house built of red bricks. A negro man opened to their knock, dressed as fine as a lawyer in knife-edge pants, boiled shirt, and roundabout. "Harrison," said Lin Dill, "we got a complaint to set afore the Jedge." The negro went away and came back, and admitted them to a room at the left of the central hall.

The walls of this room were all shelves and the shelves all books. Light came from windows opening on the front of the house. The Judge sat at a wonderful desk full of little drawers and pigeonholes. He was writing, and kept them standing in the door till he finished. Then Squire Pate turned his chair around and beckoned them in.

He was a small, spare man, with a thick head of white hair tied in a club behind his head like George Washington in the history-book pictures. Clean-shaved, with a chin balled like a child's fist. He had spectacles hooked to his ears. When he took them off you could see his sharp black eyes. "Well now, Dill," he said, "what's all this about?"

Lin Dill held his cap in his hands. "Well Jedge, we have got a license to ferry 'cross the river ..." He fumbled out a paper and handed it to Pate. "An' Jedge, this Yankee been runnin' passengers out to boats in the river there, which he hadn't no right to done. On account it's ours, accordin' to that paper there Jedge, Your Honor." Dill was talking too much, putting jabber between himself and whatever it was made him uneasy. The fineness of the house? the negro? the Judge himself? Maybe the Dills were like Pap when law come a-nigh him: afeared how unaccountable it was, and a man could lose everything by it.

Judge Pate peered over the top of his spectacles at Abe. "That the right of it, son?"

You didn't lie to this man. But what could he say that wasn't a lie yet would keep the law off him? His heart was banging. Danged if he'd show yellow though. "Well," he said, "I ain't no Yankee."

Did the Judge smile the least small bit? "No," he said, "you sound Kentuck to me. What's your name?"

"Abe, Abraham," he said, glad of something easy to say. "I'm Thomas Lincoln's son. We live in Pigeon Crick, but I was born in Knob Crick, Kentucky."

The Judge nodded. "And is it true what Mr. Dill says, about you running passengers out to the steamers?"

Wasn't but the one thing to say. "It's true." He thought for a minute. "I don't make more'n two bits a go for it."

Pate poked his bottom lip out, considering. "Not your boat, I reckon."

"It's Mr. Taylor's boat." Was the Judge opening a hole in the law for him to crawl through? There was a clock somewhere in the house. Tick. Tock. If it *was* a hole, did he want to *crawl* through it? "It was his boat, but my idea to use it."

Pate nodded. "Well then: Mr. Taylor doesn't come into the case."
But he smiled as if he liked something in what Abe told him. Abe
wished he knew what it was, he'd give the man all he could swallow. He had another idea. "I never knowed it was against the law."

Lin Dill snapped, "Well you ought to! Didn't I holler at you . . ."

Judge Pate shook his head. "It doesn't signify. Ignorance of law
can't excuse the breaking of law." He rose up out of his chair and
ambled across the room, picked a thick volume off a shelf. "This
here," he said, "is Littel's *Statute Law of Kentucky*." He looked at
something in the back, then riffled forward till he found what he was
looking for. "Here 'tis: 'If any person whatsoever shall, for reward,
set any person over any river or creek, whereupon public ferries are
appointed, he or she so offending shall forfeit and pay five pounds
current money for every such offense.' " Finished, the Judge looked
over his specs at Abe. Waiting on him, watching him squirm.

Abe was in a sweat. Five pounds was better than twelve
dollars—more than he'd earn in two months, and which wasn't
even his to keep but to hand over to Pap. "Sir," he said, "would it be
all right if you read that over again?"

Judge Pate considered him further. "Do you know your letters, son?"

"Yes sir."

Judge Pate set the book down on a small table and said, "Go on
and read it yourself if you like. Section number eight on page three
hundred sixty-three."

Abe bent over the book. It was smallish print, but numbers made
the law easy to find, like Bible verses. He read Section 8 over once
fast, then again slow, the careful way he read river-current for the
wrinkle he could slip into and ride to shore. *There it was.* Abe raised
up and looked at the Judge, who was watching him with a mild
look. "Says here 'set any person over any river or creek.' I never set
'em *over*. I jest rowed 'em partway out."

Judge Pate nodded with ponderous slowness, stroking his chin.
He took up the book and read the law out loud again. Then he
looked over the top of the book at Lin Dill. "Dill," he said, "did this
fellow ever carry anyone over to the Kentucky side?"

Dill was red in the face. He glared at Abe. He glared at the floor. He looked up at Judge Pate like a man who knew he was due for a whuppin'. The words came wrenched and grudging: "Not that I ever see."

"Nor any witness you might bring?" asked the Judge.

Dill shook his head.

"Well then," Pate said, setting the book down, "I have no choice but to find for the defendant. Case dismissed." He gave the Dill brothers a cool smile. "Harrison will show you out. Lincoln," he added, "I would like to talk with you a bit."

They were alone. The Judge sat down in a stuffed chair and motioned for Abe to pull up a ladder-back. He smiled, plain friendly now: only, you had a sense of his quality, a man would have no more feelings than a hog to presume on his friendliness. "You won your case at law, son. But I recommend you keep an eye out for the Dill family."

"Yes sir, I will surely do that." Relief had just about unstrung him. He was grinning like an eejit, too embarrassed to look at Squire Pate till he got his face under orders again. His eyes kept running over the shelves and shelves of books; for a man who liked such things it was Ali Baba's Cave.

Squire Pate stuffed tobacco into a pipe with a long curved stem. He didn't offer any to Abe. Probably on account of him being only a boy. Abe didn't mind, he hadn't used tobacco anyway since Konkapot died. The Squire puffed up a fragrant cloud of smoke. "Dills are like a lot of western people: they have got used to making their own way, and doing things as they please." Squire Pate screwed his face up into a mockery of Lin Dill with a quid of chewing in his cheek. " 'The *minn* thet made the *lawr* ain't no better'n whut *I* be. So why should *I* mind *hit*?' " Puff puff. His eyes narrowed. "Men like that: only way is to show them they haven't any choice *but* to obey the law. Even so, they will go outside it when they can. All they want is force enough, and the chance to use it."

The Squire was mulling something over, the energy of thought working his lips and mouth so his pipe fumed like a kettle. He looked past Abe. "So what you have is a community of people that is either afraid of the law or mad at it, but don't have an *understanding* of it—most don't even know what the law *says*." He jabbed the bill of his pipe at Abe. "We're supposed to be a self-governing people, a republic. But you can't have a government like ours if people don't respect the law they make. Used to be no man in the country had any more freedom than his rifle could hold for him—and none at all if the other man got off first shot. We have not got past that yet, not entirely."

The Squire looked Abe up and down. "I judge you work hard to earn your wages," he said. "Know your letters—look to improve yourself. But when you came in here, you were mad on account of being took to law—now weren't you?"

"I was mad how they took me," Abe answered.

Squire Pate waved that away. He leaned towards Abe through the smoke, pecking the stem of the pipe at him. "You were afraid what the law might do to you. Afraid, because you were *ignorant*"— the word *ignorant* sounding ugly and harsh as he said it. The Squire fanned away some of the smoke that had gathered around his head. "But you can read," he said, "so you don't need to *stay* ignorant. The least you ought to know is the law that pertains to your business."

He launched himself out of his chair and across the room. Scanned a shelf. Took out a slim volume with an odd shiny cover. He crooked a finger and Abe rose and stood looking down at him from his great height, which embarrassed Abe as somehow improper. But the Squire paid it no mind. He put the book in Abe's hand. *The Western River Pilot; Being a Compendium of Navigation on the Ohio, Mississippi, and Missouri Rivers, and Major Tributaries, with Maps.* The cover was oil cloth to keep out the wet, for it was intended to be used by pilots on the rivers. The author was a Mr. Zenas Cradok of Cincinnati, and he had included *an Appendix Containing a Complete Statement of the Marine and Riverine Law, Respecting Commercial Regulation, Salvage, Charges and Duties, &c.*

"You may keep it," said the Squire. "The account of down-river navigation is two years old, but I don't guess that concerns you just now. The section on law will serve—there has not been much change."

Abe stuttered his thanks. He was bowled over by Squire Pate's generosity. How could a day that started so poorly turn so lucky? The Squire brushed off thanks. "You mean to improve yourself: good. So does just about every man in the country. What they mean is, they want to *get ahead*. And the way they go at it is every man for himself and devil take the hindmost. You can't go on that way— every man taking and no one putting in—and expect to keep your self-government. What's good for one man isn't necessarily the public good. Keep up that way and, in the end, the rich men and the gun-men will govern themselves, and the rest have to knuckle under and go along." He glared at Abe to drive his lesson home. "The way I learned it, in a republic no man ought to get too big an edge over the rest. A man that gets advantages ought to give something back."

Troy, Summer 1828

All the rest of that season at Troy he kept Cradok's *Western River Pilot* with him, wrapped inside his shirt as if it was a talisman. It was a book to dream on, like Pilgrim and Shebazade—but it had more power than these, because the rivers it told actually ran right at Abe's feet. Zenas Cradok had got the whole of the Ohio and Mississippi Rivers wrote down: on every other page a picture like a cut section of snake mapped five or so miles of river, with instructions how to run each riffle and chute, what settlements there was, the kinds of trees and animals, and what Denton Offutt would call "prospects"—evidence of coal deposits, gold mines, sugar-cane ground, cotton ground, places to get rich in. Evenings Abe read Cradok's rivers into his head, and ran them every night in his mind when he laid down to sleep: the Hanging Rocks, the Chute above Number 10, Memphis Napoleon Natchez New Orleans. And if any man along the way challenged his right to pass, why, he'd haul out the *Complete Statement of the Maritime and Riverine Law* and *whup* him with it!

Beyond the voyages, he treasured the *River Pilot* most because it

reminded him of a place he'd been once, and meant to come to
again: a quiet room of light and books, which he entered as a no-
account boy under accusation of wrong—but where a hard little
man had set force and prejudice aside, weighed all in the scales of
reason, and gave Abe Lincoln *justice*.

It took him weeks to work his courage up to it. Then he knocked on
Lawyer Pitcher's door.

The lawyer's heavy hairy eyebrows rose right up his head in surprise, then clinched down. His eyes ran Abe down head to toe, and
when he dropped his eyes Abe saw he was dripping mud-water on
the lawyer's braided rug. "Well?" said Pitcher.

"Sir, Mr. Pitcher"—once he got his jaws working he'd do fine—"I
was wonderin' how does a man git to be a lawyer."

The lawyer considered what Abe's question might imply.
Couldn't think of a thing. "You need schooling," he said. "Then you
need an established lawyer with whom to read law."

"Like a man might take on a 'prentice," Abe said.

Pitcher nodded to suggest the likeness was close enough.

"I was wondering— Sir, it come to me I might ask if you
wouldn't take *me* on that way."

The lawyer ran his eyes on Abe, head to toe and back again, taking account of his jacket rough-cut and splotched with dried mud
pork-grease and charcoal, patches in the knees of the worn-out jeans
that his ankle-bones outgrew by a good hand-span. "To *read law*?"
Pitcher said.

"Yes sir." Pitcher said nothing, only looked some more, so Abe
guessed he'd best throw in the extras now: "I don't mind chores
beyond readin' and clerkin'. I'm a good hand with an ax . . ."

"Not much schooling I don't think."

"Not much"—honesty the best policy—"but I write purty fair.
I've practiced eelocutin' out of books. I can cipher to the Rule of
Three and read anything set afore me."

The boy was slow to take Pitcher's meaning. He'd have to spell it
out. "Tom Lincoln is your Pa, ain't he?"

"Yessir."

The Lawyer nodded: *Point one.* "I recollect you ain't of age yet."

"No sir. I will be twenty next Febr'y."

The lawyer nodded again: *Point two.* He leaned forwards, as he liked to do clinching a deadly cross-examine. "Do you reckon your Pappy would give you permission to come in as my 'prentice?"

"Well sir," said Abe. "I can ask him."

The lawyer looked smug. "What d'you reckon he will say?"

He could have throwed Lawyer Pitcher through his own window, but what use would that have been—except to prove Abe Lincoln was just what Pitcher thought he was, a no-account father's no-account son.

And he couldn't whup the whole of Troy. It didn't take but a day or two for every man and boy in the settlement to hear how Taylor's Abe had walked into Lawyer Pitcher's office in his hog-butcher clothes and asked to be took for a lawyer. If Abe was waiting on tables they'd holler, "Bring me another whiskey, Jedge!" If he was gutting hogs they'd say, "I got a case for you to look into when you're done with that'n." "Wrassles good for a lawyer, don't he?" "Ever see a lawyer dance like *that*?"

He had got above himself, and this was the price of it. Troy Landing was going to laugh him back into the mud. He was the fool of his own books: Robert Owen and Frances Wright and their New Harmony school, Judge Pate and his justice—they were no more for him than Baghdad was, or magic lamps.

Even Denton Offutt had no better thing to say of him than that he could be the biggest man in Pigeon Creek if he put his mind to it. It had took him cold in the heart when he heard it. Pigeon Creek was a mean small place, and big men there were like bullfrogs in a slough: push the next frog into the mud then brag on him.

But if Pigeon Creek was all there was, he'd put his mind to making sure someone else was bottom frog.

Vincennes, October 1828

Early in the morning the sour wail of bugles and the rattle of drums
summoned the militia of the Southwest District of the State of Indiana to muster in the fields south of the old territorial capital of Vincennes. Boys and men rolled out of their tents, stretched, pissed in
their campfires, took up their rifles, and moseyed into ranks.

This year James Gentry wore the sword and the clutch of pigeon-
feathers in the band of his new beaver stove-pipe that marked him
as Captain of the Pigeon Creek company. Reuben Grigsby had failed
of election for the first time in the history of the settlement. The company had chosen Reuben Jr. as lieutenant to keep the peace, but Old
Reuben was unappeased. The settlement was his dunghill to crow
on, his money and his sons made sure of that.

Then without warning Pigeon Creek started laughing at him and
his boys. Someone had wrote out and handed around a thing called
"The Chronicles of Reuben," which sounded enough like Scripture
to fool a preacher, but was meant to make a joke and a scandal of the
marriages of Reuben Jr. and Charlie, and their ways with women.
*"Now there was in those days a man named Reuben, and the same was
great in possessions, having swine in abundance, and sons. And it came to
pass that the sons of Reuben cast their eyes upon the daughters of men, and
saw they were fair. They bethought themselves, saying: 'Would that we
might have some of those—for a man's delight is not in swine alone.' "*

The "Chronicles" was in the nature of *special* revelation, vouch-
safed unto the young men of Pigeon Creek not long after the feast
at which Reuben Jr. and Charlie were married to (respectively)
Jemimah Hardin and Dorcas Whitman. *"So the sons of Reuben gat
them each a woman for wife. And Reuben prepared a feast in the midst of
the neighbors, and a great slaughter he made, of fowls and cattle and every
creeping thing that crawleth upon the earth."* But something went awry
at the point in the festivities when the grooms were to leave their
friends and go in unto their wives, waiting in the upstairs bedrooms
of Grigsby's great house, *the wife of the younger upon the left, and of the
elder upon the right.* There was some mix-up. Whether the boys were

fuddled with drink, or someone somehow mis-informed or mis-directed them no one could say exactly, but *it came to pass that the sons of Reuben knew their wives, and yet they knew them not.* The settlement was laughing at them yet, the women ashamed to go in public, and the men . . .

Reuben Jr., his sword at port-arms, stomped down the ranks. "Lincoln, con-sarn you! Didn't I say shoulder arms?"

Abe looked at him, mild and puzzled. "I wasn't jest sure if you wanted the piece upon the left, or upon the right." The Boys poked and whacked at each other, laughing fit to bust.

Junior shook his lieutenant sword. "Dang you, Lincoln! When I give an order . . ."

Abe looked cool. "Danged if I'll take orders from a man I never voted for." Behind him the Pigeon Creek Boys went *Woooo!*

Captain Gentry stomped over to the trouble. "Lincoln, stand to, dad-rat it!"

Abe considered that. Then: "Danged if I'll take orders from a man I *did* vote for."

The Boys elbowed each other and chortled, *Got 'im ag'in!*

"Dang it boys!" Gentry pleaded. "Get in line here. Don't let them Bucktails get ahead of us!" The Bucktails were from the neighboring county, natural rivals of Pigeon Creek. They wore white-tails in their hats the way Gentry's company wore pigeon-feathers. "Where in tarnation is Dennis Hanks!"

Here came Dennis, slinging his blanket-roll, a sheepish grin on his face. Someone had hid his musket for a joke, so he was carrying the busted parasol the joker had left in its place. Abe called out, "Denny ain't no Minute-man—more like a some-time-next-week man." Denny grinned, opened the parasol, a few scraps of cloth on naked ribs, shouldered the thing, and stood to attention.

Captain Gentry glowered at the ranks. "Drummer . . . ," he started. John D. said "Yowtch!" and slapped himself. A spot of blood on his cheek—someone had stung him with a pebble fired out of a pea-shooter. You could not have sat a Pigeon Creek jury that wouldn't have convicted Will Grigsby. The Captain got the drum going, and the company turned "on end" and headed out to the muster ground in a column of ones, twos, and threes.

The belated Bucktails came grouching up behind, muttering darkly about *dead pigeons*. "Say there, Cap," Abe called out. "Why do you wear ass-wipes in your hat?" Abe's people whooped and hee-hawed for that, and the Posey County company joined in. Score another for Pigeon Creek.

The militia of the Southwest District of Indiana made a various appearance as it drilled: hats no more uniform than heights, weapons as peculiar as hats—long rifles, muskets, and shotguns, but also pikes, axes, splitting-mauls, boathooks, peavey-poles, and what-all—at right-shoulder, carry arms, or arms amidship. The ranks kept breaking up on account of the men naturally wanting to watch the parade and be in it at the same time. Through a course of tangled evolutions they finally found themselves assembled before a raw plank reviewing stand decked with bunting. They gave themselves a cheer. The Mayor of Vincennes praised their martial ardor, and introduced the celebrities who shared the platform with him. Chief among these were the two candidates for Congress, Ratliff Boon and Thomas Banks, who would debate each other as soon as the Mayor closed shop. Everyone was looking forward to that: Banks was a boiled shirt, and Boon was a regular old rip—Dan'l's nephew or some such, he'd killed his man and scalped his Injun.

But there were two others up there, whose faces Abe recognized from illustrations in the *New Harmony Gazette:* the well-turned-out gentleman with side-chops was Robert Dale Owen, son of the original Robert; and the woman next to him, with wicked black eyes and sunburnt the way no lady ought to be, was Frances Wright. *Looking on while the Pigeon Creek militia made an ass of itself.* The Mayor introduced them, and said they would offer a lecture this evening, free to the public, in the Oldham Tobacco warehouse.

Abe told himself he must hear that lecture or die trying.

After the troops were dismissed, Allen Gentry came over to join his father. He was one of the men himself now, was Allen, with his own farm at Rockport, the next settlement downriver from Troy. A little fullness under the chin showed him well fed, a good coat showed him prosperous. His Pa whispered him something, he nodded and came over to greet Abe. "You ain't still growin', are you?" Allen stood no higher than Abe's throat now. He didn't wait for an answer. "You mind how I said I might take a flatboat downriver? Well, I'm bound to go this winter. I'll want a hand to build her and buck bow oar for me. We'll go all the way to Orleans—trade at the plantations once we get below the Arkansaw. Two dollars a week and found."

Now he could shuck Pigeon Creek and get back to the river—not just at it but on it, all the way to New Orleans! "I won't go higher than two dollars," Allen added, "and you'd best understand there ain't but one Captain on the river. I'll give orders. You'll take 'em."

That was the Allen Gentry Abe remembered. But it was a chance. "I'll do it," Abe said. He stuck out his hand—

Allen hesitated. "I picked you on Pa's say-so. Because you stood up for Matt when Will Grigsby was deviling him." Then he shook Abe's hand. He couldn't give any without taking some back. Abe had an inkling of what it would be to have Allen looking down from behind that "Captain" for two months. "Who-all is comin' with us?"

Allen gave him a sharp look. "Jest us two."

Two hands was short for a flatboat, especially if you meant to make landings along the way. You generally wanted two hands on the sweeps and one on the steering oar. Either Allen had a higher opinion of Abe's strength than he let on, or he was pinching pennies. But be the reasons whichever or both, "You're the Captain."

Lute Casebier whumped Abe on the back. "C'mon, Abe! Let's go to town and git our rifles cleaned!" The others swarmed in, declaring themselves pokey as a bull, primed for squirrel, ready to set a wedge and drive it. Abe had lost his taste for funning, but it wouldn't do to let his Boys see. He grinned and whumped Lute right back, "Git a start, hoss," he said. "I'll ketch up and pass you."

Vincennes was an old French village set at a place where buffalo used to ford the Wabash. The last buffalo were hunted out twenty years ago, but you could still see where their million hooves, season after season, had beaten a groove in the banks. The ruin of Hair-Buyer Hamilton's British fort sat on the edge of town. (The Injun that murdered Grandpa Lincoln was out for Hamilton's scalp-money.) The old French houses clustered along the river— odd-looking, with walls of wattle-and-daub and thatched roofs. Past the French houses was Niggerville. The Frenchies kept slaves before the Americans came, and though the legislature forbade the Thing it was winked at in the old settlements. Niggerville was low shacks and shanties, not much to look at nor many people to be seen. The negroes had seen musters before.

Abe and his Boys did what all the backwoods companies had done before them: walked to the brick courthouse, tilted back to see it rise fabulously high above them—then looked around for excitement. There was plenty of hooraw in the courthouse square. The candidates set out barrels of whiskey to treat their supporters. There was a tug-o-war, Boonville Eye-Shooters against Evansville Gully-Whumpers, hauling each other back and forth over the mud-wallow that was Wheatland Street. Scattering shots in the distance told where marksmen were shooting targets. Up the street a hilarious mob was trying to grease a pig, the critter's wheezing scream cutting through the cussing and laughter.

There was a *little* buzz over the Owen-Wright lecture. Most of the militia had no more notion of going to a lecture than to a camp-meeting: this was *muster*, by God, time to let the dog howl and the rooster crow. But word got around: that *lady* wasn't just going to set on the platform and look purty, she had clear intent to *public speech*. Ain't *that* spit in your eye! *If I don't find nothin' better, might jest go see has she got the nerve to do it.*

Abe and the Pigeon Creek Boys were working their way towards the refreshments when a bunch of Bucktails stepped out of the crowd and blocked their way. Their sergeant Collins was in front, his right cheek swole most remarkable by a quid of tobacco—a string of which he shot neatly between gap-teeth right at their feet. "I smell dead pigeons."

The Pigeon Creek Boys followed Abe Lincoln. It was on him to answer. He didn't want to get throwed in the mud just yet, not if he meant to go to Frances Wright's lecture. But the Boys were counting on him. He raised a finger and pointed at the white-tail in Collins's hat. " 'Tain't pigeon—it's that ass-wipe on your head."

Collins grinned and rubbed his hands. "Longshanks," he said, "I reckon we'll take a piece o' you right now." Abe's choice: general brawl or man to man. Collins had called him out personal, so: "If you think you're man enough, why don't you try it yourself." Collins emptied his mouth in the street and rolled his sleeves. The Boys and the Bucktails whooped as they backed off to make a circle. Abe shucked his moccasins, bare toes take better hold in the ground.

Abe and Collins crouched and circled carefully in the slidy mud of the street. They held their arms like men planning to hug a bear, every once in a while swiping for a hold. *Go it, Abe! Sic 'im, Bucktails!*

From the crowd behind Abe there was suddenly an explosion of yells, a shrill wheezing scream, and here come the greased pig honking and shrilling with a dozen men after him, broke into the circle and slammed Abe into Collins's arms—the two grabbed and held each other up in the sliding slop. The leading chaser leaped flat-out, grip-slipped off the pig, and put his face in the mud. The pig zigged on skittering trotters, spooked, zagged through a gap, and scooted off down the street—Bucktails and Pigeon-Shooters joining the mob of Pig-Chasers with a whoop.

Abe looked at Collins, who nodded. They let go of each other and started after their boys.

The pig saw Niggerville ahead and scampered between two of the shanties. The mob came piling in after, no man giving way so they slam-jammed all together in the slot between the shacks. Worn boards cracked, weak posts rocked. The wall of the right-hand shanty buckled, there were screams from inside as the roof folded down into it in a cloud of dust—then the militiamen were clambering and piling over the wreckage, and sweeping down through the shanty-town towards the river.

Abe had mostly saved his clothes so far, so he hung back. Below him the mob came to a check between Niggerville and the river. Where in tarnation had that pig run off to?

A big man in a slouch hat—his beard thick and stiff with mud—threw a couple of men aside, hiked up his right leg, and kicked in the door of one of the shanties. He disappeared inside—yells, screaming.

A negro woman scrambled out, a small child plastered to her front with arms and legs wrapped round. A bunch of men—Bucktails, Pigeons, Pig-Chasers—pushed past her to get a look in the door. There was the sound of wood being busted up.

The men at the door backed away sudden, but not fast enough—a negro man fell backwards out the door, knocked one of the Pig-Chasers ass-flat with the negro on top of him. The white man yelled, the negro rolled off and got to his feet. Slouch-hat came out the door hollering where had the nigger buried that pig? He slammed both fists into the negro's chest and knocked him back on his heels.

There wasn't a sound from the other shanties, nor a face showing.

The white man who had been knocked down got to his feet. He looked down his muddy front. "Well I'm damned," he said, "would you look what that nigger done to my go-to-Meetings?" He got a wonderful round of hee-hee and haw-haw for that one.

The negro stood in the middle of the mob like a man froze just as he thought to run.

Abe knew what was in the man's head, he could almost hear it, *Git out of here git out of here,* his eyes running everywhere and not a hole to slip through. The man knew and Abe knew what was coming and there wasn't anything to be done about it, no more than if it was death by Milk-sick.

Abe looked at the woman: she stood there looking at the man, her back hunched to curl her over the child that clung to her yowling.

He ought to do something, but there wasn't anything he could do any more than the black man could himself.

The militiamen let out a gleeful whoop and swarmed the negro under. A clutch of men burst out of the mob, three men each side holding arms and legs and the black man slung facedown between them as they stumbled towards the river. Lute Casebier had a near leg along with one of the Bucktails. The negro screamed and twisted like it was fire they meant to throw him in and not just the river, so the white men wrenched his arms and legs out, spreading him open.

Abe felt a sickly disgusting down-suck inside, like it was himself spread-eagled helpless his own belly swung that way naked over the ground, *I'd kill them I'd die afore I let them do me that way, you might's well* kill *a man as shame him that way to his people.*

But this is only a nigger, it's just the Boys, *my* Boys, having their fun with a . . .

And me just standing watching like the Grigsbys watched Sary twisting and mewing in the hurt she was dying of . . .

Suddenly the woman rushed past him, the child clinging to her hip, and she was yelling and grabbing at the men with her free hand. The Bucktail who had the negro's near leg laughed and brushed her off. She grabbed at Lute, he yelled dropped his leg of the negro and swatted her back with a full swing of his arm. She sprawled hard on the ground. The carrying party rushed the river with a whoop and launched the black man out, splash-flat into the muddy shallows. Lute and a couple of Pig-Chasers rounded on the woman.

Just then the baby got its breath and let out a long wavering peeping sort of cry. The brown woman had cushioned the baby's fall with her body, was curled partly over him. She turned her face up and glared at the men, lip bloodied: glared at them, her eyes wild with a hate so deep it *shrunk* them.

The men backed off. Something gone wrong. Couldn't say how—but their fun was spoilt. The very next thing they wanted was to get out of Niggerville as fast as they could so they could find their fun again.

Abe hesitated—would have liked to told the woman he was sorry and offer her a hand up. But the time to *do something* was gone. He heard Lute calling, "Abe? Abe where you at?" He ducked behind a shack, shy of his followers.

Abe washed his muddy feet in the river, put his moccasins back on, and kept out of trouble the rest of the afternoon. When the hour came he drifted down to the tobacco warehouse where Owen and Wright were to lecture. He was surprised at the press of people. There were citizens of Vincennes in frock coats, but also militia looking the worse for fun: bound to go in and see if it was true, that *that Woman* meant to speak in pure shamelessness from the platform.

The warehouse smelt like the inside of an old dirty briar pipe. At the far end a stage had been hammered together, a row of chairs sat under a swag of bunting. A pair of well-dressed men, organizers of the event, came on stage and the crowd whistled and stamped feet on the packed earth floor. Then Robert Dale Owen strode on stage, a beautiful high-crowned beaver hat set at a jaunty angle on his head—someone hollered "Oh what a *hat*!" and right on cue some boy spanged it askew with a chewed apple.

One of the organizers, sweating badly, raised his arms to calm the waters. The crowd started to hush, then someone said something that got a laugh, someone else hooted and yelled "Fetch her out!" The hubbub rose like water in a cistern. Owen started to speak—Abe could see his lips move, but couldn't make out a word he said. Owen's face flashed red. He roared, "Will ye nawt give me a hear-r-r-in'?"

Oh, they'd give him *plenty*, all right, but not *that*. "Fetch her out! Fetch her out!" Owen folded his arms and stood his ground, glaring.

Suddenly—there She was: a good head taller than Owen, in a dress of fine blue cloth which swooped from her broad shoulders to a waist nipped tight by a red sash. She was as dark in the face as Owen was fair, her black hair a mass of curls heaped all around, nose like a hawk and eyes like a catamount. She flashed her smile into the heart of the big room, black eyes alive touching things as they moved.

Silence rolled back from her like a wave.

They'd hooted her to come in and bellered to keep her out, and here she was in spite of all. What would she do next? Owen bowed to her and stepped back.

She moved her eyes slowly over the room, marking things. Then she spoke, a voice with an odd penetrating tone like a long bow-stroke on the deep string of a fiddle:

"Are there *true* Patriots here?"

There was a burst of astonished laughter, a scuffle down in front. One of the organizers stood and pointed at the crowd—"Shame there! For shame there!" A militiaman with a raccoon cap jumped up on stage and began flapping his arms and strutting back and forth. "The hens is crowin'! The hens is crowin'! Buckbuck *buck* adoodle doooo! Buckbuck *buck* adoodle-doooo!" Miss Wright stood there—looking steady at him, with a little smile on her face. Chicken-man bugged his eyes at her and said "Buck-buck." She never moved or blinked. Just looked at him some more.

Then she said: "Quite." Abe could hear her all the way at the back of the room, because at the sight of her staring down the chicken-man the place had gone still as Sunday.

The quiet came down heavy on the man. He discovered himself suddenly alone up there on stage, making chicken-noises at a most respectable looking lady with a whole town of people staring at him. He dasn't look at that crowd. His face froze in its mocking grimace. She said, with a little nod, "Good evening then, my man," and turned away.

The chicken-man let himself down to where his friends waited to comfort him. Whipped like a dog.

Now she lifted her head and beamed over the crowded hall. "I knew *you* would not refuse me! You are, after all, *Americans*! And *free* men do not fear to let *any* person's thought be spoken." She looked them over again, sure of herself, smiling with pleasure at the attentive quiet. Then she began, not hollering like a preacher at camp meeting or a candidate on the stump, but letting the odd penetrating ring of her voice carry clear through the wide room.

"The Fourth of July, 1776, which dates the national existence of the American people, dates also a mighty step in the march of human knowledge. The frame of government sprung out of the Declaration of Independence is one of the most *beautiful* inventions of the human intellect. It has been in government what the steam engine is in mechanics, the printing press in disseminating knowledge. If imperfect in any part, it bears within it a perfect principle: the simple machinery of representation which allows the people to mold their institutions at will, to change them peaceably, to fit them with the knowledge of the age, and so guarantee their improvement and ultimate *perfection*."

She had them now, and Abe could see she was enjoying it. She smiled them a mothering smile. The crowd sighed and hummed dreamily. So she took up the tale: told them their own history over again, from the colonials that came for freedom of conscience, to George Washington, right down to Henry Clay. But never before had Abe got the *sense* of it so clear, the meaning of all that had been accomplished.

Which still was not enough:

She paused and reared back, her catamount eyes snapping here and there to every part of the hall. "But we must not mistake the mere lighting of a candle for the coming of dawn! Who may speak of liberty while the human mind is in chains? Who of equality while laboring millions live in squalid wretchedness? Who of justice while the negro African is held in degraded bondage; and *woman*—even the so-called *free* woman of these States—in a bondage no less degrading in spirit though different in form!" She rose out of herself stretching her body upward, and shook both fists in anger and warning: "I tell you there is nothing more certain than this: *The bondage we inflict on others merely educates our children in the molding of chains.*"

She had stung them, she had set them back, some looked mad as hornets but some was ready to come to the mourners' bench. Abe felt something twist and jerk inside him, and it come to him sharp that this was what Mam felt when the Preacher hollered *Sin!* and *Jeee-ssuss!* and remembering wrung him so hard his tears sparked.

But her truth was merciless. She raised her arm slowly, and pointed into the heart of the crowd: "The founders of this state did but sketch the theory; it is left to *us* to discover its true practice! *They must not rest satisfied with* words *who can seize upon* things."

It was on all of them to finish the work: all of them, even Abe Lincoln, you couldn't cry off your bounden duty just because you had no better father than Tom Lincoln.

"We are not free simply because we vote office-holders in and out. A nation . . ."

He knowed it in himself, he was bad as the rest, ignorant of the law, wouldn't take orders from Grigsby because he didn't vote for him, nor Gentry because he did.

". . . a nation, to be strong, must be united. The jealousy of sectional, party, and class interest—the distinctions of wealth, and color, and sex—must give way to a true patriotism, in which the interest of each becomes the interest of all." She paused. She breathed deep. "I ask more of Americans than that they love their country as she is. We must go further. We must nourish here a nobler patriotism, which concedes to *all* humankind the right of popular government; which takes for its object the achievement of a Great and Universal Republic—a republic which shall include and equally empower all classes, all races, all sexes—all *colors*."

Her hand dropped, her shoulders eased. She bowed her head. It seemed she was done. The crowd suddenly found its voice and its hands, clapping, stomping, yelling, whether angry or pleased it made one sound. The men on the platform rose, Owen took her arm, and together they went out the door they came in.

He wandered back towards camp through streets full of hilarious militia, lit by burning tar-barrels. His ears were ringing with the aftersound of her voice. *A Great and Universal Republic . . . They must not rest satisfied with* words *who can seize upon* things. But what was his words more than "Chronicles of Reuben"? What was there for him to seize upon in Pigeon Creek but whiskey, greased pigs, niggers to throw in the river . . . ?

"Abe! Hey Abe!" Lute Casebier was hollering and waving to him. "It's Will Grigsby and John D. . . . ."

They ran through the camps towards the Pigeon Creek tents. Abe broke into the circle that penned the fighting ground. John D. was sprawled on his back. Will Grigsby strutted around him, flapping his arms and crowing like a rooster.

Pigeon Creek had split. Some stood with Reuben, Reuben Jr., and Charlie on the Grigsby side, others backed John D., Lincoln, and Gentry. Tom Lincoln was glowering and pounding fist in hand, James Gentry demanding John D. get up and fight.

John D. got to his knees, braced on his arms. The bigger boy kicked his arm loose so he side-flopped, helpless. "Cry uncle!" Will crowed. "Cry uncle or eat dirt!" John D. was overmatched—Will Grigsby had heft on him, and height, and meanness. "John D.!" Pap cried. Was he begging the boy to get up and fight or stay down so the whupping would stop?

Hate and disgust exploded in Abe's chest. "Grigsby you little weasel!" He fairly puked the words and next thing he knew he had thrown Lute sideways with one careless swing of his arm and in two strides he was on Will Grigsby.

The smaller boy looked up at him and squinched, fear wringing every muscle in him. "No fair!" he squeaked—too late. Abe stooped in, slammed his right hand into Will's crotch got his neck in the left and heaved him straight up into the air the whole height of Abe's body and length of his arms, and with Will crying and twisting in his hands slowly turned round the bug-eyed hollering circle till he found the Grigsbys standing froze with outrage—

—and suddenly fear: they saw a Thing there was no stopping nor pleading with, a Thing huge and raging, face of bone eyes of mica, *No man gets vurry far in this life if he can't* kill *a man when he needs to.*

Abe gathered and *Haaah!* heaved Will Grigsby headlong through the air smash into his brothers, knocking Reuben Jr. and Charlie backwards together to the ground as their friends peeled aside.

Abe glared down at the Grigsbys sprawled helpless on each other. "*I'm* the big bull of *this* lick!" he cried. Then he raised up and glared at the people backing them: "Any of you want to try me?"

None of them did, not one, they were too afraid, afraid of Abe Lincoln, a man that size who don't think twice about slinging a boy headfirst right into his own brothers and all their friends. They wished they were brave enough, but they weren't. Abe could see it, *everyone* could see it . . .

Might as well kill a man as shame him to his people.

John D. was leaning on Pap, face blubbered with the shame and hurt of his whupping and joy of Abe's revenge. But Pap looked at Abe, as sick and scared as the Grigsbys, like he didn't know which was worse, if this *was* his son or if it *wasn't*. James Gentry was tight-lipped with shock, even Abe's own Boys stood white-eyed and scared stiff.

The Bull of the Lick walked past them out into the dark.

He went down to the river, below the camp. The water ran by, whispering. "Go on," he told it, "go tell Ma how I turned out. Tell her I'm mean, all right. But I ain't *keerless*. I go at it *scientific*."

A rustle in the brush behind him. A man cleared his throat. "Say there—Lincoln? Abe? Is that you?" Offutt. It sounded like Denton Offutt.

"It's me," Abe said.

Denton Offutt, in the flesh, popped out of the brush like a genie out of a bottle. "I thought it was you back there at the lecture. Isn't Miss Wright a stunner? I've been staying with them down at New Harmony. She'll do that any night of the week if you give her a chance. I wasn't sure it *was* you. So I followed the crowd. Then I saw you heave that little monkey—I think he's the little bastard put a pea-shot through my hat." He took off his low-crowned beaver and showed Abe the hole. Offutt cleared his throat. "I hope you didn't get in trouble with those Kentucky boys on my account." The Dill brothers were trouble from another age of the world. But Offutt didn't know that. "I'll be plain with you," he said. "I don't mind taking advantage in a trade. But I'm not one to ruin a man, or get him in the clutches of the law. If I can make good your fine . . ."

It seemed he felt a little guilty on Abe's account. Abe smiled in the dark. *Soon as you touch bottom, things start looking up.* "Well, the fine wasn't *too* steep," he allowed. "But now, I recollect we had an agreement—concerning sang-roots? You said: *if* I dug a mess of roots, and *if* there was a boat to ship 'em in"—he was really grinning now—"and *if* I ever see'd you again in *this* life—you said you'd go partners with me. And here you are!"

Offutt scratched his head. "Well, strange as it may seem, a sang-root speculation might be just what I want right now. The woolens did not yield the return I had a right to expect. A voyage to New

Orleans could be the very thing to set me up again. But do you have the roots? And can we get a boat?"

"If you can hold out till winter you can buy in partners on a flat I'm building. Between now and then me and my brother John D. can dig out every root in southern Indiana."

Offutt said, "You aren't building it in Troy."

"No sir: in Rockport. For Allen Gentry, brother of a good old friend of mine."

"Rockport? That's just as well. If I had to explain to Taylor and the rest why the woolens didn't sell it might delay our sailing." He put out his hand. "I'll talk to your Mister Gentry."

Abe took his hand and shook it. "Cap'n Gentry," he said, grinning, "I reckon you might have to call him *Cap'n* Gentry."

BOOK V:

Father of Waters

Chapter 12: **The Old Man**

Rockport, December 1828

Abe had seen flatboats a-plenty at Troy and knew the breed well
enough to build one. He built it bottom-side up, starting with the
framing of the cabin / storehouse which made up most of the flatboat's nearly thirty-foot length. For the bottom he squared heavy
oak timbers and laid them atop the cabin frame, pegging all tight.
Then Abe and Gentry's man set poles under the flat and levered her
over, whump-splash on her bottom in the shallows of Spanker's
Branch. After that it was easy to set courses of squared timbers all
around, to give the loaded flatboat two-three feet of freeboard.
These side timbers closed a small well or cockpit in the stern: a place
for the steersman to stand out of the wind, a shelter to fire rifles from
if they should be attacked by river pirates or Indians. A wide double
door in the well gave access to the cabin and stored goods.

Gentry's hands loaded her with barreled pork and corn, whiskey-
kegs, withe-bound stands of hoop-poles—sacks of sang-root on top
out of the wet and handy for trading. They set in a tool-chest and a

rack of armaments: a long rifle, two muskets, and a bell-mouth blunderbuss. Then Abe roofed her over with timbers strong enough so you could drop a bull on the roof and not crack 'em; boiled pine-tar and pitched her snug against the wet. He set thole-pins at the stern and several points round the deck, so an oarsman could bring his pull to bear from any angle; shaved sweeps out of solid beech logs—a pair of twenty-foot sweeps with broad paddles for steering, and six bow oars or sweeps upwards of twelve feet long. Gentry had a half-breed skiff, lean as a canoe but with oak ribs and over-lapped strakes: Abe built a rack for it to sit in upside down.

Rockport to Cairo, December 1828–January 1829

There was chill smoke on the branch when Abe unhitched and pushed them off. They glided past the Hanging Rocks at the gate of the creek and the river opened broad from bank to bank, cold sun shattering sparks on her ripples. They broke into the main current, the river buoyed the heavy-timbered flatboat from beneath: they were light and loose in the rush of water, free and in peril of life and property.

The Ohio ran a beautiful straight reach fifteen miles down to the big bend at Owensboro. They worked their sweeps to get the feel of the loaded flat in the current. She was considerably less handy than Abe's scow. If you showed her hind quarter to the current the river's big unforgiving push would start her turning broadside, they had to dig hard to stop her broaching.

They came up to the bend just after noon. The fast water and deep channel were on the outer sweep of a bend, but if you went too far out you could catch the eddy that always waited in the bight. An eddy could broach you, swing you around. Out on the Big River were eddies three acres across, with a current so strong and tight it could break a keelboat through the spine. Yet if you stood off from the eddy and shaved the point too close you risked striking on the sand-bar shallows that ran out from a point.

After Owensboro the river curved gradually north and west.

There were swift runs where the banks pinched in, narrowing the riverbed, slower passages where the river spread out. The air was clear so it was easy for Abe to spot the spikes of snags and wallowing drift-logs. Only, the glitter hurt his eyes after a while. He thought Allen might take a turn at lookout and let Abe steer, but Gentry said no.

The short day was closing as they came abreast of the mouth of Little Pigeon River, about twenty miles above the Evansville Mounds, where they were to meet Offutt. Allen eased the flatboat into slack water and grounded her on the Little Pigeon bar. Abe had built a sand-filled fire-box just aft the middle of the cabin roof-deck. They cooked supper; then banked the fire. Abe pegged a pair of uprights into the deck, Allen stretched a tanned hide over them to make a half-camp, back to the wind and face to the fire.

It was strange camping at the mouth of the stream whose water came from his home. Of course the mouth was wrote down in Cradok's book, and Abe had took note of it: but reading a thing and living it was different. Abe fell asleep to the sound of Little Pigeon whispering old secrets to itself.

It was mid-afternoon when Abe saw the three tall bare Mounds rising above the trees on the Indiana shore. Offutt hailed them from the beach. Behind him a wagon-track slanted up through a break in the bench that marked the high-water shore. Gentry swung the flatboat into the slackwater and sidled her along the beach, scraping to a stop in the pebbles.

Denton Offutt was dressed as near to work-rough as he would go: wool pants tucked into boots and a wool cape over all, with his grease-stained beaver hat still up top. He was full of heigh and howdy, praised them as men true to their pledged hour, punctuality the courtesy of kings. "My goods are up on the bench. I've been camping on them two nights." He had four kegs of sang-root, which he had brewed up with the aid of a New Harmony chemist past any mere "tonic"—it was a genuine *Elixir*. He also had two bales of woolens and a large ironbound trunk: "A cash commission, boys—

that is the papers scientific philosophic and political, with other prized possessions of *Miss* Frances Wright. Mister Owen has paid me a good fee to deliver same to her plantation Nashoba, outside Memphis." Abe was thrilled. Allen Gentry cocked an eyebrow. "Which I will of course divide with *you*, Captain, as my partner in the voyage."

It was near evening of the short day when they finished wrassling Offutt's goods down the slope and stowing them on the flatboat, so they decided to lay over that night. Offutt said why didn't Abe walk up with him and take a look at the Mounds while the light lasted?

The nearest Mound rose out of the brush a quarter mile in-shore. From the river Abe had seen the Mounds end-on, and they looked like bee-hive ovens with flattened tops. Seen from the side, this one was the shape of the earth you pile on a grave, only this was the grave of a Creation giant. Offutt pointed, proud as if he'd built it: "Ever see the like?"

Abe shook his head. "It's out of nature."

"It *isn't* nature," said Offutt. "The man that drove me down from Harmony is a scholar. Told me it was Injuns heaped these mounds, thousands of years ago. *Civilized* Injuns, if you can believe it."

The sharp rise and smooth sides of the Mound had them breathing too hard for talk till they got to the top. Up there the ground was smooth as a table, wind scoured and sun baked. Far below they saw the shining curve of the Ohio.

"They had an eye for location," said Offutt admiringly. "Nothing could come by here without them looking it over." Abe looked across at the other two Mounds. "It must have took years to heap these things. Hunderds of people, thousands."

Offutt nodded. "And there are dozens more just like these scattered from Pittsburgh to the bottom of the River."

Abe was trying to make a picture of it in his head, hundreds of Injuns hauling stones and shoveling earth. "What did they want Mounds for?"

Offutt shrugged. "Place to fort up? Climb out of a flood? Or like the Pyramids of Egypt: to bury a king under."

"Ha!" said Abe. His old idea came back to him, Injuns and Egyptians were someways alike.

"Nobody can say for sure," Offutt continued. "The people that built them are all of them gone, and left not word nor whisper to say why or how. Makes a man think: all this work, and it came to nothing."

They pushed off in the morning, Abe on the bow oar and Allen Gentry on the sweep, Offutt perched on the roof with his fiddle to play them out like a chantey-man. He was in high spirits, the others were doing all the work. He sawed up a tune on his fiddle then threw back his head and sang:

> "Yankee gal will take your money—*mind* how ye row!
> Yaller gal is sweet as honey: long—time—ago!"

Denton Offutt had a fine tenor voice.

> "Western gal will work your land—*mind* how ye row!
> Yaller gal makes you a man: a long time ago!
> Hard upon the beech-oar—she moves too slow!
> Way down to Shawneetown, a long time ago!"

On the point opposite Henderson Island a dam had been built out into the river that banked the flow so steamboats could pass the riffle there. At the end of the dam the river piled up and combed back on itself, a three-foot wave churning out into the channel. The flatboat "smelt" the backwash at the end of the dam and her head swung away—Allen hollered for Abe to "Drive her hard!" Abe dug in on the port side, Allen backed the steering oar to hold her stern against the sideswipe current off the dam. Abe took spray in the face as her blunt head banged into the chop, Offutt cussed and snatched his fiddle in under his cape. They straightened her into the current and went racing down the chute of fast water between the dam and Kentucky.

The chilly air bit through Abe's wool shirt and pants where the water wet him. Offutt took his fiddle from under his coat and looked at it solicitously. "Dang me if I looked for breakers on a river trip."

Gentry gave him the laugh. "This ain't nothin', Offutt. Wait till you run a Mis'sippi chute with the wind across."

There were islands and sandy shoals to slip among as they rode past Posey County. "Let me steer her awhile?" Abe was getting the hang of the river.

"That's all right," said Gentry. "Jest you tend bow oar."

They ran the boat into the willows on Slim Island, the thicket of lithe saplings gradually braking the boat. The Ohio was too "bony" to run in the dark unless they had high water.

Offutt took Abe below-deck to help him shift his woolens and Miss Wright's trunk. The waves at Hendersonville Dam had impressed him. They split the bale of woolens in three and cleared a space to lay them atop the barrels. Then Offutt grinned and said, "Long as the deck's dry, why don't we lay these out for mattresses and sleep like kings?" Abe's notion of a good bed was a corn-shuck tick. He felt the layers of woven cloth and savored the notion of their warmth and quiet under his body. "Just make sure you stow them out of the wet when you go on deck in the morning," Offutt admonished. It wouldn't do to let the boy presume on their partnership.

Abe tipped up Miss Wright's trunk so Offutt could slip blocks underneath. He reckoned the trunk was proof against damp, but wouldn't like for it to set in water "if they shipped their bilges full."

"She's a fine, intelligent lady, Miss Wright," said Offutt. "Maybe a little set in her ways—but she will *do*, where others only *talk*." The ceiling of the cabin was low enough so Abe had to hunker while they talked, and Offutt rested his hind end on the trunk. "Those philosophers would talk days on end and never come to business. 'Man is selfish by nature.' 'Man is selfish by education and training.' 'It's society makes the man.' 'It's man makes the society.' 'Round and 'round, Owen and his son as woolly as the rest—how that man made such a pile of money is more than *I* can tell. Is the negro a slave by instinct or training? If you cut him loose is he going to die? run crazy? join the Church? or go make money and run for Congress like the rest of us? Then *she* says: 'Only way to see is try the experiment. And I mean to do it.' "

Offutt looked smug and cagey. "That was what I wanted to hear. I said if she was ready, I knew where she could get a dozen candidates prime for education—delivery in Kentucky across from Evansville." He rubbed his hands together. "Donaldson brought the negroes down on an old flatboat, him and that Sephus of his. She paid *cash*." Offutt sighed. "Abe, I'm bound to say I *admire* that woman."

There are negroes in the world with more luck in life than I expect to have. Abe took a breath and faced up to it. "Well, you made a good thing of it anyway."

"Well now, Abe," he offered, "our speculation got *some* good of all that philosophy." He crouched over an Elixir keg that he'd bunged and spigoted, and eased the plug to let some drops onto Abe's hand. The smell was pretty high.

Abe touched his tongue to it, bitter as sin—then the tip of his tongue went numb as if he'd licked a hard-froze gun-barrel, and something fluttered behind his eyes as if he'd got a moth caught inside his head.

Offutt patted the keg. "My boy, this is the genuine article: she's got the soul of an angel and the kick of a mule, and will cure every ailment from ague to zymositis. The Chinamen themselves couldn't do better."

They ran the complicated channel below the wild bluffs of the Cave-in-Rock, where (according to Cradok) river pirates used to lurk in the old wild Daniel Boone days. Abe was all for internal improvements, but he *almost* regretted the pirates. After the bluffs the land went flat, they had days of frigid steady rain. Then the big rivers poured in from Kentucky, the Cumberland and the Tennessee, bulking up the current. Gentry trusted the water enough to run at night past Grand Chain and the Monkey's Eyebrow.

Abe was looking forward to Cairo, the big town at the junction of the rivers. Cradok spoke highly of it: said that with a little ditching and draining the town was sure to become "the great *Deposit* for all the rich produce of that Terrestrial Paradise, the Illinois . . ." But Cairo itself was a disappointment—that is, the parts of it still above water. The buildings were drowned to the eyebrows, shingled roofs like a line of rocky bars. A huge raft was anchored at the far end of drowned Front Street, a hundred feet long and half that across, with wigwams tents and clapboard shanties pitched aboard her. Smoke curled from stove-pipes. The light breeze offshore brought the town's smell of shit and wood-smoke. Gentry snickered. "Yes—I reckon she *does* want ditching and draining."

The river swung south, the Great Raft of Cairo faded into the dark line of drowning trees that failed out along the last point, then just rain and river water . . .

. . . and just like that they lost the Ohio, suddenly the Big River was rushing along to starboard, a huge prone expanse of open water that stretched two-three miles across to the low gray line of the Missouri shore, the sky above high wide and barren, no sound anywhere but the susurrant wash of water alongside.

Off to starboard a lean furrow of turbulence ran alongside them on a gradually converging course. Gentry called orders, they gave the boat an extra push, and she ran across the furrow—a faint vibration ran through her as she crossed. As abrupt as if they'd struck a patch of ice they slid forwards at speed, the boat rocking a little in the muscular coils of the new current. The water overside was milky with churned-up mud and sand. When they crossed a rip the River didn't chuckle under the bow, it growled.

Ahead and to starboard a slick-topped circle of flat water appeared in the middle of the current. Allen pointed them for it with a peculiar grin on his face. As they rode up to it Abe could see it was a huge bubble of smooth water wide as a cornfield, bulged-up in the middle so it stood markedly higher than the river around it. A wrinkle of turbulence ran round the outside of the thing. "Stand ready!" Gentry called and steered the flatboat to cut a slice off the outer edge of the circle. "Stroke hard!" he called, seemingly intent on driving them into the huge glassy boil.

"Hold on!" yelled Allen—and they hit the edge of the glass bulge with a jarring bang that made them stumble. The head of the boat was shoved tilting to port as if she was riding over an ice-smooth rock, something seized the boat by the bottom and ran her round the furrow of turbulence that marked the circle.

Abe gouged his oar into the smooth face of the boil to drive her out—some huge living strength wrung it, nearly wrassled him out of the boat. The flatboat was racing across the face of the current heading for Missouri at unbelievable speed. Allen dug the steering oar hard to drive her stern out of the furrow, "Backwater starboard!" Abe pulled on his oar instead of pushing, Offutt drove the port side forwards, the flatboat swung backwards out of the spinning water.

Allen kept the boat swinging till she turned full circle and her head was pointed downstream again. Offutt gave Abe a poorly kind of look. "What in hell's name was that?"

"Call 'em *boils*," said Gentry. "They pop up anywheres in the River. I'd have steered well clear of this'n. But I wanted you to git the feel of Him."

You couldn't trust the Old Man. You had to read his face closer than ever you read a book, every squint and shift of eye-light, to see was He a mind to kill you. The Ohio had taught Abe her ABCs: the sketchy V's in the surface that said there was a rock or snag below; the slick of fast water, dimpled if it was shoaling. But the Ohio was clear as glass, and only half the size of this Thing. On the Big River the surface was roiled even over deep channel, muddy so it whorled thickly. And *fast*. The dangers here were the same, but the speed and weight of the River made them worse.

Rocks of course, rooted in the riverbed, smash your boat's brains out rock don't move. Then the killer trees. The River was constantly caving in its forested banks, you had to watch for drift-logs and floating islands. And *snags:* dead trees with split limbs or roots like sharpened stakes, rip the bottom out of a steamboat, hang a flatboat up and broach her. Below the surface were *planters*—great tree-logs jammed endwise in the mud with the butt-end pointing into the current like a battering ram, waiting rooted and still just below the rush. Then there were *sawyers*—planters that lifted and sunk, lifted and sunk to a regular rhythm like two men sawing wood in a saw-pit. Bang into one with the full shove of the Mississippi at your back and it will crack your flatboat's oak brow, bang her seams loose, pop

her pegs, and send a mess of logs hogs fruit furniture and family
floating down the River.

As for bends, the Old Man had twists in Him that made the Ohio
seem like a bee-line. He'd loop and twist Himself into bights crimps
and double-backs like a rattlesnake winding among a bramble
thicket. The current through his bends was complex and sneaky, the
bottom broken with reefs and underwater dams of mud and boulders, if you didn't watch yourself rounding a point the current
would throw you where a claw of shoal could grab and spin you, a
tentacle of eddy swipe you in. There were eddies in the Big River
wide as plantations, with a suck-hole in their heart that went straight
to the bottom of the earth. Where the bottom rose and the water
quickened and shoaled, where the banks squeezed in or an island
plugged the stream and drove the current fiercely down a chute you
had to stand ready at the oars and look sharp. But even if you did . . .

The air chilled and sucked fumes off the face of the River so they
floated on a carpet of smoke. The air suddenly turned white and
packed their eyes with cotton wool. It was like being in a lightless
cave under the earth, only white instead of black. They reckoned
they were drifting but couldn't prove it. No way to get out of the
River either—the nearest shore might be China for all they could
tell, they wanted more Columbus than they had in them to go sailing off to look for it. Nothing to do but drift, whanging on tin pots to
warn off any steamboats foolish enough to be blundering around in
the white-out.

The Old Man grumbled under the bows.

Towards evening a wind stirred the thick cold white soup,
thinned it enough for them to see a tow-head to starboard where
they could tie up for the night.

In the middle darkness something disturbed Abe's sleep—a rhyth-
mic pumping sound. He slipped out the cabin door, his blanket
thrown over his head against the chill. It was clear dark, the River

an oiled gleam of almost-black between far black banks of trees—
and riding on it was a double-stacked steamboat: a building big as a
courthouse cut loose to sail like one of those Aladdin palaces, the
white-pillared tiers of her decks illuminated by lanterns and the
gold of lighted windows, black smoke from the stacks overwriting
the stars and throwing a fiery spray of orange sparks in their place.
The throb of her engines pulsed the air, and her wake sent small
waves breaking against the side of the flatboat.

There were people on board of her: he could see shapes move in
some lighted windows, saw a man emerge from the door of the
pilot-house and stroll aft. What was their life like, what kind of people were they, living in such a place?

It was a . . . *huge* grand country, wasn't it? You might *think* you
had a notion of it, seeing it set down in a book or drawed on a map,
United States of America—but that was no more notion of it than
you could get of the Old Man by taking a swim in Little Pigeon
Creek. His ignorance came home to him. Out in the republic the distance was like China, and a world of strangers living in it. The most
of people had no more notion that Abe Lincoln existed than Abe
Lincoln had had of Mound Injuns. If he was to die, they wouldn't
even have to forget him.

The steamboat showed him her hind parts, orange gleams of fire
in the furnaces, the petticoat flurry of white at her paddlewheels—
she was turning into a further bend. Then a wall of solid black slid
across her gleaming, erasing her as she rounded the point.

Days and days they drifted south, thirty to forty miles a day
depending on the difficulty of the bends. The January air was raw-
cold, a wind you could lean on, burning your cheeks numb and biting your knuckles. The reaches were lonely, except now and then far
across the water the low dashed pen-mark of another flatboat drifting south. The shore was distant, low black streaks far off to port
and starboard of the mile-and-a-half or two-mile width of the River.
When they drew close to shore, all there was was reed-flat and half-
drowned forest. No sound of axes, no thread of chimney-smoke.

They floated past the mouth of Bayou de Cheen, looking for a grove of pines that was Gentry's mark to cross the channel. The water was smooth as a pond and dead quiet.

Then the flatboat seemed to skid forwards, Abe felt the suck of horrible motion in his innards, and suddenly the woods were racing past, the smooth look of the water exposed in an instant as the glaze of a terrible rushing speed. "Jesus!" Allen Gentry's cry and a cuss from Offutt told Abe they noticed it at the same time.

Abe threw a glance backwards. The broad beaten-silver path of the river rose visibly behind him, upwards, up on a line as even as a gangplank. At the top the water ended and sky began, and they were falling, rushing away from that sky. "We're in a cut-off," Gentry hollered. "Stand to your oars, and ready when we hit bottom!"

Abe hesitated one breath, mesmerized by the awfulness of that rising sky-line. Then he hollered and turned and ran down the tilting deck, snatched up his sweep and nocked it. Up ahead the left bank's overlap of the right was sliding steadily back the way you might draw a curtain—there was the gunmetal gleam of river between the opening lips of the cut-off's mouth. Abe held his oar poised ready to drive ahead or backwater when Gentry hollered.

Down at the bottom the roaring current of the cut-off slammed sideways into the slow water that still ran in the River's old course, a slanting scar of rucked-up water marked the long seam. The currents would be wild as a mare's nest in there, and if there were stumps boulders or trees washed down the cut-off that's where the backing churn of the water would drop them. At this runaway speed they couldn't rein in the boat nor turn her worth a damn, if there was a rock or a planter in their way they were dead men.

Gentry leaned into the steering oar to help them ride the near edge of the wave-bank till they could break across. Abe tried to help him by backing water to starboard—the steely rip of the current nearly broke his oar.

The boat dropped suddenly, the starboard side lurched up into the wave-bank and soaked Abe with spray, Offutt whooping and plying his oar to snug them into the curl of the seam—then the boat was level, the seam was gone, Allen hollering for starboard oar.

The low wet crocodile head of a planter seethed past, a drift-log pounded them like a drum.

They were clear. The Old Man had come that close to killing them, and let them go with a warning.

Gentry said afterwards the River must have made a new cut-off below Bayou de Cheen, and they had run into its chute. Abe thought he ought to have recognized it himself: he'd read in Cradok how the River wore away at the neck of a point till it broke through in a rush and cut a new channel through the woods. But it was one thing to read about it, and another to come on it suddenly face to face.

And cut-offs weren't the worst of it. Waiting down the River were all manner of monsters, human and otherwise: sawyers and planters, reefs and rocks, strainers and floating islands, pirates, wreckers, rogue Injuns, alligators, snapping turtles as wide across as a tanner's pit. "Then there are the *bayous*," said Cradok, "streams which may, at any time, sally forth from the main river through a break in the levee, with astonishing rapidity, and whose vortex extends some distance into the stream. Boats once sucked into such bayous are next to lost, it being impossible to force so unwieldy a machine as a flat-bottomed boat against so powerful a current." Just knowing the name of the thing didn't give a man any notion of its strength, or how to fight it. Words on a page can't run fast enough to catch what they hunt. Abe put his book away and set himself to keep wide-awake from here out. He mustn't let the Old Man get the jump on him, more than he could help.

Gentry was stingy about steering, it belonged to his authority as captain and he felt uneasy without it. But he had to relent: had give his back a twist, and was anyway wore out. He'd rather Offutt steered, who was a partner not a hired hand and had experience with boats. But Offutt preferred head-work to hand-work, so he gave most of his time to Abe and stood by to advise.

Days of anxious look-out had taught Abe to read the squints, frowns, and wrinkles of the Old Man's face. Steering oar gave Abe a new touch and deeper feel of the River. There were currents under the currents that showed on the surface, boils and cross-rips that never saw light of day. The Old Man's bed was deep down, it must be full of caves and humps and fissures, a whole territory you'd never see, wracks and sunk logs, bones of bears and wolves and buffalo, man-bones—the last man the River et was down there, and plenty of those long-time-gone Mound Injuns. And every one of these long-ago lost and drowned things gave its little bump or drag or twist to the Old Man's run: couldn't stop Him, but they made their mark. You could feel them as a vibration in the long paddle and stem of the steering oar. Konkapot used to say if you want to *hunt* you have to *listen*. Well Johnny, I am learning how to *listen dhat River*.

Let the Old Man teach what it is to hold your purpose and keep your ways through the earth, never mind rock or tree, earthquake or hurricane, the 'ruptions of Nature or the makings of man. Then, maybe, you will be the kind of man She wants: "Once launch the animal man on the road of inquiry, and he shall, he must hold a forward career. To hold him still he must be chained. His master movement is always in advance."

Gentry reckoned they would make Memphis tomorrow or the day after. The sun was stronger, and took the chill off the January air. They were feeling pretty well pleased with themselves. Allen Gentry set his back against the skiff and his face to the sun and bit off a chaw. Abe leaned on his oar and played push-me / pull-you with the Old Man, working out of slow water. Offutt brought out his fiddle, sat on the roof facing Abe, tuned and tested her a bit, then sailed off into a brightened-up version of *Shenando' I long to see you— Way-hey! you rollin' River!*

Another flatboat, a large one, was coming down fast with the main current behind her. There was a crowd of people on her roof, must be passengers as well as crew. Some of them were waving and hallooing. They had heard the fiddle, the oarsmen were pulling hard and the steersman slanted them across the current to come up with Abe's boat.

Abe made out that most of the people were negroes, including the sweep-oars, but there were three white men, and one gent with a top hat was waving it. Gentry waved for them to come on, and at the same moment Abe recognized the gent with the hat as Captain Donaldson. It was the custom on the river that when boats from neighboring settlements met, they would tie up and float together as long as trade took them the same way. Abe held the boat steady in the current and let Donaldson's negroes pull his boat alongside.

Donaldson was taking another boatload of negroes to sell off south. The two white men were hired to keep watch—as the boat came nearer Abe could see that one, standing in the bow, had a blunderbuss slung by a rope over his shoulder. The second sat on an upturned canoe amidships, with a musket leaning handy. As the two boats came level Abe saw Sephus was steering. He grinned at Abe and hollered to the oarsmen, who checked the boat's way with a backwater stroke, then in-oars as Sephus eased the boats gently together. One of Donaldson's white men threw Gentry a rope to hitch them.

Donaldson, his red face beaming, jumped across, shook hands hearty with Offutt and Gentry, and said they ought to celebrate the well-meeting with something suitable. He flourished a bottle. Offutt and Gentry clapped him on the back and they sat down on the sunny side of the skiff to share it.

It rankled Abe a little that Donaldson hadn't give him greeting too, nor invited him to share a drink. Not that he wanted any. Offutt ought to have asked him—but then, Offutt probably knew Abe didn't like liquor. He guessed it was all right. Donaldson hadn't invited his own white crew over neither. Nor Sephus. The black man nodded to Abe, and did a little stamp and shuffle to show he recognized him. For just a tick Abe wasn't sure if he ought to howdy back to a negro, but it come to him he was glad to see Sephus out here, someone that knew him from home. Sephus, as if he read Abe's mind, called, "You de pilot?" He stood easy, one hand resting on the shank of his sweep. He reached a twist of tobacco out of his shirt and offered some to Abe, who shook it off (he didn't chaw neither). Sephus shrugged and looked away forwards.

"I don't chaw," Abe called out, and saw Sephus nod, in profile—not looking Abe's way. Abe cussed himself. Now he'd said howdy and as good as apologized to a black negro. No wonder he wasn't asked to have a drink with the gentlemen.

From forwards Abe heard Donaldson crowing how Yessir, he finally seen his way clear to sell off more o' these damn *niggers* been eating up his property like a plague of locusts. Planters were paying top dollar at Natchez, wanted all they could get for the Red River, *that's* the country for cotton. "But the climate?—uses up niggers faster'n they can breed, you can't season but one in five. Fifteen hundred for a prime field hand, two thousand for a breeding wench, that's what I heard. I'll see enough to pay out what I owe and plenty left over. Why, I might give the Red River a go myself."

There were a dozen negroes on the roof of Donaldson's flat, eight men and four women—most within a year or two of Abe, one older hand that might be twenty-five, and Sephus the oldest by some years. They bunched around the fire-box in the middle of their boat. The two guards, sharing a word between themselves, still kept an eye on them. Sephus lounged easy by his oar and spat tobacco-juice in the River.

The three magnificoes wandered back to the stern. Donaldson wanted the others to consider with him the prospective value of his goods. "Look there: four wenches in the prime, two has had healthy-born before this. That's what? six–eight thousand? And eight prime hands. What d'you think? No worse'n nine hundred, a thousand on average, wouldn't you say? That's . . ." He tried to add it up but couldn't.

"Thirteen thousand at least," said Offutt, and Gentry whistled. "If you git 'em all to market."

Donaldson waved off worry. "With Starkey, Penn, and myself that's three rifles." He took thought, then gestured proudly at Sephus. "And Sephus, of course—that's *four*." He beamed at Sephus, his voice took on a soothing-syrup sweetness. "Couldn't get on without Sephus. Best steersman *I* ever had, and he ain't lost a nigger for me yet! Have you Sephus?"

The black steersman gave a broad smile. "Dat's so, Cap'n. Ain't lost one yet."

There was too much sugar in Donaldson's mouth. Abe reckoned he was diddling the negro like he'd done back in Troy: pretending to put Sephus in charge and give him a chance at freedom while all the time he meant to sell him like the rest. Unless he was an eejit, Sephus must *know* Donaldson was lying. He knew Donaldson better than anyone. But negroes were unaccountable. If he wasn't fooled, why hadn't he run off? Maybe he wasn't as smart as he seemed. Or maybe negro thinking was that different from a white man's that what was plain to one was dark to the other. Negroes would put up with the kind of thing a white man would generally kill you for—shaming, insults, blows, or worse: your family broke up and sold away. They would do things a white man or Injun wouldn't—hadn't Sephus helped Donaldson sell one boatload of his kind south? Sure, the buyer was Frances Wright—but what would Sephus know about Frances Wright?

Offutt had Abe bring up a pail of whiskey from the hold, and they offered Donaldson and the two white men, Starkey and Penn, the hospitality of the boat.

Donaldson threw back his drink, dipped another, and looked around for fun. His eye lit on Abe: "Hey now, why ain't you got nothin' to drink?"

Starkey grinned, gap-toothed. "Ain't lost your taste for the tit, have you boy?" And everyone laughed.

Donaldson stared at Abe with eyes that went in and out of focus, puzzled. "I 'member you," he said, "Tom Lincoln's boy: hired out to Taylor. You used to speak out a piece for comp'ny, didn't you?"

Starkey haw-hawed and poked Penn in the ribs. Penn, who took his liquor quiet, was annoyed.

Abe had no mind to speak his piece for this bunch. He gave Offutt a look, but Offutt was puzzled by his whiskey.

Donaldson squinted as he brought his whole mind to bear: "You used to say that piece about the Jews got eyes."

Whatever happened, he wasn't going to sit up and bark on Donaldson's say-so. "No," he drawled, "I 'druther hear fiddle-music. How about some fiddle, *Offutt*?"

Hearing his name in Abe's mouth without the "Mister" attached woke Offutt up. He blinked: what was wanted?

"I bet he don't know how," said Starkey. It come to Abe that Starkey was looking to start a fight with him, and the man a complete stranger Abe hadn't had no more to do with than to dip him a drink of whiskey.

Donaldson slurped the last of the juice from his cup and shook his head, satisfied. "Yep," he said to no one and everyone, "I 'member perf'ly well. Boy spoke it out good as any Jew." He nodded emphatically. "Maybe better!"

"Maybe he is a Jew," said Starkey.

Offutt was awake at last, and moved to head off trouble. "How about some fiddle-music instead?" He reached his fiddle out from under the skiff.

But Donaldson wasn't interested in fiddling. "What about wrasslin' then? I recollect I lost a pile on you *wrasslin'* too. But I'm bound an' 'termined make it all up this voyage!" He hauled out a leather purse, and slapped it down on the deck. "Let's wrassle him 'gainst Penn or Starkey," he told Gentry. "I'll give you odds."

Starkey got to his feet. "I'm the man for it, Cap!" He rubbed his hands and stepped out into the middle of the deck.

Things had gone too far. Offutt said, "The boy has no mind to wrassle neither." But it was too late.

"You ain't afeared are you?"

Whether it was Starkey said the words, or Donaldson, or whether nobody ever actually spoke them at all, they were so obviously the *next words* that Abe and everybody else heard them plain.

It made Abe mad to spitting, mad to stamping and cussing, how he'd been pushed into this against all his will and wanting, and now couldn't get out of it without being shamed: shamed to the white men if he backed down, shamed to himself if he went ahead with it. It made his head ring he was so mad, sick-mad—and it made him wobbly on his legs, like the spirit in his bones was loose and flighty instead of cold and strong like it needed to be.

He was going to get whupped. He knew it. Starkey knew it. The man was near enough Abe's height and heavier muscled. He moved like a cat, toe and heel sideways as they circled each other. Then he rushed, Abe caught him, and they grappled arms around. The stink of his breath and raw sweat filled Abe's nostrils. Starkey had wrapped a leg around and was kicking for the bend of Abe's knee. Abe's leg buckled and he went down, Starkey's weight bearing him to the deck. Starkey worked an arm loose and punched Abe hard in the back—a sharp pang when he hit the tender spot over the lights. It was dirty fighting, Abe knew the next he'd go for was an eye-gouge so he grabbed an ear and twisted it hard as he could. Starkey rolled back, and as Abe staggered up Starkey stepped in and slammed a hard forearm against the side of Abe's head . . .

The world blinked.

He was in the air, cut loose from earth.

Then with a splash he was in the River—first a blank wash, then the sudden bite of cold. His back and the side of his head were throbbing against the cold press of the water, he was glad for the cold on them. His head broke surface. The side of the flatboat moved by him and he heard Starkey's voice, ". . . haw haw, whupped his ass and threw him in the river for you, how's that Cap'n D?"

Whupped. That piece of white trash. Captain Donaldson's bad dog. No fair fight, but just what did he expect? This was the River, not Pigeon Creek: Uncle Mordecai's kind of fight.

A hand reached down. Black hand. He looked up and saw Sephus's face. "Best let it be, Longshanks." He spoke in a whisper, not moving his lips. "You ain't scairt, but he a mean son a bitch."

The River was cold but it wasn't any colder than Abe. *Let the Old Man teach you, teach you patience willfulness stubborness treachery, find your way any way, back front or roundabout.* He gripped Sephus's wrist and the black man hauled him up to where he could get his arms over the freeboard and pull himself up the side. Abe looked at Sephus and Sephus looked right back. It wasn't the first time it had seemed to Abe they understood something together. "All right," said Sephus, "only mind his right boot. Got a knife snuck in it."

Offutt was standing on the break of the cabin roof looking down. "You all right, Abe?" he asked anxiously. "That wasn't any fair fight. You've nothing to be ashamed of."

Abe climbed up onto the roof-deck. His clothes clung cold like a suit of iron and he dripped a storm onto the decking. Offutt was solicitous. "Get on over to the fire, I'll fetch you a sup of that Elixir, set you right up again." He threw a blanket over Abe's shoulders and ushered him over to the fire.

Starkey stood next to Donaldson, grinning with pleasure in himself, and a sneer in his eyes. Starkey was the kind would spit on any man he could whup, fawn on any man could whup him. Abe's whole body felt icy-numb but it wasn't the cold air on cold wet skin, the ice came from inside him.

"No hard feelings now," said Donaldson, "my man whupped you fair and square."

It was all plain, Abe could read these men like they were a book. Gentry looked uneasy: didn't like the way Donaldson's man whupped, but he wasn't proud of Abe neither. Offutt returned from below and handed him a cup of Elixir. The fumes lit a fire behind his eyes. He took the cup and said, "Well I reckon I will, this time."

Starkey shot a sizzle of spit into the fire and said, "Least now you'll drank like a man."

Donaldson nudged Starkey and beckoned Abe. "You boys come on now and shake hands. Fight like gentlemen," he said, "no hard feelings."

Abe stepped over to meet Donaldson and Starkey. Starkey had a cup of whiskey in his right hand. Abe's heart pulsed steady but his nerves were sizzling. He made a small, sheepish smile on his face. He was in front of Starkey now, and Donaldson stepped aside to let them shake hands.

Abe shifted the cup to his left hand to clear his right for the shake, and said, "No hard feelin's." Starkey of course just grinned and kept his whiskey in his right hand a little longer to make sure everyone knew which of them had put out his hand first to beg off a grudge-fight.

Abe threw the sang-root Elixir full in Starkey's eyes and grinning face with his left hand, and when Starkey slammed his hands over his eyes blind-burnt with raw forty-rod spirit Abe pulled back his right and punched Starkey hard in the guts, right in the eye of the belly where the blow stops you breathing. Donaldson said, "Hey now—!"

Starkey was half-bent, wheeze-choking for breath. The ice in Abe's blood was burning fire now. His head was full of it. *Beat him so he stays beat.* Abe took a step back and kicked Starkey hard and most deliberately in the balls. Starkey fell down, gasping, kneeling on the deck. Abe went down next to him, snatched the sneak-knife out of his boot and showed it to Starkey—held it under his blinking eyes. "I could cut your throat with your own damn knife. Couldn't I?" He grabbed Starkey by the hair. "Tell me I could do it if I wanted to."

Starkey was fighting for breath, but shook his head yes. But Abe wasn't done. Couldn't be done, the son of a bitch was still there, a sack of shit and bones. *Feed him to the River.* Abe dragged him by his hair over to the side of the boat, and kicked him till he went over the side. Then he threw his knife in after him. *Go down and stay down you son of a bitch.*

He felt a hand on him: Offutt. "Abe, Jesus Christ, Abe." Offutt was scared. "You don't want to kill anybody, Abe."

But of course he did . . . There was just the little bit of that icy-fiery rage left, riding up top of a darker, down-plunge of feeling that he knew was coming—shame for losing control of himself like that, no better than an animal, drunk on his own blood-rage like a damned wolf.

Offutt patted him on the back. "He never fought you fair, son. You paid him back his own coin." Gentry was pacifying Donaldson, easing him back over to his own boat with lots of assurances, no offense, young men got no more sense'n a set o' seed bulls, but we best not camp alongside . . . Sephus cast loose the hitches that bound the boats together. Splashes from aft told how Penn was hauling Starkey out of the river.

The boats drifted apart. It was coming dark—they'd run tonight to put distance between them. Gentry was angry, he didn't want trouble with Donaldson and Abe had made some for him. "Now you have to watch your back. You can bank on it, that Starkey will be laying for you."

With the last bit of living rage Abe said, "Not to my face he won't." Then he stomped off to the cabin to shuck his wet clothes; to close the door so the dark inside the cabin would cover the rush of black shame rising inside him.

When he woke his back and the side of his face hurt. He didn't feel so bad inside anymore. Was a little embarrassed to have took on so after the fight. So what if he had got mad? Wasn't *whupped* better than *got-whupped*?

He went on deck. There was a cold morning light on the River. They were coasting the levee, a row of cottonwoods as regular as if they'd been planted a-purpose. Gentry was at the steering oar, still mad. "If I was lookin' for trouble on your account, I wouldn't have guessed that kind in a hunderd years." On the other hand, he had a wary look in his eye like he didn't want to rile Abe.

Offutt was boiling coffee. He give Abe good morning. "Well," he said, handing him a cup of the bitter brew, "you don't rile easy, but when you do—watch out." It was good as a flourish on the drum and three cheers. Abe's face broke out in a grin. Too bad there was only the two of them to enjoy it.

He realized he wasn't all that sorry for what happened. Only felt bad he hadn't throwed *Donaldson* in the River.

Chapter 13: **Queen of the Nile**

Memphis, January 20–22, 1829

They rounded the wooded end of Loosahatchie Bar and there she was: Memphis. Small houses were scattered along the top of the high bluff like a random spill of dice, with a couple of big buildings—the courthouse, probably, and a hotel—looking down their chest-fronts at the River. Keelboats and flats nuzzled the river-front like piggies swarming the teats. White steamboats with sun-bursts, heroes, and women painted on their wheelboxes stood apart from the riffraff: *Ben Franklin* had found himself a place alongside *Cleopatra*, and was letting on to think about philosophy while gaz-ing at the Queen over the tops of his spectacles: there was a lot of her to see.

Their plan was to tie up long enough to deliver Miss Wright's trunk and give Offutt a chance to sell her some of his woolens, then cast off for the plantations downriver. Offutt put on his town suit before going up the bluff to meet her. He might travel by flatboat, but he would look like a steamboat passenger. Abe was to meet

Offutt later in the day to arrange for bringing her goods up the bluff. Maybe Offutt would introduce him, he *was* Offutt's partner after all. The swelling on the side of his face was down and not much bruise. She mustn't think he was a brawler.

Down the riverfront a small crowd was watching as a rank of soldiers—regulars by their blue-and-brass—filed up the gangplank of a one-stack sternwheeler, *Red Rover*. A stubby brass cannon was mounted in the bow.

Offutt followed his curiosity that way, Abe in his wake. A well-dressed man in the crowd took in Offutt's go-to-town suit and extended his hand. "Jasper Kent," he said, "that's my hotel up the bluff." Anticipating Offutt's question, he said, "They're sending the soldiers down to Helena to clean Murrell's pirates out of the swamps." He smiled at Offutt. "I hope I may have the pleasure of showing you the hospitality of my house while your boat lays over—you and your man there." He nodded at Abe.

Abe went hot in the face at being mistook for Offutt's man. He expected Offutt to correct Kent's error, but Offutt merely inclined his head. "I'd be delighted, but I suppose we will be leaving again this afternoon."

Kent looked surprised. "Why—ain't you heard? Steamboat travel has been suspended three days, and they advise flatboats lay over the same: you don't want to be on the River till those boys get well off it, with their cannons and all."

Red Rover hooted, her crew threw the gangplanks ashore.

"Do they need the army to catch a few pirates? I thought Murrell was safe in jail and his gang broken up."

Kent gave Offutt a look. "I reckon you ain't from *these* parts. Murrell's ain't a gang, it's a *combination*. There's men back of Murrell too smart to get caught—or too rich to catch, if you understand me."

Red Rover hooted again, and backed into the stream.

"Got *him*, but there's gangs over in Arkansaw, in the swamps up the Franzwah and the Langwee—raidin' flatboats, runnin' niggers off the river plantations." The man was in a sweat with his story. "They planned to raise an insurrection. Burnt a plantation by Helena, kilt the owner and what-d'you-reckon to his wife and daughters. Their *own* niggers done it, but Murrell's men got 'em up to it." The man's eyes were hot. "The army will clean 'em out."

Some ladies along the shore waved handkerchiefs at the troops that lined *Red Rover*'s railings. The regulars' fife and drum struck up a jaunty tweedling tune. The Stars and Stripes ran up the flagstaff and streamed flaring on the cold breeze. Abe wished he was going with them, a soldier among soldiers, hunting pirates through the jungles of the Langwee with a cannon in his bows and the Stars and Stripes overhead. But he was bound by his word to his partner and his employer. And there was that chance of Miss Wright.

Offutt went up the bluff with Kent. Abe helped Gentry make some minor repairs, then he was let free to loaf along the docks till Offutt sent for him. There were half a dozen big steamboats ranged along the waterfront. They couldn't get away, and Abe meant to look his fill of a steamboat for once in his life. *Cleopatra* was grandest of the lot: lacework decorated her railings and filled the corners where pillar met deck like spider-webbing. It would take Pap a month to make one such piece—if he even had the tools for it, or the skill. Gangs of Irishmen were rolling a few bales of cotton, last of the winter gleaning, up a broad gangplank. He tailed on and lent a hand, which got him onto the main deck. The mate in blue uniform coat and cap was hollering directions for stowing the bales, so he didn't notice Abe slip inside.

Here was the steamboat's engine deck—six furnace and boiler combinations ranged three and three, heaps of fire-wood laid ready for use. It was right warm: there were banked fires in the furnaces. No stokers about, just a man in a peaked cap who walked about checking the furnaces. Abe stood out of eyeshot and studied the engines. He remembered what Miss Wright said about steam engines being the most beautiful and *advancing* of mechanicals, so he tried to puzzle out the workings: furnace boils water to steam, steam runs through the pipes, something in the pipes lifts the arm that cranks the wheel . . . but how does up and down in the pipes become round and round for the wheel?

If he could have studied some more he might have figured it

out, but "Hey you!" hollered the man in the cap, and Abe ducked outside.

He skulked along the side of the boat. As he crossed the foot of a staircase someone called, "You there boy!" A short fat nicely dressed man stood three steps up, beckoning him. In his other hand the man held a sheaf of papers and a leather sack, which looked to have a hammer and nails in it. "You boy," said the fat man, "how'd you like to earn yourself half a dollar?" With a flourish of his podgy hand, he produced as if out of thin air a dollar clipped in bits.

"I don't mind," said Abe.

The man held up the sheaf of papers: "I want these put up around town. Trees, posts, shit-houses, any place a man is likely to see 'em. Ask the shop-men and saloon-keepers would they put one in a window." He shook the paper out to display a printed poster the size of a newspaper:

PERFORMANCE TONIGHT!
The Great AMERICAN Tragedian,

JUNIUS BRUTUS BOOTH,

Just returned to his Native Land from his recent
TRIUMPHS in the LONDON THEATRES of
COVENT GARDEN AND DRURY LANE

Performance this evening at *Seven o'Clock,*
In the Grand Salon of the Steamboat **"Cleopatra."**
Admission 50 cents.

The time and place of the performance, and the price of admission, had been written in by hand.

"Tragedian," said Abe. "What's he do?"

"Shakespeare, my boy. If I had to guess, I'd say *Richard Third*, but the day is young and Mister Booth is stalking the muse through the streets of Memphis even as we speak. Who knows to what she will inspire him when he catches her?"

"I'm your man," said Abe. *Shakespeare!* The half-dollar would buy him a ticket. And he was bound up the hill anyway.

The man handed him the sheets, the hammer and nails, and one two-bit snip. "Other one when you bring back my hammer."

The main street of Memphis straggled along the bluff, its center a clutch of stores, grog shops, and the hotel where the dock road topped the rim. Abe picked his way through the mud street and nailed his first poster on the side wall of *Jepson / DRY GOODS &* *Negroes*. The next three buildings down the pine-board sidewalk were whiskey-houses. Decherd's let Abe tack one to the wall, Cassiday no, Beale put one in his window. He stepped up on the boardwalk outside the hotel and nailed a poster to one of the wood pillars that supported its portico. A couple of farmers peeped politely over his shoulder to see what was wrote.

Just then a man in a plaid wool coat bustled round the corner of the building. " 'Scuse me, gents," he said, "if you wouldn't mind stepping back a bit . . ."

Then a man stepped out from the alley alongside the hotel. He was short, bandy-legged, and peculiarly stooped, and had on the queerest hat—a soft dark-green thing like a mushroom with a ruff around it, and a shiny brass ring for a hatband. He was grossly deformed, a swollen hump loomed over his left shoulder, his whole body twisted as if the hump were screwed into his spine.

Abe expected someone to holler *Oh what a hat!* and make fun of the hump. Then he saw the man's face and understood the silence. The face below the hat was brilliantly pale. Blue eyes glinted under delicate arched eyebrows. The man paused and glared around—his head projecting tensely from below the hump like a snake leaning out of his coils: fixed his eyes first on one man, then another—then on Abe. A pulse or throb seemed to run through the man, sharpening his eye-lights like breath on coals. Abe was fixed where he stood. Never seen a hump-back before; didn't know, was such a man loony? Abe felt a little fear at what might come out of the twisted lips that scarred the man's beautiful face.

"Now is the winter of our discontent made glorious summer by this sun of York. And all the clouds that lowered upon our house, in the deep bosom of the ocean buried."

He *was* loony. The farmers eased back, glad he was looking at Abe. But soon as they did he shifted his glare to them, and they froze. "Grim visag'd war hath smoothed his wrinkled front—" He glared now at each of them in turn, and a backwards sweep of his left hand revealed he was armed, a long straight sword swung at his left hip. "And now—instead of mounting barb-ed steeds to fright the souls of fearful adversaries . . ." He paused: and a sneer of horrible contempt twisted his face into the mockery of a grin: "He capers *nimb*ly in a *lady's* chamber, to the lassscivious *pleazzing* of a *lute!*"

A crowd was gathering, loafers drifting through the mud from across the street, guests stepping out of the hotel door to see what the to-do was. The man strode forwards to stand face to face with Abe. The soft green hat stood no higher than Abe's breastbone but there wasn't any question which of the two was in danger of the other. The by-standers gave Abe credit for standing his ground.

The man stared Abe up and down; turned himself a little this way and that, for all the world like a flirty young girl admiring herself in a mirror. "But I," he said, "that am not shap'd for sportive tricks. Nor made to court an amorous looking-glass—I!" A noise, something between a laugh and a sob, broke from the man's chest. "I, in this weak piping time of peace, have *no* delight to pass away the time, unless to see: my *shadow* in the sun—and *des*cant on mine own . . . *deformity.*" His body was seized by a paroxysm of rage and disgust. "My eye's too quick! my heart o'erweens too much! unless my hand and strength could equal them . . ." His eyes lowered and searched out along the street, and he began to stalk slowly along the boardwalk like a wolf slinking in on a kill.

He had let Abe go and passed on down the street. *Who? What?* Abe heard the buzz rise behind him. Abe had recognized his words as one of the Shakespeare pieces from the *Elocution,* so he reckoned he knew what the little man was before the man in the plaid coat offered the people his reassurance: "Don't be concerned, gentlemen. It is Mr. Booth, the tragedian." He tapped the sheaf of posters in

Abe's hand. "The greatest actor in the English-speaking world—
and an *American* born."

The crowd followed Booth as he "stalked the muse" to the end of
the boardwalk. He turned suddenly—the crowd bumped into itself
as he turned and came stalking back, ". . . like one lost in a thorny
wood—that rents the thorns and is rent with the thorns—" He
turned and his eyes found and seized a well-dressed woman in the
crowd, lifted a hand to her, beseeching, "Not knowing how to find
the open air but toiling desperately to find . . ." The lady involun-
tarily reached a gloved hand in his direction. But Booth's own
hands instantly clawed, and fist-clinched he cried, "And from that
torment I will free myself—or hew my way out with a *bloody ax!*"

The woman recoiled in fear. Booth grinned, and turned—to discover himself standing outside a grog-shop, the Golden Buck. The
proprietor stood in the door goggling. With a swoop of his forest-
green cape the actor sailed through the open door, his rich voice
booming, "A round for the house!" The crowd looked at each other,
then piled in after him.

But Abe saw Denton Offutt beckoning him from the door of the
hotel. There was a tall lean-faced man with him. Offutt looked
quizzically at Abe's sheaf of posters.

"Man paid me to put these up for Mr. Booth."

Offutt smiled, "I like enterprise," as if it had been done on his
say-so. He turned to his companion: "Judge, this is Abe. He'll show
your boy down to the flat."

It wasn't exactly an introduction, and the "Judge" didn't offer his
hand, only nodded—with a real polite look to him, though. He
spoke easy and slow, Kentucky-like. "Abe," said the Judge, "my boy
Jordan is out back in the stables. There's a hand-cart you can use to
run your goods up here." He flicked his pointing-finger, just that little bit, the way Abe was to go, turned, and went inside without giving Abe a second look.

It was like a slap in the face but done so quick the man was gone
before Abe felt the sting. *Reckon he thinks the wag of his finger is enough
to make a man jump.* But it was Offutt's fault if the "Judge" treated
him off-hand. Offutt ought to have introduced him, and named him

"Lincoln"—*Abe* made him Offutt's boy when Abe was supposed to be his partner.

Offutt ignored Abe's look. "When you go for our goods, tell Gentry Miss Wright's people never showed up. But Judge Davis is riding out to visit her, and has kindly offered to help us carry our goods to Nashoba." Offutt rubbed his hands together, and his eyes lit with appetite. "He's a man worth knowing! They often spoke of Joseph Davis at New Harmony: a disciple of Robert Owen—owns a great plantation below Vicksburg, and manages it according to the most scientific principles."

Abe didn't care about Judge Davis. "You're going out to *Her* place?—I'm going with you."

"Of course," said Offutt, "you don't think I can carry the goods myself, do you? Tell Gentry we'll only be a day or two—we can't leave anyway on account of the army. And when you get her trunk, fetch up a bundle of my woolens and a pint jug of Elixir. I mean to do some business with the lady."

That first day in Memphis was long on promise, but short on satisfaction. The promise of Frances Wright was still alive. But Davis's "boy" Jordan—a forty-year-old colored man—was no joy to work with. He helped Abe carry Miss Wright's trunk and Offutt's woolens up from the landing, but never said anything but *yassuh*, and sidled around like he was afraid Abe would shy a rock or kick him if he turned his back.

Then Abe forgot till too late to bring the fat man back his hammer—got hollered at and the two bits throwed at his head. To top it off Allen Gentry said he must stay aboard as boat-keeper, he'd been gallivanting through Memphis all day and it was Gentry's turn.

So he sat on the roof of the flatboat looking along the docks to where *Cleopatra* burned on the black water—not able to make out a single word, only the faint rise and fall of a voice speaking genuine Shakespeare oratory, and sudden volleys of applause. He read over the speech Booth had been speaking out in the street—there was a piece of it reprinted in the copy of the *Elocution* he'd brought along.

But he wished he was there to hear, to see that oratory done the way
it should be, in a place set out special for it, everyone in Memphis
there to listen. He could imagine the ugly twisted-up little hunch-
back with the beautiful eyes and voice, proud and angry, lost in a
thorny woods, swinging his bloody ax to hack his way clear. But he
had more going for him than that ax:

> I can smile, and murder whiles I smile . . .
> . . . Add colors to the chameleon,
> Change shapes with Proteus for advantages
> And set the murderous Machiavell to school.
> Can I do all this and cannot get a crown?

"Tut!" Abe said: "Was it further off, *I'll* pluck it down."

It was fifteen miles along Wolf River to Nashoba, through willow
thickets and under dark cold stands of pine, over some sad and
sorry ground. With Abe and Jordan walking to drive the jackass
mule that toted their goods, they went slow. By the time they got
there it was near dark.

Maybe it was the gray dusk or the leafless oak and hickory all
round, but something in the look of Nashoba struck a chill in Abe.
What he saw didn't suit his notions of a plantation, nor of Miss
Wright. There ought to been at least a good white clapboard or brick
house like Judge Pate's. What there was was a large clearing with a
zig-zag worm fence round the border. There was a barn in one corner, a corn-crib and hog-pen, and half a dozen log cabins set to face
in from the sides of the clearing. A double-barreled log house sat in
the middle, and there was another larger building, perhaps three
cabins cobbled together, towards the rear of the clearing. The clearing itself was full of stumps.

The cabins were poorly made: glints of inside light showed
between the logs and tendrils of smoke sifted out of gaps in the
chimneys. They had set the cabins on *pilings*! Well that was one way
to keep out of the wet, Abe reckoned, but a cabin without a mud-sill

was a cabin loose on its pins, especially on soft ground. Better to double your sills . . . or pick a better piece of ground.

A tall man with a lantern strode through the mud to greet them. "Friends! Welcome to Nashoba!" He held the lantern to show his face, "I'm Richeson Whitby." Davis was well known and warmly greeted. He introduced Offutt to Whitby, who was Miss Wright's manager. "Let your men set animals and baggage in the barn, then join us for dinner. Judge, your boy is welcome to eat with our people in the Refectory."

Whitby and Davis walked towards the Main House. Offutt paused—Abe stood there glaring down at him instead of taking their horses to the barn. Offutt sighed, he had seen this coming. "Listen Abe: I didn't mean things to happen this way. Truth is, you haven't got the clothes for the Judge's kind of company. If I'd thought that far ahead I'd have seen to it—and I *will* see to it. But when you do business with folks like these, you don't want to go against their notions of what's proper. So will you just play along . . . partner?"

Abe considered it. It wasn't like it ought to be. But it was no worse than playing the fool to get an edge on someone. As long as it was an open agreement between him and Offutt, which meant Abe Lincoln was nobody's man but his own . . .

Well: his own and Pap's, at least for one more year.

The business with Offutt distracted him so it wasn't till he approached the door of the Main House that he realized: *She* would be in there. In the same room with him. Face to face. Breathing the same air. *You ain't got the clothes for it.* No, and now he come to it he didn't have the schooling neither, nor anything else he ought to have. There was a rainbarrel near the door: he splashed icy water to clean his face and hands, dried himself on his pulled-out shirt-front.

She was seated at the head of a long plank table. Even sitting she held herself like a soldier. Her dark heavy hair was wound in two thick plaits about her head. She saw him at the door and her face brightened, she lifted and slightly opened her arms as if to embrace his presence. "Welcome, sir!" He remembered the low thrilling note

of that voice. "Please, do take a seat. We do not stand upon cere-
mony at Nashoba. I am Frances Wright. You are . . . ?"

He had to admit it was only "Lincoln, ma'am. Abe Lincoln.
Abraham, that is, ma'am, Abraham Lincoln." *And dang Abe Lincoln
for a fool!* His face burned.

"Well then Mister Lincoln," she said, his heart said *Mister Lincoln!* and she gestured where he was to sit: an unoccupied three-
legged stool next to a young woman. "Let me introduce you to Miss
Mariah Connors of New Orleans." The young woman looked up at
him and smiled friendly. She was peart, rosy in the face, and gave
him a nice straight look with her blue eyes. She gave him her hand
too, in a kind of "over the top" way, which was how they shook
hands in Orleans he reckoned, so he turned his hand under and give
hers a good little shake, and she chuckled, "Sir, good evening." She
held his hand longer than he expected and he felt a thrill run up his
arm. Her hand was warm, and small in his though not small for a
woman's, and he guessed her fingers had worked a needle: they
were wiry strong with flattened calloused tips.

Sitting down seemed to be the thing. He feinted at his chair with
his hind end, and when no one objected, sat down. The others all
had food on their plates, but he wasn't sure how they had got it
there. He snuck glances left and right. Miss Connors caught his
eye—"Help yourself, Mister Lincoln. There are no servants at table
in Nashoba."

"Ma'am," he told her from the heart, "I am much obliged." He
reached around and hauled his pig-sticker out of its sheath and was
about to set to when he noticed knife and fork set by his place. The
others were working their vittles with those implements. He wished
he might shrivel up and die. But it didn't happen. There was nothing for it but put the knife back and start over, so he did it. He set to
his food and regretted putting his own knife away: the fried pork
was gristled and stringy, the corn bread full of cob and grindstone
grit. Ma would have called it dodger.

"Mister Whitby said you were feeling poorly," said Denton
Offutt. "I hope it is nothing serious."

She gave a hard little laugh. "It is *merely* 'shaking ager.' The doctor says it is so common that were a household not visited, they

should feel snubbed." Abe had recognized the janders color of her cheeks.

Judge Davis said seriously, "Change of climate, ma'am. New settlements are often decimated until the settlers become *seasoned*, as we say. I've just come from visiting my youngest brother, Jefferson. He is posted to Minnesota Territory. I am not certain whether four years at West Point have thickened Jeff's blood against the northern chill."

"Well now, Judge," said Offutt, "and ma'am, if I might be so bold: I have been experimenting with an Elixir—with the able assistance of Mister Lincoln here, who is a su*perb* practical botanist—which I venture to think, ma'am, may alleviate the ager, and what you may call your seasoning disorders. Judge, if you'd like a bottle for your brother, I'd be happy to oblige."

Abe was grateful for the acknowledgment, which made up some for Offutt's treating him as "my man."

"Thank you, Mister Offutt," said Miss Wright, "perhaps tomorrow, when you join me for a tour of *our* little 'experiment.' "

Davis asked after the health of the enterprise. Miss Wright's brows came together: "Not altogether as I would wish."

"If I can advise . . . ?"

She beamed at Davis, took him up in those shining black eyes: "I have been counting on your generosity!" But then she lowered at Offutt. "But I must complain of you, sir!"

"I?" Offutt was shocked.

"Those people I purchased on your advice have given nothing but trouble. The woman Dilly in particular!"

Dilly? The feisty-looking woman that kept camp for the saltmakers. Sounded like she had wasted *her* chance to go to school to Frances Wright.

But Miss Wright suddenly paused: Offutt had gone red in the face, and looked horribly mortified, almost frightened—staring past her at Judge Davis. Davis sat rigid, his face gone hard: "I was not aware sir, when you introduced yourself, that you were a negro-trader."

Offutt swallowed. "Sir, I assure you I am not. Captain Donaldson, a friend, asked me to speak to Miss Wright . . ."

Miss Wright glanced from one to the other and said, "Bah!" Then to Davis, "You should know, Judge, I would never offend you in that way. Mister Offutt has done nothing for which a gentleman need apologize!"

Davis held rigid for a moment, then inclined his head. "Your pardon, ma'am . . . Mister Offutt."

"No offense taken," said Offutt, vastly relieved.

"I must say," said Frances Wright, "it is an aspect of American manners I do *not* understand. Why, in reason, is it so offensive to trade in negroes that the man who does is an outcast from polite society? When it is no dishonor, but the contrary, to own and use what the trader sells?"

Davis answered, a little heavily (it was hard to recover their light tone), "Well, every people has its customs. They may not be reasonable, but they run deep and are held dear. It isn't always wise, or safe, to go against them."

"Safe or not, they must be gone against if the race is to progress. One expects aristocratical pretensions of the English. But in this country there ought to be perfect freedom of intercourse between all reasonable persons." Miss Wright beamed and spread her arms to embrace her guests: "As we at this board exchange introductions, enjoy dinner and conversation," she smiled archly, "and *other pleasures*—without distinction of birth, or rank, or trade, or sex."

"Leaving only," said the Judge, "the distinction of color. Without which we Americans might, perhaps, be more inclined to make English distinctions among ourselves."

Frances Wright clapped her hands and laughed. "Your point, Judge—but we shall see tomorrow what may be done in the matter of color."

That night Abe rolled his blankets in the straw of the barn, and savored the luxurious prospect of another day at Nashoba. Just sharing supper with Miss Wright and the Judge had been as educational as a chapter of the *Orator*—"Dialogue Between a Philanthropist and a Slave-Master," let's say: Miss Wright arguing the slave should be educated for freedom and colonization, the Judge saying it couldn't be managed and even if it could, how would they

get the cotton picked? Of course, *you* had no more chance to put a
word in than if the two *were* printed in a book.

He closed his eyes and pretended Nashoba was a huge flatboat,
like the Great Raft of Cairo, in the morning they'd cut her loose and
sail off together, he'd be steersman, She'd come out of the cabin to
talk with him, to argufy and explain ... Abe fell asleep with the
memory of Miz Wright's throaty musical voice thrumming in his
brain, and of Mariah Connors's lively, friendly eyes shining at him
in the dark.

Nashoba looked worn and sloppy in the thin winter light when
Miss Wright showed them around the place. But her talk made you
look through it to the splendid success it ought to be, once the sys-
tematics were worked out. She talked wonderfully, mostly to the
Judge and Offutt, who squired her left and right. Abe walked
behind with Mariah Connors, daring to offer his arm to help her
jump a slash of muck-water, tickled when having once took she kept
it. She was frowning, though. Abe guessed she wished it was herself
arm-in-arm with Miss Wright, and he thought he knew how she felt.

They looked in at the Schoolhouse and Refectory, stood in the
work-shed and watched half a dozen glum-looking negro women
scraping dried kernels from a bushel of cobs. Miss Wright went on
arguing with the Judge as if the negroes were deaf and dumb: "Yes
yes, but the children, if taken from them when young, might be educated for a life among the white race. They have not been so
degraded as their parents ..." If the negro women heard her they
didn't let on. Abe didn't think there was a human being in the world
could keep countenance, overhearing such things said about them.
But I reckon negroes are used to it, he told himself, *reckon they ain't the
kind of people takes offense at such treatment.*

Miss Connors seemed to share his discomfort: she rolled her
eyes, as if the sight was a trial to her. "Lord but I am sick of her
negroes," she breathed, "when it is her own sex that most need
her efforts." Abe couldn't think what to say to that but "Yes ma'am."

They strolled down to the negro cabins—built as poorly as the
other houses, but no worse, which showed fairness. An old negro

woman was sitting on her front step with her arms crossed. She was small-made, wore a tattered linsey dress too thin for the weather. Abe recognized Aunt Dilly, and nearly said howdy. But when she saw them coming she went inside and shut her door. Miss Wright shrugged: "That is a specimen of our Dilly."

"I see," said Judge Davis.

Miss Wright paused before the cabins. "Slavery," she pronounced, "turns men into swine. I mean to reverse the process by educating their reasoning faculties." Over each cabin door was an odd ornament: a square block of painted wood which turned on a wooden spindle. There was a different color painted on each face of the block, black (facing outwards), red, yellow, and blue. "Ah," said Davis, "the Owen System."

"Bravo, Judge!" said Miss Wright. "Yes: the same that Robert Owen used with the Scottish weavers of New Lanark." The heat of excitement washed the sallow ager-color out of her cheeks. "The negroes are instructed how they should keep their quarters clean and healthful; how order their family government; given all needful education; assigned their tasks. The governors—myself, Mister Whitby, or who we shall appoint—observe, inspect, appraise their progress. The negroes are rewarded: a red chit, let us say, for a well-swept cabin or a good day's work with the hoe. When ten red chits are accumulated, they are presented to the governors, and . . ." She borrowed the Judge's walking-stick, reached up, and turned the wood-block on its spindle, so that the red face showed outwards. "Thus the individual's progress—or lack thereof—is apparent to all." She turned the block to its yellow face, and last the blue, and looked triumphantly at them.

The Judge was nodding. "Yes indeed. But you've not been successful applying it to your people."

"Not entirely." Her brow grooved with puzzlement. "I confess I was not prepared to be so stubbornly resisted. Despite our best efforts, it is Aunt Dilly who sets the tone for the people here." She reached up with the stick and turned the wooden block so its black side once again faced outwards, advertising to all the low condition of this household's achievement. She returned the stick to the Judge.

Davis looked pleased at the exchange. "The error, ma'am, is in how you apply your theory. You promise these people a future equality and freedom—and the effect is to make them unmanageable. *My* people understand from the first that their condition is permanent; but if they accept my governance—which I order upon the best principles I can discover—they can be comfortable in their station. So I propose an experiment: let me have your Dilly for a season at Hurricane. Reclaim her when you visit on your way to New Orleans. If you do not find her much improved," he grinned, "I will *consider* throwing over my system and adopting yours."

"Done!" said Miss Wright.

They were a *pair*, Abe thought admiringly. Other people *talk* about a problem, they go right *at* it. He wished he could think of a way to ask Miss Connors what she thought of the idea—he was so alive to the feel of her hand on his forearm it was like his skin was glowing. And she must have sensed his wish, because as they left the shed she said: "Science is wonderful, to be sure—but more pleasurable to the experimenter than to those experimented upon."

He hadn't considered the thing from that side. He turned it over in his mind: there was good sense in what she said. It reminded him: "My Ma has a saying: 'A chicken, a pig, and a man don't get the same good of a ham-and-egg breakfast.' "

Miss Connors played a musical scale with her laughter, "Your mother is a wise woman!" Her eyes touched his and flashed away, teasing friendly.

He was the happiest he'd been in ages to just be walking with Miss Connors like this, her hand as light as fire touching his arm. He wished he knew something to make her laugh some more, just that same way . . .

But Miss Wright called, "Mariah!" and she dropped him. And Offutt beckoned Abe—they had to make a start for Memphis: Judge Davis had a steamboat to catch.

Abe went to the barn to saddle their mounts. He was stirred up and disappointed. It didn't look like he'd get any more good of Frances Wright than old Dilly, though he'd have showed himself a sight more grateful for the chance. And he was sorry Miss Connors had run off like that.

As he slung his blanket-roll and Offutt's pack across the jackass's back the door creaked, and when Abe turned there was Mariah Connors standing hesitantly in the entry. "Mr. Lincoln?" she said. "Miss Wright asked if I would not fetch her some of that Elixir Mr. Offutt spoke of."

Abe was glad to see her again, and happy to oblige. He reached into the saddle-bags and pulled out the pint jug with a flourish. Mariah Connors stepped carefully through the hay and horse droppings. "We are very much obliged," she said, and held out a small bottle to be filled. She had the same lilting singsong to her voice as Frances Wright.

He carefully poured the bottle full. "I reckon you are English, same as Miz Wright?"

Her sweet-looking mouth went wry. She dropped the bottle into a small purse slung from her belt. "English yes—but not *just* the same as Miss Wright." She looked up with a kind of defiance. "And I have been American a good deal longer."

Abe was sorry to have poked a sore spot. "Well," he said, "I reckon you are well seasoned then"—then blushed, because he wasn't sure being seasoned was a proper compliment to a lady.

But Mariah Connors seemed to like it, for she laughed. "I *reckon* I am. Still, it would do no harm to take some as a preventative."

Abe scrounged a tin cup out of the saddlebag and poured her a little. "Jest wet your tongue at the first. She's got a bite to her."

Miss Connors blinked at the smell. Her pink tongue darted out to catch the Elixir at the lip of the cup. "Good heavens," she sang, "it tastes *awful* enough to cure *any*thing!"

The look of that little tongue made Abe's heart go bump, and nerves lit up all up and down the front of his body. He felt scared and happy both at once. To prolong the moment he asked, "Are you going to teach in the school here?"

"I!" she snapped. "I want nothing more to do with her interminable *negroes*! I own my shop in New Orleans, Mr. Lincoln." Her eyes suddenly flashed with tears. "At least, I *did*. I expect I will have lost my trade by the time I return. I am fairly ruined on *her* account!"

"Miz Wright?"

"Who else!" Then she noticed his hang-dog look and drew herself up. "No," she said, "that is unfair. Indeed, if I have any *self* to support, I owe it to her example. You cannot imagine what it is like to have educated oneself, to be skilled at a trade and earn one's bread by it, to have ambition—and yet be a *woman*." She glared at Abe. "To the *gentleman* and *lady* she is a tradesperson—they are offended if one makes formal introduction. And to the common lot she is a beast to keep house and breed with! I'd rather whore for money than be some man's slave by marriage!"

Common lot. Cold water in his face. What had he been thinking? But the remark stung. "Well ma'am," he said, "I don't know about the common lot. I know I value readin' in a woman. The best part of what I ever learned come to me by women."

Miss Connors came to herself with a jolt. The Elixir was volatile in her veins. She took hold of herself. "I'm sorry," she said, "that was a dreadful thing to say!" She touched his arm and looked in his eyes. "You'll pardon me?"

The look in her eyes was soft, earnest. He remembered how Judge Davis made apologies, and briefly bowed.

For a wonder, that seemed to make her *happy*. She beamed sunshine at him, and wet her tongue again with the Elixir, which brought up the color in her cheeks. "So you value reading in a woman?" She arched one eyebrow like there was a joke somewhere. "What sort do you most like?"

No one had ever asked him such a question. "Well, books are hard to come by. I've liked whatever I could get my hands on: Grimshaw's history, *Pilgrim's Progress, Arabian Nights*. But I can't ever get enough Shakespeare. There's only speakin'-pieces in the *Orator* and *Elocution*, and Mister Taylor—the man I worked for—he only lends me his Shakespeare book now and again."

"Well," said Mariah Connors, "you are rather an *unusual* backwoodsman."

Abe grinned: "Somethin' out of the *common*?"

"A touch, Mister Lincoln!" She dipped her head. "But if you

were a woman, you might understand. Even in America, when equality is thought of *woman* is never its object. The *negro* is thought of first. Yet see what Frances Wright has done! Then ask yourself: Cannot a woman learn as well as a man? Become as wise . . . ?"

Her words rang up an echo in his head, "Fed with the same food! hurt with the same weepons!".

Her eyes flashed at that, and she gave Abe a look that went to his spine and played the bones on it. "Well!" she cried. "You *are* an uncommon backwoodsman." She looked as proud of him as if he was her making. "But if a woman can do that, why should she not vote as a man? Why should she not have her will . . ."—she was all on fire inside, the words came blazing off her tongue—"and her *pleasure* too—that pleasure men are afraid even to *hear* of, let alone *learn*—just as a man does! Just as Frances Wright has done!"

No woman ever gave him such a look, no woman nor man either ever gave him so much argument—as if he was the man of all the world that had to be persuaded. "She is a *buster*, I reckon," he said enthusiastically—then blushed. It was so easy talking with this woman he forgot she was a lady from New Orleans. "*Beg* pardon, ma'am."

Mariah laughed. "No need. She is indeed a *buster*." Then her eyes turned, a look both wistful and aggrieved: "I see our modern *Circe* has charmed you. I have yet to meet the man, or woman for that matter, who *could* resist: provided they were open-minded enough to have ten minutes' conversation with her."

Abe could understand that. But for his money, Mariah Connors would do as well as Frances Wright. She might be as smart, was kinder and *considerably* easier to talk to. But he had no idea how to say such a thing.

Mariah Connors was feeling quite happy. Offutt's Elixir *was* invigorating: one's outlook brightened. "I have made up my mind! If I cannot maintain my millin'ry shop, I shall transform it into a book-shop. Classic authors, and the best of the moderns. My premises will be a home to the most enlightened thought of the age! And you must visit me when you get to New Orleans!" She fumbled him a card out of the purse looped to her wrist.

He looked at the card with her name and address written in

the most spidery elegant script. "Well," he said, overwhelmed. He imagined Miss Connors standing in her store, a gorgeous Shebazade in an Ali Baba cave jeweled with a hundred books. When he raised his face she saw that its crude features had been transfigured by something like joy—and blazed with a blush that gave the poor boy away *entirely*. She tilted her head and smiled at him: "Why Mr. Lincoln!"

Abe swallowed his Adam-apple to clear the way, but didn't have a word to say for himself. He was froze between the most awful wonderful exhilaration and the worst afraid he was ever in his life.

Mariah saw and didn't mind. Enjoyed it, actually—how easily she could disconcert and excite him, this boy, young man rather. The bitter bite of the Elixir, the slightly sick feeling it gave her at first, had lifted off. She actually felt quite . . . quite *healthy*, as if the tonic invigorated the blood rushing beneath her skin. Now this Abe was as rough a diamond as you could want, a gawky oversized boy whose shins and ankles had outgrown his worn dirty trousers. But then, he was an imposing physical specimen, toweringly tall, and the muscle in his forearm felt like corded steel, *heroic* proportions really . . . was clever, liked books, he had that natural unscripted courtesy one often found in American men. He *listened* to her: she was *full* of unused conversation—after those first ten minutes Miss Wright was not, in truth, a devoted listener.

And this *Abe* was looking at her now, a yearning intensity in his pale eyes it almost hurt to look at, like sun behind an overcast. The way men, and women too, looked at brave beautiful glorious Frances Wright. *Well and why should not I take my pleasure as she does?* "Well but a boy like you," she said softly, not talking to him as he was now but as he might be, *the most I ever learned come to me by women*, the Elixir making her dreamy. "Maybe I could teach you . . ."

There was a mischief in her voice that sent a cat's-tongue burr of excitement thrilling up the skin of his belly. His heart was banging. He was suddenly as pokey as a buck in rut and ashamed that she should see it. Her eyes were half-closed so he could not tell if she saw him or merely a fog of eyelash-flutter. Her long fingers touched the buttons that closed her blouse at the neck and she gave him a smile . . .

"Abe! You Abe!" Offutt calling from the yard.

She blinked. She glanced down at the cup of Elixir in her hand as if she had never seen it before—then thrust it back into his hand. She said, "My God!," gathered her skirts, and rushed out the door.

He was not sure himself if he was let down or let off.

Before he could figure out which, the voices outside began hallooing for *Mariah?* and *Abe?* He wanted to run after her, but recalled his dignity just in time. He packed the pint jug away, and made himself amble slowly out into the yard, leading the jackass. *Brother, this makes two of us.*

Miss Wright and her guests were gathered in front of the Main House to say their good-byes. Jordan led up the saddle horses. Miss Wright had lent mounts enough for all to ride, even Jordan. Offutt gave Abe a nod and patted the bulge in his weskit-pocket—Miss Wright had paid off for the woolens.

"Excuse me," Mariah Connors was saying, "but if you do not object, Miss Wright, I will take advantage of the Judge's protection to return to New Orleans."

Davis bowed. "It will be my pleasure to offer my protection, ma'am, as far as Hurricane."

Frances Wright's eyebrows rose in surprise. "Of course, Mariah," she said, "you best know how to manage your affairs. I will miss you greatly," she added wistfully.

As they spoke, Whitby brought Aunt Dilly forwards. A small crowd of negro women and children tailed after, but stopped a little distance from the white people. Miss Wright stood on the stoop of the Main House, looking down at the black woman. "Dilly." Frances Wright was sadly severe. "Dilly, you are to go with Judge Davis to his plantation in Mississippi."

A low moan ran through the crowd. Dilly's fice-dog eyes sharpened suddenly, her lean small muscle-knotted frame stood stiff. "Sold South," she said bitterly.

Frances Wright clapped her hands. *"Not at all!* Judge Davis has agreed to help in your education! You will find him as kind as he is just: but you will be sure to obey him."

The black woman stood her ground. She knew better than to talk sass. But if ever a body *looked* sass, Aunt Dilly did. Abe knew that look: it was Ma's look when Pap was scowling on her to do the thing *his* way or else.

That snapped him short: it was an ugly thing to see, even for a blink of the eye, the same face as Ma's on a little old nigger-woman. It was . . . it was *disrespectful*. He was mad at himself, he was even madder at Dilly for putting him in mind of Ma that way.

A child gave a small cry, and a woman said, "Hush chile: Awnt Dilly ben sont to de Breaker."

The sun was sinking into the woods across the river when they splashed through the mud of Main Street. They parted in front of the hotel. The Judge would put up there, Miss Connors too, and take the steamboat *Huntress* south next morning. While Offutt and the Judge were exchanging invitations to future hospitality Abe sidled next to Mariah Connors. He'd have liked to apologize, but didn't know what to be sorry for. "So long, ma'am," he said.

She gave him a puzzled, sad look. "Good-bye." She thought a moment, then added, "Abe?"

He made himself smile. "Abe it is. I wanted . . ." He had ransacked his memory of their talk for words he knew she liked: "It was a great *pleasure* to talk with—to be havin' sort of a 'conversation' that way? With you? I reckon you could teach anyone whatever you'd a mind to, and . . ." She looked startled again, *was he going too far?* "If you get that book-shop started, when we get to Orl'ns I will come buy a book first thing."

He had gone too far: tears sparked in the corners of her eyes. She smiled, kind of sickly, and said, "Thank you." Then she turned and vanished through the door of the hotel.

Abe looked after her. He couldn't make her out. He wished he could. She left a great big empty hole in the air behind when she disappeared.

There was another itch he couldn't scratch. Aunt Dilly stood in the mud, waiting for the Judge and his man Jordan to take and lock her in the jail for the night. Her feisty look put him so much in mind of Ma that he felt sorry for Dilly and mad at her at the same time. If she was, under the black skin and strange woolly hair, a woman anything at all like Ma, then she'd be full of grief and anger and hurt to be took afar off from her home and children and kin and all she loved—but would never let on, never give *them* the satisfaction, she'd go still inside and out so's to be *ready* for what come next.

But it *couldn't* be Ma and Dilly was the same, it would be too terrible if they were.

A notion came in his head. He reached into his saddle-bags and found the pint jug of Elixir. Offutt was still playing the gent with Judge Davis. He stepped up alongside Aunt Dilly and without looking at her gave her arm a poke with the jug. He felt the quick brush of a warm very dry hand as she took it, heard cloth rustle as she hid it. "It's yarb tonic," he muttered, "good for what ails you."

"Praise Jesus," she murmured quickly.

Gentry was glad to see them "at last!" but pizen mad all the same. Two days wasted. Plus he'd been seriously put out on Abe's account. "Donaldson's boat come in last night," he said as they pushed off. "That man Starkey? Quit Donaldson soon as they tied up. He was goin' to lay for you in town, only I told him we'd have him up for murder. So he took his part-pay and skedaddled." Gentry shook his finger at Abe. "He'll be layin' for you regardless. A man don't forget what *you* done to him. I thought better of you, Lincoln."

Chapter 14: **The Greatest Actor in the English-Speaking World**

Memphis to Helena, Late January–Early February 1829

The land fell away behind the levees. When they drifted close they could see the River was noticeably higher than the swampy cane and reed flats that stretched away into the distance. Towards evening they floated past a place where the levee was worn thin, the cottonwoods that lined its top had their toes in the water and some were leaning to wash their hair in the flood. Gentry said they needed to work further off. It was a timely notion, for not long after they saw a gap in the cottonwoods and felt a strong suck of current towards it. It was a levee break, luckily a shallow one, for even so they had to buck the sweeps hard to keep out of its draw. Abe guessed that was how those "bayou" monstrosities worked: if the River was high, and the bayou low enough, the draw would be bad as a chute. Throw you into the trees, break you, and leave you to rot.

Off beyond the Arkansaw levee they saw the shine of a broad open stretch of water. "That must be the Franzwah," said Offutt. As if to confirm his navigational guesswork they heard a flat *bang!*

across the reeds and cane to the southwest, not loud but marked against the silence all around. Abe said, "I reckon *Red Rover* has found some pirates to shoot at." Offutt hoped the gunboat wouldn't drive them this way.

They drifted along the delta of the François and L'Anguille Rivers—Arkansaw swamp shredding out into skeins of cottonwood and willow-covered islands and tow-heads. The winter evening was coming on fast. The channel ran quick among islands here, it was tricky, they ought to lay by, if they ran on a snag or sand-bar in the dark . . . but the idea of pirates made them shy of tying up.

Gentry sent Abe to stand in the bows and look sharp as they came among the islands. Offutt brought Abe the rifle, and took his own stand with musket at the ready. Gentry in the stern had the blunderbuss in case they were boarded.

"Starboard a mite—hold her," Abe called, and the flatboat eased into the quickening run between two islands. In the dusk Abe could not see much more than long rifle shot, but he could read the heavy current that marked the channel.

Offutt said, "Dang it, look there!"

Abe tore his eyes away from the water: he saw a thick drift of smoke above the trees on the Arkansaw side, a big fire burnt down to a heavy smolder. "Think it's the army?"

"No," said Offutt, "that cannon was a good way west of the river." Neither one said *Then it must be pirates*, but they cocked their pieces. "Gentry!" Offutt called, "I'd get that blunder-gun ready."

Abe's eyes held the water now with fierce intensity. The Old Man wouldn't forgive a mistake, not with this big current running, and if they hung up on a snag or struck a bar they'd be setting pigeons for whoever made that burning.

Long rifle shot ahead Abe saw a dark narrow shape marked against the dull sheen of the river. *Drift-log?* There was lots of floating timber. Then he saw it wasn't running downstream but holding in place—*a snag?* In the dim it was hard to tell. "Ease her la'board . . ." They were riding up fast on it, already within easy rifle-shot.

"Hey!" yelped Offutt. "Hey now!"

The snag was moving deliberately against the stream—and Abe

recognized in just the same breath that Offutt hollered, "It's a canoe full of them!" Offutt threw his musket up to his shoulder and took a bead on the lead paddler, if he shot him the canoe would go over, and in that current . . .

The flatboat was rushing down on the canoe, there were three of "them" in it, but if it was pirates they were too few for business. The middle figure was waving a long piece of cloth, beckoning with full-arm swings, pointing to the wooded shore to starboard. There was a break in the shoreline ahead where a side-channel sliced an island out of the woods. The heavy slow drift of smoke was coming from back in the trees where that channel looked to run.

The canoe was within musket-shot and closing when the bow paddler noticed Offutt leveling his piece on them. The man froze with his paddle cocked, and now Abe recognized the man as a negro, and that was a negro woman behind him streaming the unwound cloth of a turban.

The front paddler in a panic hacked into the chop to turn them away from the armed men in the flatboat, the canoe swung broadside to the current, the woman opened her mouth wide to scream, the man in the hind seat threw his paddle and grabbed the thwarts as the canoe broached and flipped bottom up as quick and nasty as if the Old Man had slapped a pot-lid over the screaming woman and the two men.

Abe set the loaded rifle on deck and jumped to the starboard side. The dark was shutting down overhead but the canoe showed sharp against the flash of water, and a black ball bobbing in the welter alongside, a head. Abe guessed it was the stern paddler, quick-thoughted enough to grab a-holt. The flatboat gained fast on the canoe, the difference in speed between a big boat in the push of the current and driftwood bobbing and ducking. Abe dropped down onto the timber curbing that ran around the outside of the flatboat. He crouched, took a hard left-hand grip of the cabin frame. They came up on the wreck at the pace of a trotting horse. Abe yelled, the black ball turned, was a face, white eyes in black skin. Abe reached out, the man in the water reached his free left hand while his right kept its hold on the canoe. They gripped, hands to wrists. Abe leaned back and pulled the man across the millrace to where the negro could get his elbows up on the timbers. His woolly head sparkled with water. Still hip deep in the river, he looked up at his rescuer—his eyes went wide but he was too breathless to speak.

Abe said very softly, "Well I'll be damned."

The half-drowned negro was Captain Donaldson's Sephus. For one deep breath he looked up at Abe, astonished but steady.

Then Sephus wrung his face up and let his body sag on the timbers. "God bless you, Mas' Abe," he blubbered, "God bless you savin' po' Sephus." Abe reached down and hauled him all the way out of the water. Offutt came over to help Abe. While Abe was saving Sephus, Offutt had managed to catch the canoe with a boathook, and hitch it to a thole-pin.

Sephus sprawled limply where they dropped him. He was soaked through and shaking—with fear maybe, which come on him after a delay, but it was chilly too. Abe ran below, hauled out his blankets, threw one over himself, and took the other for Sephus. He remembered the Elixir, tapped the bung for a cupful, and hurried back on deck.

Offutt and Gentry stood over the negro, who sat hunched by the fire-box. Abe threw the blanket over Sephus and gave him the cup of Elixir. Sephus was blessing and thanking them over and over, bursts of gratitude fired out of a storm of teeth-chattering and body-shakes. "All dem people," he moaned.

"Nothing we can do for 'em," said Offutt, "they drowned when the canoe went over."

"Damn it, boy!" snapped Gentry. "I asked what were you doin' on the river? Where in *hell* is your Master?"

Sephus looked up from under the cowl of Abe's blanket, a flash of white eyes. He began to shake again, his voice quavering, "*Dead* Mas' Gentry! Cap'n an' Penn *both* dead! Pirates come an' kilt 'em, oh lordy lord . . ."

The three white men exchanged looks.

Sephus sobbed, "You got to go back an' help 'em Mas' Gentry, you . . ."

"Damn it!" said Gentry. "We told you it ain't no use, the niggers are drowned!"

"Not dem, boss," said Sephus, "de people back on de flatboat." He threw the cowl off his head and looked pleadingly, eagerly into their faces. "It's why we come out—flatboat is burnt to cenders. People is lost on an islan', no food, some shot—water risin'. You got to go back!"

"Ain't no way we can go back," said Gentry, and Abe had to agree. There was no way they could drive the flatboat upstream against the whole weight and force of the River. Nor the skiff nor the canoe. *Poor Sephus.*

"Wait now," said Offutt. "You said pirates killed everyone."

"No suh, jes' white folks and Uncle Jack." He looked appealingly from face to face, Gentry, Offutt, Abe. "It was jest two snuck on board. Cap'n Don'lson asleep in de stern, Penn 'spose to be on guard, I reckon pirates jump him. Us men is all down below, only womens sleep on deck. Fust I knows a gun go off *blam*, I hear Cap'n say 'You's kilt me.' Jack an' me bust out." He stared off into the dark trying to see it all again. "Cap'n leanin' on his side, bleedin' out his mouf—a man by him, cut in his guts, reckon Cap'n got him. Other pirate is up on deck—Jack *goes* for him, he put his knife in Jack. Meantime I find Cap'n's pistol—shoot de man dead." He dropped his head and moaned, "I swear dat's how it happen."

Gentry said, "Damn!" and turned to stare into the dark woods that always floated backwards and away from them.

Abe was respectful: "So it was you killed the pirate." He remembered how Sephus took out his knife and let Kenton have a look at it. He had no show in Troy, but out on the River he had showed white.

But Gentry looked truculent: "It was white men you say?" As if he didn't believe Sephus could kill a white man, or wasn't pleased to hear he had. Offutt was skeptical too. He cocked an eye: "How'd the boat come to be burnt?"

Sephus looked up. "I 'spec somebody knock a lantern in de bedstraw. I's on deck, fixin' wounds. Done my best fo' Cap'n, but he was gone." He shook his head mournfully. "Time we smell smoke, burnin' got too strong a holt. So I beach her up a channel. Boat burnt right down." Sephus lifted sad eyes to Gentry's face. "Burnt up po' Cap'n, an' Mist' Penn, an' Jack. Never had no time to git 'em off."

Offutt, out of Sephus's sight line, jerked his head to pull them away for a private talk at the stern.

"What do you reckon . . . ?" said Gentry.

"It *could* have been pirates," said Offutt.

Gentry groused, "That Sephus is a smart nigger," like it was grounds to suspect him.

But suspect him of what? Selling Donaldson out to the pirates? How in blazes could he have done that, unless . . . ? Abe began, "You don't say he . . . ?"

The look the two men gave him set him back: they were angry and frightened. So it was as much to defend himself as Sephus that he said, "It ain't possible he done it. Donaldson was goin' to set him free . . ." But he stopped, he saw what was wrong with that line of thinking.

Offutt saw it too. He shook his head. "The good Captain meant Sephus to steer the boat and guard his people all the way to Natchez, then he'd sell him out. He was *always* cheating that boy— and everyone knew it."

Gentry mused, "You think *he* knew?"

"You said he was a smart nigger," said Offutt wryly. "He was a smarter *nigger* than Donaldson was a *Massa*."

Gentry glared over at Sephus, who sat hunched by the fire. "A nigger will lie for no reason, and this one's got reason. I'm goin' to get it out of him." And with Abe and Offutt following he stalked over to stand hulking over Sephus.

The negro looked up. His face wore a mournful look, but seemed settled, as if he was getting used to his loss.

Gentry kicked him in the side. Sephus grunted and cringed. It was a hateful thing to see. "Damn you lyin' to me," Gentry snapped. "You think you kin fool me, better think again." And he kicked him again.

"I ain't lyin' Mas' Gentry, it's de tru—"

"How did they get the jump on Penn, hey? How'd they get the jump on both white men at once?" He kicked Sephus again, the black man shot him a look of rage and hate—then closed his eyes, shook his head, and moaned, "I ain't gon' say one word mo', I ain't say one word ag'in my Cap'n." He looked appealingly from white face to white face. "I git *home*, say de same to Young Mas'r Don'lson: his daddy went down fightin'." He set his face stubborn, folded his arms: "Go on kick me again if you want, it's all I gon' say."

Offutt grabbed Gentry's arm. "Leave it. That's all the truth we'll get out of him." He pulled Gentry aside, Abe followed. Offutt looked closely into Gentry's face. "You know what it is he's *not* saying, don't you?"

"Dang it," said Gentry. "Donaldson was prob'ly drunk. Prob'ly got his throat cut sleepin'. And Penn . . ."

"There was women on board," said Offutt. "Sephus was below with the men. Only 'womens' on deck."

"Dang it!" said Gentry again. "I don't want to have to tell Donaldson's people . . ."

Abe caught on: "Neither does Sephus. When Donaldson was drunk, he always took care to keep the man from shaming himself."

They all three looked at the black man, sitting cowled and hunched by the fire, nursing his kicked ribs.

"What are we goin' to do with him?" Gentry said softly.

Offutt hushed them. "Leave it to morning. He can sleep on deck. We'll run all night, steersman can keep an eye on him. Keep the blunder-piece handy."

"He can keep my blanket," said Abe. "I got another."

Offutt and Gentry gave him a look. Gentry said, "You didn't aim to take it back, did you?"

They drifted through the night, putting distance between themselves and the pirates or whatever it was that murdered Donaldson and burnt his boat. Abe drew first watch for a change, and so got to sleep right through to morning. When he came out of the cabin Offutt and Gentry were sitting together in the stern. He heard Gentry say, ". . . long as we had the trouble and expense of savin' that nigger, might as well get some good of him."

Abe said "Morning," and they turned to look at him. "Morning," they said together.

Abe saw Sephus by the fire. He had built it up, set coffee on to boil, threaded chunks of bacon on wood spits for toasting, and was set to spoon corn-mush into a fry-pan for hoecake. Offutt pointed at him with pleasure: "All I ever did was tell him to set coffee on for breakfast." So Abe reckoned that was what Allen meant by getting some good of Sephus.

Sephus smiled over at them, bobbed his head, and called, "Mornin', Mas' Abe!" He was in pretty good spirits for someone that just seen his dear Master killed, and his own people killed or left to die, and almost been drowned himself and kicked to death the night before.

They made a little circle round the warm fire. The morning mist off the River closed them in as if they were in a quiet, somewhat drafty room. Sephus's hoecake was done just right, with bacon and coffee it was a much better breakfast than their usual mush and fatback. Sephus modestly waited to be told to help himself, then sat back a little way out of their circle to show he knew his place.

As the mist lifted Abe saw they were in a broad straight reach, coasting the edge of slack water along the Arkansaw side. Abe could see a good-size town ahead, steamboats and other craft clustered along its front. Offutt said, "We have to put in at Helena and tell the army about poor Donaldson. They'll send a boat up to bury the bodies, salvage what they can." His eyes flicked to Sephus. "If there's anyone alive, they'll take 'em off."

Sephus gave Offutt a quick close look, then dropped his eyes. He was setting himself to say something. When he raised up again he had a yearning smile on his face. "You gon' set me down wid 'em, suh? I kin guide 'em right *to* de place. Den dey send me home to Young Mas'r Don'lson . . ."

Offutt gave Sephus a cool look. "No need of that, Sephus. Army won't need a guide to find that boat."

Sephus looked watchful, but he still wore that yearning smile and his voice was sweetened. "So you give me a pass, I kin go back myself. I got a wife at home, boss—and children." He squinted like a man taking aim. "My ol' Mas'r, he'd trust me to git myself home."

Sephus was pushing. Abe expected the next answer would be

short. But Offutt opened up: "Can't give you a pass, Sephus. We don't have the right in law. We'll have to keep you with us down to Orleans, then bring you home with us." He smiled. "Go home in style, Sephus—deck passage on a steamboat."

That was a deal more answer than Sephus was entitled to. Sephus smelt something; kept smiling, but his eyes went dead. "Dat be fine, Mas' Offutt, fine jest fine jest fine." He kept nodding his head like he was agreeing with someone invisible who was argufying at him. Then his mouth wrung up, and the look he gave Offutt was desperate. "You gon' sell me down de River, ain't you boss. You gon' sell me out de Red River." His fear was plain and a little horrible to see. Abe thought Offutt would shut him up.

But instead Offutt spoke hearty. "Nothing of the kind, my boy! You aren't ours to sell, you see? But when we bring you back to Young Donaldson, I expect he'll pay our expenses, and something over for recovery. You just do your work, same as if we hired you from your Master. Tell you what: we might even pay you out some wages, if there's anything left after what it costs to feed you. Now *I* call that fair."

Sephus seemed to agree, for he suddenly started bobbing his head and smiling again, saying "All right Mas'r" and "Thank you Mas'r" and such, glancing quickly at Abe from moment to moment. Well, Abe had to allow it *was* fair, more'n fair considering they owed Donaldson nothing and Sephus less. If there was any botheration in it, it was just it's being that *little bit* more than fair, both the deal itself and the way Offutt set it out: as if Offutt had something to sell and needed to persuade Sephus to buy it—though Abe couldn't see what Sephus brought to the trade beyond the black skin over his bones, and that was more *lien* than *crop*.

As they drifted up to the landing at Helena Gentry sent Sephus below-deck. Offutt came up wearing his shore-going outfit for his talk with the army. Abe said, "Partner? What you told Sephus: is that *all* the good you mean to get of him?"

Offutt gave Abe a shrewd look and conceded. "Yes, it's the truth—far as it goes. Allen *was* for selling him, but we don't have the papers." He saw the look in Abe's eye and added, "Besides: you heard what Judge Davis thinks of nigger-traders. I'm not about to risk my standing as a gentleman. But we ought to get *something* for our trouble and expense."

"It was mostly *my* trouble and expense, I recollect: it was me went in the water for him, and my blanket he slept in."

"Now now," said Offutt, "we'd have given you your share."

Abe was disgusted. The two of them had *thought* of cheating him anyway—cheating Sephus too, if you thought about it. Every time negroes got into the story, you couldn't trust anybody. "Hang my share, I'd as soon be shut of the whole business. Why *not* let the army take him back?"

"What makes you think they wouldn't sell him quick as the next man? Army officers don't get such a windfall every day."

"Then give him a pass and send him home. Young Donaldson would know who sent him back, he'd pay our expenses anyway."

"He might or he might not. Listen, you know Donaldson was broke, and meant to sell Sephus. What makes you think his son would pay to get him back? And if he did, he'd just take and sell him again. And while you're worrying about Sephus's welfare, you might ask yourself if he really wants to guide the army to that wreck. No telling what they'd find. It might have been pirates, and again it might not."

Helena to Napoleon, Mid-February 1829

At first Sephus made things easier and more pleasant. An extra hand meant less work for everyone, shorter watches, more time to loaf and speculate. The negro went out of his way to be cheerful, you never had to tell him twice to do a thing. The eating improved considerable: hoecake with bacon instead of warmed-over mush with fatback, and he had the knack of catching big juicy catfish and frying them tasty in corn-meal and grease.

Sephus was a skilled riverman: you could trust him with the steering as well as the bow oar. So Offutt left off steering and pulling oar entirely and became more of a supercargo, taking inventory of their goods and speculating on the best way to trade 'em. Allen

Gentry—who had been so stingy with Abe over steering privileges—now left almost all the steering to Sephus and Abe, as if it was a no-account sort of work, and set himself to "navigate": leaning at his ease for'ard, letting on to be minding the channel.

Abe used to love taking his turn as steersman. It was a mark of how much he had learned of the River, a sign he had won admission to share-alike with two growed men—one the son of the second richest man in Pigeon Creek and captain of the vessel, the other an educated merchant gentleman. Sephus spoiled all that. He turned steering into nigger's work, something the quality didn't soil their hands with. And as for free and easy—

Before Sephus they all three slept in the cabin except when they floated at night and one stayed awake at the stern oar. But now, of course, Sephus had to sleep on deck. The idea of sleeping side by side in the small close cabin, and breathing unconscious the same air as a nigger all night long—it made their skin crawl. But if he was let loose on deck in the dark, what was to prevent him stealing the skiff or canoe and running off into the swamps? And there was worse chances: suppose it wasn't pirates killed poor Donaldson? They began to be more careful how they kept the guns and axes. Yet they couldn't bring themselves to tie Sephus at night. They weren't nigger-stealers or nigger-traders, they weren't jailers, and they resented that Sephus by his presence made them feel so. But then, he was so obliging and friendly it was hard to think as bad of him as, with due regard for safety, they knew they should.

So with this and with that it came out they couldn't all three of them sleep the night through ever again, but one must always be on watch whether they floated or laid by at night.

Instead of free and easy and share-alike, the flatboat had grown an invisible line which ran right through her, Sephus on one side, Offutt and Gentry on the other, and Abe a-straddle of the middle—sometimes doing grunt-work along with the negro, sometimes joining the quality to guard Sephus and keep him in his place. Offutt and Gentry seemed perfectly happy with the arrangement—why shouldn't they be, when Sephus made their lives easy and comfortable? But he had spoiled the voyage for Abe.

Sephus saw it, of course, and worked his wiles to win Abe over too. He smiled and called him *Mas' Abe*, worked past the end of his watch so Abe could sleep, tried to slip him the first best cut of fried catfish or spit-roasted duck before the others came to supper. It only made Abe dislike Sephus more, made him begin to hate him: hate in particular the smile that split Sephus's face, smile when he spoilt Abe's joy in steering the River, smile when he ducked and bowed and *Mas'-Abe'd* him when it was plain to everyone on board that Abe was just hired hand to *Cap'n Gentry* and *Mas' Offutt*.

Sephus found him off-watch for'ard, sitting with the canoe between him and the rest. "Mas' Abe?" (Smile. Duck the head.) "Mas' Abe, how you like a piece o' dis nice . . ."

Abe had enough. He rounded and glared at the black man. "Don't want your fish, and I'm sick of your damn smile. If you think you can make fun of *me* and get away with it . . ."

Sephus's grin got sick, but didn't quite die. "I ain't makin' fun o' you, Mas' Abe."

Abe spoke in a tense harsh whisper so the others wouldn't hear: "I ain't your *Massa*! I ain't *nothin'* to you! Call me *Abe* or call me *Lincoln*, call me *Mister* if you want, but if you call me *Massa Abe* one more time I will throw you *back* in that river!" *And now the son of a bitch is going to cringe and hunch and give me that grin and I swear I will throw him . . .*

But Sephus regarded Abe calmly, his eyes considering. "I ain't makin' fun," he said, and Abe noticed the difference in his tone and language. "We are South and goin' South-er. If I call you *Abe* down here, it mean *you* ain't *white*, or else *I* is a dead nigga." He nodded, seeing Abe understood. "You save my life, and I owe you for it. So I call you any way you like."

"Mister Lincoln," said Abe.

"Mist' Lincoln it is," said Sephus. Then with a look: "Or Mist' *Abe*, if it won't rile you." He grinned. "And I won't smile on you no more'n I kin help."

Without thinking Abe put out his hand. Sephus looked at it. Then gave it a quick shake with his big dry sandy-palmed hand, turned, and went to call the men to supper.

Abe was embarrassed. It was thoughtless to shake hands like that. If the others seen him, they'd give him the laugh.

.   .   .

About a week south of Helena they rounded a bend and saw a big twin-stack sidewheeler aground in the shallows, standing like a derelict castle in its moat. It was *Cleopatra*—run hard on a sand-bar. Gentry told Sephus to ease the flatboat over so they could pass close and give the steamer a going-over. But before they could compliment the Cleopatras on their choice of bottom-land, an officer in a blue uniform hallooed them through a speaking trumpet. "Ahoy the boat! Will you come alongside please? We shall make it worth your while!"

Offutt perked up and Gentry steered them to *Cleopatra*'s side. A hand tossed them a line and Abe threw a hitch round a starboard thole. The Mate of *Cleopatra* hopped gingerly across. "Captain," he said to Gentry, "I mean to ask a favor, and I'm willing to pay for it— any price in reason."

Gentry wouldn't say *yes* or *no*, he was enjoying the fact of a high and mighty steamboat officer in blue coat and silver-badge cap begging favors of a humble flatboat skipper. The Mate took breath: "We've had the worst trip I ever heard of. Held up three days at Memphis for the army, six more at Helena with a ruptured steampipe, now two on this reef."

Gentry give him a sweet innocent look. "I wonder how you come to pick this *particular* one?"

The Mate swallowed that. "It wasn't entirely our fault. We have a passenger, a famous man—the actor Jun'us Booth in fact. He took a notion our Captain was a tetch bilious."

Offutt clucked, "Poor man, was he indeed?"

The Mate turned red. "I can't say—I ain't no goddamn sawbones. What I'm getting at is that Mister Booth, he's a man will take liquor regardless. And when he's in liquor he's the devil. He took it on himself to physic the Captain. In the pilot-house! When the Captain told him to get himself below-deck he whips a horse-pistol out of his belt and claps it under the Captain's chin: *'Drink and be healed or by all that's holy I'll send your soul to a better world!'* " He paused: his hearers were impressed. "We were just entering the bend. The pilot jumped out the window and broke his arm. The boat ran herself aground."

"Where were you while this was goin' on?"

The Mate spat over the side. "Off watch. If 't was me I'd let him blow a hole in the old bastard before I'd see my boat wrecked." His eyes blazed. "I come running in my unmentionables soon as I felt her strike and run up. Time I got there the Captain had physic running out his nose and was begging Booth not to physic him to death nor shoot him neither. So I lammed the son of a bitch with a wrench and laid him out."

"Which son of a bitch was that?" Offutt inquired mildly.

"Booth," said the Mate in all seriousness. "We've got him locked up. By rights the man ought to be hung for interfering with the officers and wrecking the boat. But the truth of it is, he's kind of a sweet and sorrowful gent now he ain't drunk. And he's Jun'us Brutus Goddamn *Booth*! My owners won't like it if he was to get hung on their account."

Offutt nodded sagely. "And your underwriters would have some peculiar questions if this business came out."

"That's it," said the Mate. "I see you are a man of some understanding. I'll make you a straight proposition: you take Mister Booth and his associate off our hands and drop them in Napoleon. The rest of his people can join him there in a day or two. There should be another boat downriver tomorrow or next day—they'll haul us off or else take the rest of the passengers down to Napoleon. The officers of the boat will pay you twenty-five dollars, gold and silver, to take them."

"Make it thirty," said Offutt, and the three of them—Offutt, Gentry, and the Mate—clapped hands together to seal it. It seemed to Abe his luck was turning: here was a second chance to meet Junius Brutus Booth.

The two men who hustled across the gangplank had cloaks about their heads like fugitives. One was the man who had shilled for Booth's street performance in Memphis: "Flinn's my name, Tom Flinn. I am Mister Booth's Feedus Ackayties," which none of them understood but was danged if they'd let on. Booth himself, small frail and greenish, dropped by the fire-box and stared vacantly into space.

"I've seen jimjams afore," said Gentry, "but that is one of the worst cases I ever see."

The crew tumbled a pair of leather trunks on the deck of the flatboat. Abe and Sephus tied them down while Flinn talked things over with Offutt and Gentry. "He won't be any trouble now," said Flinn appealingly. "He's a lamb when liquor ain't in question. I make myself responsible for him."

"He ain't got that pistol," said Gentry. "I won't have him armed."

"Secured," said Flinn, spreading his coat to show two silver-mounted dueling pistols stuck in his sash. "Gentlemen, I would not have you think badly of my friend for all the world. When he is at home he is the gentlest soul imaginable. Why, he will eat none but vegetable food; won't suffer a creature to be killed for his sake, not even a musqueeto." He glanced at the slumped tragedian. "Indeed, on that subject he can be quite ... quite passionate I'm afraid."

The idea of never eating no meat, and not having critters harmed on his account, struck Abe as interesting. Was there any good in it? And how far was it practical? He glanced over at Booth, then murmured, "What about them boots, I wonder?"

Flinn was distracted, "What say? Boots?" He too looked at Booth. A look of anxiety came into his face. "Boots indeed—leather of course. It never occurred to me ..." He glanced at Abe. "Nor to him, I don't think. I'd take it kindly if you wouldn't call it to his attention."

Gentry gave Offutt a look that asked what he had got them into now. Abe's eyebrows lifted all by themselves as he took Flinn's meaning. "Glad to oblige," he said. He heard Offutt tell Gentry, "It's not much more than a day to Napoleon, and that's thirty dollars specie you got there."

They cast off and drifted away from *Cleopatra*. Passengers and crew lined the ornamental railings to see them off. Abe got next to Offutt and asked him did he know what day it was?

"Well into February, I guess. Might be the tenth or so. Why d'you ask?"

"No reason," said Abe. It was his birthday, or near enough. Don't it signify if particular good luck come on such a day? Ain't it nearly providence?

Ordinarily they'd have left Sephus to tend the guests, but Abe wanted to get next to the Shakespeare actor any way he could. He couldn't say, even to himself, just what he expected. Booth was a man who had absorbed all that Shakespeare, took all the best of words and speaking into himself, so that he *was* those books turned into the flesh and bones of a living man. He was like a magic lamp—rub him and who knew what genie might pop out, and grant you wishes if you had the brains to ask the right things.

So he fetched food and drink, rigged the lean-to to shelter them. Booth sat up but remained silent and pale. Flinn sat by him and said something heartening. The little man didn't answer, only reached out and took Flinn's hand in both his, and sat there with him. Now and then a tear would gather, ripen, and run down his cheek. Once he looked up at Flinn, very sad and solemn: "We know what we are, Flinn, but not what we may be." Then for an hour, nothing.

Abe only had a day to get the good of the Great Junius Booth. He needed to get him started. "Say Mister Feedus," he said, "we got some Elixir on board, I bet it'd set Mister Booth to rights in a flash." It was no lie: whatever the Elixir did was generally done in a flash. He assured Flinn there wasn't any but vegetable matter in it.

Abe fetched up a cupful, and Booth took a tentative sip. It made him sit up like a man wakened with a pail of ice-water. Then he dropped his head back opened his jaws and threw the whole cupful down his throat in one swallow.

Abe blinked at the sight, afraid the dose might blow out the back of Booth's head. He ought to warned him to take it a sip at a time, only he'd never seen anyone who could stand to take it faster. Booth looked about fiercely. "Flinn!" he snapped. "If I am not mistaken, the flesh of slain creatures is secreted aboard this vessel!"

Flinn looked desperate. Then he hissed, "Say nothing of it, my lord! We are in *cognitto* here. I would not have the sailors see through these our habits."

Booth looked down and studied the clothes he was wearing as if he was surprised to see them. Then he tipped Flinn a wink, and turned to Abe with a great hail-fellow grin on his face. "Much thanks, good sir, for this assistance." With that he rose to his feet and walked briskly over to palaver with Gentry and Offutt. Abe tagged along, hoping to get Booth to act them a piece—but his luck was out. Booth talked nothing but fertilizer and hog prices, as if he never read anything but the *Farmers' Almanac*. Abe was disgusted, but Gentry was pleased. "If you hadn't told me he was a high-toned Shakespeare actor I'd never knowed it. No airs about him, and he knows a thing or two about *soil*."

They tied up for the night and Sephus made ready for supper, Booth still downright hearty, Flinn pleased to see his friend set up again. Whatever the cognitto was, it was doing the trick. Only, when Booth out the corner of his eye caught Sephus moving around, he became uneasy. Sephus was making a certain amount of fuss over serving for company, smiling most agreeably to show the hospitality of the boat. It made Gentry more than a bit proud to have a servant at such a time.

Then, in the middle of talk about the price of corn in Natchez, Booth broke in, "Is it your slave?" His smile had gone dead and there was a shine of sweat on his brow.

Gentry looked at Offutt. Then he said, "Well no, not mine. We're out of Indiana, where it ain't allowed. Sephus belongs to a neighbor from Kentuck. He's hired for wages."

True and not true, Abe thought, but it took some of the edge off Booth's manner.

"I do not oppose the institution," said Booth. "I cannot conceive any other relation of the races, if they must be in contact. But I will not have one in possession, no. To work *in*, yes, but not to be *of* my household—*decidedly* not." He began brushing at his clothes, as if they were full of dust.

Sephus served Booth first, a dollop of succotash made of dried corn and beans. Booth looked suspiciously at the vittles, glancing rapidly from the plate to Sephus and back.

Sephus said, "No meat, suh, not a speck."

Booth's head drew back as if there was something repellent in Sephus's being mindful of him. "Why should you say that to me I wonder?" he said in quiet alarm.

Flinn said, "I spoke to the boy on our account."

Booth watched Sephus intently as the black man went off to eat by himself. "This King of Smiles," Booth murmured. "I have set it down: that one may smile, and smile, and be a villain."

Abe thought that was shrewd—Sephus the King of Smiles. Booth had put a name to the thing about Sephus that made Abe most uneasy. The negro slave is our King of Smiles. See? already he'd got some good of having Booth on board. He remembered the actor Richard-Thirding up and down the streets of Memphis, *I can smile and murder whiles I smile, / And cry, 'Content,' to that which grieves my heart . . .* King of Smiles again, except with King Richard it was *murder* back of those smiles, where Sephus was only a . . .

Unless Sephus was lying about those pirates.

Chapter 15: **The Crossroads**

Napoleon, Arkansaw, February 1829

The two biggest rivers in Arkansaw are the Arkansaw that rises
in the Rocky Mountains far to the west, and the White that drains
the country north to Missouri. Both come down to the Mississippi
through a broad belt of drowned forest that covers most of the east-
ern half of the state. Twenty or so miles west of the River they ooze
almost into each other, but hold their own current and pour into the
Mississippi by separate mouths. Between the mouths is a sandy
bulge of land, built up by deposits the same way as the natural levees along the River. And on that bulge sat Napoleon.

Napoleon was a buster of a town. The waterfront was jammed
with downriver flatboats and keels bound for the north and west. A
steamer with her fires banked was loading passengers, another
gathering way in the River. Front Street boasted a little brick courthouse with a bell-cupola, a two-story yellow-painted clapboard
hotel, and a straggle of one-story stores workshops and whiskey-
parlors trailing off south towards the Arkansaw. At the south end

was a house that looked like it had been chopped in half with an ax. The broken side opened on a mud-flat carpeted with a drift of sodden house-trash—shakes, timbers, dead cats, snakes of cloth, busted crockery shells, rusted kettles. A recent spate of the Arkansaw had swashed off the southern third of the town. But what was left was booming and bustling.

Gentry conned the flatboat to a landing near a trio of keelboats. Banners swung between their masts advertised ARKANSAW RIVER FUR COMP'Y. Rough-looking men lounged on the boats or stood around the landing: some bearded to the eyes, some clean-shaved but with long hair to their shoulders, some with Injun braids. They wore loud plaid shirts or fancy hunting-shirts fringed and beaded. Most were carrying cleaning or otherwise fussing over long lean Kentucky or Hawken rifles. Three men in town suits and stovepipe hats sat at tables on the landing signing men up on long sheets of paper.

Abe threw a rope hitch round a piling and snubbed her to with a creaking and whining of the hemp. Offutt leaped ashore and scurried over to the keelboats to find out what was afoot. Gentry hollered for Abe and Sephus to lend a hand with the gentlemen's goods. Booth and Flinn were shaking hands with Gentry to thank him. "Perhaps you'd lend us your boy to help with the baggage?"

Gentry sulled. "I don't like to let the boy out o' the boat by hisself."

Sephus let on to be deaf. Flinn nodded understandingly, some niggers would take any chance to run. Abe said, "I'll go along and see he gets back."

"Well that's white of you," said Flinn. "Of course, we'll give you something for your trouble."

Flinn stepped ashore, turned to hand Booth down. The actor's face brightened as he looked alertly around. "Ah good," he said, "what time is the performance?"

Flinn, standing like a statue with hand extended said, "No performance in this town, I'm afraid."

Booth stopped as if struck by a blow. The color left his face and his lips went pale. "My God," he said softly. His limbs went loose, he stumbled, nearly fell into Flinn's arms.

Sephus passed the trunks down to Abe, then hopped ashore himself. Abe swung Booth's trunk up and balanced it on his shoulder, Sephus did the same with Flinn's. Offutt came bustling back to the flatboat. He jerked a thumb towards the keelboats: "They're bound to the mountains to trap furs. Signing up boatmen, hunters, whoever they can get." He rubbed his hands together. "We will lay over a day or two. I never saw such a good spot for the Elixir."

The big hotel was full up, as were the two rooming houses on the waterfront. Back of Front Street were other rooming houses and whiskey-shacks, mostly double cabins built of cypress logs. Women sat in front of these, and a brisk trade of rivermen and hunting-shirts went in and out. Napoleon was a buster of a town all right. If Abe was any judge, every third resident was a whore and every other house a whiskey-mill. He had a notion of women now, after talking with Mariah Connors. A notion, and if truth be told a hankering as well. *A man don't know a woman's pleasure? Well I don't even rightly know a* man's *pleasure yet. But I got an itch to find out.*

Booth perked up himself, sluffed his tired shamble for a grenadier strut. The women gave *him* a look.

All sorts of women: blond girls with baby-fat in their cheeks and muddy bare feet, tall rangy women in ragged calico with straight brows and deer-hunter's eyes, Injun women with black hair cut in level bangs, coal-black women with slick features like water-smoothed pebbles, and strange ivory fawn and honey-colored women whose every feature—dark eyes with no pupil, bee-stung lips, pigeon-breasts, delicate fingers—was rounded and soft and full. Quadroons they called them, yaller gals, mulattos, *Ain't a man till you've . . .*

There was a rooming house on the southwestern edge of town. Flinn and Booth went in to dicker for a room. Abe and Sephus stayed outside to guard the trunks. There was a high-water line five feet up the side of the building, and she smelt of damp and mildew. They heard Flinn tell his name, but not Booth's, and sign them in.

A tall man in a wide-brimmed hat with a turkey-cock feather stepped out of the double-cabin across the way. It was right smart of a hat, and his hunting-shirt was slathered with fancy beadwork and belted with a red sash, pistol, knife, and tomahawk stuck in it. Abe noticed the man wore good knee-high boots and wool trousers. He picked his way through the mud towards the rooming house. Behind him a red-haired woman in a black dress stepped into the open door, put her back against the frame, lifted and set her right foot against the opposite side, and hiked her skirt up to show her calf—then (when she saw Abe staring) her thigh.

Flinn came out and tapped Abe on the shoulder. "Our thanks, sir. Mr. Booth and I will board here until the rest of our company arrives. We will not need your services further." He put a silver dollar into Abe's hand, nodded, and disappeared inside. A little negro boy came out after him, grabbed the handle of Booth's trunk, and dragged it complaining across the boards into the house.

Meanwhile the tall man in the big hat had come up to the rooming-house porch, stopped, and stood looking Abe and Sephus up and down. "Paid off are you?" he said. "If you're lookin' for work, I've got an offer you'd be crazy to turn down." He stuck his hand out and Abe shook it. "I'm Fitzgerald, call me 'Big Hat,' Arkansaw River Fur. You boys must've seen us signin' recruits by the River. We want watermen to pole us up the Arkansaw, close to the mountains as we can get. Then we'll want men to build the post. We'll pay . . . say what was you boys gettin' for wages?"

"We ain't interested," said Abe. "Already hired on a flatboat for N'Orlins."

"What can they pay, ten a month and found?"

Actually, it was six a month—not counting Abe's share of his partnership with Offutt.

Fitzgerald clapped his hands. "I'll go twelve," he said, then when he saw Abe wasn't interested, "make it thirteen, fifteen if you stay to build the fort." Abe shook him off.

Fitzgerald took off his Big Hat and wiped his brow. "You drive a shrewd bargain, friend. But I like that: it shows you got sense. Besides, what's a young man like yourself want with sittin' 'round some pokey old garrison out in the Great American Desert? What you want is adventure, excitement—and a chance to make more'n *wages*. So I won't beat the bresh and try to get 'round you, I'll make you the best offer I got. Fifteen a month to pole us up to the fort. That should cover the cost of your outfit and somethin' over, or if it don't why the Comp'ny will lay it out for you on credit."

"What kind of outfit?" said Abe, caught by curiosity.

"Why a *trappin'* outfit, what else would I be talkin' about? I'm the Arkansaw River *Fur* Company, or a piece of her, ain't I? We got 'most ever'thing we need: trade goods, presses for the pelts, burgeways to sell all we ship. What we need is boatmen to get us upriver—and trappers to bring in the fur. I won't lie to you: trappers ain't easy found, most of the old mountain men signed with Ashley and the Rocky Mountain Fur to work the north end of the range." He gave Abe a wink. "Our hard luck, but you get the good of it. If you sign, we'll outfit you for the mountains: traps, rifles if you ain't got your own, blankets kettles and buffler skins to see you through winter, it gets godawmighty *cold* up them mountains. Horses and a jackass mule to haul it with—throw in a gallon or two of whiskey and another of trade beads so you kin make friends with the Injuns." He gave Abe a close look. "No offense, friend, but I don't reckon you could get that much credit for any other speculation you might have in mind." Then a thought occurred to him and he added, "They's friendly Injuns, mostly, in the mountains we aim to work. They don't know Americans—yet."

"We ain't interested," said Abe.

Fitzgerald shook him off, "Naw naw, you ain't thinkin' straight. But you ain't seen the mountains, so I don't blame you. You'll see 'em, though," he said. Abe shook his head *No*, but Fitzgerald held his sleeve. His mouth had run away with him, his eyes were hazed like he was looking through Abe instead of at him: "You'll see 'em: a ghost line on the edge of the flat world at the first, but ever' day closer, and one day there they are—like a wall right up to the sky, snow shinin' on the top-spikes. And next you're among 'em, the walls close 'round—and then my boy, then you are on your own: take what you please and leave the rest." His eyes gleamed. "The Shinin' Mountains," he said. "They call 'em Rockies, but that's to scare off the tenderfeet. Shinin' Mountains, that's what we call 'em that knows 'em. Air is light and clean in the lungs, sage and balsam pine, a man feels like he's floatin' when he walks. Water clear and clean as glass, cold as snow. Ever'thing bright sharp clear to see. No women sez you? Well, not too dang many, I'll admit. But if you want 'em, there's women there." He looked round him, a little dazed, and scratched his crotch. "Not like these-here," he said. "You want mountain-Injun women: they're clean and tall, takes their pleasure and let a man take his. And when you want shet of 'em—why you jest up and ride away!"

Big Hat paused and looked Sephus speculatively up and down. "Your boy here, he'll be worth plenty to you in the mountains. Injuns think the black skin is big medicine. He'll be like a bull in a herd of heifers. You won't do so bad yourself, as high off your moccasins as you are."

Those words fanned Abe's hankering like breath on coals. But there was no way he could leave the flatboat in the lurch, Ma and Pap counting on him to come back, to go floating off into the Shining Mountains. And if he ran off with Sephus that would be niggerstealing. "*He* ain't mine," Abe told Big Hat.

"Free nigger then?" said Big Hat to Sephus. "Well good on you. Then you can keep your share, buy you a wife when you get back— or trade yourself a squaw and stay in the mountains. Hell if I was black, Gawd forbid, that's what I'd do."

"Ain't free," said Sephus.

"Ain't interested," said Abe, "and we are obliged to get back." Abe give Sephus a little push to start him.

"Ain't interested?" said Fitzgerald incredulously. "Well I took you for a man of more brains than that. More 'magination." His voice rose to follow them: "It's all new country! Valleys big as Kentuck and twice as purty, and they ain't been discovered yet! You could be first on the ground, like it was C'lumbus discovered America—only *you'd* keep dark about it, wouldn't you? So's to have it *all* to yourself, or the best of it anyways." He raised his voice to call after them: "You could make a *fortune* in beaver. We'll pay cash money! Specie, by God!"

As they walked away between the cabins a long-faced woman

with straggly brown hair stuck her head out a window and called, "You, the white boy! Do you for a dollar!" and as they kept on, "Do you for six bits!"

"You got a dollar," Sephus reminded him.

Too bad it was only the one. He had to bank it against New Orleans, and Mariah Connors.

Gentry rigged an awning off the flatboat, and they sat beside their Elixir kegs, selling doses by the spoon the cup and the flask. Offutt in his yellow suit paraded up and down, singing her praises: "Friends, this is the Genuine Chinese Gin *Sang*! Double-tried double-dyed and double-rectified! A certain specific against what ails a man, be it the scrofula, the cholera morbus, the measles, the ee-ri-sifilous, the shaking ager, the dumb ager, the chills ager, or the four-week ager." Then in a confidential whisper, "She'll wipe the venereals out of a man as sweet and thurra as an oiled rag will clean the bore of a rifle. Gentlemen!" cried Offutt. "I do not sell this potation to *ladies*! It is a masculine pejorative *exclusively*. I *dare* not sell it to a woman—on account of its *erotageous* propensities." Eyebrows up. Eyebrows down. "My friend, she will stand a man's pecker up like it was President of the United States on the Fourth of July. And *keep* him standing, and saluting too, through frolic and fireworks regardless."

With evening coming one keg was about empty, and they had made fifty dollars. They concluded to close shop for the night. Gentry had taken the day to enjoy the pleasures of the town, so he agreed to stand watch. Sephus had no choice but stay aboard. Abe meant to spend his dollar, now he had two more to put with it (an advance on his share of the Elixir money). If there was a Booth performance he might have spent it on that. It was still more or less his birthday. What else did he hanker for that a dollar could buy?

He walked up Front Street with Offutt, who looked the women up and down and smiled and tipped his hat. The women in the Front Street houses had rouge on their cheeks and a smell like honeysuckle, all the different kinds there was, long and rangy, short and plump, white brown black gold. He had an itch, he had a hankering, but it was too big, it rustled up his insides so that he couldn't settle his eyes on one face, one body. If he did choose one, what would he say? How would he ask when he had no idea what to ask for? *Evenin' ma'am my name is Abe Lincoln I have got a dollar here would you please, that is if it ain't too much to ask . . .*

"My boy," said Offutt, "don't take this unkindly, but—am I wrong in thinking you are as yet *unknown* of woman?"

Abe could see it was kindly meant, but he was a little embarrassed.

"Just so," said Offutt. "And from your purposeful look, I surmise you mean to repair the gap in your knowledge?"

"I reckon," said Abe, only half-committed.

"But you have scruples! The harlot has a bad name among Christians. But consider it in the light of science: it is called the world's oldest profession; it has stood the test of time. Take it as it is, and what is it?" Offutt waved a hand at a saloon, in whose porch stood four women, like horses to be looked at for a swap. "A humane and reasonable institution. The man takes his pleasure, the woman her wage, and perhaps some pleasure as well. They go their ways, well satisfied. I wish all business could be conducted on such a basis."

That sounded fair. Abe remembered that even Mariah Connors said she'd rather whore for money than be some man's married slave. He began to think a little better of himself for wanting to try it.

Offutt beamed. "Then let me advise you, as if I was your . . . uncle, let's say. You may like the notion of a girl your own age." He nodded toward a threesome of such on the porch of a rooming house. "The young are frisky, but not all that sympathetic; haven't learned the value of a gentle manner."

They passed a bright door inside which they heard fiddle playing. The women who lounged by the door were bare to the cleavage of their breasts, black hair piled in thunderheads or draped in serpent-loops framed their soft oval faces, their naked skin glowed amber or acorn-brown in the door-light. "Colored women now, they will cut loose the *dog* in a man. Yellow gals especially—if they are *cat* enough to purr and white enough to fool you. But you want to know your way through the woods before you go howling at the moon."

They were at the end of Front Street now, the end the Arkansaw River had bit off. There was a small frame house nailed up alongside the wreck, a woman standing in its doorway. She was tall and rangy, she had straight brows and deer-hunter eyes that drooped at the corners. She wasn't young—not old, but she wasn't young. Offutt said, "What you want is a grown woman. Maybe she's gone whoring to pay her way till she finds a man to settle with. Not a bad speculation, seeing there aren't women enough in the western country. Or a widow woman that needs to get by—and *is* getting by, so she isn't grudgeful. A woman like that? Likely she's clean and *careful*, you know? With a boy that's new to it, and means no harm? Woman like that will teach you something for your dollar, like a . . . like an aunt, sort of." He laughed. "If you got that kind of aunts."

But Offutt's advice put a chill on Abe's hankering. Whether it was the horse-trade dollars and cents of it, or the idea of whores that used to be someone's aunt or mother teaching him where to gore his horn and how to gouge it—or maybe just the look of the tall woman standing by her broke-down shanty waiting to see if one of them was going to ask her to lie down and spread her legs for a dollar poke—what would Ma think of his doing such a thing, and Sary, and Mam?

But Sary and Mam don't think anything anymore.

"I reckon not," Abe said. "I ain't got the inclination jest now." Offutt looked disappointed, then amused.

Abe walked back along the waterfront. The whiskey-mills were running full bore. Drunks sprawled in the street, having lost the use of their legs or fallen asleep. The street was wet enough that a man face down could drown himself. A man in a cape was stooping to turn a drunk on his back. The light from a doorway struck his face: Feedus Flinn.

"Mr. Flinn?" said Abe. The man's hair was wild, he had a black eye, he looked frantic. "Jesus Mary!" said Flinn eagerly, then blinked to clear his eyes of light-blind: "It's . . . Abrams, isn't it? From the flatboat?"

Abe started to say his right name, but Flinn grabbed his shirt.

"Listen," he said, "you've got to help me find Booth. He's on a bender and liable to get himself killed, lecturing these river toughs on the vegetable diet or . . . I can't find him by myself, there's more shebeens and whore-houses here than fleas on a dog!"

It seemed Abe was going to get another crack at the man of Shakespeare. "All right," he said, "I'll look into the ones next street back."

"If you find him, stay with him and watch out as best you can. If you aren't back here when I finish the waterfront, I'll come look for you."

The fourth whiskey-mill was the one: a low room yellow with tallow light. Junius Brutus Booth was seated at a round table in the middle of the room, a pair of hard-looking characters with him and a bottle of whiskey as clear as spring water on the table. Men and women crowded around, sitting on chairs or stools, leaning on the table-planks.

The clear whiskey was the kind called "forty-rod," because the recoil would kick a man that far. As Abe stood in the door, taking in the lay of the room, the little man fired back a shot, then grinned all round, his blue eyes twinkling. You had to look twice to see if the whiskey had any effect on him. His face had that numb swollen look as if it was frost-bit. Abe reckoned he was probably paralyzed from the waist down. And even if Booth could still walk, the crowd would never let him go: he was buying. No sooner did he knock one back than they filled him another.

The man behind the plank bar was a dandy-looking hard case, with oiled hair and arms like haunches of beef. The crowd was keel-boatmen and trappers in dirty shirts and slouch hats, they'd reach out and give one of the women a pinch to make 'em squeal. The women? They were all sorts, lean bony girls in stained shifts like they just rolled out of the cribs in back, some of them so white they might never go out of doors; colored women too—one tall girl black as coal and lean as a post, with those same river-stone-smooth features Abe was beginning to recognize as the pure shape of black faces.

The men at the table with Booth were a cut above keelboat hand or trapper. The lank-haired one in greasy buckskins might head a gang of trappers, the bully-looking red-head next to him might be boss hand of a keel. In his own mind Abe called them "Rough" and "Reddy." They were egging Booth on to buy another round, laughing at whatever he said—which wasn't Shakespeare. "So the Irishman says, says he, 'Begorrah!' ..." They all howled so Abe never heard the snapper.

Abe had made up his mind to wait for Flinn, when things took a turn. "Scammon!" hollered Rough, "bring us out a cut o' ham, an' some bread to hold this here whiskey *down*!"

"No meat," said Booth, suddenly cold as ice.

Rough looked him up and down and said, "Well pass if you like, old hoss, but I mean to have me some."

Booth's eyes had a queer light and his numb cheeks twitched as if he tried to grin and couldn't. "You may eat human meat, as I do, sir. None other will I permit to be eaten in my presence."

No time to wait for Flinn. Abe eased his way to the table. "Mister Booth," he said politely, "I been lookin' all over for you. You're wanted down to the steamboat office, agent said there ain't a minute to spare."

Booth adjusted his head painfully upwards till by squinting he could just make out the tall boy rearing miles into the ceiling above him. But if he understood a word he gave no sign of it.

"Longshanks," said Rough, "you are blowin' smoke. My friend here don't *have* to go nowhere we don't want. And his name ain't *Boots*, it's *Bowlegs. Shorty* Bowlegs, ain't that right?"

Booth didn't answer. He had forgot why he was looking up at Abe, but kept looking anyway.

"Sir," Abe told Rough most respectful, "I don't like to say it, but you are mistook. This here is Mister Junius Brutus Booth, the famous Shakespeare actor—there's a *passel* of his friends waitin' on him down to the steamboat landing."

Rough poked Booth in the arm. "Well what do you know," he said. "Longshanks says to call you 'Juney-buggy Boots.' Hee hee hee! That is funny as hell." He held the bottle out to Abe. "Take a pull, Longshanks. Set down and jine the fun."

Booth woke up sudden. He snatched the bottle out of Rough's hand and crashed it on the table in a spray of glass and the sudden sharp tang of raw spirits. He sat glaring at Rough with the broken bottle's neck in his hand, claw out—cocked an eye at Abe. "Give not thy strength unto women," he said, "nor thy ways to that which destroyeth kings." He nodded, as if approving his own sentiments. "It is not for *kings*, O Lemuel, it is not for *kings* to drink wine, nor for princes strong drink: Lest they drink and forget the law."

Rough and Reddy looked sadly at the wreckage. "Breakin' bottles don't mend matters," said Rough, and Reddy said, "You got to pay fer the broke one anyways—and one to pick up whar it left off." He motioned the bartender to bring another bottle, which he did: and his bung-starter with it.

"Lemuel," Reddy said to Abe, "set on down and take a drink. Then we'll see 'bout givin' your strength to these women here." He reached out and grabbed the pole-thin black woman and jerked her to him. He lolled his tongue out and gave the woman a shake. The black woman let him shake her. She widened the line of her dark lips, but didn't smile; her eyes were like river-stones, flat dead.

Reddy grinned. "Or maybe Bowlegs Juney-bug wants to take a bite out o' *this*!" He gave her a shove that sent her sprawling across Booth.

Booth reared up out of his chair, eyes wild with horror and disgust, slashing at her with the broken bottle-claw—sudden flash of bright bright red blood on her black arm. Two white women closed round the girl and her first shrill cry came from behind a wall of women.

Booth glared fearfully at the spot she no longer stood in as if her ghost was still there. Every other man in the room was froze with the shock of it. Booth began a sort of low incantatory hum. "For the lips of a strange woman drop as a honeycomb, her mouth is smoother than oil, but her end is bitter as worm, as worm . . ." He seemed to lose the thread. Then his eye found Reddy and he muttered, "As food for worms great Percy." His eyes lit nastily and he took note of the bloodied bottle-claw in his hand.

Then Abe heard Flinn's voice, calling heartily, "Well Booth, there you are! Time for bed, old man!" Flinn stepped carefully into the room. His coat was open to show the pistols stuck in the sash round his waist, his right hand resting on the butt of one. "I'm sure this company will excuse you. We must take our rest, and prepare for the performance."

The pistols put a chill on the fun. A dissatisfied grumble went through the room, but no one took particular responsibility for it. Only Rough was man enough to protest: "Dang you all three! If he *is* Mister Famous Booth, why don't he speak out a piece for us, right here 'n now!"

Booth blinked, and for a flash there was a lucid look in his blue eyes. "Bowlegs may drink and joke with your sort," he said. "Not Booth."

Abe got an arm under Booth's elbow and eased him to his feet. Flinn stood off, smiling most friendly with both hands on his pistol-butts now, saying politely, "I hope you will excuse Mister Booth, I fear he is not in the best voice this evening. However, when our company arrive we will perform a proper tragedy for your amusement." He smiled at Booth. "Will we not, sir?"

Booth smiled around the room—a full-faced smile, as patently false as a tin dollar. "Yes yes, trippingly on the tongue. We shall suit the word to the action, the action to the word . . ." He felt Abe's arm supporting him and turned his face up to glare at him. His forty-rod breath nearly blew Abe over. He pushed Abe away, wolf-eyed with hate, turned totteringly to Flinn. His voice was wrung tight with rage and menace: "I will, sir, flatter my sworn brother the people. Show them the scars which I should hide, as if I had received them for the stinking hire of their breath." He glared at the whole room of them. Then he sneered. "Bid them wash their faces and keep their teeth clean!"

A nasty murmur ran through the whiskey-mill. Abe got Booth on his arm, Flinn stepped between them and the room, hands on his pistols. He took a bag of coins out of his pocket and threw it on the floor. "There's for the damage," he said.

They were out the door. Flinn swung his shoulder under Booth's arm, and with Abe lifting on the other side they rushed Booth swiftly round one corner, behind the next house, up an alley. There was hollering behind them, but none coming their way. Booth sagged on their shoulders, a nerveless dead weight. "I had forgot myself," he muttered. "Is not the king's name twenty thousand names? I will from henceforth rather be myself, mighty, and to be feared, for these are things a man might play! But I, I will, I will be, I will have such revenges on you—!"

There was a horse-trough near at hand. They heaved Booth splash into it, face down full length. Flinn hauled him up by the hair, nose to dripping nose. "There was a crown offered him," Booth said. "He put it by with the back of his hand; but for all that, to my thinking, he would fain have had it." He had begun to weep, the tears lost on his dripping face.

"You owe the boy some thanks," said Flinn, tilting his head in Abe's direction. "It's Gabe—from the flatboat."

"Abe," said Abe.

"Short for Gabriel then," muttered Booth. He sat up in the trough and fumbled at his pockets, but they were sealed with the water of his immersion. "Put money in thy purse," he said distractedly. "And if thou wilt needs damn thyself, do it a more delicate way than drowning." He squinted at Abe in the dim light of the stars. "Make all the money thou canst. The rest is . . . is vanity, and vexation of spirit." He hung his head over the side of the trough. Something shook his body like a terrier shakes a rat, and Booth puked splatteringly onto the ground.

Flinn took his arm and helped him out of the horse-trough. He slumped against it as if he had lost the use of his legs. "And that which should accompany old age, as honor, love, obedience, troops of friends, I must not look . . ." and then he was asleep: a deep rich wet snoring in-suck of breath.

Flinn looked up at Abe. "Don't judge him by this. All he wants is a part to play, and the stage to play it on. Then there's no one can touch him. In London, once, a great and famous actress actually turned tail and fled the stage when he said: 'Put out the light—and *put out the light.*' She knew he *meant* it. But off-stage—" He looked down at Booth, asleep and smiling like a baby. "It's even odds whether he plays the part or the part plays him. He's going to drink himself dead or get himself killed some day. And what a wounded name . . ."

Abe said, "He don't know the difference between what he is and what he plays at."

Flinn sighed, "All the world's a stage . . ."

Booth's eyes popped open. "No!" he snapped. "No it is not! If it was I'd be King of England—or President of the United States of America." He smiled. "Thank you, *kind* friends," he murmured, and passed out for good.

Chapter 16: **The Dead Reaches**

Napoleon to Greenville, Late February 1829

The Elixir business played out a little after noon next day. Offutt allowed he was satisfied. They cut loose of Napoleon and headed south again.

Abe wasn't sure if what had come to him on or about his birthday was providence or something else. He reckoned he'd learned something of the Great Booth, though not the educational matters he expected. *A part to play and a stage to play it on.*

A different sort of "providence" was bothering Sephus. The two of them were fishing for mud-cats off the bow, Sephus edgy and fidgeting, throwing looks at Abe now and again like he was casting for a bite. Finally Abe asked what was eating him. Sephus looked watchful. "Do you reckon what Big Hat said is true? 'Bout Shinin' Mountains an' hidden countries?"

Abe had been thinking about them too. "He might have stretched some, but I reckon the main of it was true enough."

"Damn," Sephus breathed. He sighed and stared off at the shoreline forests. "Ain't you sorry you miss dat chance?"

"Some," Abe admitted. "But I'm bound to finish what I started. I reckon the mountains can wait a year."

Sephus shook his head. "If it was me, I wouldn't count on no second chance."

Talking with Sephus stirred Abe's discontent. Maybe he *had* chose wrong. Missed his chance to be Columbus, or Boone, or Uncle Mordecai, to discover new country, make it any way *he* liked, it's *your* land if you come first.

He let his mind dream on that for days as the flatboat floated south. If you wanted wilderness that had the look of never been discovered, this stretch of the River would satisfy you. South of the Arkansaw the swamps drew down to the banks, a uniform wall of trees stood right behind the levees. No settlements, not even a cabin or wood-lot, nothing back in the woods but wildcats, pizen snakes, and 'gators. It was the rawest country they had seen yet.

With Sephus at the tiller, Abe stood lookout forwards scanning the empty River and the blank of the forest. The River wound in wide loops so there was never a clear run or sight to the south, only short reaches of water ending in a level wall of trees, which would slide apart like curtains at the last minute to reveal the next reach.

As they rounded a point Abe saw at the bottom of the reach the bare bulge of one of those Injun Mounds, peering over the trees like a bald man's dome. He had borrowed Offutt's spy-glass to play Columbus with. He whipped it up to his eye as smartly as if it was the first *Land ho* of America—and by God if there wasn't someone up top of the Mound, keeping lookout like the Aztec Mex'cans used to on their great old temples . . . and there he goes a-running, took by surprise no less than Montezuma himself, back in the Spanish days. "Hey below!" he called. "There's a settlement ahead!"

Gentry came out of the cabin, hauling on his coat. "We're still well above Greenville," he said, squinting at the Mound that loomed over the trees and marked the next bend.

Abe said, "I saw a man keeping watch up there—run down when he saw us."

Gentry thought that over. It might be a chance to do business, or a chance to get robbed. "Ease her over to shave the point,"

Gentry called out to Sephus. Then to Abe: "Go fetch the guns up, and Offutt too."

The Mound looked down on the bottle-neck of the next point. It was smart how those old-time Injuns put their Mound where it controlled the neck and watched the reaches upstream and down. The boat rode up level with the Mound, then swung past and up to the point, Sephus steering to shave the bar that ran out from its tip. The three white men stood on deck with the rifles and musket ready to hand.

The point was a broad one, wooded to the levee. A light breeze, a little warm and wet, swamp-funky, blew off it as they rounded it slowly. From the look of the bank Abe judged the river would have cut a bay just back of the point. They rode the slow water, watching the bay begin to open up.

The first warning came when the little swampy off-shore breeze threw them a quick curling whiff of some awful yellow rot-shit stink. Then the bay opened up—

At first look it was the wreck of a landslide down the bank, but at the next they recognized two dozen ragged bark huts huddled on the levee in the cusp of the point. Dirty brown ragged shapes, Indians, scrambled in heaps along the levee, some waving, some sliding down the bank, two dugout-log canoes already shoving off from shore: and cries, shrill piercing wailing cries. Then the whole breath of the village hit them like a wave, yellow-thick with a stink like hog-pens if human beings were the hogs, rotted shit offal and dead flesh, that knife-sharp yellow piercing stink that runs up your nostrils like needles into the brain.

"My God!" cried Offutt. "My God what is it?"

Humped shapes scrabbling or falling down the bank, wading out in the water with their hands clawed at the boatmen—three canoes now, paddlers flailing, coming out to get them.

"Look out," hollered Gentry, "they're a-comin' for us! Sephus Sephus for God's sake shear off!" He raised his piece and leveled it. He fired *pow!* and the water spat under the bow of the nigh canoe. Gentry dropped the butt and reloaded quick with shaking hands.

The canoe sheared off. The men in it waved their arms back and forth, showing they had no guns. Two other canoes came flailing up to them, the lead paddler in one stopping and holding both palms out in sign of peace. The canoes were about four or five rods off, Abe could see the lead paddler clearly: the arms spread in peace were bone-thin, and the bare chest of the Indian showed his rack of ribs. The three canoes drew along parallel to the flatboat, not trying to catch them only following from the shallows as Sephus steered them, at the slow current's pace, on a long slant back to the quick water of the main channel.

"Show 'em your guns," Gentry snapped. "If they rush us all at once in them canoes they can be aboard like *that*. Shoot the lead paddler or steersman, we might make 'em flip. Abe, take the far one, Offutt the middle, I'll take the nighest."

"Where's the blunder-piece?" said Abe, thinking what would happen if they got aboard.

"I got it, Mist' Abe," said Sephus—he was standing in the stern-well with the blunderbuss in his hands, the steering-oar tucked under his arm, and Abe's first thought was relief, he should have knowed they could count on . . .

Then he saw Gentry whip his head around and look at Sephus kind of sick. Then look at Offutt, who shrugged and said, "Wasn't me." Meaning he never gave Sephus the blunder-gun—the bell-mouth shotgun that could fire a spread big enough to kill all three of them at once if the range was right.

The Indians were crying again, shrill birdlike cries. Gentry tore his eyes off Sephus and leveled on the first canoe. "Spread out!" he said. "Don't shoot 'less they come for us. I 'druther keep 'em off than fight!" They had drifted the length of the village and the woods closed up to the shore again, but the three canoes still followed them. Abe couldn't tell if some in the canoes might be women— wild thatchy mops of black hair over dark faces. Injuns wouldn't take women with them if they meant to fight—would they?

An Indian in the lead canoe had risen wobbly to a kneeling position, his upper body bare. He was bony as death, the corners of his shoulders sharp-edged as a pane of glass. He was signing something with his hands, the left cupped below his chin the right wafting over it towards his open mouth. He chewed air with the whole force of his jaws. He clawed both hands into his stomach. Then he went through it again.

"Food," said Abe, "they want some food."

"Horse-shit," said Gentry. "Injuns in the woods and they got to beg food off a flatboat?" He made a pushing-away movement, then leveled his rifle and took a bead on the man making sign. The Indian behind gave a bundle into the sign-maker's hands. He took something out of the wrappings. He held it out to the white men in the flatboat. It was a small child. By the hang of its head and drop-straight arms—dead. The signing Injun laid the child across the thwarts of the canoe. He clawed his hands into his belly and writhed. He slammed the palms of both hands against the sides of his skull.

It wasn't words but Abe could read him plain. "Starvin' I'll swear," he said, "starvin' and sick," *the claw in the belly the mouth that can't take food, like Mam like Milk-sick* only here it was more people and worser sick. "We got to give 'em food—give 'em some Elixir for medicine."

Gentry grabbed Abe hard with his left hand and swung him around. "Keep your piece leveled! If that mob gets aboard they'll tear us to flinders to get the food. Shit if they ain't starvin'-crazy enough to eat us too!" Abe hollered right back in Gentry's face, "They ain't rushin' us! Jest drop 'em a barr'l of meal and some meat and a keg of Elixir!"

"Point your gun that way, goddamn your eyes, or I'll throw *you* to 'em . . ."

Abe stopped still and said: "I'd like to see you try." He had his rifle ready and full-cocked.

Gentry blenched and worked his jaws to say something, couldn't spit it out. He wrenched away and leveled his musket at the first canoe and fired. Abe heard the bullet plunk the wood of the dugout. The Indians wailed. Abe saw them stop paddling. Some were looking after the flatboat, others slumped forwards, their paddles useless stuck out at odd angles. They hung there in the slack water watching the flatboat go.

The boat swung into the turn of the next bend, and a curtain of forest swept forwards to close the reach in which the Indians still sat, not turning back to the village till they were sure the flatboat was gone for good.

Abe was froze himself, shaking, unbelieving that such a thing could be, and then believing—but then, refusing to believe that it could be, and they see it and pass it by, and not do a solitary thing but Gentry firing two shots at them. Gentry stepped up to snatch Abe's rifle, but Abe came awake and held on. Offutt stepped between them. "Let be, Abe—Gentry, let be. The boy only meant . . ."

"Meant?" said Gentry. "What do I care what he meant? Ain't I captain of this . . . ?

"Course you are," Offutt soft-soaped him, "he just wasn't thinking, he's upset is all, he's only wanting to do right and help those poor . . ."

It was shoot Abe for mutiny, throw him overboard, or shift his fire—Gentry shifted. "For a boy s'pose to be smart, you can be thick as a post! How far do you reckon a barrel of meal and a cut of fatback would go with that crowd?"

"There ain't Elixir enough to dose the least part of 'em," Offutt chimed in. "They'd drink it all and die anyway—and leave us nothing for trade." He gave Abe a pat on the back. "You have a share here, son. You have to think about protecting it. We're all in this together, aren't we?" he said, smiling around to include Gentry.

But Gentry was staring aft with that sick look on his face again. Abe turned and saw Sephus standing on the stern-timbers with the blunder-gun in his hands. It wasn't exactly aimed at them, but it wasn't exactly not—and the 'buss was not a weapon that wanted more than a hint to hit everything in the neighborhood.

Gentry said, "Sephus." In the quiet they heard the Old Man chuckling under the timbers. Gentry made himself a smile and put it on: "Sephus, you done right well. I will remember it of you, Sephus, when we get you home to Young Donaldson."

Sephus stood with the gun in his hands and looked at them. Abe felt Offutt's subtle nudge, and he eased away, spreading the three of them.

Suddenly Sephus grinned, bobbed his head a few times, "Thank 'ee, Mas' Gentry. My Mas'r always found me ready." He quickly reversed the blunderbuss and held it out butt first. Gentry walked over—"Thank you, Sephus"—and took it, to stow it below with the other guns. Sephus nocked the steering oar and leaned on it to keep them in the heart of the current.

Abe looked upstream. The green wall of the last point had closed over the Indian village and its death-stink, erasing it. If you didn't know it was there you would never think it was possible. But it was. Then his stomach went sickly, his innards heaved. Blood hammered painfully back of his forehead. Cold sweat. It was like they'd struck utter disaster—only nothing at all had happened to them. They were sailing along, the River easy, the air clean. Something in Abe's head turned over. He looked at the river and the woods: they were still there, only they looked *thinner*, mere floating images on the skin of the water and nothing behind but the black bones of the river-bottom.

They stopped at Greenville long enough to find out what the Indians were doing camped under the old Mound. They'd signed a treaty to give up their land in Mississippi and move out to the back of Arkansaw, come down to the River where a gov'ment steamboat was supposed to bring up rations and carry them West. But the steamboat never showed. They'd et up their provisions waiting, hunted and et every critter in the region down to frogs and spiders. The Greenville militia was mustering to go on up there and drive 'em out. "If we don't they'll be raidin' down this way." Their informant showed his long teeth when he grinned: "Agent says the gov'-ment won't like it if we hurt its Injuns. I say: gov'ment that cain't or won't keep its word ain't no gov'ment at all."

South from Greenville, End of February–Early March 1829

They ran day and night now, drifting broad empty reaches, on the Mississippi side nothing but the thick airless jungle of the Yazoo Delta, on the Arkansaw side a drowned forest of cypress and gum four hundred miles across. The River was bare, except now and again a steamboat beating its way upstream through slack water, ribbon of smoke by day, coal of fire by night.

Dog-tiredness and the flat monotony of the drowned forest blunted Abe's attention, trying to think was like trying to breathe under water, Mis'sippi water too thick to drink too wet to plow. He couldn't sleep. Was dead tired but at the same time his insides itched intolerable, fleas jumping and fidgeting in his nerves and muscles. Offutt and Gentry murmured on their watch. Secrets. Below-decks no feel of movement, only the sense of being afloat, cut loose of all moorings in an empty place.

Offutt shook him awake for his dog-watch. He went on deck and took the steering-oar. Sephus was for'ard to watch for snags. Darkness canceled the shoreline, trees and their reflections one black blot. Stars like foxfire. But it was the empty spaces between the stars that drew Abe's eyes, sucking at the spirit inside him, drawing it out and out. The River kept sliding them away and along. Nothing could hold them, nothing good, nothing evil, nothing they done nothing they ought to done, the River wouldn't let you dwell on it nor go back and do it again, do it better, make it right. The good was lost and the bad lost, erased by the green sweep of a point or the fall of dark or the relentless blind brainless push of the River.

Abe felt it was himself dimming, sinking, floating down. An effort to keep his mind on steering—to believe the boat needed steering, the blanked-out shore the still River gave no proof of motion. The night air was lightly tainted with the breath of invisible swamps: a ghost-stink of the Milk-sick out of the Indian village, the dead breath haunting him, invisible, everywhere—the sign of Death hiding everywhere in all things, secret, till suddenly there it is, cruel stinking and complete. A man could run over the world, go to the Shining Mountains, discover new countries, find a magic lamp, marry a princess, lead his people through a desert, build himself a great big Mound to sit on and look down on the world—and in the end it all come to nothing.

He was suddenly aware that Sephus had come back and was sitting on the cabin roof, looking at him. In the pale starlight the negro's eyes were hid in oil-black pools of shadow. "Bad, ain't it?" said Sephus.

"It's bad enough, I reckon." No point keeping secret. Talking to a black man in the dark was no more than one haunt talking to another. "Don't seem like it's worth goin' on."

Sephus leaned in eagerly, the liquid shine of his eyes became visible. "Made us a bad mistake, didn't we?"

Abe shook his head, Sephus didn't know what he knew. "Wasn't a thing we could do would have made any difference."

"No difference?" Sephus hissed. "If we'd a' signed Big Hat's book, be on our way to Shinin' Mountain right *now*!"

Abe came back to himself like *that*: mistake to think Sephus was thinking the same as he was. He was a free white man, and this here was Captain Donaldson's negro. "Sephus," he snapped, "I ain't runnin' off, and neither are you!"

Sephus let himself go slack. He shook his head regretfully. "Course not, boss," he said. "What's I thinkin'?" He backed off and went for'ard again.

But at least he had woke Abe up a little. Whether the blue devils had him or not, he'd better keep a closer watch on Sephus.

It started to rain, and forgot to quit. Rain poured down with only an occasional break, day after day, steady drizzle and then a soaking downpour. Sometimes a wind out of the west would blow the rain in sideways, whip a mean chop out of the River, bully the flatboat towards the eastward bank—the Mississippi bank they would have said, only the way the Old Man humped and twisted and wrung Himself around it was anyone's guess whether the wind was driving them into Mississippi or—it must be Louisiana by now.

The Old Man was rising to the rain, bank-full mud-heavy and moving fast, clawing great chunks and sides off the banks and levees. His face was marked with floating timber, house-wrack. Great old trees washed down out of the north, their root-ends like a mane of frozen snakes, reared and plunged in the current. Alongshore suddenly a rank of cottonwoods swayed and dropped all together feet-first into the run of the River, which tipped and swung and tangled them in a rustling mass the water seethed through. As Abe watched, the leafy raft swung off from shore and floated in a current turned bloody by the mud of the caved-in bank.

Gentry was at the stern-oar with Offutt to help pull in an emergency, Sephus on port sweep, Abe on starboard trying to read the scars and wrinkles of the River's face.

Then they heard the Old Man roaring—a hoarse full-throat roar like they had never heard in their lives.

The current picked up sudden speed, Abe felt that awful suck and dip he recognized as the start of the long fall down a chute. He peered downstream, looking for the straight corridor between the trees that would mark the chute. There was a wall of forest ahead— no, not a wall: there was a bite took out of the wall off their starboard quarter and they were sliding sideways at it, rushing down on that hole in the wall like a demon homing on hell.

Levee break. My God.

Abe hollered to Gentry, *"Sta'board swing her sta'board!"* He scrambled across the deck joining Sephus to throw double weight on the oar to turn the boat against the slam of waves so she'd face head-on the gap of the levee-break. Offutt, Gentry, and Sephus were crying and hollering to shear off but Abe saw it was too late for that, the only thing left was to hit the break head-on, if they broached into the woods they'd be rolled over smashed and drowned . . .

The forest rushed bang at them, the nose of the boat burst over the break on a lifting surge of river, Abe saw trees behind the broken levee leaning away in fright—Something snatched his oar and the Other slammed him head and shoulder, he went down mind fogging body numb the deck was cottonfeathersoftbed . . .

He thrashed, tangled in something. It said "Easy!"—Sephus. The deck beneath them slanted up at a low angle. They had fallen and rolled together against the skiff, arms and legs mixed up. Sephus's breast was hard as planks under that soft-looking black skin, his weight considerable, his breath rich with smoked ham and chawed tobacco.

The flatboat was stopped. The air was blue-gray with rain, soft and pervasive. A rushing sound filled Abe's ears.

Abe said, "Get off!" Sephus rolled away. Abe hauled himself up. Down the slope of the cabin roof, Gentry in the stern-well floundered knee-deep in a banked-up rush of tobacco-stained water. *Where was Offutt?* The top branches of a cottonwood sailed up and nestled against the stern, pushing in closer and closer like a pup snuggling for the tit, Gentry swatting the branches as the thing stubbornly worked its way aboard. Gentry gave up. He turned and batted through crackling twigs, bending to haul Offutt to his feet, soaked but whole.

The starboard bow was canted up, the whole of the bow lifted just out of the rush of water. The flatboat must have jumped the levee on the wave of pent-up water that piled through the break, rode it ten rods or so down into the woods—then run up on the trunk of a tree whose roots had lost hold and let it tip head down into the stream. It would hold them there, the Old Man would pile driftwood and floating snags in after them to pound and beat the boat to pieces, pile them under along with their goods if they didn't abandon the boat and try to get away in the skiff.

All this work for nothing. Abe looked around for words to cuss it with, but couldn't find any equal to the job. It was awful enough to make a man cry—or laugh. *Look at all these damn trees,* he thought, *I run a thousand mile from Pigeon Creek and here I am stuck in the trees again. I reckon if a man is meant to die in the woods, it won't do him no good to try and drownd himself.* He looked up—there was a broad swath of gray smokey sky overhead, the trees didn't come near overarching the rush of water alongside.

Then his mind began to work. His first notion was that the levee break had blowed a hole in the woods and shot them into it. But that wasn't so. A clear sweep of water ran past them and ahead, no broke-off trees sticking up in the middle. Without disrespect to the Old Man, Abe didn't judge the water he saw running could have gouged that much forest clean in one blast. And water don't bust down a wall if there's a door handy. This here must be a regular bayou, a piece of the old riverbed with water standing in it year round, with every now and again an overflood to wash out any second-growth that might have took hold. Off in the trees he saw the dull metal sheen of still water standing among tree trunks. But the water in the slot tore past. Water didn't do that unless it had somewhere to go and a channel to take it there.

Maybe just a slough back in the woods. Maybe she just shallows and thins out and leaves you in swamp.

On the other hand, maybe she keeps running. Cradok said some bayous were regular by-ways, twisting along till they come back to the River. Maybe this was one of that kind?

Then he came to a certainty: *no use thinking this-here is anything but the luckiest kind of bayou a man could get stuck in. If they could just get off this tree . . .*

Yes. *Then the next thing I want is an ax.* Abe inched down the sloping roof and dropped into the trough of the stern to stand knee-deep in water. Gentry gave him a look: death-pale, ruined. Offutt clung to the roof-timbers, dazed. "Get the skiff," he said, " 'bandon ship."

"No need," said Abe, "it's just the one tree."

Gentry's haggard face twisted as if he would weep, but he raged: "One tree? One tree?!"

The cabin doors sagged. Abe waded in, sodden blankets snatching his ankles, found the carpenter box along the starboard wall; grabbed two axes by the necks and sloshed out.

Gentry had climbed up on the roof, stood gazing back up the way they had come, watching the water piling in behind them, the driftwood beginning to back in behind the cottonwood that clutched the stern. Offutt by him, groggy, a cut on his forehead. Useless the both of them. Abe picked his way up the slanted deck to where Sephus stood looking over the bow. The black man nodded when Abe handed him an ax.

He put Sephus to work on the up-tilted bow timbers, striking down to notch the partly submerged section of log under the bow. Abe clambered out onto the trunk, his bare feet gripping the slimy rough bark; braced himself and began to swing his ax. Careful. Upswing easy—like a man trying to chop balancing on the ridgepole of his cabin—downswing easy till the last hard flick of the wrist did the work, *whunk!* The river hissing like snakes all around him. *Whunk!* Now the carefulness was coming easy to him, coming natural. *Whunk!* Turning his edge this way and that to pick his notch clean, deepen it, drive it in.

Sephus stood on the up-tilted bow: his notch was cut. Abe said, "Get the spare sweeps, and tell *them*. When she goes we'll have to fend off everyways."

It wasn't but a dozen swings after that Abe felt trembles run through the wood—then the little springing thrill under the palms of his feet. He whammed his ax into the bow timbers and jumped for the boat as the tree cracked under him and the boat slid, a muffled crunch saying the trunk had broke again where Sephus notched it . . .

The boat was alive again, buoyant in the current. The tree's claws scrabbled their belly timbers as they went over, the cottonwood branches crackled as the stern pulled out of them. They were loose. Abe and Sephus fended off with the last two spare sweeps used as poles. Offutt's busted head made him too poorly to do much, and Gentry just gave up and sat there with his head between his knees. Up ahead was a wall of trees, if it didn't slide aside and show a bend they were done . . .

The left bank swung aside as they came up, but the reach on the other side was short, another wall at the bottom that might not part for them, and another after that. But the water kept moving, and they kept moving with it. The woods threatened to close in alongside and overhead, to shut the door in front—but so far it was just brag. And as Ma always says: Brag is a good dog, but Holdfast is better.

The waterway narrowed and the spate in it lessened as the floodwaters spread into the flat country behind the levee. But the channel never gave out completely, and though the water stilled and stilled it never stopped moving that least bit that gave Abe a direction to follow.

They tied up at night to a water cypress, bulbous at the base like a trumpet bell-down in the water. The rain had given way to drifting mist. Abe hated to lose any high water, if it dropped and they grounded again they'd never get the flatboat off. But it was no good drifting in the dark without a clear channel.

Sephus tended Offutt's head and shared out a tot of Elixir to firm them up. It didn't help Gentry. As the dark shut down a strangled feeling came over them, as if the trees were creeping in. Weeks and weeks they had slept in the breeze and wide sky of the River. The forest stifled the air, closed all but a band of sky light. Then in the dark, instead of wind and river: constant whisperings of leaves, rustles and wood-creaks. Scrabble of paws. Sop and drip of water. Rank raw smell of swamp-wash. Something back in the trees said *Whooo-coooks! Whooo-coooks-f'yoooou!* It barked like a fice, yap yap yap, then shrieked high and piercing, and chopped the shriek into a raucous eejit laughing, *Yee-hee-hee-haha.* Battering of wings in the branches.

"What the devil is that?" said Offutt.

"Don't say his name out here."

Abe said, "Owl I reckon."

"Squinch-owl. Lawd if it's de squinch-owl . . ."

Offutt said, "Not any owl *I* ever heard."

Sephus was astonished at Offutt's ignorance. "Man don't hear de squinch-owl but once."

Whooo-coooks-f'yoooou! Whooo-coooks-f'yoooou! Ark ark. Yee hee, yee hee, yeehee-haha!

Gentry rolled on his face and little riffles ran through him. If he wasn't a man you'd think he was crying. If it had come on him slow and steady he'd have faced it square enough. It was the speed of the thing undid him.

The owl cut loose again, further off. Maybe it was and maybe it wasn't the worst sign a man could get. But there was nothing gained by thinking it was. "Naw," Abe said, "that ain't no squinch-owl. It don't *screetch*, it's more a *scrootch*. I reckon it's jest a scrootch-owl."

Sephus considered the alternatives; then allowed he was satisfied. Offutt shrugged. Gentry lay still, face down.

In the morning the water was awful quiet but sun slanted through the high leaves. They took a little time to cut and trim some spare poles. Then Abe dropped a curl of dried leaf in the water and watched it move off. "That way," he said, and they pushed off the way the leaf pointed.

Dug their poles in the riverbed: for the first time since Rockport their own muscles were stronger than the current. With the sun up it got warm in among the trees, no breeze and the air steamed off the bayou. Little bright green birds with hooked beaks, parro-keets Offutt called them, flicked like sparks through the trees alongside.

Woods-swamp: the same trees repeated endlessly in every direction, same branches clogged and draped with hanging moss, deadfall—but that rot-speckled branch was the edge of something alive. *Copperhead. So pizen it make you sick jest to see him.* Heaps of muck and dead branches piled like beaver-lodges against the cypress knees: inside one of them the gleam of a yellow eye, snick of a tooth. "Jesus," Offutt hissed, "a nest of alligators. Do you think they sleep the winter like a bear?" An arrow homing towards them across the thick surface: cotton-mouth. *Git his teeth in you, good night.*

The channel forked. Abe floated a chip of bark; another; then another. Three out of three said take the right-hand channel, so they did it. A little way on the trees squeezed in, then at last dead trunks dropped criss-cross to block the way. Offutt and Sephus stood at the bow with Abe. Gentry slumped against the skiff. Offutt said, "Pole back and take the other channel?"

Abe shook his head. "Current goes this way. Other channel, we'd get the same trees and less water." He considered the criss-cross trunks, then: "You and Allen pole us right up against the trees. Sephus, roust out the axes."

Abe and Sephus went at the deadfall with axes. The trees weren't all that thick, the wood soft, but there were a lot of trunks to cut through. The channel was just wide enough to let them pass, and the water moving enough to float the bark and chips off ahead of them.

On the other side of the block they came to a long flat pond, hairy with saplings and reeds at the lips. Lily-pads floated to either side of the channel, in the harsh new sun their beds glistened like the surface of a river frozen in riffle. But the air was warm, wet, and still. They poled the length of the pond, following the path between the lily-pads. On the other side was a slot into the woods. Wide enough for the flatboat. Green flashes in the trees. Abe and Sephus stood in the bows with their axes ready. The water bubbled just a little under the bows as Gentry and Offutt poled them ahead.

They came to an understanding, though they never put words to it. Abe took charge, Sephus was his right hand, Gentry and Offutt would go along as best they could. Sephus even managed to boss the white men, when he had to, without showing out. Abe tried to pick up the trick of it when he could spare a look that way. The black man would say something like it was to himself—"Got to pole out to sta'b'd" or such-like—then start in, straining at it till Offutt or Gentry felt their obligation to join.

The bayou slung a curl to the north, looped south, snaked east, threw a set of corkscrew curls west. Were they moving away from the River or slanting back towards it? Water spread out everywhere, trees standing in it to their knees as far into the woods as a man could see. Still. The difference between dead water and living was so small it took a thing as light as a down-feather to find it: Abe set it in the water and in five minutes watching saw it creep a foot ahead. Abe said it must be the current, wasn't no breath in the air to speak of. But he knew when he said it he might be trimming his judgment to suit his hankering, or quiet his fear.

Maybe there was no channel. Maybe the Old Man was just playing to the last laugh some terrible, disgusting joke, holding out just enough fool's-hope to keep them slopping about in the muck. If they ever forgot that possibility, the scrootch-owl came back at night to remind them, whoooing and barking and laughing like a maniac in the trees.

Three ponds later—each pond just a little longer than the one before—they pushed out into a broad opening. The water ahead was neither pond nor swamp. It looked like a shriveled version of the Big River they had lost so many days ago: only twenty-five to thirty yards across, but it bent this way and that, it had banks, there was a current in it. They hallooed, crack-voiced after days of mutter and mumble. Even Gentry raised up and looked around. That was the first night they went to sleep without worrying if they'd wake up in the morning and find they'd run out of water.

But they were afraid to trust their luck. Whatever they had found, it wasn't the River. If the Mississippi was a river with too much mud in it, this here was a lot of mud with just a little more river than it could handle. But there *was* higher ground, low ridges back in the trees that curved to follow the line of the bayou. Their height was marked by a different sort of trees from the cypress and water-tupelo they had come through: overcup oak, water hickory, sweetgum on the crests. The ridges had a *made* look, like serpent-shaped versions of the Injun Mounds. Or they might have been the remains of old levees, grave-markers of dead channels the Old Man left behind.

Then finally: they rounded a bend and saw a cabin with smoke at the chimney, a plowed field bony with picked-over cotton plants between it and the trees. Abe leaned on the sweep and let the pleasure of that seeing run over and through him like sweet water and sunshine. *Done it.*

"Done it, by heaven!" Offutt echoed his thought from the stern. The merchant was capering on the deck. He jumped down to where Gentry manned the steering sweep and whacked him on the back. "Done it done it done it!" he crowed. "By heaven, Gentry, we have come through after all!"

Gentry stood there, trying get hold of the truth of it. He was still back in the jungle he believed he would never see the end of. Then it come to him of a sudden, and made him want to bow down and rise up at the same time. "Come through," he said, "well by God." Offutt patted Gentry on the chest, like he was patting a dough-boy into shape. "Cabin to sta'board, Cap'n." Gentry hesitated—looked to Abe. Then he grinned too and called out, "Take her to land, and mind she don't ground."

Abe looked at Sephus.

Sephus was waiting on him.

Well what was he supposed to do? It was Gentry's boat, wasn't it? "Let's turn her in," Abe said, and without a word Sephus looked to his oar.

Chapter 17: **The Scrootch-Owl**

Roundaway Bayou, Louisiana, Early March 1829

They were afraid to ground the boat, if the water dropped they might not get her off again. But the current wasn't much so they threw a loop over a stump that stood in the shallows. Abe and Offutt waded ashore through the sucking muck.

No sound from the cabin, only the curl of smoke to say it was lived in. Offutt hollered, "Hello there!" A shutter slapped open and a rifle poked out a slit in the door. "Come ahead, but keep yoah hands where I kin see 'em." Offutt and Abe shared a look. But if the rifleman meant harm he could plug 'em running. They spread their arms to show palms out and walked slowly towards the cabin.

When they were two rods from the door it opened, and a white man stepped out. He put up his rifle and smiled apologetically. "Howdy, an' welcome. Sorry to been so *prev'ous* with the rifle. But we'ns be keerful, out hyeah." He was an awful lean man, janders-looking, with a lantern jaw and teeth missing in his smile. But the smile was friendly.

A black man stepped out behind him. He had a rifle too, and his shirt wasn't any worse than the white man's: both raggedy. "This here's Thomas, calls him *Doubtin'* Thomas on account he's so *skittish*." The two men were of an age, height, and leanness, but Thomas had the edge in teeth and Caldwell (which was the white man's name) the better of the two rifles.

Caldwell waved for Gentry and Sephus to come ashore. To show his joy in company he had Thomas butcher a hog. Sorry he hadn't no strong drink to offer, too wet here for corn. So to be hospitable, Offutt sent Abe for a jug of whiskey. Caldwell said that was *right* kindly. They set the hog in the fire and poured a round. The cabin was too small, so they hunkered or laid out on the ground, each as it suited him. Thomas sat right amongst the white folks, like it was his custom. Sephus sat next to him, so as to keep the custom without putting himself forwards.

What had Caldwell busted was how they never saw the flatboat poling up, and the cabin set to look right down the bayou. When Offutt told him they came from *up* the bayou, out of the swamps, Thomas said *Humpf*. Caldwell stilled, whiskey cup in hand. Then he deliberately drained his cup and set it down. "Thomas *doubts* y'all. But I took to ye on jedgment, an' will stand *by* that jedgment." He shook his head. "Only—we don't look to see no one comin' *down* that bayou. Not no *safe* individual, if you take my meanin'?"

Offutt explained how they were carried through the levee break, and were able to poke through the swamps on account of the high water. But they had no notion where they had got to.

"Calls it Roundaway Bayou," said Caldwell. Four-five days poling would get them back to the Big River maybe thirty miles below Vicksburg. Plantations were bigger closer to the River, they could do a fair piece of trading lower down. Too bad the boat come today—Caldwell had just come back from trading at Colonel Cahoon's store, at New Carthage by the mouth of the bayou. "He will charge *his* price, will Colonel Cahoon." It was on account of what he heard at New Carthage that Caldwell had been so "keerful." "Someone's been stirrin' up the niggers and Injuns in the backwoods. Talk is it's Murrell-men. Army gone after 'em in the Arkansaw kentry, ain't no

one to keep 'em down *this* end o' the River." He paused consideringly, then added, "You want to walk a leetl *small* with folks further
down. They mought not be so glad of comp'ny as Thomas and me."
In his courteous way, Caldwell was telling them they might be mistook for Murrell-men.

Offutt said, "With all this Murrell-talk, you weren't afraid to
leave your place alone?"

"Not with Thomas to keep watch," said Caldwell. He saw
their skeptical look, grinned: "Where's he run *to*, out in the
swamps? Besides"—he gave Thomas an affectionate poke—"we in
this together! Come out together; staked the claim and cleared her
together; plowed her, put in the cotton, picked the field together.
Didn't make but a short bale, but once we git her goin'—this is
bottom-land, rich as a man kin want—we'll make ten bales easy.
Then we'll see some cash money I reckon." Caldwell smiled beatifi-
cally, half-closed his eyes to savor the vision. "Buy us some more
people—women fust of all. Thomas, he will boss the lot, same as if it
was me. Now: what's he want to run for? Nigger don't want no better sitch-ation than this!"

Thomas give Caldwell a sideways look. "Got to make cotton fo'
you spends de money."

Caldwell went *hee hee hee*, and shook his head. "Didn't I tell y'all?
Doubtin' Thomas, hee hee hee."

As they bedded down, on straw ticks laid on the cabin floor, Sephus
gave Abe the eye. The black man showed Abe his fist, flashed it
open to show a shiny silver piece, then shut. "Thomas," he said, "he
want some E-lixir." Grin. "I told him how she fix what ails you."

Abe whispered, "I'll draw him a cup."

Sephus nodded agreement. "It's what I said you'd give." He put
the coin in Abe's hand. "Give it to him *sly*," Sephus murmured.

Abe didn't see the need of that.

Sephus hissed, "Mas'r don't know he got money." But something
else was working inside him. He gave Abe an angry look and said,
"Don't want it hisself. Wants it for Mas'r Cal'well."

It was too many for Abe. Sephus leaned closer, his whisper just this side of silence: " 'A nigger don' want no better sitch-ation,' " he quoted. "But Mas'r has got janders. If he die—whut den?"

They poled down the half-dead water of the bayou. Working at it, they made less than a dozen miles a day, and were worn out. They tied to a dead tree for the night and tucked into their blankets like they meant to drownd themselves. But in the middle of their snoring one of those laughing shrieking barking *Whoo-coooks-f'youuu*'s cut loose overhead and brought them awake with their hearts between their teeth and good-bye sleep for that night. Every time they put their heads down the critter, or maybe it was a whole gang of critters, would start up somewhere else: now deeper back in the swamp, now across the bayou, now in the trees overhead.

Sephus rolled out of his blankets cussing quiet and steady. They heard him rummaging in the cabin. When he came up again Abe saw he had the pole-snare in his right hand—he'd made it to catch birds with, out of the shaft of a fish-gaff and a loop of twine—and a sack, which he let drop on deck. He stood listening. Then he put the back of his hand to his lips and made a soft kissing sound. There was a rustle back in the trees, a limb creaked.

There wasn't but a sickle moon and starlight to see by. In the blue light Sephus's smile showed wolfish. He poked Abe with his foot, pointed forwards, and mimed the hand-kissing motion. Abe slithered forwards. Then he put his hand to his lips and kissed his palm with a soft smacking sound. A limb creaked overhead and astern, a whoosh as a black shape winged out of the trees . . . a loud scream, *bump!* and quick hard feather-muffled thumping. Abe looked back and saw Sephus wrassling a big black bird to the deck, snatching at his wings. "Help me, don't bust his wing jest grab it, keerful now . . ." Sephus got his arms around the thing. "Watch his beak!" Abe whipped the bag over the struggling bird.

A few flutters and the creature stilled.

The noise roused Gentry and Offutt out of their blankets. Gentry said kill the dang thing, but Sephus said it was bad luck: "Swamp-

owl is kin to squinch-owl. Kill one, t'other come lookin' for you."
No need to say more: you hear the squinch-owl, best get right with
your Maker and not waste time neither. "He won't make no noise
long as we keep him covered. Believe he in a holler-tree, it's his
home to sleep in."

They tied the owl by his leg to the stump of the lantern-post, a loop
of twine bound his wings to his body. They took the bag off him in
the morning and set him to perch up on the broken end of the post.
He was about as long as your arm from wrist to elbow, feathered in
brown and white bars with bits of black. He had a small mean sharp
hooked beak and huge dark eyes framed by arched panels of white
feathers. Blinking in the dim morning light, he'd swivel his head
almost all the way round, like a thing against nature, which made
Abe discomfortable when he saw it. The owl's eyes were way too
bigger than his body called for, and dark like a dog's or a man's,
where a regular owl's eyes are yellow like a cat's. Sephus teased
him, kissing his hand with a soft squeaking, which was how a
mouse would sound, scared of owls. The owl would rouse up and
glare. Sephus would laugh, he'd fooled that critter bad and wanted
him to know it.

Night-time he'd go into his fit again, jerking and bobbing on
his tether, shrieking and *Whoo-cook*-ing and barking like a dog, till
you got the notion it wasn't a bird at all but a possessed critter with
a spirit inside it—an eejit spirit, Gentry complained, or a whole
menagerie of spirits was Offutt's opinion. The owl tore up the sack
with his beak; so Sephus took a small empty keg, knocked a hole for
air and food, and they put the owl in it and stowed it below. The
critter thought he was in his holler-tree and went to sleep, expecting
to wake up at nightfall and hunt. He was quiet then, and let them
sleep the night. Only, if you dragged something across the deck the
sound would rouse him up fierce and he'd start in caterwauling and
barking and hooting and shrieking inside the barrel in a way to
make your hair stand up if you didn't know what it was. When Abe
tried to replace a busted thole, he discovered you could get the same

effect by banging on something, rap-rap-rap. He got a good deal of amusement waiting till Gentry or Offutt had drowsed off in a noonday snooze, then give the keg a rap-rap, sit back and enjoy how that owl would roust them out. But he overdid it, and they made him quit.

The shore was mostly swamp jungle, with now and again a clearing: a brown field haggled out of the canebrake, the cotton just rows of brown skeletons, last pickings gone and a month till planting; a sorry-looking cypress log cabin with a spavined roof; a bare yard with always a peeled tree-trunk planted in the middle—nothing hitched to it, it was too heavy to fly a flag and no good for shade. If there were people about they didn't hail the flatboat ashore: stood with rifles to watch it float past. One, maybe two white men on each place; two, maybe three blacks. If there were women they never showed.

Finally a plantation that had some size to it. A big double-cabin sat on a little rise looking down to the bayou. There was an open-faced shed with horses stalled in it, a plank-sided gin, and some small cabins with roofs made of dried grass and branches. Small knots of people stood here and there about the yard watching the flatboat pole up. A half dozen white men armed with rifles waited at the peeled stump that served for a landing. They were woodsy-looking for farmers: skinned-out pole-cats and mush-rats for hats, dirty shirts and pants busted in the knees—barefoot. A runty man, oldest of the bunch, jerked his arm to beckon them in. The rest stood fingering their triggers. Pappy and his tribe of sons. They all had the same face, small eyes close together, stick-out front teeth, the whole face tapered to a point at the nose. Might be one or two of the sons weren't old enough for a beard, but with the dirt on their faces it was hard to say. Offutt put on a great old sociable smile and said, "Gentlemen, I see you have been expecting us!"

Pappy spit: "Had word o' you since you passed Bal'win's. You

ditn' stop to say how do." Abe heard the Mountains in his voice.
People up this bayou came from all over.

Offutt chuckled like they were in on a joke together. "I hope
Brother Baldwin will pardon me," he said, "but to speak truth,
we're a trading boat. And yours is the first plantation we've seen
that looks prosperous enough."

One of the boys said, "No sech of a boat ever come *down*
the bayou."

"Son, I don't fault you asking such a question. Truth is we come
through a break in the levee, during the rains. Followed high water
through the swamp to Mr. Caldwell's."

Pappy spit again.

Offutt never quit grinning. "Got corn-meal, hog meat smoked or
pickled. Hoop-poles. Got some—Sephus my boy, bring up a keg of
our best *Kentucky* whiskey." Of course it was Indiana whiskey, but if
Offutt wanted them to seem a little less Yankee—well, he wasn't
turning water to wine.

Once they had drunk Offutt's whiskey they talked more free. The
weasel-faced man allowed that Jones was his name, Asahel Jones,
and these was his boys: Young-Asa, Morgan, Lafayette, Seth, Jefferson, Calhoun, and Bob. They *could* use some corn-meal and hog
meat—they were an awful lean bunch. Offutt began working Pappy
up to serious trading, Gentry pitched in to help. Sephus made himself scarce below-decks.

Now they weren't in danger of getting shot, Abe gave Jones's
plantation a look-over. *One double-cabin and all them rank-looking
menfolks to live in it, must be a treat to keep clean.* Couldn't see any
white women—in Indiana a woman would have stood in the door,
at least, once she saw it was no shooting. In the middle of the yard
was one of those bare logs, higher than a tall man, planted upright
in the beaten ground—no use for it Abe could see, or think of.

The other people in the farmyard were negroes. Two men and an
older boy, with harness for mending laid out between them. Two
women standing straight, three young'uns leaning back into their
skirts—boys, naked, and a little girl in a ragged smock with her hair
tied in two tufts. Three young men in a bunch by the gin. All of them

stock-still, like they had froze that way: staring at the flatboat. If the Joneses were lean, these black people were plain gaunt. Shoulder-bones on the women looked like they been squared with a draw-knife. Their heads of hair were wild tangles of black wool. Skin looked queer—dull and dusty. Abe hadn't seen negroes enough to know if that was usual. These looked different from any he'd seen in Kentucky or Indiana—blacker for one thing, coal-black. The little ones though, one was black but the others kind of mud-brown.

Mud-brown and a little bit rat-faced.

Wasn't there any white women? There was a blur of white at a window of the main cabin—there it was again. One woman inside anyway, mother of the clan. There was something queer about the cabin: twiggy yellow brooms were pegged over each of the windows, and hung like scraggly blond bangs. Another pair of brooms was pegged crossways over the shut door.

The Jones trade turned out more talk than swap. Joneses didn't have much cash to hand. They could pay for a barrel of meal, which Abe and Sephus rolled out most obliging. But they could use another such, and the rest of that whiskey keg to keep out the wets. Offutt spread his hands, helpless to help.

Pappy Jones tried bluff: Offutt didn't have no right notion what a thing cost down here. Then he tried bullying: he'd took Offutt for a white man, but now he come to think about that levee-break story ... When Offutt shrugged like he didn't care what Jones believed, the man scuttled backwards. "No offense, no offense, I liked the looks of ye the fust I see'd . . ." Then he tried wheedling: a man ought to he'p his even Christian. If he gives, 'twill be give un*to* him, ain't that Scripture?

Then Jones looked shrewd. "Say now: s'pose I trade you a picka-ninny for that kag. I kin let you have that little 'un—she'll breed in a few years, in Natchez you'll git a hunderd *easy*."

"Friend," said Offutt, "I don't trade negroes."

"All right, all right," said Jones most agreeable. "No offense askin'. But"—he winked—"why not take a fuck on one? One o' the wenches I mean." His boys rumbled a laugh all around, liking the idea.

The black women standing near did not move or change expression, stood stock-still like planted posts.

"Go on," said Jones hospitably, "take your pick. Have 'er all night if you want. As many of you as you like. A man kin get a lot o' satisfaction out of a nigger-woman in one night, ain't that so boys?" The man could see Offutt was reluctant, maybe scared, which was gratifying to Jones, who had been feeling put down some. He was taunting now: "Take a fuck on 'em, any one you like. Ain't a man till you've had one, ain't that what they say up North?"

His boys said Haw haw, it sure was.

"No trade," said Offutt, and stepped back aboard. Abe was ready to push off, Sephus standing at the outboard sweep to get them started. Gentry stood near the cabin door: the blunderbuss leaned against the frame, plain to see.

Jones's face twisted in a nasty sneer. "Well get on then! *I'm* done with ye!"

Abe pushed off. Jones shook his fist, full of spite and righteous contempt: "Too proud to take a poke? Reckon you are niggerlovers at that. Go on to Rowell's, he's *your* kind. He *'malgamates* his niggers—that the way you like it?" His voice went up the scale as the flatboat drifted further away, "Go on to Rowell's, he's another nigger-lovin' Yankee sumbitch!"

Offutt had been scared enough so he had to give Jones a cussing now they were safe away. "That crazy skunk-eater! Calling us *'malgamaters* for not wanting to jump his niggers! What does he think those boys of his have been doing? Did you see those mixblood children standing around?"

Offutt had evidently forgot Captain Donaldson's wisdom on that subject—that it wasn't 'malgamation unless the woman got some "advantages" of it. It didn't look to Abe like they got any advantages at Jones's.

Sephus was the only one who didn't seem bothered by Jones's offer, or his cussing. His face got a queer look, sort of smug: like he knew something the white men didn't.

"What are you grinnin' at?" Gentry wanted to know.

"You see dem brooms, hangin' over door an' winders? It's to keep off *witches*. Witch can't pass a door got a broom in front—got to count *straws* afore she go by." He considered a moment, then added, "Must be a *sight* of witch-trouble 'round here." The idea seemed to please him.

The next plantation gave them a warmer welcome: a squatty dark little man standing on the shore, his squatty dark little wife next to him, waving all their arms to call them in, " 'Allo-'allo! 'Allo-'allo!" The short man wore a knitted cap with a dangling tufted tail. Instead of a shirt, a smock that covered him to his knees, and his wife the same, and they both wore little bags of bright red cloth on plaited loops around their necks. The man grabbed the thrown line, his negroes tailed on and pulled them up, then laid a plank for them to come ashore dry-shod.

" 'Allo wel-*cawm*," said the knit-cap man. He was LaFeem, Fren-*shee* they call him, Americans, ha-ha! He had good monnays, buy-trade, ness-pah? His wife reached down into the bulges of her bosom and hauled out a long leather sausage—shook it to make the coins clink and laughed.

Abe took to the LaFeems right off—only, when he got close enough to shake he smelt a stink coming off of LaFeem and the Missus that made his throat clench up and his eyes water. It was like dead buzzard—and not fresh neither. It set Gentry and Offutt back though they were too polite to say anything. But Frenchy just laughed and waggled the red-cloth neck pouch at them. "Is assa-*feet*, you know? Is mah re-*med'*. Is keep off da Vo-*doo* man-*yan*, ver' bad, ha ha ha!"

"Herb med'cine," said Offutt, interested right away. "I never heard of Vo-doo *man*-yan, but I got some Elixir that will cure any ager or miasmals this swamp could throw at a man."

"Vo-doo manyan, he's not malad'." His smile faded a little. "He's con*jho'*, ness-pah? Dese negg', from *Afreek* some o' dem? From 'Aye-*tee*? Dey will make a workin' on you, compron'? Put *ouangah* where you find." He made the cut-throat gesture and a snick-sound. "Dis re-*med'* she say, I am up to dere trick—don't work no t'ing agains' LaFeem."

Meantime Sephus had gone ashore and drifted over to where he could talk a little, quietly, with LaFeem's negroes. There were more than at Jones's, a lot better fed, livelier, and more sociable. The only feature LaFeem's place had in common with Jones's was the peeled log, planted upright in front of the slave cabins, like the sign of some peculiar local religion. No brooms over the doors and windows: but there was something nailed to the porch, a critter of some sort, black fur and a tail. Pole-cat?

House cat. Dead black house cat skinned and dried and pegged to a post. Maybe some more re-*med'*.

They pushed off from Frenchy's, Offutt and Gentry feeling pleased with themselves. What had started out like ruination with the levee-bust was turning out lucky. Sephus was pleased too. He had done some trading on the sly with LaFeem's negroes, couldn't understand the most of what they said but he'd sold a pint of corn whiskey for two dollars in bits, and a cut of root for *this:* he drew a silver candlestick out of his shirt.

Offutt turned the candlestick over and over in his hands. "Where would a negro come by silver candlesticks?"

Sephus shrugged, he didn't care, it warn't his business.

"Stole from LaFeem," said Gentry. "If he notices . . ."

"No." Offutt was thoughtful. "LaFeem don't seem the silver-candlesticks sort. If they had any it was only the one pair, he or that Missus would notice it missing and know where to look." He told Abe, "Hide this back in the hold."

Rowell's plantation was the biggest yet, higher out of the water, and boasted a new gin and enclosed storehouse. Offutt reckoned the bayou was deep enough here for small steamers or barges to take on cargo. They were almost back in civilization. Rowell didn't have the peeled log planted in his yard, so evidently he was not of the local religion.

The master waved to them from the porch of a big two-story cypress-log house. Rowell ambled down the yard to meet them, a large fat man wearing his lunch and a chaw of tobacco on the front of his baggy white cotton coat. He was the friendliest they had met—a Virginian, he said, and Virginia is famed for her hospitality. His negroes dropped whatever they might have been doing and flocked to him, crowding so he had to tell them back off and let the gentlemen ashore. "You there, Jer'miah, fetch the rest of that jug for our guests. And don't drink any yourself, leastways no more'n usual!"

If Rowell was a Virginian, Abe was hard put to understand Pap's grudge against the tribe. The man wouldn't hear of trading until they'd took drink with him, then supper. "Boys," he called to the colored crowd in general, "get over the pen some o' you and kill us a couple shoats—let 'Liza get to cooking on 'em," and off a bunch of them ran.

A fawn-colored woman, her head wrapped in a calico turban, came out onto the porch and hollered after the boys they better not let loose any them pigs and then she find they cookin' them in quarters!

"That's my 'Liza," said Rowell proudly. "Runs the place as well as any overseer I ever had." She knew trading too. Between gutting the pigs and setting them to roast, whipping up corn bread, and boiling greens, she came out on the porch and stood with Rowell. If he was about to shake hands on so much for a barrel of meal she'd clear her throat, *Hraaaff-hrrm*, Rowell throw her a look, grin sheepish, and say, "Well ain't that a little too dear?" Abe reckoned he understood why Jones said Rowell was a 'malgamater.

Guests meant *holiday* at Rowell's. They saw no work done there the livelong afternoon, only people rustling up an early supper in front of their cabins. And there were things they might have done. The farmyard was slovenly, busted wheels boxes and trash strewed all around. The big brown cottonfield back of the place—a good twenty acres bony with picked-over plants—could have used weed-

ing. There was a rough road, not more than a trail, separating the
yard and the cottonfields, and a fence run along it. But if it was a
snake fence, the snake's back was broke. There was a gate, but only
a man enslaved to formal courtesy would have thought to use it.

But Rowell wasn't bothered by the mess, so why should they
worry for him? They traded the afternoon away, Rowell's "boys"
pitched in and rolled the boughten barrels of meal and pork, and
two kegs of spirits, off the flatboat up to the shed. Offutt had a word
with Sephus: he appreciated the trading he'd done at Caldwell's
and LaFeem's, and suggested he try his hand with Rowell's
negroes. Sephus gave him a grin, and ambled over to chat with the
oldest man on the place.

They took supper in the cool porch ('Liza's was the best cooking
since they left home) and watched the sun melt towards the straight
line of woods on the far side of the bayou. They slung lanterns from
the porch-beams, tilted back in their chairs, swatted flies, and let the
pork settle.

There was a stir by the cabins. 'Liza stepped onto the porch and
looked down towards the quarters, her brow knotted. "Sim come
back," she said.

"Always does," said Rowell complacently.

Two men approached the porch: a young man with cut-off pants,
and an older man who wore one of Rowell's old coats (fit him like a
tent). Rowell nodded to the delegation. "Sim is back," said the old
man. "Paterollers 'most git him."

Rowell said, "Hm. You say howdy to Miss Cassie for me?"

Sim grinned, missing a dog-tooth on one side. "Sho' did, Marse
Gee-awdge." His smile went out like a blown candle. "Paterollers
somethin' *strong*."

Rowell yawned. Vittles slowed him. "Well. Y'all got back no
trouble."

Sim and the old man hesitated, then ducked their heads to the
company and turned back to the quarters. Sephus had been squatting below the porch: the old man gave him a look and he rose
eagerly, as if he'd been waiting for Sim to get back. Abe heard him
laughing as they strolled to the quarters.

. . .

A little later, just at dusk, they heard horses in the road. Someone out by that wreck of a gate called, "Hello! Major Rowell, suh!"

Three men on horseback let their tired animals walk them up to the big house. The three held rifles across their laps; wore hunting-shirts and slouch hats. Each had a coil of new rope slung from his saddle. The leader was thick through the body, clean-shaved, eyes hid by the shadow of his hat-brim. He had a short length of whip looped over his saddle-horn.

Rowell said, "Crowe." The man answered, "Rowell." He looked at the fat man awhile. Then: "Rowell, I come for your boy Sim. Caught him in quarters with my Cassie again. Makes four times. Four times I know about," he added. "Four times I come to tell you, you need to take a hand with your people."

"My people are mine, Crowe. I do as I think fit. In Virginia we don't bother about niggers visitin' their women, one plantation to the next."

Crowe looked at Rowell some more. "This ain't Virginia. Folks is fed up scarin' your niggers out their quarters and chasin' 'em over creation. There's things been stole. Niggers passin' it to someone to sell. Someone whose master don't mind what his people get up to." Crowe took the limber whiplash off his saddle-horn and slung the loop over his wrist. "I saw that boy duck under that so-called fence o' yours. He run from the pateroll. Bring him out. I mean to have the whuppin' of him here and now."

Rowell said, "I'll take care of my own any way I see fit. And pateroll or not: you are trespassing on my land."

Crowe sat quite calm. "That how you want it, Rowell?"

"That's how 'tis."

"Well then," said Crowe, "ev'nin'—*Marse Gee-awdge*." He touched his hat and turned his horse, the two others following, each in turn throwing a look at Rowell as they passed, and rode out at the "gate."

In the quiet they left behind Offutt said, "Well sir! We thank you for your hospitality, but we must be getting . . ."

Abe jumped up. "I'll get Sephus and see to the boat, Mr. Offutt"—speaking formal so it would be harder for Rowell to stop them.

But Gentry was sleepy with vittles. What was everyone getting up to leave for? He hadn't no notion of poling the flatboat off into the dark when there was hospitality to hand. As Abe went across to the quarters he heard Gentry's puzzlement, Rowell protesting, insisting they take another drink, he had some N'Orlins brandy in the house somewhere.

The negroes had disappeared, whether into the cabins or the brush Abe couldn't tell. He stood off from the row of cabins and hollered, "Sephus!"

The black man popped up behind him like a spirit and scared him half to death. "Let's git on board," Sephus said. "People says Regulators comin' for Mas'r George." Abe started for the boat, but Sephus checked him, grinning. "Look what I traded us!" He pulled a crescent moon partway out of his shirt—the edge of a heavy silver plate. "Rowell's Sim, he give me . . ."

Abe grabbed his shirt and shook him. "Chuck that thing in the bayou!" Sephus was so surprised his rage flashed and he shoved Abe off. But there was no time for that: "It's stole! You want to have it on you if the Regulators catch us?"

"I give him a hand o' roots for it!"

"Hang the roots!" Abe said. *And us too if we ain't careful.* He jumped for the boat, Sephus with him.

Abe's thinking ran fast: not runaway but as if everything else was slowed to a crawl while his own thought sped point to point: shore hitch undone save the loop he could loose with a flick; musket rifle and blunder-gun set handy just inside the cabin door; poles and sweeps set by the tholes.

Offutt and Gentry were still saying their good-byes, easing out of the yellow light of the porch, but slow, slow, like bugs caught in reezin. What was keeping them? Trouble might wait, but Abe couldn't see any reason it *should.*

Then, just like that, it was too late. Abe's keyed-up senses picked up the drip and chuckle of water off in the black dark. Wasn't any critter: woods and water were dead still, sign that men in numbers were in the woods or paddling up the bayou. Offutt and Gentry were ambling across the yard, fending off Rowell's hospitality.

Abe hissed, *"Sephus!"* He put his lips next to the black man's ear and whispered, "Regulators comin' on the water. Let 'em take us. Show out you been took by surprise. But be ready." He gave Sephus a little push to go stand in the stern-well. Abe sat down by the skiff and waited. His back hairs were all a-prickle for the canoe to bump and the men in it to swarm up onto the flatboat.

There was a sudden cry from the quarters, a rush from the dark gate! Rowell turned and shook his fist at it, Gentry and Offutt took one look and bolted for the flatboat.

Abe heard something butt the water-side timbers, Sephus cried out, Abe held himself calm as he half-rose—then froze at the rap of iron on wood: a man stood in the stern-well pointing a musket straight at Abe. Abe recognized him as one of Jones's get. Abe got slowly to his feet, raising his hands. The man in the stern-well climbed up onto the roof-deck, careful to keep the drop on Abe. Two more riflemen scrambled across the stern-well and onto the landing: Gentry and Offutt skidded to a stop in their rush for the flatboat and raised their hands. Sephus, down in the stern-well, cringed against the timbers while the fourth man out of the Regulators' canoe (another Jones) pressed a rifle up under his chin.

Someone set torch to one, then another, of the slave cabins. Shadows humped and popped like bladders in the red firelight as Regulators swarmed into the yard. Rowell stood at bay maybe two rods from the flatboat, armed men on horseback circling him, looking down on the fat man from the height of their horses.

Abe dropped to his knees like he was hamstrung. "Oh lordy lordy lordy," he moaned, so scairt his wits had flew the coop, man with a gun don't worry about someone who shows out yellow like that. "Oh lordy lordy lordy." He was so scared he couldn't move, they'd have to haul him off the flatboat, that would need two of them at least and they were too busy enjoying their lynching-bee to have time for such work. Whatever he had to do, even hugging knees and crying, Abe meant to stay on the flatboat. That was their getaway. He had no notion yet how to get the drop on the

Regulators: only knew that was what he had to do, one way or another.

More Regulators swarmed out of the dark, hooded and masked, spooklike in the fires. Maybe forty all told. Some had driven Rowell's negroes—or as many as they had found, eight women and some kids, two older men—into the yard, where they made them get on their knees so they couldn't run, and set three men to watch. Others were battering the door of the house, which 'Liza had barricaded against them. The leader of the Regulators—in the fired darkness Abe recognized Crowe by his horse—called for them to leave off, she warn't goin' nowheres, they'd give her what she had comin' *after*.

Rowell gave himself up and stood stock-still. The circle around him opened so they could push Offutt and Gentry into it. It was quite a show: they brought torches in close to light Rowell all around, but the Regulators were behind the torches: black shapes, only their voices and the dull flash of light on gun-barrels to show them. Three or four Regulators heaped a bunch of the wood-trash that littered the yard and made a hot fire. They set a kettle in the fire, and stood tending it.

"George Rowell," said Crowe, "you been warned. But you ain't one to listen, are you Marse *Gee*-awdge? Not to a white man. Listen to that yaller wench you keep house with, let her run your place, but won't stop your niggers runnin' the roads at night. Stealin' your neighbors' goods. Roost'rin' in another man's hen-house. Stirrin' up every man's niggers, think they kin get away with anything at all." There was a grumble of assent from the horsemen and catcalls from the Joneses on the flatboat.

Crowe moved into the fire-light now, still a-horseback, his hat pulled low to black out his face. He took the whip off his saddle-horn and pointed its drooping limber length at Rowell. He gave his voice a deep, portentous tone, as if hidden powers spoke through him. "Someone burnt Crawford's barn. I lay it on your niggers, Rowell. And I lay it on you." He swung his head around the circle, "And how say you all?"

"Guilty," rumbled round the circle.

"Someone run off three of my niggers. Run 'em off, and sold 'em

to that Red River trader come through last fall. I lay it on your niggers, Rowell, and I lay it on you."

"Steal your niggers?" Rowell cried. "What do I need to steal your
niggers for, I got plenty of my own."

"Only you don't sell *your* niggers," Crowe said, " 'cause you love
'em too much." He pointed at Rowell and said, "I lay it on George
Rowell. How say you all?"

Guilguiltguilty "Guilty as hell!" chanted the Regulators. The uni-
son of their voices, massed and hooded in the night, gave them a
superstitious power and terror that went beyond their numbers and
evident malice. The Regulators themselves seemed to feel it. Every
time they spoke they became more restless and eager, jerk-reining
their horses, barking their responses.

Rowell looked up at Crowe. He knew he was a goner. Nothing to
do put play it out strong as he could. "Crowe, there ain't any man
has the right to tell me how to run my place or rule my people."

"String him up," yelled someone.

"No hangin'," said Crowe. "We ain't here to do murder." Crowe
paused. Then said, slow and pleasureful, "No. Punishment has got
to fit the crime."

A man in the shadows hollered: "What about these others, ain't
we goin' to fix these sumbitches . . . ?" and the crowd seemed hungry for it, muttering *nigger-stealers* and the like. But Crowe was in
charge. "Strangers after. Neighbors first."

Half a dozen Regulators swarmed in on Rowell and laid hands
on him, the great fat man swatting and beating them off with his
arms till someone kicked him behind the leg and buckled him down
to his knees on the ground. Two men took hold of each of his arms,
held them straight out and give them a twist that forced Rowell to
bow his head. They hauled up, forcing him to stand. Another man
stepped up behind Rowell and slit his coat up the back, peeled it,
then ripped down his shirt. He cut Rowell's belt and ripped Rowell's trousers down around his ankles. Two more Regulators stepped
up, limber willow-switches in hand—whooshed them experimen-
tally. The big man was trembling in the holts, his fat naked smooth-
skin body quivering.

The willow-switch men wrenched up and swung, and Abe heard the nasty skeeter-whine/spat of the switches as the whippers rocked one after the other in the fire-light and lashed Rowell left and right across his broad white back and fat ass, whee-*spat* whee-*spat* again and again and again, not blows, not stabs, not hard pain a man could go down beneath and still have some dignity, even a strong man can lose to strength and numbers—just the spiteful incessant whine and sting, you ain't a man you ain't a man you are a puling snot-nose, the men are laughing at you as they switch their marks, X and X and X, on your fat ass and nekkid back, till Rowell broke out in little chokes, wheezes, then "Oh," then "Oh-God," as they cut him and cut him again, till he began to fall in pieces, till he didn't have no pride no more, only wheezing and crying, snot blowing out his nose and hanging down, only "Stop it oh Jesus oh Jesus . . ."

Then long after it should have been over it was over. They let Rowell's arms go and he fell on his face in the dirt. There was a rush of men from the fire, carrying the hot kettle between wooden poles. They tipped the kettle and poured some sticky smoking black liquid on him, pitch-pine tar by the smell—Rowell hollered and tried to roll away but one man stepped on his hand to hold him. Rowell was croaking something. Two men turned a cotton-bag over and snowed feathers all over Rowell.

"That'll whiten him some!" That set them all laughing. They'd turned Major Rowell into a goose, the biggest fattest goose you ever see. A growed man! turned into a goose!

Abe couldn't stand to look at Rowell. He hated what was done, and the men that done it, but he couldn't stand to look at Rowell. *As well kill a man as shame him to his people.* He wished Rowell wished he was dead, and that he could be dead for the wishing. What must his spirit be now inside the shame, the whipping, the goose-ifying, the laughter? What could it ever be, now? Better be dead. But Rowell was still alive, a fat mound of filth and feathers, moving a little in the dirt.

Crowe said, "If you kin hear me Rowell? Won't a white man in the district know your name after this. Lay up three days if you want; then sell out and *git*. We'll hold your people 'gainst the sale—all but the ones burnt the barn. Our own people give out who they be. If they run tonight, we'll ketch 'em—and fix 'em."

Then it was their turn. Crowe shifted in his saddle to look down at Offutt and Gentry. Silent. Waiting for Offutt or Gentry to say the first words, and so mark themselves guilty or . . . well, what could they say that would be took for proof of innocence?

Gentry said, "You got no quarrel with us. We are strangers here. Jest tradin': corn, pork—"

The Jones in the stern-well called, "Got a nigger up here." He lifted his rifle under Sephus's chin, hoisting him like a fish on a gaff. The torches swung to illuminate them.

Crowe said: "Got papers for that nigger?"

Gentry was buffaloed, Offutt jumped in: "Papers? We never needed papers before this."

"Kin you prove you didn't steal him?"

"Can you prove we did?"

"I don't have to," said Crowe.

A man in the mob hollered, "I'll prove they stole the nigger." The crowd parted to let a burly man through. The torches swung to red-light his face:

Starkey.

Of all the bad luck turns in creation, Abe would never have guessed Starkey. It was worse than bad luck: it was like they'd been singled out for a peculiarly mean providence. *Starkey quits Donaldson and works his way downriver, hears some Regulators are looking for an extra gun* . . . It was almost funny if it wasn't so likely to get them hung.

Starkey stood in the torch-light. He grinned open-mouthed at Offutt and Gentry. He peered into the shadows to see where Abe might be. "Last time I see that nigger, he belonged to Cap'n Donaldson. That was his prize nigger—takin' him and dozen more south, to sell for the Red River. These ain't no planters: they are Yankees out of Indiana. They sure never paid no Red River price for that nigger."

The crowd muttered. Crowe motioned for Offutt to answer.

"We are near neighbors to Captain Donaldson—his place is just over the river. His boat was wracked, and we hauled his boy out of the river. It's all of his property we could save—him with a wife and son, and heavy in debt. All we are doing is to carry the boy back to Donaldson's people."

Starkey's turn: "Horse-shit."

A rumble of laugh all around. Offutt saw he was licked. Abe reckoned they were done, if he couldn't think of something. They had fallen into the black hole and would never get out. *Forgetting and forgot.*

Starkey said: "I say we horse-whup and hang the lot of 'em. Then divvy out their goods—it's prob'ly all of it stole off of pore Cap'n Donaldson!"

A rumble of assent went around, and Abe's Jones brother pounded his rifle-butt on the deck to signify his enthusiasm, *bonk bonk bonk.*

And at that a horrible scrooching scrawk sounded out of the belly of the flatboat.

Everyone froze: Crowe, the Regulators, Starkey, Offutt, Gentry, Rowell in his misery and shame, the negroes on their knees, the Jones brothers on the flatboat—the one with his gun under Sephus's chin whipped his head around, the whatever-it-was come from just behind him. From behind *that door.*

Next was a shriek that went all hollow-booming as it echoed through the belly of the boat. Then the dog-bark, *ark! ark! ark!* Then that horrible neck-strangled shriek and an awful scrabbling of claws on wood.

"Oh lordy," Abe moaned. "Oh lordy you have woke it up!"

"Jesus Christ," said Crowe, "what *is* that?"

Abe clinched his insides to hold the sudden extreme joy that nearly exploded in him. He had the play in hand. Abe got slowly to his feet, pointing at Offutt. "It's your fault," he moaned. "I told you not to take that Thing on board! Black cat that size—and what's a house cat doin' out in the swamp I want to know?"

"Sacr' diab'!" A voice that might have been LaFeem's.

"But you wouldn't listen, wouldn't let me throw it back where it come from!" Abe appealed to the crowd, they were reasonable men: "Wasn't I right? But he! *He* said the Thing promised him *riches*, and he meant to keep it *regardless*." He sobbed, "Now *look* what we come to!"

There was a muttering now, some Regulators had sympathy for Abe and give Offutt a nasty look—beginning to take sides between them, where before it was all sides against them. But Abe wanted a *leetl* more—

And got it:

"Whut kind o' riches did it give?" Old Man Jones!

Abe ignored him, his voice cracked. "It ain't *my* fault," he appealed to the Regulators, "I wanted shet of it. I told 'em, throw it back and set brooms to keep it off. But the Thing—the Thing promised *them* riches, all they had to do was *feed* it. Feed it! Oh lordy, it was *me* had to go down and *feed* that Thing!" He dropped to his knees, sobbing, pounding the deck with his fist.

Which called up a long, rageful, claw-scrabbling scrootch from the depths of the cabin. That snapped the Regulators to: they had got so fascinated by the spectacle of Abe's blubbering cowardice, they forgot the Thing itself—but there it was again, scream like a cat, bark like a dog, scrabble like a crab, what in hell *was* it?

Abe looked up at the Jones boy that stood over him. His jaw was sprung, staring down at the thin deck that was all that kept the Thing from running up his leg. Abe said, "You can't make me go down again! I 'druther you shoot me!"

Then he heard Offutt: "For pity's sake man, make him go down and feed it. It gets mad if you don't, it might bust out." Abe felt a rush of thankfulness—Offutt had took the game up smart.

Crowe sat his horse, couldn't decide what to do.

"Crowe, dang it!" yelled Old Man Jones. "Ask him whut *kind* o' riches it give 'em!"

"Give 'em the dang boat," Abe moaned. "I don't want no gold at *that* price." He emphasized his words by pounding his fist on the deck.

Which summoned a rising string of hoots dog-barks and wildcat-shrieks enough to stand your hair on end. "Son of a bitch," said

Crowe. "Jones! Make him go down and feed it. But keep your eye on the door in case it tries to get out!"

"I ain't goin'," Abe whined. " 'Druther die."

The two Jones brothers on the boat looked at each other, terror-struck and afraid to show it.

"Asa Jones!" hollered Old Man Jones. "Take that Yankee son a bitch and make him feed that Thang. Do it or you know whut!"

Young Jones said *shit* under his breath and poked Abe with the rifle. "Get on and feed it," he said, " 'r I'll blow your haid off." Abe cringed over to the stern-well, dropped into it. Asa Jones was close behind—Abe heard Old Man Jones call out, "And look-see whut kind o' *riches* it give!"

Abe cracked the door. He saw the other Jones, the one with Sephus, lean back as far as he could against the side timbers, then climb up on them so's to jump for the woods if the Scrootch-Thing got loose. Abe cringed his way into the door, Young-Asa hung back, he was afraid to go in—the rifle-barrel lifted off Abe's back . . .

Abe twisted, snatched the rifle-barrel with both hands and jerked Asa through the door sprawling across an out-stuck leg. He snatched up the blunderbuss where it leaned by the door, right where he'd put it. A splash outside, yells, no shots, reckon Sephus throwed the other Jones in the bayou. Abe kicked the owl's keg. *Whooo-coooks?* shrieked the owl. *Yark yark! Yeehee-hahaha!* Abe laid the bell-mouth of the blunderbuss alongside Asa Jones's head and told him quite seriously, "Why don't *I* just blow off *your* 'haid,' and feed *your* guts to that *Thang* in there?"

He wondered if he meant it, would he kill Asa Jones if his bluff didn't work and the Regulators rushed the boat? *No man gets vurry far in this life if he can't kill a man when he needs to.* Uncle Mordecai's wisdom. Abe had played the blubbering coward. Now he had to *be* a man who wanted to kill someone, kill him even if he couldn't get no real good of it, kill him if it was the last thing in his life.

He motioned Asa Jones to rise and step into the stern-well. Sephus crouched in it, sheltered from rifle-shot; he had the other Jones's rifle—the Jones himself was just now floundering ashore. Abe pushed Young-Asa up to where the Regulators could see him plain, and waved the blunder-gun so they'd know what he had against the back of Asa's neck. "Jones!" Abe hollered. Crowe might not care if Pappy Jones came home short a son, but Jones would. "Jones! Send my people on board or I'll blow the back of Asa's head out the front!"

"It's jist your one shot!" Jones yelled. "One shot and we rush you."

"Well all I want's one shot," said Abe reasonably. "One shot from this-here blunder-piece and you will be combin' Asa's *brains* out your hair, hee hee hee." He goosed Asa with his knee and the boy said, "Pappy he's a-gonna *kill* me!"

Jones gave a strangled cry, grabbed Gentry, and shoved him viciously at the pier. Offutt followed. Crowe tried to block the two men, but Jones pushed in and leaned against Crowe's horse. "Back off, Crowe! It's my boy he's got a-holt of!"

Gentry and Offutt were aboard. "Musket and rifle by the door," Abe told them, and when they came back out he told Sephus to cast off. "Use the sweeps," Abe said, "I want to get out o' the light. They won't shoot while we got Asa." Gentry and Offutt set their guns handy and went to the sweeps.

They glided off, the Regulators staring after them. The torch-lit ground of Rowell's receded in dead blackness. When Abe judged the distance was right he said to Asa, "Can you swim?" and when the boy said he could Abe shoved him splash into the water. They heard him thrashing his way back to shore. Across the glassy black water new fire surged brightly at Rowell's. Abe reckoned it was his house going up. He remembered what Crowe said about seeing to Rowell's 'Liza, and hoped she had got out before they lit it up. But where could she run? Then the sweeps took them round a point, blackness covered them at last.

Then he remembered: poor fat Major Rowell. Why hadn't he told them to sling Rowell aboard? Well, it might have spoilt his play: Rowell wasn't *his* people, he was the Regulators' and they might have got hard if Abe tried to take him. But the truth was, the idea of saving Rowell never crossed his mind. As if the man was as dead already as Abe supposed he must wish himself to be.

Abe shook off the image of the friendly Virginian, and his trans-mogrification into a human goose. There was one more thing he had to do. He went below, and brought the scrootch-owl's keg on deck. It was full dark on the bayou, they rowed under a black overhang-ing wall of trees. Abe wedged an ax and popped the lid of the barrel. The owl scrootched and barked. Abe reached in and took the critter out; held it under his arm while he reached out his knife and cut the cord that bound its wings. Then he lifted and threw it at the trees. The owl scrawked and dipped, then rustled out its wings and soared up disappearing into the black.

Abe said: "Now we're even." Then he broke up the owl-filthy keg with the ax and threw the pieces in the bayou.

Chapter 18: **The Trial**

New Carthage, Early March 1829

They swept and poled through the night. Offutt, Gentry, and Sephus worked with energy born of joy at their escape. But the glooms came down on Abe. Maybe it was Rowell. Maybe it was that the dull sheen of the water-path, clogged before and behind by overlapping points, made it seem that they still labored without progress. He had a notion the bayou wasn't done with them.

So he was not took so horribly by surprise when at first-light he steered them round a point and they saw the broad shine of the Mississippi beyond the last sand-spit of the bayou's mouth—and also a big log-raft squatting in the channel, riflemen on board, cutting them off from the River. And rifles along the landing at the mouth of the bayou.

Sephus turned to wood. Gentry slumped to the deck. Offutt threw down his sweep, glanced at his gun, then gave it up. He looked round at water, woods and sky and said, "Well, we give 'em a run." Abe turned them in towards the landing. Nothing else *to* do—for now. He reserved judgment as to the future.

The ambush-raft was a rope-haul ferry that operated across the mouth of the bayou. Abe scanned the reception committee. Maybe a few more than forty Regulators all told, a dozen on the raft and the rest on shore. They were armed to the gizzards with rifles knives muskets pistols and shotguns, but in the thin morning light the Regulators didn't look as spook-scary as they had when they were shadows in fire-light. They looked mean enough, but scraggly. Some boasted themselves forwards, others looked like they'd as soon be somewhere else now there was light to see them by.

The Regulators formed a gauntlet and they had to walk it, poked at and punched, till they got to Crowe, who sat himself on a nail keg under a big old cottonwood, Pappy Jones at his side. The cottonwood had straight projecting limbs dismally suggestive of hanging. They were bullied into line facing Crowe, Abe uncomfortably prominent because he towered over the others. The Regulators closed in behind. Crowe gave them a long cold look intended to scare them witless.

Off to the side of the cottonwood was the log-built store that served the landing, CAHOONS NEW CARTHAGE, also a cotton-shed and a small cabin. The Regulators' horses were hitched to the rails of a pen behind the store. On the bare ground nearby, one of those peeled upright logs was set in the ground. Two other prisoners stood against the wall of the store, guarded by a pair of Regulators. The white man's bare shanks stuck out below a dirty nightshirt. The negro wore a clean white shirt and good trousers, but his feet were bare.

Starkey abruptly pushed his way into the open space by the tree and slid a long knife out of the sheath in his boot-top. "Longshanks," he said to Abe, "you are *my* meat."

Crowe jerked his thumb at Starkey and snapped, "Get back in ranks! This here's Regulators, not no private grudge-fight." He was mad Starkey had broke into his stare-down.

Offutt spoke up. "I don't know what you think we have done. But if you have charges, why not take us to court?"

Crowe said, "This is all the court you get. It is our kentry, and we keep it as we see fit."

Gentry looked like he was strangling. No way out. If they got off with their lives they'd be lucky. If they got off without the whipping the mob give poor Rowell, they'd be blessed. "Offutt," he said, "don't rile him."

Offutt tried to keep his voice under control. "All right," he said to Crowe, "it's your game. But if you're a gentleman, you'll play fair with us. You haven't said what we're charged with. You don't give us a show to answer."

Crowe frowned. "You'll get your show all right. First off, you are charged with armin' and incitin' niggers."

Offutt was flabbergasted. "Why in God's name would we do that? And what niggers did we ever give guns to?"

"*That* nigger there," Crowe pointed at Sephus. "Every man in this assembly seen that long drink of water"—meaning Abe—"give that nigger a rifle. And tell him to point it at white men: white men, and Regulators in the course of their duties. That is what I call *incitement.*"

Pappy Jones said, "Plus the nigger took my boy at a disadvantage and throwed him in the river."

Crowe said to tie the nigger up. One man kicked Sephus behind the knee to buckle him. Two more grabbed him by the shirt and dragged him to the hitch-post in front of the log store. They whipped some thongs around his wrists and cinched them hard to the rail.

Offutt said, "That wasn't inciting. How'd we know you weren't robbers? Hasn't a man got the right to defend himself? Yes, and order his boy to help, if it comes to that?"

Crowe said, "Things has got to be purty hard, and plainer'n what this is, afore I'd say a man can give a nigger a gun to shoot a white man with. Besides, you ain't proved that *is* your nigger." He smiled. "Which brings us to the rest of the charges: that you are Murrell-men, and been incitin' niggers to rob our houses or run theirselves off, so you could take and sell goods and niggers both!"

Offutt spread his arms helplessly. "But none of that happened while we were here!"

Crowe said, "That's 'cause we was on to you since you come out the swamp." Crowe leaned in, his eyes wolf-lit. "We got Rowell's Sim, that carried the goods." He waved his hand at the two men held against the wall of the store. "We got Cahoon's Octavius there, that kept and sold 'em."

"Well then ask Sim, ask him . . ." Offutt hung fire—he remembered in mid-speech that Sim had traded silver (probably stolen) to Sephus. "Ask him whether he ever saw us before this," he finished lamely.

Crowe showed his teeth. Jones said, "Ax him yo'self." He gestured towards the pen where the horses were hitched. On the ground was a dirty cotton-sack cinched at the ankles, waist, and neck, and hitched by the neck to the pommel of a saddle by a length of rope. The cotton-sack was stained with blood.

Gentry's voice ran up the scale: "Sir, Mister Crowe—it's a mistake! We ain't Murrell's. We're Kentucky-Indiana men! Look at the boat—she's oak built. Go on board, look at our goods: its all Indiana-Kentucky produce we got there!"

Pappy Jones went red in the face. "Go on board of her! I like *that*! We ain't forgot that critter you got down there!"

Crowe was annoyed at the distraction, he dropped Gentry and give Jones a look.

Abe perked up. "Go on and look, why don't you?" His grin jeered Jones's cowardice.

Crowe shot his point-finger at Abe and snapped, "Now you *shet*." He twitched his mouth around, uneasy. "Ain't no need to look at your goods. You could have stole 'em same as you did the nigger. That's the last charge: that you stole that nigger of Cap'n Donaldson. Got a *witness* for that."

"My turn!" said Starkey, stepping into the judicial space between Crowe and the accused. He was working a quid of tobacco in his jaws, his smiling mouth overbubbled with brown spit. He unloaded it on the ground between himself and Abe.

Abe smiled friendly. "Starkey," he said, "you forgot to tell these folks the part where I kicked you in the balls and throwed you in the river." There were splutter-laughs and a burst of haw-haws in the crowd. Abe turned to Crowe. "Plain truth is this: we hooked up our flatboat to Donaldson's north of Memphis, on account we are neighbors. Starkey picked a fight with me—and like I say, I kicked him 'twixt the uprights and throwed him in the river."

"Son of a bitch," said Starkey, pelted by the laughs.

"When we got to Memphis, Donaldson give Starkey his *dis*-miss for bringing shame to the boat."

There was a rumble in the crowd. They were beginning to look forward to Abe and Starkey squaring off.

But Crowe was still set. "It's your word against Starkey's," he said. "You can't prove none of that."

Abe thought a moment: "Well, I can kick Starkey in the balls and throw him in the river any time you like."

"I will kill you for that," said Starkey, but was rolled under and drowned by a wave of the hee-hawing back-slapping and thigh-pounding.

Crowe had risen to his feet and was about to pound his gun-butt on the keg again—when a sudden rapid drumming of horse-hooves sounded from behind the store. A dozen men on horseback swept round the corner at the trot—breaking into the Regulators and driving them back.

Their leader was a small man, erect and easy on a beautiful blood-horse. The man was neat as a pin: a white boiled shirt with paper collar and ribbon necktie, wide brim beaver hat, dove-gray riding coat, and britches tucked into soft-gleaming knee-high boots. He folded his small clean hands on his lap. He looked down at Crowe the way a man looks at some unaccountable nuisance his dog has made in the parlor.

Under that look, Crowe slowly got to his feet. "Tate" was all the greeting he offered.

The little man said, "Colonel Cahoon to you, Crowe."

The men behind him (they shifted their horses, easing out to either side of the leader) were armed with rifles, pistols, and shotguns—all but the small man himself, who carried no arms, and carried himself like he didn't need any. Three of the men looked to be sons of Colonel Tate Cahoon. The rest of Cahoon's men wore dirty shirts and gallus pants—Cahoon's hired men or tenants. From what Abe had seen of the South, it took a man more than ordinary rich to employ that many white men.

"Crowe," said Cahoon, "appears to me you and yours are trespassing on my land." He nodded at the two prisoners by the store: "That's my 'Tavius you've took; and my man Priest."

Crowe stood his ground. "This is Regulators, Cahoon—*Colonel*. You got no right to interfere with the law."

"Law," said Cahoon. "You have no more sense of law than a weasel. I know what you did to Rowell. What were you thinking of, to whip a white man in front of niggers?" He shook his head at the stupidity of it. "I won't have you lynching flatboatmen at my landing. You'll hurt my trade."

Crowe slipped from judge to plaintiff: "Your 'Tavius was tradin' stolen goods. Rowell's Sim brung him the stuff, and he traded it off to steamboat niggers and flatboatmen. If your man Priest wasn't in it, he must've . . ."

Cahoon paid him no mind. He dismounted gracefully, and his three sons after him. Their retainers stayed mounted and watchful. Cahoon stepped over to the two prisoners by the store. He looked the white man, Priest, slowly up and down; then nodded, as if the look satisfied him of something. Then he turned to the black man, 'Tavius. As soon as Cahoon's eyes touched him 'Tavius broke out, "Mas' Cunnel, I don't, I nevah, I ain't . . ." Cahoon lifted his hand and he shut up. Cahoon nodded to himself again, as if he was satisfied.

"Priest," he said, "did you know about this?"

"No sir, Colonel sir, I never . . ." The man was trembling and sweating.

"If you are not dishonest, you are a fool," said Cahoon. "Get your pants on, and be off my land by noon."

Then he leveled on 'Tavius: the black man stood straight, his face gone slack and still. Cahoon pointed his little chin at his oldest son and said, "Jugurtha!" The son gave his orders, and the two Regulator guards grabbed 'Tavius by the arms and rushed him to the high bare log driven upright into the ground in front of the store. "Give it a hug," said Jugurtha Cahoon, and the black man embraced the post. As soon as he did one of the guards bound his wrists crossways with a leather thong. 'Tavius's face was pressed so hard sideways against the log that his features deformed. The other guard ripped the clean white shirt down to show the man's broad unmarked black back.

The little colonel placed himself where he could observe the expression of 'Tavius's face. Cahoon assumed a dignified pose with lifted chin and cocked head, right fist on his hip and elbow jutting. "Hannibal," said Cahoon, which was the name of the next oldest son. The young man unlimbered a short snake-whip, flexed its muscular length, flirted it with his wrist, and cracked it across the black man's naked back. The man twitched hard and took his lip in his teeth. Hannibal Cahoon made the whip whistle *whee*, and cracked it again into that back, blood jumping out in the broad smile it cut. Whee-*crack*! again. Whee-*spat*! the stripes crossing each other, blood bright in the crotch of each cross-stroke, whee-*spat*.

Abe's own skin jumped and twitched at the sound of the whip's whine and sting. His mind snatched at distractions, the Regulators standing mesmerized, tongues lolling, pup wolves watching the boss wolf work the carcass, *Well*, he thought, *now I know what them peeled posts are for.*

" 'Tavius," said Colonel Cahoon mildly, "is it true you are a thief?"

"No sah, no sah ain't a thief . . ." He knew it was worse than useless to deny it, but he couldn't help himself.

The Colonel raised his eyebrows, "Do you give me the lie, 'Tavius?" He looked ruefully to his son. The young man grinned, flourished his whip, whee-*crack*! like a rifle-shot, and the pain made the bound man jump in his bonds, mashing his face into the post— grunting at the next crack, then a choke at the next, his nose and face beslobbered. Between whip-slashes, he sucked his lips into his mouth to hold the outcry, but spat *pooh!* anyway at the jolt.

" 'Tavius!" said the Colonel mildly, " 'Tavius, do you mean to say *I* am not speaking the truth?"

"No sah," the black man's voice was muffled by his cheek mashed against the log, and he was weeping. "Yes sah. You say troof sah . . ."

"Do you tell me so?" the Colonel asked himself, wonderingly. Now he was disappointed—not angry, just seriously disappointed. Hannibal Cahoon grinned, flirted the whip, and snapped the negro again. And again. And another. And a right *smart* one.

Abe found himself sucking in his own lips, holding his breath, twitching in horrible sympathy with the black man lashed hard to the post. There was no right thing to say would make Cahoon quit, *yes* was as bad as *no*. And not a thing to be done about it: Law nor reason wasn't worth a damn as long as Cahoon had the whip, and all those guns behind him.

Abe felt the ice rising in him, and the rage, murderous. He had to stop himself grinding his teeth together. *No good looking like a nigger-lover.*

Cahoon raised his hand, and Hannibal let the whip loll. " 'Tavius?" said the Colonel. 'Tavius was blowing and crying through the slobber of his face. " 'Tavius. I will not have you tell me what is, or is not, true: do you understand?" The black man started to speak, then by some inspiration held silent. That made the Colonel smile. He considered the slave judiciously. "Octavius, you *are* a thief. I judge you are not alone. After a time I will speak privately with you, and you will tell me who has helped you in this."

Young Cahoon curled his whip, finished—for now.

As if that was a signal, the Regulators came back to themselves. "Let him tell all of us!" hollered Jones. "We all of us has lost by it!"

"We got our rights," said Crowe stubbornly.

Tate Cahoon considered Crowe's and the Regulators' rights. It didn't take long at all. "You're on my land. I'll sit judgment on what passes here."

"Well, set with us then," said Crowe, gesturing towards the judicial keg.

Cahoon's time was his own. He spent a little of it. Then he said, "I won't sit with you. I might sit *here* awhile, and listen." He gave Crowe a look. "I might even let you pass a judgment: as long as you remember who is the court of appeals." He waved his hand for Crowe to proceed.

So they went over the charges again, and Starkey told his story same as before.

Then the Colonel looked over the culprits, noticed Offutt had the best clothes. "You seem to be a gentleman," he said by way of inviting him to speak.

Offutt's face lit with inspiration. "Colonel, I wonder if you are acquainted with a gentleman I know, who lives hereabouts. I mean Judge Joseph Davis, sir. Joseph Davis of Hurricane."

Cahoon nodded approvingly. "I know him well. His plantation is just over the River. We differ in politics: but the Judge is as fine a gentleman as there is in this country."

Offutt's gratefulness shone in his face. "Then sir, if you would, send to him. I believe he will vouch for me, and make my word good with you."

Cahoon looked genuinely astonished. "By gadfrey! Do you claim acquaintance with Judge Davis?" He pursed his brows. "This puts a different light on the matter." He considered Offutt with his mild, deadly gaze. "A man *might* pretend to such acquaintance—but to what end, when it is so easily put to the test?"

"Hang it, Colonel," Crowe complained, "we've had testimony the nigger was stole. If he ain't, why don't they prove up?"

Cahoon admitted the point. "Sir." He addressed himself to Offutt again. "Whatever your acquaintance, it would be better if you had papers . . . some legal show of title to this boy."

Offutt spread his empty hands.

Abe said, "Beg pardon, Y'r Honor, but I don't reckon title is necessary in sech a case."

Cahoon raised an eyebrow at that. He looked Abe up, then down again: coarse ugly face, ratty thatch of hair, ragged clothes, no shoes. White trash.

Abe reached into his shirt and took out a book: Cradok's *Western River Pilot*. He remembered Judge Pate, and tried to speak to Cahoon the way he'd have spoken to the Squire, hoping to *bring out* the 'Judge' in the little colonel. "Law of salvage, Colonel sir. She's writ in the back parts of the book, 'Abstract of the Maritime and Riverine Laws.' "

"I know the law of salvage," said the Colonel. "What's it to do with niggers?"

"Well, I might be mistook, sir, Y'r Honor: but if a boat wracks, and a man saves the property, then the property goes to him, no matter who had papers on it."

Cahoon still looked puzzled.

Abe prompted him softly, "Slave is a kind of property, sir. Colonel. Your Honor."

The Colonel stared at Abe, then on through Abe off into the woods. He came back shaking his head. "Well I'm blessed," he said. "I never thought of it." He balanced the *Pilot* in one hand against nothing visible in the other. *Pilot* won: "Point well took," he said. "But look here son: we have nothing but your bare word that that is how it happened."

"Ask the nigger to bear him out," said Starkey. He stalked over to where Sephus crouched by the hitching rail. He kicked him hard in the ribs with his booted foot.

Cahoon missed Starkey's humorous intention. He gave the man a short look: "We don't allow nigger testimony down here," he snapped. He turned his mild expectant gaze back to Offutt. "As I said, sir, your appearance is that of a gentleman, and I am inclined to believe you. I will myself go across and talk to Judge Davis. If he vouches for you, I am satisfied. Meantime my boys will guarantee to hold your boat safe, and your goods. I'm afraid we will have to put you in our lock-up." He indicated a windowless cabin across from the store. "But it's for your protection—my boys will see no harm comes to you."

Crowe broke in: "Dang it Cahoon, you can't jest bust in and take over . . ." Cahoon gave Crowe a dead-fish stare. Crowe, red-faced, added, "Colonel!"

Cahoon turned his back and addressed the Regulators. "Boys!" he said. "This gentleman here, a stranger, makes claim of acquaintance with our neighbor Judge Davis. You know Judge Davis"—he glowered a little—"and you know me. These men are under my protection, until I can satisfy myself of their truthfulness. If they show out liars, you can hang the lot for all I care. If they show true, they go free. I give my word as to that. If harm comes to them, or their goods, before I get back, well: you know *me*."

Poor Crowe, he saw it all slipping away. The Regulators were feeling low-down. They'd gone from running the show to watching the quality conduct business. But they had no stomach for standing up to Cahoon and those boys of his, and his hired men. Too many guns. Best not show too sull neither: a man didn't make money getting wrongside of Tate Cahoon. The Regulators' ranks began to fray and dissolve: they were not backing down, but they had better things to do than—

A loud voice by the store, Starkey: "Nigger, didn't you hear me? I said, 'Boy—you give me the *lie!*'" The drift of Regulators had begun to clot up again around the hitch-post where Sephus was tied. *Sephus.* No one thought to bring him inside the Cahoons' circle of protection.

Sephus had got to his feet, and stood facing Starkey and Jones. His back was hunched because of his wrists bound low to the hitch-rail. Jones grinned: "You lifted your hand on a *white* man, boy! You pointed a gun at a *white* man . . ."

Sephus stood, his eyes fixed on a point far off in space.

Starkey kicked Sephus's legs out from under him, he fell sidelong his bound wrists over his head. "I'm talkin' to you boy. When a *white* man talks to you, answer up!"

Offutt and Cahoon were deep in discussion of Offutt's claim on Judge Davis's friendship, and the terms of their imprisonment. If they were aware of what was going on by the store, they gave no sign of it. Only young Hannibal and some of the hired men glanced that way, like men bothered by being left out of the fun.

Starkey said, "I'm gonna teach you a lesson, boy." He kicked Sephus alongside the head, changed position, and kicked him a jolt between the legs. Sephus's arms twitched as he tried to clutch his balls, but his wrists were cinched above his head. He curled into himself, his breath strangled with hurt. The Regulators called and shouted encouragement.

The sound got Cahoon's attention. He held up his hand to interrupt and glanced towards the store.

Sephus had got hold of the hitch-post and hauled himself up to it, kneeling. Starkey strutted around him to take an angle for his next kick.

Cahoon saw nothing to concern him. "Well then," he resumed with Offutt, "if you'll give your word . . ."

Abe grabbed Offutt's sleeve: "Why don't you stop 'em?"

The *hunk!* of another kick.

Offutt went pale. He turned to Cahoon: "Colonel—if they kill that boy—he's all that's left of Captain Donaldson's property. If they kill or ruin him, his widow and orphans will get nothing."

Cahoon nodded. "Yes—that's reasonable." He turned to his oldest son, Jugurtha: "That's enough now. Go tell those men to quit. And bring that boy here."

Jugurtha Cahoon and his brothers waded into the crowd with a couple of hired men, dragged Sephus back through the dust by the thongs around his wrist, and laid him at the feet of Cahoon and Crowe. The two had muttered some agreement, and stood together as the mob came up.

Crowe said, "That's all the whuppin' for now. We got to settle whether these strangers are all right or not. If Judge Davis vouches for 'em, the nigger is theirs to send back to the Donaldson family. We don't want to send no dead niggers back to the widow and orphans." There was a grumble of agreement—the Regulators weren't pleased, but what Crowe said was reasonable and just.

Abe didn't give a damn what they thought was reasonable and just. Down here reason wasn't worth spit unless it had guns to back it. And if it had the guns, the worst crazy meanness could pass for justice. Something inside Abe was beginning to howl, not dog-miseries but dog-rage, *If I had the teeth I'd rip that son a bitch's throat out, Cahoon and Starkey one after the other.* But Cahoon was their hope to get out of this trap, and Starkey had the mob behind him. He took a twist on the mad dog, *Curb him, make him heel.* One moment more and they were safe, the crowd was stilled waiting for Cahoon and Crowe to make benediction and dismissal.

"Starkey!" Abe barked, throat tight and raw as if he'd been rope-choked. "Starkey, you lying son of a bitch!"

Starkey woke suddenly, shocked, from his soft aftermath. Then his face lit. He drew the long Arkansaw toothpick out of his boot-top. "Longshanks, I'm gonna gut you like a fish."

The Regulators perked up and cheered for the fight, maybe this day warn't entirely gone to waste! Crowe looked at Cahoon, Cahoon looked annoyed at things took out of his hands.

Abe heard Offutt's plaintive whisper, *Abe!* but ignored it. He didn't care what happened to him next, or any of them. He was sick with anger, trapped in that black hole, bullied by these crazy skunk-eaters and now this dandy little colonel with eyes like a snake— sons of bitches all of them, they were as bad as Milk-sick, but the difference between men and Milk-sick was you could kill a man, *and no man gets vurry far in this life if he can't . . .*

He looked to Colonel Cahoon. "It ain't but right, is it Colonel? Accordin' to your notions?"

The Colonel nodded sourly and stepped back with a permissive wave of his hand.

Starkey stepped out at a half-crouch, making little slashes at the air with his knife. His face had a put-on snarl, his eyes were wary: he didn't like Abe's death's-head grin.

Abe said, "Don't need no knife to whup my dog." There was an ax jutting from a stump where someone had been splitting fire-wood. Abe wrenched it out, then banged the ax-head loose leaving himself with the helve—a two-foot club of smooth hard hickory carved with a slight graceful arc. The mob would think he was giving Starkey the edge. Whereas Abe calculated the length of the helve plus his long arms gave him the reach over Starkey. If Starkey and the rest were too stupid to figure that out, so be it. Fair play had nothing to do with this. This was Uncle Mordecai's kind of fight.

He stepped into the man-fenced arena facing Starkey. Some of the Regulators hollered for Starkey, some wanted Abe to bust Starkey's head, and some just said *Kill him,* never mind which one they meant. The two stalked each other round the circle, watching for the chance to strike. Starkey held his knife in front of his body, making little cutting motions in the air. Abe held the ax-helve in two hands gripped close to the base.

Abe stopped circling. Grinned. Stood easy: daring Starkey to rush him, *and here he comes—*

Starkey ducked his head and dodged in at Abe, slashing at

Abe's left side with the toothpick. Abe slashed the ax-helve quick and popped Starkey's knife-hand—the knife flashed away. Starkey jumped back grabbing his broken hand. Just like that Starkey was knife-naked, half-crouched—he raised his hands a little to ward off. But Abe never moved.

The crowd was still. Almost happy: waiting to see how the show turned out.

Starkey said, "It's done, Longshanks! It's done if you want it to be!"

Abe said—or did he just think it?—"No. I ain't done with you." He was cold as death inside. He swung the helve up over his right shoulder and went in, his mind moving with a terrible speed that made the work of his body seem slow: Starkey threw his arms up to save his head just as Abe expected—Abe dropped the helve and swung low from the side, the straight waist-level swing with the whole force of his long body whipping through it like he meant to sink an ax-blade deep into the heartwood of some oak or maple that was in his way—slammed it into Starkey's ribs and felt the bones buckle, Starkey cried a piercing cry.

Abe stepped back to watch the man fall.

Starkey twisted to the side. He went down on one knee. His face was bloodless and his lips were green. He was making a kind of sighing whine as he knelt there. A look come into his eyes: Abe could see the man knew, the man knew Abe had busted him up bad inside. Starkey dropped to his knees. He gulped a little. A bright line of bloody spit showed along the dead green line of his lips.

A spasm of disgust shot through Abe's whole body, he swung his arms and the ax-helve up over his head, one pure purging swing and he'd smash the son of a bitch to flinders, drive him helpless into the black earth like a spike . . .

Abe yelled and slammed the ax-helve hard into the ground, driving it deep enough to stick upright—missing so close Starkey shut his eyes and every man in the mob sucked wind.

Abe felt something, something sick inside only it didn't make him want to buckle and puke it made him feel like his head was rising high and higher and drawing his body out after it rising dizzy and high and all the men in the clearing looked shrunk and puny.

He turned to Cahoon and Crowe. To keep the bile down he made himself smile. Then a notion came to him. He jerked the ax-helve out of the ground and offered it to Cahoon: "I submit my argument to the jedgment of this honorable court."

Cahoon took the ax-helve. "I guess that's settled."

Abe said, "I'm satisfied."

It would have been truer to say he was fed up—fed up to puking. But he never let on.

Chapter 19: **City upon a Hill**

New Carthage and Hurricane, Early March 1829

Next morning Cahoon was back, and Judge Davis with him—who took Offutt's hand without hesitation. "Offutt, I am sorry we meet under such circumstances." With Davis to vouch for them they expected to be let off at once. But no: not without a fine for damages.

"Damages!" cried Gentry. "Why Jedge, we're the ones damaged! There ain't a court wouldn't—!"

"I don't say you are not entitled to bring the case to court. You understand such an appeal is not immediately practical." Davis hesitated, looking a little discomfited, then continued, "But I wish you would forbear the exercise of your rights at law. There are certain *peculiarities* in the situation which, if put before a court, might expose your friends as well as your enemies to . . . *embarrassment*."

Offutt laid his hand on Gentry to quiet him, and told Davis: "We are in your debt, Judge. The last thing we want is to embarrass you. But I hope you do not think there is any truth to the accusations against us."

Davis looked troubled. "I do not believe you did, or would do, *intentional* wrong." He hesitated. "But you see, if you arm a negro against a posse and we let you off—or if a federal court were to support your action—why, there's the appearance our negroes don't *have* to obey us. And we can't live with that. Our situation is uncertain: a few white men, their women and children, on farms and plantations in the woods, and many more negroes than kinfolk around. Our safety depends on instilling in the negroes an absolute conviction that there can be *no* appeal from the Master's judgment."

Offutt and Gentry looked at each other, and at Abe. They owed Davis so much ... Besides, they were still a long way from any court. "All right," said Offutt. "Sephus grabbed the gun himself and has been properly whipped for it."

"Yes," said Davis. "And since you accept this understanding of the case, you might acknowledge your ... *negligence* by payment of a fine." Gentry and Offutt looked alarmed, so he added: "In goods, not to exceed a hundred dollars value?"

A hundred dollars might be forty percent of their voyage so far, but it was plain Davis thought this the best way out. Gentry and Offutt agreed. "Let us finish this business," said Davis. "Then you must be my guests at Hurricane. Perhaps I can show our institutions in a better light."

Hurricane plantation occupied a broad tongue of land in the crook of a grand loop of the Mississippi. A leveled path of white sand rose from the landing to the grove of old liveoaks in which Davis had built his great house: a large two-story house of red brick, with heavy white pillars to give its front grandeur.

A young woman stood in the doorway—small and delicate, black-haired, plump as ripe fruit. She was Abe's age, maybe younger, likely the Judge's daughter. She cried the Judge a welcome home and came to him with little dancing steps, and he took her hands. "My dear one," he said, and gave her a husband's kiss full on the mouth. Abe and Gentry blenched and Offutt shot his eyebrows up. Davis gracefully introduced Mr. Offutt and Captain Gentry to Mrs. Davis—who gave them a perfectly lovely little smile and dipped a curtsey.

The door of the house filled with girls: three of them, in fine muslin dresses matched in a pale peach color. "And these are my girls," said the Judge proudly, waving them forwards to greet their guests properly. The littlest was no more than eight, the middle girl rising twelve. The oldest was about the same age as Mrs. Davis and held herself with careful dignity, one eye always on her young step-mother. There was no way any of those girls were daughters to *this* Mrs. Davis. It softened Abe a little towards the Judge to think of his loss. And it was plain he'd made it up to his girls, for they appeared to dote on him.

In fact, just about everybody on the place, black or white, kin or kitchen-help, looked at Davis like he was made of sugar-cake and they didn't want to miss no crumb of him. Davis was like an old bull in a herd of heifers, or Sultan Shariar amongst his hareem.

The house Davis showed them through was both luxurious and comfortable in its scale and furnishings. Thick brick walls kept the house temperate in all seasons. The library was a small palace of readables. The Judge even boasted an indoor privy, built for him by a Cincinnati craftsman. Offutt had seen plenty such, but it was a wonder to Abe. Not just the workings of it, for the piping was logi-cal and easier to read than steamboat engines. The wonder was that anyone should have thought to *want* such a thing. It showed how mean Abe's ideas were—just what you'd expect of Pigeon Creek.

They took supper at a long table in the dining house. There was a muslin cloth, silver eating tools, and fine plates of potter's ware— finer than ever Abe had seen, yet not the finest Davis had, which were ranged in a glass-front cupboard. The Judge sat at the head and his Missus at the foot. Offutt got the Judge and Gentry to talk to, and the oldest of the three Misses Davis to look at. Mrs. Davis got Abe and the little girls, whose notion of conversation was to glance at Abe then bust out giggling till the Missus made them hush and say what was so funny?

"Oh nothing, ma'am, only Mister Lankton . . . he's even higher off the ground than Uncle Jeff!" This set them off again, and Mrs. Davis hushed them and told them to apologize. "That's all right ma'am," said Abe, "I'm used to it. Tallest nail is the one you hammer." He was more embarrassed by the fuss than the giggling, which was just a little girl's way of flirting—only, he wished it was the oldest girl doing it. She was pretty and soft and clean, and put him in mind of Mariah Connors and that dinner at Nashoba a long time ago.

The mention of "Uncle Jeff" caught Davis's ear, and he reminded Offutt that they were speaking of "my younger brother, Jefferson. Graduated from the Military Academy, and posted to the North-west to keep watch on the Indians."

"A military career is the very thing for a young man of spirit."

Davis nodded. "The profession of arms is a noble calling. But my hope, perhaps a selfish one, is that Jeff will return to Hurricane. The army will have taught him to *command*—there is no more needful education for a planter. I mean to divide my land equally with him when the time comes."

The generosity of the notion made Offutt rear back a little in his chair. "Why sir, that is noble . . ."

Davis waved the praise away, embarrassed. But it took Abe the same as Offutt. Pap wouldn't let him keep a tithe of his own earnings, but this man was ready to give his brother the half of his kingdom. Under the Judge's plain-gentleman exterior there *was* a kind of Sultan or Caleeph hiding—and a mighty free-handed one.

"My father left Kentucky and risked his all to build a plantation near the Lou'siana line. He never made his fortune. But he put his children in the way of success."

Gentry looked around at the signs of that success, his mouth pursed as if he was regretful his own pappy had chose Indiana instead of Mississippi. Abe understood the feeling. Lincolns and Davises both started in Kentucky. Pap thought God was ag'in slavery, so he went north into the trees; Davis didn't mind the Thing, so he went south to the cotton. Now Davis was lord of his own kingdom and Pap one crop away from a dispossess. A man might *begin* to wonder if Pap hadn't been a trifle *mistook* in his calculations.

Offutt said, "It seems almost magical you should have built all this in—was it two years?"

"Well well," said Davis, slightly embarrassed, "it has required more than that. I guess it is seven since I first saw the land, five since I began buying out the settlers. And then, one needs capital to buy people to work it. My brother Isaac occupied the ground and began clearing while I stayed in Natchez to earn the wherewithal. The foundations of this house were laid more than a year before I moved here."

"Mister Davis was head of the legal profession in Natchez," said his young wife proudly, "and author of our state's constitution."

Davis bowed to her. "Madam, you praise me beyond deserving." He sat thoughtful for a moment. "Natchez may be the finest city of the South—our city on a hill, so to speak. But it was not what I most wanted." He gave Offutt a straight look: "I wanted a world according to my own will. Not to share in a world made by others, not even if it was the best good place on earth. But to have everything just as *I* wished: built and managed by myself, on the most scientific and progressive principles I could discover. And in this bend I saw how I could make it so: the wilderness easily displaced, the soil rich and amenable to the plow, the River at hand to serve my need of commerce, and a race of men submissive in the service of a careful master." He looked consideringly at Offutt and asked him seriously: "What man would *not* wish to have all things as *he* chooses, if it were in his power?"

It was a good question, and Abe thought it over as he lay in his blankets that night. What man *didn't* want a place of his own, where he could make all things to suit himself? Even Pap, in his mean Pigeon Creek way. But this flatboat journey had opened Abe's eyes to bigger possibilities. Nashoba, the Arkansaw River Fur Company, now Hurricane: which showed what a man could do if he went at things scientific—and if his notions were *large* to begin with. Maybe if Abe put his mind to it he could work up to a place like Hurricane, shiny glass plates and indoor privies, rooms full of books and pretty young women, *Maybe small at first like Caldwell and Thomas, maybe on the River maybe in the Shining Mountains, maybe he and Sephus . . .*

Early next morning Offutt and Gentry went to say good-bye to the Judge, and Abe went down to the quarters to fetch Sephus. He followed a worn path past a fruit-tree garden. Beyond that was the white-washed log house that belonged to Davis's white overseer, and past it two long rows of cabins. The negroes came spilling out of their cabins, men women and children in family groups more than a hundred all together, some with hoes and mattocks hupped to their shoulders, flowing together in a column that marched to the fields like it was to a muster. The smaller children darted in and out through the column raising dust and a *little* Cain. As Abe came up to them, the negroes went quiet, and gave him nothing for his best *Howdy* but an uneasy respectful duck of the head. But they told him Sephus was at Aunt Dilly's: that tough little woman who Miss Wright sent South with Davis. She and Sephus were both from Donaldson's, it was natural she should get the care of him.

Aunt Dilly's yard was gone to weed. As Abe came up to the cabin door he heard Sephus's low-down chuckle and a woman's *hee-hee-hee*. He stopped to listen. Dilly said, "Sephus, I be sorry to see you go. I miss home folks somethin' *bad*."

"Old woman," said Sephus softly. Then: "Yo' *Missus* say she come take you back."

Dilly snorted. "An' send me to die in *heathen* lands."

"Maybe she let you stay. People here say Jedge Davis a good man."

"He de Lawd Jesus if you ax *him*!" Then she was still. "He don't 'buse yo' body. But yo' *spirit* must bow down."

"Ain't no satisfyin' you . . ." said Sephus.

"*Humpf!* If *you* like it, go ax de Jedge to buy him *yo'* pitiful self!"

Suddenly she slammed the door open—and caught Abe listening, froze with surprise. The wiry little woman glared at him in pure yellow-eyed fury. "God damn yo' soul an' what does *you* want?"

" 'Scuse me, ma'am," Abe said.

"Ma'am!" she snorted. "Who does you think I *is*?"

"I come for Sephus."

But Dilly stood blocking the door with her hands on her hips. "You must be his home ticket. My my my." She shook her head and enjoyed a mean chuckle at the foolishness of men. "So you's who he got fo' his home ticket, my my my." She left the door and stalked away across the weedy yard.

Sephus sat up out of bed, bare to the waist except a band of cloth around his ribs where Starkey kicked him. Half his face was swole and his eye on that side closed. He greeted Abe but with a watchful look. Abe guessed he was wondering how much Abe overheard. "Don't pay Dilly no mind," he said earnestly, "got a mouth like a pizen snake."

That didn't put Abe off, it made him prickle. *Home ticket.* Why should Sephus call him that? "Offutt and Gentry said we would take you home to Donaldson's."

"Which is all I's ever sayin' to her," said Sephus, and opened his arms to show his true heart.

"And another thing: don't take what that woman says about Miz Wright for gospel."

Sephus went still. Why should Abe care what *he* thought? But if there was a trick in the words he couldn't find it. He shrugged. "All right, Mist' Abe, I won't."

The Judge had got up early to see them off, sorry they wouldn't stay for breakfast, but he'd had cook put up coffee and vittles for them to take. He shook hands with Gentry, and lingered awhile speaking with Offutt, put a paper into his hands. Abe had got over expecting more than a nod from the Judge, so he just hefted their baggage and walked it aboard. He liked the rise of the boat under his foot. Sephus clambered painfully aboard, and Abe told him to set out of the way while they got ready to push off.

The sun burned through warmly and yellow as Offutt jumped aboard. Abe set his oar against the dock and pushed them into the stream. They turned to wave to the Judge, who raised his hat to them. Gentry took the stern-oar and Abe manned the in-shore sweep and moved them out to the current. The River muttered again under the timbers. Sephus leaned against the skiff, worn out just walking to the boat.

Offutt stood looking back to Hurricane, patting absent-mindedly at the pocket of his coat. "What's the paper?" Abe asked. Offutt beckoned Abe to follow him aft, and they dropped into the stern-well with Gentry. Offutt spoke soft so Sephus wouldn't hear: "The

Judge says we can't go on carrying Sephus without legal papers. He took our word we were holding Sephus for the Donaldsons . . ."

"Well it ain't no lie," said Gentry.

"Of course not," said Offutt, "of course it isn't. But he couldn't write us a paper naming us agents for the Donaldsons—not unless they were here to sign." He glanced at Abe. "So I told him your salvage idea."

Abe wondered if he told Davis whose idea it was.

"He wasn't easy with it. No precedent he knew of, and he seemed doubtful about setting one." Offutt looked a little puzzled. "I asked him what was the danger, and he said: 'We are breaking new ground down here. Suppose a court was to recognize right of salvage in a negro. Any man that saved a negro from drowning could claim him.' "

Gentry grinned. "You'd have people throwing niggers in the river every time one crossed their path."

"What did he write?" Abe wanted to know.

Offutt looked solemn. "Well, he wrote we made salvage of Donaldson's wrack, and are holding Sephus as earnest for a claim on the Donaldsons. It ought to cover most situations. But the Judge didn't feel entirely right about it. He asked us, on our honor, to do our best to keep it out of court. I told him we would: we owe him that much."

Gentry said, "So as far as anyone down here is concerned, we own the nigger." Offutt said, "I wouldn't put it just that way." But they left it at that. Offutt put his hand on Abe's arm and said, "I'm not forgetting what we owe *you*. The Judge pulled us out of the water, but it was you kept our heads from going under. I make you a promise: we will see you get some good of it before you are much older."

Hurricane to Natchez, Mid-March 1829

They let the Big River take them south, sweeping no more than was needed to keep them in the main current. Sephus was let to lie in the

sun for a few days so his ribs and face could mend. The memory of
the bayou haunted Abe a little, the choking closeness of the trees,
the way his wolf had got loose when he went for Starkey. But the
darkness faded with distance. The sun was warmer every day,
higher in the sky, slower to set. It was only March, but the air was
already April-soft and coming on to May-sweet. The poplars willows and tupelos along the river tipped out in sprays of new green.
Geese went north overhead following the river, brants and ducks
rafted in the shallows.

A week out of Hurricane they entered a broad curving reach at
the bottom of which a high sheer-sided hill rose above the River,
crowned with white spires and gleaming cupolas set in a froth of
green trees. Natchez looked grandly down its three hundred feet
of height as they drifted up to the waterfront. Flatboats swarmed
the upstream end, beyond them were the steamboat docks: eight
grand boats a-loading, twin-stacked sidewheelers slathered in white
filigree.

The Natchez waterfront ran along a muddy flat below the Hill,
nearly level with the River. Nestled against the cliff were the hotels
and gambling halls, the warehouses and whore-houses of Natchez-
Under-the-Hill: the glory and shame of the River trade for a generation. It had a seedy look in the afternoon light. Maybe the brimstone
showed to better advantage after dark.

Offutt's notion was to set out a sign and see if Gentry could sell
any Elixir to the riverside traffic. In the meantime he and Abe would
go up-Hill to talk to some folks whose names the Judge had given
him. Gentry got a kick out of that, even Sephus saw something to
grin at. Whatever the joke was, Abe was left out. Well, the way to
take a joke, when you can't get out of one, is let it come—and wait
your chance to play one back.

Abe and Offutt climbed the steep-pitched road to the top of
Natchez Hill. Offutt carried a wrapped parcel about which he said
nothing. At the top of the bluff the road became a broad "Promenade," with the River far below on one side, and on the other rows
of great tall old trees, heavy in the trunk and thick of limb—oaks
and liveoaks and peccans, all of them in bud or leaf in the early

Southern spring. Behind the trees were splendid houses, buried to the gables in flowering shrubs. Abe used to think Squire Pate's was all a man could want; then he saw Hurricane, and that was more than any plain man would think to want. Now the first house he saw in Natchez made Hurricane look rawboned. Every time Abe believed he had seen the finest house ever built, the next turn of the River showed him something finer. He was no fool: you couldn't trick him the same way more than a dozen times.

At the edge of the bluff, space fell away as if the world had been cut in two. Abe had never in life been that high off level ground. The gold light of the sun dissolved in the humid air softened all edges and gave everything a glow. At their feet was the huddle of shipping and Under-the-Hill business. The River spread wide, in grand curving milky reaches between green forests broken by broad brown sweeps of plowed land. On many of the fields mule teams and gangs of negroes were plowing and hoeing and ditching, at that distance they looked like beetles scurrying about. There were great white and red-brick houses set in the cleared fields. Offutt rubbed his hands: "Isn't this a *location*?"

Beyond the Promenade, Washington Street was lined with fine buildings of brick or clapboard, stores had signs with letters of gold hung over their doors. The street was full of people, more than half of them black. Every wagon or coach that spattered by had a negro in the driver's seat. Every well-dressed man or woman that passed was tailed by a train of two or three colored servants—carrying packages, holding a horse, laying a plank over a puddle. There were negroes standing behind counters, taking down boxes. The negroes were dressed for town, most of them. Their clothes looked *made* rather than *found*.

Offutt led the way to a shop with a red-stripe pole in front of it, grinning fit to bust as he bowed Abe in, "After you, my dear Mr. Lincoln." The Barber rose to greet them: a light-skinned negro with a broad grin. "My good man," said Offutt, "my friend here is to have your best: hot bath, shave, and haircut!" Offutt hauled cash money out of his pockets and laid it in the Barber's hand. The Barber's clothes were *all* of them store-bought, and he had on leather half-boots. In Natchez even the negroes were rich. The Barber looked Abe up and down and said, "I ought to charge by the yard," and they all had a laugh on Abe.

In the Barber's back room two negro boys were pouring buckets of kettle-heated water into a large cast-iron tub. Abe was to strip. He balked.

"Come come," said Offutt, "you have read of Kings, haven't you? David and Solomon and so on? Bathed and anointed? Well: do you think they did it in their clothes?"

Well why not? Abe thought. *Why not enjoy a taste of the rich life right now, and earn his own piece of it later?* He gave a whoop and hauled shirt and jacket together off over his head, then unslung his belt and dropped his pants. One of the boys poured a powder into the bath and stirred it. Abe stepped in—it was right warm to his feet— let down into it easy, the water rising above his hips. He was scrunched, knees up under his nose. The Barber said, "I'm sorry, it's the biggest tub in town."

But they managed: Abe hunching while the boys washed his back with a brush, then hanging his shanks over the side to lean back and let the water rise to his neck while the boys poured warm water on his head and the Barber massaged his hair and scalp with cunning gentle fingers.

He put on a clean set of clothes—which was what Offutt had in the parcel. Then Abe let the Barber lather his cheeks and shave them with careful strokes of the razor, trim his hair with careful snips, then a quick rub with aromatic oil.

"Offutt," said Abe, "is this for a weddin' or a funerl?"

"Hee hee," said Offutt, "maybe a little of both."

Offutt treated to an early dinner. When they stepped out again on Washington Street it was evening. The air was soft—March was April down here, April was likely June, and June might be heaven. Abe felt a little bit drunk, though he hadn't tasted anything stronger than what they called lemon-water. His head was floating above his shoulders, and his body stalked along under him like a long-legged horse he happened to be riding. Offutt looked like the fox that et the rooster, he was that pleased how his "show" had knocked Abe over.

Well, let him enjoy his chuckle: Abe was satisfied. More—he was grateful. But when he tried to say as much, Offutt just said to hold on, for the best was yet to come.

Offutt stopped at a white gate. It was the last house in the street. There was a large stable across the road. To the north the trees and houses seemed to fall away and broad fields opened out under the stars.

But Offutt had opened this gate, and his moonlit face was smiling. "Son," he said, "you have showed yourself a man this voyage. Gentry and I agree: it is time you came into a man's estate, and took yourself a taste of a man's privilege."

The face of the house was masked by a pillared porch. Glass side-lights blazed in the dark framing a red-painted door—which opened before they knocked, a negro pulling back the door to show a splendid old woman in an emerald dress, who welcomed them. As Abe passed the threshold the spirit inside him dropped down and flew up at the same time, like it did when the River suddenly tipped and dropped you down a chute and you knew you might smash up and die but you were riding the fastest water in the world, hold on a little longer you'd be flying. Offutt said something to the emerald-dress woman, Abe caught the mention of "Judge Davis," at which the woman became overjoyed to see them.

A pair of double doors slid aside. They opened a room whose color and odor hit Abe in a sudden blaze and a wave of sweet perfume. The room was *full* of females, at least a dozen, girls gliding sinuously about, women draping themselves across luxurious couches or perched on the arms of stuffed chairs. There were men mixed in too, you could miss them easy because they were so few, maybe one for every four women, and dark clothed where the women and girls flashed and glimmered with colors of skin and bright clothes and lace froths, women's hair braid-bound or let loose, women's plump breasts bare almost to the nipples, women's legs naked from ankle to thigh, all to be looked at and no shame.

Pap Lincoln's boy *couldn't* be in such a place. The swish of the spirit-ax went through him again, sweet and thrilling this time, it cut him loose from himself, Pigeon Creek Abe dropped away

and a new man, a new Abe—call him *Mister* Lincoln—floated free
and sailed out into the light, tall as a tree and strong as a bull and
smart as a whip, ready for his first taste of a man's privilege—and
more to come after, more and more of it the rest of his life long, *Mister* Lincoln, *Judge* Lincoln, *Lord* Abraham Lincoln of the Shining
Mountains . . .

A woman was coming towards him—seemed to recognize him:
look how she smiled at him! A small oval face on a long bare neck,
she was uncommon tall for a woman, she wore a loose watery dress
that looped over one shoulder left the rest naked and ran down her
in ripples when she walked. She walked right across the room
directly to him. Her whole face was smiling and her eyes set on him
in a steady level deep-friendly look. She looked really *truly* happy,
happy to see him *again*, like she had missed him and was just so
plumb to the bottom pleased he come back—so happy that Abe
found himself guessing whether he *had* met her and somehow forgot? But if he'd once seen such a woman he'd never forgot her in a
hundred years. "Well now," she said in a low voice that made Abe's
heart bump. "I reckon you are *Mister* Lincoln."

Abe swallowed his Adam-apple and tried to say *Ma'am*. The
woman smelled like sugar and flowers. She was the softest-looking,
cleanest-looking person he had ever seen in his life. There wasn't a
sharp edge to her anywhere. Her skin looked like flower-petals, that
plushy softness. Her hair was gathered up all round her small head
except for a long piece that flowed sudden and straight like a water-
fall down the side of her face and across the little moon of her right
breast, which Abe couldn't help but look at. Yet she didn't mind:
only lifted herself a little so the soft hair slid apart and the curve of
her breast rose in it.

He stood there paralyzed with looking at her breast. If she hadn't
took him by the arm, and given him a start towards the doors,
he might never have moved again. "You can call me Ruby," she
told him.

He cleared out his throat enough to say, "Abe."

She give his arm a squeeze and said, "Well that's real fine then,
I'll call you *Abe*." Her hand pressed his arm as they walked. He was

grateful she knew what to do for he surely didn't. He looked around for Offutt, but missed him. Ruby was saying things to him, what a tall-looking man he was, and *strong* too—she ran her free hand along his forearm in way that made the hair rise all over his body.

And maybe he would like to visit in her room?

The double doors parted like the Red Sea as they walked up to them. He let her lead him to a wonderful rising spiral of staircase. As they climbed it he felt the last of his old Pigeon Creek self slough like skin off a snake. That old boy he was couldn't imagine such a staircase, let alone going up it step by step arm in arm with a woman like Ruby. Maybe he'd have to go back to being *that* Abe Lincoln some day, but right now he was free, free when he got to the top of the stairs to be whoever and whatever he wanted, or she wanted, and he meant to enjoy it, too.

Her room was midway back in the upstairs hall. A close room, yellow-lit by a pair of tallow candles. There was furniture—a shiff-robe, a plain table with a washbasin. There was a little glass pitcher next to the basin that, from the small spike of smell, had vinegar in it; next to that a dish of spongy balls. There was a bed: made of brass spindles and posts, clean sheets gleaming smoothly on a thick mattress, woven blankets turned back, cushions covered in white cloth.

She began to talk to him then, the words didn't mean much but the sound of her voice had comfort and soothing in it, as if she saw inside him how jagged his heart was jumping. She reached up and put her two warm hands on his cheeks, looked into his eyes and smiled, and she said, "Well you are jest sweet, ain't you Abe?" The sound of his name in her woman's mouth made him stand tall and melt both at once. She smelt like more flowers than a man could smell all at one time.

Remembered only pieces of it later, vivid as things seen by a lightning bolt:

She kissed him, and let him taste the inside of her mouth. Then like she couldn't help herself no more she laid herself down on the bed and let the dress slide apart—and everything inside was out-side at last, and he had her yes to look his fill. There was the twin pear-shapes of her breasts, the nipples round and stub. There was the small mound of her belly, and the crispy fluff of dark hair where her legs divided, and the subtle hidden groove of her crotch.

Then she said why didn't he get out of those trousies.

Then he was standing there and she smiled and said, "Well now Abe you are considerable of a man ain't you" and summoned him down by moving her finger.

He lowered himself careful, like it was someone else's body and he trusted to take care of it, and all he knew of what to do next come of watching dogs go at it or Pap bring a bull to their cow. But she smiled him her friendly smile, and the next was her smooth warm hand where hadn't a strange hand touched him ever—he shut his eyes and felt himself poked root-end first somewhere smooth and warm, and kept his eyes shut, and then she begun to buck under him, buck and bounce herself around, and his mind and spirit sucked down deeper inside his own bones than ever he felt before, he felt himself bulging and churning down at the root of his groin, his pleasure was suddenly so sharp it split him in two like the spirit-ax—

—half of him up in his head wondering how he could ever say what was happening to him in words and who in this world would he say it to?—

—and other half of him some kind of animal denned in his hips, bulky and hairy like a bear that began to growl and heave itself around—

—then he *was* the Bear and only the Bear and the pleasure of it wrung through him and nearly tore him in two roaring and spurting and busting all apart all at once.

Then next he knew he was emptied out. He was kind of cold, and in the dark, and nekkid in bed with a stranger. What would Ma say, what would . . .

She said, Ruby said, "C'mon open your eyes now, honey. You done the deed. Took yourself a man's pleasure. Fust time, wasn't it. And *you* done *fine*." She began to stroke his cheek with her soft hand. He started to get up, but she said, "You ain't got to go. Your Uncle, Mister Offutt, he bought you the whole night. So you relax and don't mind a thing," like he was a boy again, in need of soothing.

The stroke of her hand was comfort. He started to feel easy. He begun to feel downright good. He *had* took himself a man's pleasure! Now he *knew*. He remembered that time with Mariah Connors in Frances Wright's barn, how she looked at him in *such* a way and told him there was no man knew a *woman's* pleasure, they were afraid to know. He wished she was here right now, he'd show her who was afraid! "Ruby," he said, "I have took a man's pleasure. But what I want to know is, what do you call a *woman's* pleasure."

Ruby drew her head back a little, like she wanted a better look at him. "Well now," she said, "ain't it sweet of you to ask?" She had a little chuckle all to herself. Then she said, "Well *since* you ask, I'll say this much. You want to go at it jest a mite *slow*. Like when there's good comp'ny, you want 'em to take their time leavin'? Treat a woman like *good* comp'ny, she will miss you when you're gone."

But while she was explaining all that her warm fingers were fiddling and fuddling him until all of a sudden he begun to feel like the Big Bear again, and words didn't seem important.

In the gray first-light she led him downstairs, stood on the bottom spiral step, and kissed him on the cheek. Then a polite negro opened the door for him. A chilly gray mist hung on the grass and bushes. A bright orange spark: Offutt, leaning against a porch-pillar, smoking a cigar. "Morning, Abraham," he said.

Abe liked the sound of *Abraham*, a man's name. He was sorry he hadn't told Ruby to call him *Abraham*. She'd have called him anything he wanted.

"I trust you enjoyed yourself?" said Offutt. Then, seeing how it was, added kindly, "No need to answer," and patted Abe gently on the back. "Yes indeed, the oldest of professions: a humane and rational institution."

They walked slowly to the gate and stepped into the street again. For the first time Abe truly understood the Adam and Eve story, when they were thrown out of the Garden. Yet the idea made him

feel lazy and sweet. He smiled at Offutt, and watched him finish his
cigar. A yellow sun glowed on the horizon eastward, the ground
mist lifted. The building across the road took on outline: a great
large stable with a fenced yard alongside, only the fence was much
higher than a body would need to pen cattle, let alone hogs—
eight-foot-high palings, sharpened at the tops and driven into the
ground with handsbreadth gaps between. Critters moved behind
the fence, seen in stripes, hard to make out.

Abe and Offutt picked their way across the road-ruts to get a
closer look. Through the slits of the palings they could see a crowd
of negroes in the corral, stretching and walking about to get warm
in the morning chill, someone yawned, someone groaned and complained, a child yipped. The look of the place shut Offutt's mouth. It
blew cold on the afterglow of Abe's pleasure.

Two black fists shot out and gripped a pair of palings, shook and
rattled the rooted fence—Offutt jumped back and Abe dropped into
his wrassling crouch. Male negro laughter, sharp as a dog-bark. A
face thrust through the palings, mashed horrible by the squeeze, a
pink tongue. "Ssssheee!" hissed the face. "Boograman, you guine
buy deez niggaz?"

A woman's hand pushed out, palm-open. "*Swee'* mon, *goood*
mon. You buyin' Massa, you buy Catrun dis 'ooman Massa, buy de
bofe chirren Massa, you buyin' Catrun bofe chirren an' I wuk fo' you
twice Massa, I wuk fo' you *two* times you buy dis Catrun, dis bofe
chirren . . ."

They backed away, scared to the bone, as if it was dangerous
to turn their backs on the faces squeezed, the hands thrust through
the fence.

Twenty paces up the street, though, when you looked back
all you could see was trees and hedges lining the road, the gilt-
roofed cupolas and captain's walks of the grand houses glinting
in the fresh sun. But they were subdued as they walked down
Washington Street towards the river.

Chapter 20: **Burning Bush**

Natchez to the Sugar Coast, March–April 1829

South of Natchez the Cotton Coast began, and they started trading in earnest. Offutt and Gentry dealt with the Big House, Gentry handling the pork and grain and Offutt working the sang-roots, Elixir, and whiskey. Abe and Sephus would help the black people haul out the boughten barrels, a negro would whisper a place and an hour of the moon. Then Abe and Sephus would do the night-trading, with field hands or drivers dusty and sweat-stinking—silver blinked in the moonlight hand to hand, corn whiskey or sang-root Elixir was tipped from the bung into pail or jug.

As they drifted down towards the sun the air melted, the light turned to butter. Offutt was in fine spirits, sawing away on his fiddle:

> "All I need to keep me sunny,
> Keg full o' corn and a poke o' money,
> Hey pretty little black-eye Susie,
> Hey pretty little black-eye Susie . . ."

Abe drifted in a warm suspension between the memory of Ruby's strange warm complaisant pleasureful luxurious body and the dreamy wish of Mariah Connors, the close look of her clever eyes, her store of books and head full of reading, her talk of a woman's pleasure. This time he'd be ready for her—thanks to Ruby! He'd have cussed the brown current for its lazy drift towards Mariah if he wasn't so reluctant to see Ruby fade in distance.

> "All I want in this creation,
> Pretty little gal an' a big plantation.
> Hey pretty little black-eye Susie . . ."

Below Natchez the River broadened, slowed, thickened to a milky-brown that broke yellow on the teeth of a snag. Mulatter water, Gentry called it: north of Natchez it was more of a high-yaller; in the swamps nigger-water, black muck. Gentry was grouchy and fretful for all the time they had lost. He had wanted to reach the lower River early, when the planters were at the dead end of their winter stores. Now the face of the River was fairly poxed with Ohio River flatboats, that started later but caught up.

It didn't help Gentry's temper to discover that some of their pork had gone off, on account of the poor cheap salt they'd used to pickle it. Abe prized up the deck and Gentry rousted Sephus out of his rest to jump down the hold and heist the barrels out. Sephus didn't balk, but he gave Gentry the dead-eye look that said he wished he could. Abe knew that look from the inside—it was the one he used to give Pap when he hired Abe out to Old Reuben Grigsby. The black man did what he was told with clenched face and stony eyes. Only once, when he was boosting a barrel up to Abe, he snapped: "Keerful—you don't want to bust up no thousand-dollar nigga."

Abe felt sorry for poor old Sephus, but he was feeling so lucky himself, what with Ruby for memories and Mariah for prospects—*and* a share in the profits of the voyage . . .

Which brought Abe up short. His dreamy drift snagged on the mean truth: Sephus had nothing to think back on but wife and child he'd likely never see again, and no prospects but to spend his life as some man's nigger.

Well, so what? What can I do about it? Not a thing. No use breaking your heart over what can't be helped—that's what Ma would say.

But once you know a thing, you can't un-know it. Against his own inclination to dream of women, plantations, and shining mountains, he began to look at the great cotton plantations that bloomed one after another along both banks of the River as places Sephus might be sold to.

The Big Houses still got grander the souther they went, the workings below got huger—broad acres cleared, muleteams six abreast ripping furrows that bled streams of red dust, and after them whole militias of men women children flailing up the earth with long-handled hoes and mattocks—white men sitting their horses to see that the work be done.

And on every plantation, large small or middling, sometimes by the Big House sometimes by the quarters, Abe saw the peeled upright log standing like an idol. Now Abe knew what it was for.

But what's the use knowing the right and wrong of a thing, if you haven't got power to change it? Better to believe the grapes are sour than stay up nights feeling ornery 'cause you can't come at them.

Or eating yourself up inside, the way Sephus is doing, when he can't change his history no more than the leper his spots.

The Sugar Coast, April 1829

Below Baton Rouge a whole new country opened, green under the yellow sun. The Sugar Coast. No more wild moss-hairy forests along the banks: but a regular line of levee both sides, the natural dikes thrown up by the River improved and strengthened with stone or bagged sand, or anchored by trees planted in regular rows. Whichever coast you rode, east or west, the land was parceled and cultivated. Plantation houses gleamed with white clapboard sides, their deep cool porches supported by white pillars. The houses were set round with flowering shrubs, magnolias thick with heavy strong-smelling flowers, and fruit trees with polished green leaves that Offutt said was oranges and lemons.

And laying over it all was a misty drift of smoke that smelt like sugar-cake burnt on the hob, like sugar-tree sap scorched in the boiling. They were burning *bagasse,* said Gentry, negroes walking the fields setting torches to windrows of smashed cane like niggering-off clearings back home, ashes are manure in the soil.

The sugar-smoke roused Abe's hankering for his Ma's corn bread with maple sweetening, all the sweet good things a woman will make. It was one awful long spell since he'd tasted anything but what men will cook: spit-broiled duck, salt-pickled pork, catfish fried in fat. But they had come out of the hard mannish wilderness to the land of women, and Abe couldn't wait to jump ashore and get him some. He wondered how Sephus would like farming sugar? *Which would* you *rather have, hominy or sugar-cake?*

Under a long shed with open sides dozens and dozens of young women with turban-wrapped heads sat at plank tables chopping roots and flags off cut cane, carving out and saving the seed-eyes for planting. All different shades of colors the women were, black and mud-brown and honey-gold and cherry-wood and yellow and paler than yellow. And every one of the dozens and dozens of them was either swole with child or had a sucking infant slung at her breast in a band of cloth. "Suckers' gang," said the Overseer, seeing how Abe stared. "We'll set 'em easy work 'long as they got bread in the oven or a sucker at the tit."

Pretty little girl and a big plantation.

. . . and in every field slave gangs hacking away with mattocks and shovels, cutting new ditches or deepening old ones, chopping and shoveling at the earth like they were bailing water from a sinking boat—dozens and dozens of negroes every shade and size, men women shirt-tail kids, white-haired grandfathers and grandmothers.

It turned his stomach—the *swarming* of them. Like it was a whole city and state and country of *people* gone black all at once, and all of them swooped together, packed in, tied down, whupped like brats and parceled out like hogs . . . A man couldn't stand to live such a way, no he couldn't, a man couldn't hardly stand to think there was men and women that *did* live such a way.

They crossed over to the left bank and tied up to a tow-head well out in the River. The bank along here was a swamp of old moss-bearded tulip-trees. Abe and Sephus slept on deck as usual. Some time in the mid of night Abe thought he heard thunder and roused up. There was a full moon up at the top of the sky. The light on the river was icy-blue, the swamp forest a wall of black. He heard the rumbling again: not thunder, but something in the swamp, upstream.

The rumble stopped like it was cut.

Off in the trees Abe thought he saw dull red light jumping and flickering. As if there was a big fire burning way out in the swamp somewhere, on a hummock lifted out of the sopping ground. *Must be a big fire to get these water-trees to do more than smoulder.*

Then from downstream in the swamp he heard an answering pulse or throbbing, irregular like thunder but it kept going after thunder would have stopped, and if you listened close you could hear that the dull irregular pounding beat was repeating itself.

The sound stopped.

Abe heard a sigh: looked over and saw Sephus rolling himself back into his blankets.

But Abe was wakeful: the pounding was out of nature, but it wasn't any human noise he'd ever heard. He had a queer feeling about it—that it woke him a-purpose, he was meant to hear and take meaning from it.

He got up on his legs and began to pace barefoot up and down the deck. He couldn't lie to himself anymore: he reckoned Offutt and Gentry meant to sell Sephus down here—had meant to do so from the first, and were keeping it from him no less than Sephus. And he had let himself be fooled because if he let himself *know* he'd have to do something about it, say *yes* or say *no*.

But once you *know* a thing, you can't *un*-know it. He knew what Offutt and Gentry meant to do, and he knew Sephus: proud, stubborn, and smart. Sephus must have known Donaldson had been cheating on the promise he could work himself free; must have known Donaldson meant to sell him South this trip. So when the chance come he killed Donaldson and made his break at freedom.

Put a man like that on a Red River plantation with a skunk-eater like Jones or a cold proud son of a bitch like Cahoon, he'd be dead in six months. Money they got for Sephus would have blood on it, and Abe was partner enough in the voyage for the blood to come on his hands too.

Unless Abe could think of a way to stop it.

He glared at the stars turning relentlessly overhead, pacing his sleepless night. They wrote a book he couldn't read, the only thing they told him was that time was passing.

But what book could help him? Cradok? This was beyond navigation. Washington? It wasn't the kind of thing you could fight the British for. Moses? Even if the Shining Mountains *was* the Promised Land, they couldn't escape that way except by steamboat, and he couldn't afford his own ticket let alone Sephus's—let alone *Sephus*, who he'd have to buy or steal.

The only book that showed slavery coming to good was the Joseph story. But from what Abe had seen, Pharaohs down here weren't as open-minded as Joseph's. Judge Davis was the best of the lot, but he wanted a lot more *hound-dog* in a negro than he'd ever get of Sephus. He'd sell him off as a bad job—and we're back to the Red River again.

Just like *that*, the answer jumped into his head. Frances Wright! She was coming down to Hurricane and New Orleans, Judge Davis said so. *When they got to New Orleans, Abe must find some way to sell Sephus to Frances Wright.*

It was . . . it was a *beautiful* plan, beautiful as *machinery*. Sephus was the very man Miz Wright needed to run her plantation. Offutt and Gentry would get their money, maybe not Red River money but there wouldn't be any blood on it. The Donaldsons would get their share. And Sephus would get an education of Frances Wright, then go free to Hayti, where he could have a republic of his own. He might even earn enough to buy his wife and children free.

It was a perfect plan. Maybe Abe would have to turn *nigger-trader* to get it done, but that was no loss—he didn't meet the Judge's notions of a gentleman in any case. And there was nothing *mean* about selling Sephus to Frances Wright. In the end, what he'd get of it was just what Abe would have wanted for himself. He lay down in his blankets to think through the details, and fell into the restfullest sleep he'd slept in days.

He woke up afraid "Frances Wright" might not stand up to daylight. His thought touched the notion gingerly while he and Sephus made ready to cast off and Offutt and Gentry came back on deck, yawning and scratching. The idea itself was sound enough, Abe decided. The difficulty was in the *how* of it: how to persuade Offutt and Gentry to give up their Red River profits? Abe didn't reckon they would do it for goodness of heart, to help Miss Wright with her abolition projects and do a good turn for someone else's negro.

He puzzled the possibilities as they worked the boat into the current. Offutt ambled across the deck and broke into his preoccupation. "Did you hear those sounds last night? I wonder what it was." He seemed uneasy. Abe brought up short with himself: he'd somehow took the notion the sounds were *put there* just to wake him up so he could find his splendid "Frances Wright" idea—and then gone back to sleep without giving the sounds a second thought! He ought to have learned by now that on the River even the tiniest break might signal disasters drifting below the surface.

Offutt asked about the noise at the next plantation. The planter looked grim. "It's swamp-niggers," he said. "Some of them been running these woods since the French and Spaniards' time. We cleaned the most of them out ten years back, but I don't guess we got 'em all, and they pick up runaways. I don't like them drumming. Wouldn't do it unless they was feeling strong. Was I you, I wouldn't tie up to shore unless it was *civilized*." The man looked down at the flatboat where Sephus stood by his oar: "And I'd keep my eye on that boy of yours."

. . .

The next day they rounded Dead Tree Point—an old dead liveoak was the steersman's mark, the squat trunk big as a cabin and four heavy limbs like giant snakes froze stark as they writhed. As they rode up on it they saw the tree was fire-killed, burned deliberately all around. But the blackened branches were hung with gourds and bottles and jugs and strips of cloth, some new-blood red, some faded with months or years of sun. Around the trunk was a belt of rust-colored vines—through Offutt's spy-glass Abe saw they were lengths of rusted chain, dangling from staples driven into the trunk.

"What the devil is that about?" Offutt asked no one in particular. "Never mind. I don't think I want to know."

But Abe knew, part of the story anyway, because it was in Cradok: "The next point below is *Dead Tree Point,* where in 1813 three negroes were burnt alive. One had murdered his mistress and her two daughters; another slew an overseer who had whipped his child, and with his wife (the third culprit) fled to the swamps; where they lived as renegades one year until captured and executed." So that explained the fire and the chains. But Cradok didn't say who it was hung the gourds and bottles and rags from the dead branches, or what they might signify.

They traded most profitably at the plantation of Madame DuChene. At dusk they dropped a little way downstream and tied up at an old disused landing. Abe and Sephus waded ashore to wait for the night-traders to slip down from the quarters. Abe was uneasy. Time was short and the only plan he had was to go for Offutt first, then get Offutt to talk Gentry around. But he didn't have a sure-fire set of arguments to use on Offutt.

Sephus seemed uneasy himself. Twitchy, and not just because of the skeeters that whined in their ears. He gave Abe a flash look, then turned away. He bit his lip like to stop himself speaking. But couldn't: "You think I'm jest a damn fool country nigga," he snapped.

Abe was startled. "I don't . . ."

Sephus glared at him, pinch-eyed. "*You* in on it. Don't fool me *none*. Ain't a thing I kin *do* about it: but I wants *you* to know." He thrust his face forwards, glaring: "I *knows* yo' game. I *knows* yo' game: *and I wants you to* know *it*! I wants one of you to *remember*—I knowed yo' game from de *start*."

There was no way to deal with Sephus except to level with him. "I reckon you're right," Abe said. "They ain't told me—they wouldn't—but it's plain enough: that paper Jedge Davis wrote gives them the right to sell you, and I reckon they mean to do it."

Sephus startled. Then he grudged, "You been square wid me, considerin'. Dat's why it's *you* I'm tellin'—*I ain't fooled*."

"They mean to sell you, and got the rights to do it. Donaldsons won't care, jest so they get a piece of money. You can't run: we're too far from Napoleon for you to join those traders. *And you know you can't go back to Kentuck.*" Abe let silence fill out his speech—watched the black man's eyes change, till they showed Sephus *knew* Abe guessed his secret—and hadn't turned him in for murder.

"Leavin' what?" Sephus said at last.

So Abe laid it out plain as he could: Frances Wright's plantation, her wanting to educate negroes up to where they could take care of themselves, then carry them to Hayti, a republic just for negroes and . . .

Sephus shook his head, he was beginning to be alarmed: "Heared about Miz Francey from Awnt Dilly. Don't know how to plant corn, but she hang a sign on yo' door and run yo' life by it. And if a body say one word, sell her South! I don't call dat *free*."

"All right!" Abe couldn't help sneering. "If you're so smart what's your idea?"

That set Sephus back. Abe took satisfaction in it.

Then Sephus said, "Well now," like he was considering what to answer. "Well now you come to *ax* me," he mused. "Well all right"—like he had settled a dispute with himself, or with some spirit hovering in the shadows—"my notion is *dis:* git yo' hand on Jedge Davis's paper—give *me* dat paper—den stand back and *let— me—go*."

Abe's heart sunk. "I can't."

Sephus said, "Didn' 'spec you would." But he was more sad than angry.

Abe's hopefulness sank down. Smart as he was, Sephus couldn't see the good of Abe's plan. *I can't count on Sephus to help, I got to do this all by myself.*

As if in harmony with Abe's discouragement, those night-trade negroes never showed.

They tied up to a planter that rose out of the shallows a musket-shot off the old landing. Abe took first watch, the darkest and so the most dangerous. As soon as the moon rose he woke Gentry, who grouched and yawned as he came out of the cabin, his blanket thrown over his shoulders against the night-dank. Gentry plumped himself on the stern-timbers. The slackwater made a glossy unbroken floor between them and the shadowy brush-furred line of the levee. Once the moon was full up a fish couldn't lip a fly off that surface without giving Gentry a clean shot.

Abe tucked into his blankets near the warmth of the fire-pit, and puzzled himself to sleep thinking of ways of selling Offutt on selling Gentry Abe's plan for selling Sephus, and then selling *Sephus* on selling Sephus . . .

He was awake. The risen moon lit the deck with a cold blaze that razored black shadows off the thole-pins, the lantern-posts, and the upturned skiff in whose shadow Sephus slept. Abe caught the gleam of eyes where Sephus was rolled in his blankets—as if the two had roused at the same time. Then Sephus rolled in his blankets to get back to his dreams. *Wonder what those are like?*

Abe was about to tuck back into his own blankets when his guts griped. He hoped it would pass, but no such luck: his gut muttered, then griped again. *Dang it.* He had drunk off a great draft of River water with supper, thirsty on account of salt pork and too gluttonish to let the sediment settle out. He'd be lucky if it wasn't squitters, Mis'sippi squitters is to Indiana as the Old Man is to Pigeon Creek.

He rose up on his legs. Sephus rolled in his blankets, but didn't wake. The boat swung on the long drift of the stern-hitch a rod off-shore, the bow downstream. Abe dropped his britches and stepped out of them. He walked soft on bare feet to the bow, dropped onto the outboard corner of the timber curb that ran round the boat. He took hold of the cabin corner-post, leaned back to the full drift of his long arms and legs, and hung his bare ass out over the River. He heard a scurry-sound on deck, and raised his head to see what was

Bang! a bolt of lightning exploded his right forehead, and he went out . . .

. . . Not out, but fighting for the light in his skull like a man stran-gling in fakes of watery rope, black suck of a whirlpool pulling at his breath—cold cold water rushed up his body, his body cold soaked except for the banging black hole in the front of his head. His heels skidded in muck and he knew where the bottom was: jack-knifed his body, paroxysm of muscles, flung himself at the air—

—and burst out of the water. Loom of the flatboat above him. There was a hole in his forehead that pulsed hurt. Someone had socked him in the head with a bar of wood, an ax-handle . . . *Starkey? Was it Starkey come back?* He threw himself forwards, got a hand on the curb of the flatboat, wallowing to his chest. He lifted himself out of the water slow-soft, droplets tattooing the timber. The cold air on his wet nekkid ass made him feel defenseless. He got his bare feet under him and raised enough to peer over the edge of the deck.

Three black man-shapes hulked on the moonbright planks, backs humped as if stooping could hide them on the open deck. A big man hunched amidships with his back to Abe, pointing the other two towards the stern, where Gentry was supposed to be on watch. *Probably dozed off.* One man went first, crouching, a second followed.

Must be one man slipped aboard and lammed me then waved the others up, but where was Sephus? and while his brain was thinking that, the rest of him was already snaking onto the deck. His right hand closed on a fish-gaff, a heavy ironwood club with a barbed steel hook in the end, someone had dropped it by the thole. *Hook will kill but club-stroke is sure.*

The first crawling man paused at the far end of the deck, a shadow hovering over the sleeping Gentry, the second a little behind him. The big man amidships hissed. The first shadow dropped out of sight, Gentry hollered, "Son of a bitch," then the second man dropped on him.

Abe climbed up on the roof, rose up and strode out one two three great rushing barefoot strides cocking the club to strike two-handed. Big man turned, *broad face, a negro* his color weird in the blue moonlight, threw up his arm to ward his knife like a slice of moonlight in his fist—

"Haaah!" Abe broke the black man's guard with an overhead slam of the club, all of his height strength of arm and the speed of his rush behind it. He felt the bone-bust, the negro's knife flew banged and slithered across the deck, the man stumbled backwards. Abe went for him backswinging the club, *Aieee! Yee! Yee! Yee!* screaming with anger pain joy of it, and to roust Offutt out of bed and let Gentry know help was coming—missed backhand then forehand as the man ass-scrabbled backwards, but the club was swung so hard the wind of it seemed to blow the man over—rolling on himself to cover his head with his good arm, the other sheltered like a baby under the curve of his body.

And it was so cold-clear to Abe, he could just turn the gaff, hook the son a bitch's throat out, and let him flop and bleed his life out like a mud-cat on the deck—

But then he heard Gentry yowl, and a pounding on the cabin door, *is it Offutt can't get out or the other two going after him?* Abe glanced at the stern: the round shadow of a head flashed above the edge of the deck—one of the black men back there had spotted him.

The big man at his feet, broken, crabbed towards the edge of the deck, just wanting to get away, no more harm in him. Abe stepped in and slammed him square alongside the head, the gaff cracked in his hand. It was a skullbreak stroke if the man hadn't been flinching and scrabbling to get away—but it was enough to stop him even if it didn't finish him. Abe kicked the man splash into the River, threw the broken gaff after him, and bolted for the stern . . .

The blunderbuss with Offutt's pale face on the hind end of it popped up over the deck combing. Abe hollered "Don't shoot, Offutt!" The merchant jerked the gun straight up and blasted its load *ba-loom!* at the moon. "Dang it to *hell*, boy!" he cried shakingly as if he was mad at Abe. "Coming at me when I am bound to shoot *something!*"

Abe dropped into the stern-well. The hole in his forehead was pulsing, the skin of his right-side face was blood-sticky. Gentry slumped against the stern-timbers. His nose was pouring blood, there were bloody rents in his jacket. A dead man lay face down at his feet, a knife stuck in his back. In the corner, crouched, was the other nigger.

Actually, it was Sephus.

Abe heard, from behind, the big negro sloshing through the shallows to get ashore. "It's that other son of a bitch. I'll go and . . ." He stopped. Offutt was staring at his crotch. Abe looked down, noticed he was nekkid as a skinned possum from the waist south, and all his parts a-dangling. Offutt grinned. "What will you do if you catch him? Whup him to death with that thing?"

The laughings hit them one after the other, first Offutt *hee hee hee,* then Abe with his horse-laugh *haw haw haw* that made the hole in his head pound but he couldn't help it, his nose scrunched up top lip curled back and his big teeth displayed to the gums, *haw haw haw*— then even Gentry had to laugh though it hurt and made him press a hand to his ribs.

Only Sephus wasn't laughing. He made a move to rise—Offutt shot a finger at him: "You *set!*"

The black man gave him a sad-eyed, up-from-under look. "Don't be mad on me, Mas' Offutt," he complained, " 'twarn't *my* watch-out . . ."

Offutt's face twisted with rage. "Don't you *watch-out* me you back-stabbing son of a bitch." And he shook the blunder-gun like to hit him with it—looked at the thing in his hands like he didn't know how it got there: then pointed it at Sephus like he meant to blow the man's head off.

Sephus lifted his chin, ready to take the blast full on. But a smile flicked. "You ain't reload dat blunder-gun, Mas' Offutt." He relaxed a bit, though he still crouched humble. "Gun ain't loaded, but I ain't make a break."

"There's loaded rifles in the cabin," said Offutt, "you know damn well we could shoot you in the water."

Sephus rose out of his hunker and stood with arms folded. "Go on, if you's a mind to. I done nothin' to be shot, 'less it's savin' de Cap'n from dat swamp-nigga." He pointed at the dead man face-flat on the boards with the knife in his back.

It was Abe's knife. How it got there Abe couldn't think, unless it was Sephus picked it up where Abe had left it, careless, when he dropped his britches and went to shit in the River. "Hold on, Offutt," Abe said, "find out what . . ."

Offutt shook Abe's hand off and turned on him. The muscles of his face were all a-twitch with rage and the back-eddies of a great fear. He glared Abe up—and down. Then he giggled again, "Don't tell a man what to do, standing there like a shirt-tail child with your nekkids all exposed." The laughing warmed Offutt, like shivering out of a fever-chill. Abe said, "Then don't shoot him till I get my britches on," and Offutt said he wouldn't: "But after that we'll see."

Gentry croaked, "Take it easy, Offutt. I reckon the nigger ain't lyin'." They looked at him, and he grimaced. "I must have fell asleep. Next I know, someone trips over the stern-oar and cusses: that nigger there, I reckon." He pointed at the body. "He had a corn-knife. Afore I could holler he come on me, I got throwed down, think my ribs is bust. Someone was yellin' like a damn Injun. I heared you bangin' on the door, Offutt. Next I know the nigger rares up clawin' at his back—and I see Sephus standin' there."

"I stuck him, Cap'n. Afore he chop you wid dat knife."

Gentry looked pained. "I reckon so."

Offutt let the blunder-gun droop. "Well I guess that's all right then . . ."

Sephus paid Offutt no mind, but went to tend Gentry.

Abe went up the deck, got his britches, and hauled them on. The hole in his head was leaking. He touched it delicate—skin felt like it been *chewed* but it was just blood not his brains leaking. Offutt called for Abe to grab a sweep, he meant to get them out in the River again before anyone else came visiting.

The moon laid an icy light over the face of the River. As he pushed his sweep Abe kept thinking it over and over, what he'd seen and when, trying to make sense of how it happened. Hadn't been a thing wrong when he went to hang his ass over the side. He'd been full awake—he'd have heard someone crawl up out of the water. But someone *had* sneaked on, and busted him in the head . . . with what? The big man Abe beat down had a knife, not a club: he must have snuck aboard, found the gaff lying there, and popped Abe with it instead of knifing him, which was . . .

Lucky? It was better than lucky, it was *providence* lucky. A murderer sneaks aboard and decides to whack Abe in the head when he could have killed him just as easy. Now: was Abe ready to believe he was entitled to that *particular* a providence?

And where was Sephus while Abe was getting his head busted? Abe squinted at the moon-flaked water, trying to remember what he had seen looking low along the deck: the big man hissing orders, two shapes crouching aft . . .

They were in the current now. Abe shipped his sweep and stalked back to the stern. Things had gone on this way too long, ever since Donaldson—something wrong at the bottom of it all, a lie or anyway un-truth like a bad-caulked seam or a mud-sill set out of true, and nobody willing to name it, till the strain begun to work the seam open and let the River in, till the house begun tilting to a fall. It was time to have it out about Sephus.

Sephus had hoisted the dead man up onto the stern-timbers. He set his foot against the man's side, rolled him splash into the moon-lit water. Gentry said, "I reckon that *is* best. We don't want dead niggers where we been known to camp."

Abe didn't care about dead negroes. "What I want to know is how this-here come to happen?"

Sephus turned to look at him. He had a knife in his hand. He flipped and caught it by the blade, held it out to Abe handle-first. "Dis yo' knife, Mist' Abe."

Abe looked at him steady. I ought to make him say his story out, make him own up to it. Then if he's lying . . . But he just took the knife and said, "Obliged." Maybe it would be better, for his purposes, to go at Sephus in private.

Sephus caught his shift of mood. "Mist' Abe," he said, "dat's a bad cut on yo' head." Offutt took notice too: "Damn it boy, why didn't you say something," and between Sephus bathing his head and binding it in a clean cloth, and Offutt's medicinal shot of Elixir, Abe began to feel easy.

And certain. Wasn't any more danger. He had whupped the danger. Offutt and Gentry were satisfied with Sephus, and grateful. That would make them likelier to go along with selling him cheap to Miz Wright instead of dear to the Red River. Sephus was feeling brash now—but Abe believed he had enough to put the negro in a close place: close enough so he'd have to go along.

Offutt said, "Abe, Sephus, get the sweeps and pull for a spell. That dead negro keeps floating after us. We want to get a start of him."

Towards morning they left off sweeping and let her drift. The pain in Abe's head had sucked in around the wound itself. It was sore and raw-feeling at the spot, but the rest of him felt sound again. Gentry was long asleep, his belly full of Elixir to heal his hurts. Offutt turned the watch over to Abe and stumbled back to his blankets in the cabin. As soon as Abe heard Offutt snoring he shipped the steering-oar and crept forwards to where Sephus had rolled his blankets by the skiff. The black man sat up. He'd been waiting.

Abe looked down his whole height at Sephus. The sky eastward was full of gray milk, and Sephus looked a little gray himself. "I want the whole story."

Sephus showed a smile. "Don't you believe Cap'n Gentry?"

"I ain't sayin' your story ain't likely." He paused for effect. "But it looked to me you were scramblin' *awful* slow if you meant to stop that man killin' Gentry. *Awful* slow—and that big man where he could jump you from behind."

Sephus showed his teeth. "So what's *yo'* story?"

"Well it *ain't* my story—yet. But if it was to *be* my story? I'd say you were in it. Watched till Gentry fell asleep, then signaled them to board us. It was *you* lammed me with the gaff. But when you saw I

had the big man down, and Offutt roused and with the guns in the
cabin, you changed sides." He paused. "Which I ain't sayin' you
done. Only—it makes sense, don't it? If what I seen was how it
happened?"

Sephus said: "If."

Abe nodded: "If."

Sephus's face smoothed. He was thoughtful. "Nigga done it
once—do it ag'in, you reckon?"

"Once?" said Abe.

Sephus grinned: "Two times. Dat's a bad nigga you got. You best
kill him—or git shet of him *quick*."

"I would. If I thought I had a *nigger* like that on my hands"—
saying *nigger* most purposeful, instead of *niggro*, to say he knew his
power and meant to use it.

Sephus watched Abe the way you would watch a snake. "But
you want to sell him for a *good* nigga, ain't dat so?"

Now Abe had Sephus where he wanted him: where he hadn't no
choice but to go along with Abe's plan. But it wouldn't do to make
Sephus eat crow: his gumption might get the start of his common
sense. So Abe nodded agreement. "That's right. So I'd keep dark till
I got shet of him. And if he kept his word to me, and didn't try to
run, then he could trust me to keep my word: that I *wouldn't* sell him
out no Red River, but only where I *told* him I would." *To Miss Frances
Wright. For your own damn good!*

Sephus was bitter. "Ain't gon' strain me none to trust you gon'
sell me somewheres. But why does *you* trust *me* to do what I say?"
He leaned forwards. "Ax yo'self *dis*. If it was me lammed you wit'
de gaff, why don't I jest stick you wit' yo' own knife you drop so
keerless 'mongst yo' britches?"

The question set Abe back. Sephus's eyes lit up to see it, and he
showed his teeth. "While you countin' de money you make on me,
you put yo' *mind* to dat—Massa Abrum."

Chapter 21: **Theatre d'Orleans**

New Orleans, April 1829

They rounded a final point and there at last was the city. Spires and domes rose out of a vast spreading clutter of houses that filled the bay of a grand crescent bend. The buildings were masked to the brow-line by the ruled level of a great levee that marched across the whole front of the city, its face sparkling in the sun as if diamonds were mixed in the grit. Keelboats and flats swarmed the city's hind tit. White river-steamers with tall black stacks were lined bows-on fronting the town, and amongst them a swarm of small craft jostling for a go at the landing. Downstream of all was a forest of tall masts, which Offutt said was sailing ships in off the ocean.

Gentry conned them into a gap in the row of flatboats—"One more pull boys, then ship your sweeps!"—and as Abe lifted his sweep out of the thole he felt the boat softly grate its nose into the mud at the levee's foot, and stick. The voyage was done. The old flat would never float again. The Old Man winked and glittered as he swooped past their stern. The sheer wall of the levee rose above them. The Pilgrim has come at last to the gate of the City. What victories and splendors are waiting for him on the other side of that wall? The city breathed upon them air heavy with a million stinks, horse-shit, man-shit, swamp-rot, clammy muck, sweet-fruit, bottle-scent, water-weeds, blackened vegetables, dead fish, wood-smoke, flowers.

Gentry went ashore to look up his old factors. They'd dispose of the remaining corn, pork, and whiskey, and the boat's timbers too—seasoned oak would bring a good price for house-building in this country of soft wood. Offutt was to go up to the Bourse Maspero to find buyers for their sang-roots. Abe and Sephus were to mind the boat.

Abe cornered Offutt as he came out of the cabin in his go-to-town clothes. "Offutt," he said softly, "we're partners, ain't we?"

Offutt showed surprise: "Why Abe, I've always said so."

"I know what you mean to do about Sephus."

"Sephus? There isn't . . ." But then he stopped. The great huge boy was glaring down at him. He spread his hands. "We always meant to give you your share."

The words stung a little. "I don't want no share in sellin' that man. He worked with us all the way from Tennessee. He saved Gentry's life. It ain't right to pay him out that way."

Offutt was alarmed. "Well, but you agree we have the *right* to sell him?"

Abe almost grinned: Offutt knew his "right" wasn't sure, he was worried Abe might spoil the game by telling tales. "Well," he drawled, "I *might* go along with that notion."

Offutt, no fool, took his medicine with a smile: "Well, we'd *like* for you to go along with it."

Abe showed Offutt his fist, as if his stake was clenched in it: "Offutt, I got a notion I want to try. I want you to swear, as my partner, you won't sell Sephus—not till I've had my chance."

"You aren't planning to set him loose, are you?" Offutt was all business.

Abe shook his head. "No sir. If my plan works, we will make money by it. Not Red River money, but money. And won't have to do nobody dirt to get it."

Offutt considered, then stuck out his hand. "All right. I promise I won't sell Sephus till you've had your chance."

Offutt came back in mid-afternoon, beaming. He had contracted with a "M'syoo" Latour for their remaining sang-roots, one hundred pounds at three dollars a pound. He supposed Gentry would do as well with the boat and cargo. "My boy," said Offutt, "if it wasn't for you, we'd never have made the voyage, never mind turned a profit. It was you dug the sang-roots—and saved our hash a dozen times or more." Offutt reached inside his coat and drew out a handbill. He savored the rush of pleasure that darkened the boy's face:

THEATRE D'ORLEANS
Announces the Appearance of the Eminent Tragedian

JUNIUS BRUTUS BOOTH,

in WILLIAM SHAKESPEARE's *Tragedy of* RICHARD III,
on Friday, and

The Tragedy of JULIUS CAESAR,
on Saturday,

All Performances at 7:30 in the evening.

Offutt's smile was a sunburst. He held out a chit with "Theatre d'Orleans" printed on it. "Take it, son, it's no more than you deserve—Gentry says the same. And we won't take it out of your wages nor share of the voyage." When Abe still gawked Offutt explained, "It's a ticket to Mister Booth's show. *Richard Three*—I know you fancy Shakespeare."

Abe's look of pure pleasure made Offutt blush. "Now don't take on"—he waved off thanks—"it's no more than your due."

But first, Offutt said, they must get him spruced up and dressed fit for such a town as New Orleans. According to the regulations a man could not come into the Theatre d'Orleans without a coat or some such, a clean shirt-front, and a necktie. They were less particular about matters south of the belt-buckle, on account of the everlasting mud (Offutt was slopped to his knees). This was just as well, since Abe's only decent pants were an old pair of woolseys dyed yellow-brown with butternut juice, which came a good handspan short of covering his shins. The soles of his one pair of boots were cinched to the uppers with rawhide.

Abe dropped himself over the side for a wash in the river, then took a turn at the bucket-mirror, Offutt's razor in hand, scraping the bristles off his cheeks. His long bony sad-horse face looked back at him. The wound on his head from where Sephus clubbed him was still raw and jag-edged. The flesh around it had turned a kind of rich yellow shot with red and purple which Offutt said was splendid as a Mis'sippi sunset, but a little *loud* for the theater. They bound it in a clean white cloth band. *Well, purty is as purty does.*

He stood bare-chested on the deck, and Offutt held out the clean shirt. "Why Abe, it looks like someone stuck the wrong head on your shoulders." He pointed at Abe's white chest. "You are black as an Injun from the breast up. But don't fret, these people don't mind a *little* color in a man!"

Offutt helped Abe into the old broadcloth jacket Gentry had said Abe might borrow. Offutt contributed a ribbon four-in-hand, five dollars cash, *and* his beaver hat for gallantry since their heads was of a size—though with the head-bandage it perched a little high on Abe's coarse thatch of black hair.

Abe in his finery looked down at the little Yankee merchant. This man had given him his chance: first the partnership; the first woman he ever; his chance to save Sephus; and now Shakespeare.

Something in Abe's look made Offutt clear his throat gruffly. "Get along now."

"Yes Pappy." Abe laughed and ran up the steps of the levee. Sephus wasn't there to see him off—below-deck, still in the sulls.

There was the city laid out below him at last: houses houses houses, ranked up in lines one behind the other behind the other as far as

Abe could see in the hazy humid air. At first look, there was a kind
of horribleness to it: put him in mind of the bayou, the crush jam
and tangle of trees that had no limit to it. But this was different: it
was a *made* tangle, not a *growed* one. And the sounds of it were man-
made too, more richer but just as everywhere as that universal hissing of trees in the big woods—a constant bubbling hubbub of talk,
hawkers crying cries, teamsters yipping horses, church-bells bong-
ing, snatches of music, laughter, shriek of ungreased wagon-wheels,
steamboats hooting.

Well, he was a man, wasn't he? If other men could build such a
place, he could make his way in it.

Below him was a ramshackle district of warehouses whore-
houses and whiskey-houses known as "the Swamp." Offutt had
warned him to steer clear of it unless he wanted his throat cut. If
he'd a mind to pleasure (the merchant lifted one eyebrow speculatively) he'd best look in the old French town, the poorer back streets
towards Rampart. "No signs out front," Offutt admonished, "the
French are discreet. But never mind. The girls will find a way to let
you know where they live." Abe had blushed and said he reckoned
not, owed his wages to Pap after all. But he suspected Offutt didn't
believe him. He felt of the money in his pocket—five dollars and
some. Was it enough?

The levee itself was the best road he had ever seen in his life: a
flat hard highway three rods across, rising eight feet above the River
on his right and twelve above the street on his left as he walked
down towards the center of the old French town—marked by the jut
of a church-spire above billows of green-leaf trees. He walked past
the great castellated steamboats bow-hitched to the levee. The water
between the steamers was a slamming jostle of scows and pirogues
piled with market goods, plank-stiff deer or 'gator hides, bundles of
cane. The booths that lined the levee sold cloth and baskets and
potatoes, raw meat butchered just the way you wanted, fruit like
heaps of Ali Baba jewels. There were hundreds of people, selling
and buying: gents in frock coats or clawhammers with dove-soft
beaver hats and gold-headed black canes, beards, clean-shaved
faces, a slick slash of mustachio stiff with grease; ladies in a rustle
of hooped skirts, powder-pale faces shaded by scuttle bonnets or

broad-brimmed feathered hats or wonderful turbans of brilliant red green yellow and blue cloth, and coal-black negroes carrying bundles for them, and farmers in heavy boots and coarse-cloth.

Most people just glanced at his hat, his boots. If they minded him more than that, they'd smile, or make a mouth he took for one, and he heard them say *Kaintock* so often that after a while he realized it meant him. Well that was all right. He was born Kentuck, and not ashamed of it.

Just looking smelling and calculating was enough to tire Abe out and make him hungry as if he'd done a day's work. There was a little Frenchy-looking man with a kettle of somewhat on to boil, and the kettle had a smell that made your nose-hair prickle and your tongue just about drownd. He held out a wooden spoonful of what looked like some sort of stew, thickish, a kind of greenish-gray look to it. Abe paid ten cents for a big cup. The first taste was kind of warm and queerly rich and flavorsome. Then all of a sudden his teeth tongue and gums and the insides of his cheeks and his lips took fire, took fire so bad the tears started and run down his cheeks. He couldn't have been more surprised if a snake had jumped out the cup and bit him. He waited for the pain to pass, *the Frenchy had played him a trick but what does a man do about it in a place like this, and him a stranger?* Only while he was thinking that, the pain eased and left behind a kind of warm pleasant tingly rich taste. The smell filled up his whole head, he'd never smelled anything so wonderful. There was sweetish crunchy fishy things in it, bits of strong meat sausage, vegetables of some sort. It was more than just food. It was a thing a man might eat just for the pleasure of it.

Abe wandered into town looking for Number 35 Dumaine Street, where (according to the card she had given him) Miss Connors had her shop. He needed to see her first thing, she'd know how to get to Miss Wright—and besides, he needed to *see* her. And for her to see *him*.

The streets were slashed with puddles and rucked-up mud from the wagon-wheels. After two crossings his feet were soaked inside his broken boots, and his shins muddied. What with picking his way through shoals, and the continual distraction of glassed storefronts and fine carriages splashing by, he also got himself muddled. To be honest, plumb lost. He came to himself standing where two streets crossed and no idea where he might be. Although the streets were all named in Cradok's map, nobody had bothered to hang out signs on the streets themselves.

The Cathedral tower was his mark for the center of town. He found his way back to it up a long street lined with commercial establishments every third one of which was in the business of negro-selling. The sight of such places was discomfortable, and he strode past with his eyes locked on the Cathedral dead ahead. Once at the Cathedral he found his place again in Cradok's map. The negro-sellers' street was Charters. Two streets over and one back was Dumaine.

But by the time he got to Number 35 the early spring sun was drooping and the streets were shadowed. The display window of the small shop was empty. On a small card tacked to the door was written: *"M. Connors, Booksellers, will be found at Bienville Street, south of Rampart."* So: she *had* switched from hat-making to book-selling. A look into Cradok told Abe she had relocated to the far side of the city, near the back end of it. So he set out cross town again, counting streets: Saint Ann, Orleans, Saint Peery, Too Loose, Saint Louis, County.

The evening lowered. A negro with an oil-torch on a pole came down the street, lighting the post-lamps. He stopped to consider the *opulence* of spending good lamp oil to light up the outsides of houses bright enough to read by.

He found Beanville and turned right, away from the River. At Bourbon Street Abe came to the city divide. Behind him the upper windows of the houses looked over their walled-in gardens like eyes above a green veil. Toward Rampart the trees overhung the houses, which were more of clapboard and less of plaster. Yet the worst was finer than the best of Pigeon Creek: glass in every window, metal hinges to the doors. He felt more hopeful about Miss Connors moving here.

But there were fewer people back this way, and fewer lamps. Abe was a little uneasy. He couldn't be late for the theater, but he had no notion when "7:30 of the evening" might be. Offutt said to listen for the bell of the Cathedral, but he'd forgot how many ringings was the part-hour.

He stopped short of what he reckoned was the corner of Dauphine and Beanville. A low brick wall ran along the sidewalk, he could smell the garden on the other side. An entryway was cut into the wall, and next to the black arch a lantern hung from an iron-lace gantry. Abe sidled up to it and held Cradok into the lamp-light to get a better read of him.

A woman glided out of the dark into the yellow light. She was small-made, with one of those bright-colored kerchiefs wound close to her head. She was bare, face neck and shoulders right down to the cleft of her breasts, which were round and smooth as apples each in its own little cup of lacy black cloth. "Bo' swa, Mishay Kaintock," she said like it was a joke between the two of them. She had a wonderful smile and gave him every last bit of it, arching up one eyebrow and *rising* herself in her lace dress so her breasts stirred like pigeons. "You want dees, Kaintock? Fi' dollar, Kaintock!"

Suddenly he was as full of hankering as a boar in rut. He couldn't take his eyes off the woman, her skin was like milk with butter in it, her lips soft and full. *Yaller gals, it's a pleasure house full of them, ain't a man till you've . . .*

"Fi' dollar, Kaintock!" she said, and rolled herself delicately on her hips, offering again the smooth swollen fruit of her breasts, letting him appreciate all that a man could enjoy for five dollars.

But five dollars was all he had and the play yet to be seen, suppose he had to lay out cash money there, and it was late . . . and what about Miss Connors, what would she think of him, and his plans for Sephus, if he stopped to take his pleasure with a whore? He backed away. "Sorry ma'am"—he showed her his empty palms—"I ain't *got* but five . . ."

"Pov' Kaintock," she commiserated. "T'ree dollar den," she said agreeably.

A bell began tolling in the Cathedral. "Sorry ma'am." He was ashamed of himself but it was late. He took his hat off, slapped it back on his head, and bolted.

.   .   .

Abe stood under the arcades of the Bourse Maspero, where Frenchies and Americans, the least of them dressed fit to be President of the United States, sat sipping coffees chocolatoes and a green spirit called *p'tee goo-ave*, crushing dead cigars into the hard-packed earth floor. Across Saint Louis Street the Theatre d'Orleans rose tier upon tier, more gorgeous and splendid than the greatest steamboat ever built, blazing with lanterns, tall windows glowing between arches and colonnades. Carriages hauled up in front of the central arches, splendid-looking men and women were handed down by negroes in fancy uniform, and drifted up the grand staircase that rose behind the arches. By the leftmost arch a line of men in rough clothes—farmers, soldiers, steamboatmen, and such—was being let in by ones and twos at a side door. At the rightmost arch was another such line, and some of these people looked nearly as splendid as the carriage-folks, but with a sight more dash and color. The men wore collars so high their heads looked stuck in a pipe, and flowing neck-bows. The women's dresses looked to be on fire, their splendid turbans were stuck with long heron-feathers that bobbed like fish-poles. Abe's shirt was clean enough for the right-hand door, but the rest of his outfit would be ashamed in such company. He puddle-hopped the street and tagged on to the left-hand line, where a little Frenchman sat on a high stool taking billets.

He walked a dank corridor into an open space, lamp-lit to a goldy brightness. A vast curtain spread across the wall ahead of him, with a picture of the city painted on it—Cathedral, steamboats, negroes hoeing in a field, everything, even the Theatre itself. With a little notice the artist could have painted Abe in the crowd. Galleries rose on three sides. The first tier was where the carriage quality sat, a pattern of black and white. The second tier was flash with the bright-colored folks who had entered by the right-hand arch.

There were no seats or benches on the main floor of the theater. Men milled about, friendly. A man came through selling pies, another whiskey wine or brandy, another oranges. "Say brother," a steamboatman said to Abe, "you couldn't hunker down some once the festivities start, could you?" That got a laugh, friendly again. Abe blushed, and eased to the back of what he called, to himself, the bear-pit. He could still see the stage: chest and shoulders higher than most of these men, with their hats off. He took his hat off, Offutt's hat, held it carefully in his huge hands.

Someone bonged a little bell, the house-lights sunk down. The City of New Orleans rolled itself up to show a broad platform that swept nearly the width of that grand room. A row of lanterns lit up along the front of the stage. A man pranced out, splendid in tall silk hat, black swallowtail, and silver-headed cane. He made a great sweeping bow, and commenced babbling in French. The bear-pit hollered for him to talk American but he paid no mind, his face raised to address the quality in the tiers above.

He flourished, a curtain behind him split, and out came a man in tights. He had three balls which he kept throwing in the air and catching again, then four balls, then five, then did it *backwards*. They gave him a mighty hooraw when he was done, quality and bear-pit the same. Then the band struck up, fiddles horns and drums, and a woman in a white hoop-dress came out spinning like a top, leaping and scissoring her feet. Then after her . . . but it was just one surprise after another, till you almost forgot what you'd come to see.

But at last the stage cleared, and a solemn quiet fell over all that great crowd of people. The drum began booming slow and sad. Then a trumpet-horn fanfare: the inner curtains split left and right with a swoosh:

And there was Booth, alone in the middle of the great empty hall that was the stage. He stood hump-backed, leaning on a scabbarded sword like it was a cane. He was thinking—no telling what. The glow of the stage-lights washed his brow and flicked in his deep-sunk eyes. He made no sign he knew anyone was there. You expected him to say something, or move, but he never did. Only stood there so still you could hardly stand it. And then he got *stiller*—seemed to condense and thicken into something heavy as iron.

Suddenly he raised up and looked straight at Abe, his eyes flashing like blades so Abe and every man in eyeshot took a step back or wanted to. "Now is the winter of our discontent, made glorious summer by this son of York." He might as well have said *son of a bitch* as *son of York*, for the bitterness of it. But he mustn't let on, no, and Abe knew why, having read the book he was one jump faster than the bear-pit as well as a good head taller.

Only knowing the words, cold on the page, wasn't anything like seeing Junius Brutus Booth act the words on stage: stalking his own shadow across the boards like it was his worst enemy, and he bent on backstabbing murder. He was a right son of a bitch, that Richard. Could give Uncle Mordecai lessons. But the way Booth did him? You caught yourself feeling sorry for the man, born ugly as sin, wanting the crown more than anything—knowing he had the brains and courage to *use* it, better than any man in the kingdom.

Well, you had to admit he went too far. Like Uncle Mordecai: it's one thing to kill strangers that attack you in war; it's another to kill anyone gets in your way, and not be particular how the killing gets done. He went too far, so the people turned on him—turned all at once: and him left to stand alone in the middle of the world with his bloody ax in hand, shoulders humped and head thrust like a bear cornered by hounds, glaring at the pack of them so they drew together back one step—

And drawing together so, they got the feel of being a *pack* again.

Then how sudden they swarmed him under all at once with a shout, chopping and stabbing—

And it was over. Richard was dead: all his tricks and cleverness hacked out of him. Dead. He had it coming. Yet you were sorry somehow—sorry he was finished, sorry you couldn't get any more of him.

It was that still.

Then all of a sudden every man and woman in the Theatre d'Orleans realized the Shakespeare was *done:* and they let out a roar that shook the rafters, storming and clapping hands and pounding their feet, some threw bunches of flowers at the stage wrapped in paper and lace. It was like the trump of Judgment: and sure enough, here was Richard III rising from the dead, blood down his face, bowing and waving to the storm.

He was Junius Brutus Booth again. Abe recognized the little man who had near drunk himself into a killing back in Napoleon, Arkansaw. Yet there was still an air of the king about him, the way he looked round at that storm of people, drinking up their cheers and stompings. He seemed to swell and rise taller in his shoes. He still had surprises in him, you couldn't hardly wait to see what the next one was . . .

. . . and just as that notion came into your head, he swooped another bow and off the stage like wind had whiffed out a candle.

The crowd bellered awhile, then gave up and mobbed the exits. Abe drifted with them, remembering what Booth had said back in Napoleon: that if the world was a stage he could have been King of England or President of the United States. All he wanted was a part to play, and the stage to play it on. Well now Abe could see what he meant by it. If the world was Shakespeare, you wouldn't want to bet against Junius B. Booth.

Abe climbed the levee and ambled dreamily downstream towards the flatboat. Just a few men were out, watchmen for the steamboats, other men homing late. Below him the River clapped the levee wall. Inside his head Abe could still see Richard crouched and smiling in the bright space of the stage, and as Abe walked he tried on Booth's/Richard's wolfish grin. A skip and a flirt of his wrist now and again was his smalled imitation of the jump and thrust of Richard in an ax-fight.

A part to play and a stage to play it on, the words and actions hitched to each other like ax-head and helve. *A bloody ax.* It always seemed to come to that. Well, in a world of wolves, if you wanted your lambs protected you had to have a *little* wolf in you—maybe more than a little. Like Uncle Mordecai, a cold-hearted cold-headedness— yet not *too* cold, nor *too* dang mean. Or the meanness well hid. Yes:

you'd have to put it over on people, wouldn't you? like Richard, changing colors, smiling while you . . .

Just like Sephus: how he smiled and smiled, and all the time thinking escape, maybe murder if it came to that.

He was at the flatboat now, looking down from the levee. No one on deck. Must all be asleep. It was moonless, pale starshine lighting the broad sweep of the River. The far shore was a shapeless black, couldn't tell the trees from their shadows in the River. Down in the Swamp, a fiddle was scraping, laughs and shouts—a sharp cry cut off.

Maybe he was wrong, setting about to dispose of Sephus like this. Maybe it was no man's right to dispose of someone else. But there was no way out of it he could see. Sephus was a slave and on their hands. Even setting him free or letting him run was a *disposing* of him—more to Sephus's liking, maybe, but still a *disposing*. So it was on Abe to find the right of it, and act according. Moses wouldn't try to duck it. Nor Washington. Abe nodded as if he was two men and just clinched a deal with himself.

But it itched at him. Something didn't set well. Something wasn't right.

He stepped slowly down the levee and onto the flatboat. There *was* something wrong. Offutt or Gentry ought to be on watch against the thieves and murderers the Swamp was full of, and to see Sephus didn't run off.

Sephus! He wasn't in his place, asleep by the skiff. *Maybe they took him into the cabin, it's almost empty now, not such close quarters.* He soft-footed the length of the deck, dropped into the stern. The cabin door was barred. "It's me—Abe." Someone lifted the bar and creaked the door. "Well," Offutt said sleepily, "the Prodigal returns."

"Where's Sephus?"

Offutt woke up all at once. "He's gone Abe." And catching the next question in the air: "Abe, Gentry sold Sephus to a trader."

A blow between the eyes. Never saw it coming. *But I ought to seen it.* Offutt had made a jackass of him. "*You* done it," he told Offutt, "you done it: buyin' me a pass to the Shakespeare. Dang you to hell for that." It was spoilt now, the whole glory of it. "You wanted me out of the way when the trader come to get him." He reached in the jacket pocket and hauled out the fistful of coins: "You even give me whore-house money to keep me away till mornin'."

"I never meant it so, Abe, I swear on the memory of my mother I never did." Offutt's voice was choked and husky. "I always meant to do something for you. Then I saw the show-bill, and remembered Booth, and how you love your Shakespeare, speaking out those pieces . . ."

It nearly broke Abe's heart to hear it. He'd wanted that show more than anything, more even than he'd wanted another woman, that yaller Frenchy woman under the lamp. But he wouldn't let it break, his mad held it together, just, he shook himself to keep Offutt's remorse from sticking to him. "I know you done it, Offutt. You're his partner. No way he could've sold Sephus without you signin' on."

But Offutt had pulled himself together. "Don't blame *me*. Gentry didn't even have to ask me—and do you know why? It was that idea of yours, that hauling a negro out of the river is the same as salvage. The crew don't *get* rights of salvage—*only the Captain!*"

Well dang me.

Offutt folded his arms. "Yes. Well you see it *now* plain enough. If it wasn't for me, you wouldn't even have got your share of the proceeds."

"I don't *want* a share in sech proceeds."

Offutt felt the force of that. Maybe the sentiment was naive, but Offutt wouldn't have liked to say so in daylight. Besides (Offutt was surprised to find) he was *sorry* to have lost Abe's good opinion. He wanted, badly, to get it back. "I understand your feelings, Abe, but there's no use taking on. If it wasn't Gentry, it'd be Donaldson. *Somebody* was going to sell him where the price was best. That's just business, son."

"Dirty business."

"Clean or dirty, the money smells the same." The boy shook his head at that hard wisdom. Offutt tried a softer tone. "Clean or dirty—there wasn't ever but the one way things could go for that . . . for Sephus."

"There was another way." Abe choked on it—he had the words, it was the action got away from him, dang himself for an ignorant fool. "Another way, if I'd got a chance to try it. You wouldn't have lost money by it—or anyways, not so much but it would have been worth it, because our hands would be clean, after."

Offutt groaned a little. "Tell me anyway."

"I was to get Miz Connors to go with me to see Miz Wright, and tell her *Sephus* was the man she needed for her experiment to work: someone to boss the hands and run the plantation. She'd have got her value of him the first year, and Sephus . . . maybe he'd have got his freedom."

"In Hayti," Offutt mused.

Abe shrugged. "His own place, his own people."

Offutt sat down thump on the stern-timbers. "Well I'm blessed." He shook his head and looked up at Abe: "You *are* a long head, *aren't* you."

"It might have worked."

"I never would have thought of it in a thousand years." Offutt looked at Abe: "I wish you'd told me."

Abe did too. If he'd trusted Offutt . . .

The merchant bobbed up like a cork. "Maybe it's not too late." He took a folded paper out of his shirt. "This here's our share of Sephus—Gentry's note of hand for four hundred dollars. Take it to Miss Connors. I don't guess Miss Wright has enough cash from that Nashoba place to buy a hand like Sephus at Red River prices. But if we go shares . . ."

It was a gorgeous gesture—more than the show ticket and whore-house money. Abe knew what it meant for Offutt to give away profits. He grabbed the man by his shoulders, so hard Offutt winced and told him, "Easy now."

Abe's ideas went running ahead. "After I see Miss Wright, where do I find Sephus?"

"I don't know. Gentry never said who it was he sold Sephus too—some French gent he met in the Bourse."

"Then you have to hunt up Gentry while I—"

Offutt shook his head. "No—I can't leave the boat till Gentry comes back." He spread his arms, helpless: "The Swamp is just the other side of the levee! If we leave the boat they'll strip her. We'll lose the rest of our profits!"

Abe danged him and jumped for the roof. "Hold on!" Offutt grabbed the scruff of his pants-leg. "You might as well wait till morning and get some rest. She won't be in her shop now. Maybe Gentry will show in the meantime."

But there was no rest for Abe, lying raged and jittering in his blankets, thinking what he would say to Gentry, *you lyin' son of a— no: got to talk more persuasive, leastways at the first—only he won't care it's the right way, all he'll care about is the money he loses by it. So then I'll say . . . and then he'll . . . and then if he still won't I'll just take him and . . .* On and on like that till towards sunup he fell asleep, deep quick and hard, and dreamed he was on a log-raft rushing down a chute between black trees towards a black wall and was it fog or was it trees? and if it was trees would the chute bend before the river busted him all to flinders among the standing trunks?

Chapter 22: **The Bottom of the River**

It was full morning when he woke, and Gentry still hadn't showed. The air was warm and soft, the sky buttered with sun, but it didn't sweeten him any. He ignored Offutt's breakfast and strode off across the deck and up onto the levee. The crowd at the market stalls was beginning to build. He bumped his way along, then dropped to street level and turned up into town, counting streets from Canal to find Beanville.

He stalked up the street blind with thinking, lost count, and walked right through town to Rampart Street. On one side a low wall ran along a dead-water canal, on the far side of which he saw boggy fields and cypress swamp. Opposite the canal, Rampart Street was lined with full-leafed liveoaks, willows, and wateroaks. Even through his mad, Abe appreciated how neat and perfect it was, the row of trees planted just so, the fine houses rising behind the trees. Ladies strolled beneath the trees, heads wound in lavish scarves, little parasols twirling in lace-gloved hands, a negro woman following with a little dog on a string.

But Miss Connors's shop on Beanville wasn't nearly as nice a place as her old one. The street was a disappointment too.

Just then he saw Mariah Connors come round the corner from Rampart Street. She had on a white dress and a black lace shawl, and the lovely pale oval of her face was framed by a wide-brimmed hat with a long birdfeather stuck slantways in it that bobbed when she walked. A young skinny black woman in worn calico meeched along behind her, kicking at pebbles.

Abe snatched the hat off his head just in time and took a step towards her. She glared out from under her brim and flicked her fingers at him. "Allay-allay," she snapped. "Be off with you, Kaintock."

"Miss Connors"—he wrung his hat in his oversized hands— "Miss Connors . . . ?"

Her eyes bulged and blazed at him in fury. "Do you think you can accost decent women in the streets?"

A passing gent in a shiny stove-pipe paused, raised his hand to still the black servant who dogged his heels, and stood watching a dozen feet away, his right hand resting on the head of his long black walking-stick. If he was to think Abe meant her some hurt or insult . . . "Miss Connors, don't you remember me? It's Lincoln, Abe Lincoln. We was introduced? at Miz Wright's place?"

She slapped a hand over her mouth to shut it, and her eyes raced round his face. "Oh," she said, "oh my. Indeed yes. Young Mr. Lincoln." She was looking all the way up at him now. "Yes, I ought to have remembered you." Then she glared again, this time with fear in place of anger. "But you mustn't speak to me in the street . . ." She startled to see the gentleman leaning on his cane, watching her closely.

That gentleman *must* think Abe had insulted the lady. Abe couldn't blame him. He set himself to make apologies.

But the man ignored him. He gave his head a little lift and said something in French to Miss Connors, his voice flat and cold.

Miss Connors turned red. "J'sui' blansh!" she cried, stamping her foot. "J'sui' blansh!"

The man stood there, looking at her, his chin lifted a little, inso-lently. Then he said something else, also French, that made Mariah Connors slump on her bones. The negro woman rolled her eyes and pursed up her mouth. Miss Connors moved her lips to speak, but nothing came out. "You are mistaken, M'syoo," she murmured.

The man flicked his eyebrows in a sort of mild surprise. He flirted his fingers in the direction of his hat-brim, turned abruptly, and walked off, his negro man following after.

Miss Connors looked like she had come all over poorly. "We must get in off the street," she muttered. "Delphine!" The black woman hauled a string with a key slung on it out the top of her dress and unlocked the door for them.

Inside it was dark till the black woman lit a lamp. It was fusty damp, dust in the air made Abe's nose itch. The shop had a small space up front with some chairs and a table with books laid out on it, and newspapers. *The Genius of Universal Emancipation.* There was a counter across the back of the room, behind that a wall of bookshelves. But Abe had no time for books now, nor money to spend on them. "Miss Connors," he began, "Miss Connors, I come to see . . ."

But she wasn't paying him any mind at all, bustling about the room in a nervous flutter, now and then pinching up her mouth and shaking her head as if a sharp pain had bit her. "You shouldn't have spoken to me in the street," she said, "you shouldn't. Of course you couldn't know, the backwoods-man, of course you couldn't." She stopped and looked at him with a kind of horrible despair: "A gentleman . . . one does not speak to a *lady* in that manner, out in the open street. And in this quarter it signifies . . ." But she fluttered both hands to wave away what it signified.

Somehow, unknowing, he had done her a hurt just by talking to her outside. Well, no wonder. He looked himself up and down: *a real Kaintock all right, just crawled out of the Swamp with his filthy slept-in clothes and his head busted in a brawl.* He closed his eyes for sorrow of it. "Ma'am, I'm jest more awful sorry than I can think to . . ."

Miss Connors rallied at that. "Oh no, no." And then with real sweetness, "No. You can't be blamed for not knowing the manners of this place. Indeed"—she stood taller—"your state is the more gracious for that ignorance." It seemed he was forgiven. But that didn't help *her* out of trouble. She snicked a bitter laugh: "He asked me why I did not wear my turban."

"I don't understand." Behind Miss Connors Abe saw the black woman hide a laugh back of her hand. She didn't seem to mind if her mistress had been insulted.

Miss Connors looked startled. "You don't? I thought all *men* knew." The look she gave him said she didn't think much of men, and what they knew. "The women of this quarter are called *milatraisses:* mulatto ladies, quadroons and octoroons. The Creole gentlemen of the city make purchase of them—there are markets for just this purpose, quadroon balls at which the merchandise makes display. They are kept in the houses and apartments of this quarter. Perhaps in the end, their master sets them free, or the children of his body—or I should say of his blood, and the woman's body!" She put a cruel smile on her small face. "You cannot always tell them by the color of their skin—some are as fair as the pure English. But you will know them: by ordinance of the city, they must bind their hair in the turban."

He nodded, but she could see he still didn't understand. So then, for the last drop of gall: "That gentleman asked me where was my turban."

He didn't understand—then he did. The blood flushed through his face with shame at his having made her explain such a thing to him. And what was worse: having done her that hurt, he had to ask a favor of her. He needed to explain himself somehow. "Miss Connors, you said, back at Nashoba, said when I got to N'Orlins I might come buy a book at your new shop."

"Well." She brightened. "At least you are here. And it is *books* that I sell." She was still arguing in her mind with that gent on the street.

"Well ma'am, I meant to. Only I can't spare the money now, on account—" He twisted his old slouch hat in his hands as if the words he wanted were in it and he must wring them out. "Ma'am, we had this niggro with us, Sephus—a good man, never shirked his duty, saved our bacon more'n once. And he's smart ma'am, you wouldn't think how smart—had the runnin' of the plantation he was on in Kentucky . . ."

Miss Connors blinked and shook herself, "I'm sorry, Mr. Lincoln—but what is this to do . . . ?"

"But you see, the Cap'n of our boat, he took and *sold* him—sold him to a Red River trader, or so I reckon—which he oughtn't to done ma'am, but we couldn't stop him. And . . . it wasn't fair ma'am, it wasn't jestice to the man."

"Well I'm sorry for the man, I'm sure, but still I do not see what it is to do with me."

He took hold of her with his eyes, it was all he could do to keep his hands from seizing—but he mustn't scare her: "But Miz Wright, ma'am! She's lookin' for a good hand, the kind could manage her place for her. That's Sephus! He's a crackerjack for managin' if he *is* a nig . . . a niggro. Miz Wright couldn't want a better man than—"

Miss Connors held up a hand to stop him. "I understand. You want me to intercede with Miss Wright, for you and this man Sephus. You want her to buy him and carry him off to Hayti—or wherever it is she means to take those poor people."

"That's it! That's it, on the nail!"

Her mouth took a bitter twist: "And where shall the money be found to purchase this paragon of *niggers*? You don't expect me to contribute!" She waved her hand round the small dusty shop. "If I had money would I be settled here? Where ruffians are free to accost me in the street? Where gentlemen inquire where my turban is? and if I should not ply my trade in the appropriate quarter of the town?"

Abe was backing towards the door. He had stepped in a hornet nest, best get out first and afterwards think what next. "Miss Connors ma'am, I am most *dretful* sorry . . ." *Ruffians in the street,* that was him. He was an ignorant eejit chested out with his knowing of women after one night with a five-dollar whore. He took a last look at Mariah Connors's furious grief-stricken face, turned, and ran like the coward he was.

He rushed through the streets, stalked by the shame of his laughingstock failure, *back to the River maybe Offutt could come up with another idea,* stomped heedless into a slimey wagon-rut and nearly turned his ankle over. He caught himself up, he ought to set and think instead of charging off in all directions. There was no use going to Offutt if he had no notion where Sephus was. Charters was the street with all the slave stores along it. He pointed his long nose that way.

He started near the upstream end of the street. COPELAND'S MDSE, NEGROES, LIVERY. A small stable with horse-stalls. At the back a bunch of people—negroes. He flicked his eyes on them, and off. Afraid to look. *Dang it.* What did he think looking would do to him? They were just *niggers.* Hadn't he seen *niggers* before?

Yes: but not to go and buy one.

You eejit: how do you aim to find Sephus if you can't look these people in their faces?

So he looked: two boys with stick-legs setting cross-legged in the straw, old man on a piece of log-wood, two young women standing sideways so he couldn't see them full face. They were all of them dark brown like plumtree bark, none of them was Sephus.

Abe said, " 'Scuse me" and ducked quick out the stable doors. In the sunlight he was all a-tremble, no cause he could understand. Six negroes setting calm and quiet, and he was scareder than when he faced that mob of skunk-eaters back on the bayou. It wasn't the negroes themselves—couldn't say what it was—just the feeling that something awful would happen, that he could never show his face again if anyone he knew was to catch him at this game.

The sunbright street was alive with foot- and horse-traffic. He "girded up his lines" and went on. HEBERT & HEBERT NEGROES, LIVE-STOCK. H ROLLINS EMPORIUM; MERD'SE NEGROES FEED. Hundreds for sale, buyers for all of them, plantations for them to be sold out to, maybe some like Hurricane but more like Roundaway Bayou. And this was only one street of one city on one day of the year.

MERCADO ROSAS, NEGRES &C. WEAVER AND SONS.

OPELOUSAS TRADING had a pen of horizontal planks. Buyers ranged along the fence, eyeing the stock. Abe found a spot next to a farmer in a buckskin shirt, green horse-shit smeared on his boots. There were two dozen negroes in the yard: old, young, babies at the tit, women, men—singly or in clumps, setting or standing, talking or keeping still, snoozing against the wall with a hat over his eyes and his feet splayed out. "You don't want a nigger likes his sleep that good," the farmer advised Abe.

"No sir," said Abe.

"There's p'ints you want to be *pertikler* about, 'specially when you are jest startin'."

"I reckon that's so," said Abe. It wouldn't do to say he didn't care about "p'ints," only one *pertikler* negro individual.

So he looked. The negroes in the pen were just doing ordinary things, like *people* would do if *people* were black in the skin. The women were gossiping, men explaining things to each other. One of the women looked more Injun than anything: tallish and narrow, high cheekbones and sad eyes that drooped at the corners. There was a woman the bright-brown of river-birch bark, skinny as a rake: her hair was little tight braids all over, cinched with strings. And there was an old grannywoman black as ironwood who looked like a smart little bird, pecking her head at this and that, giving advice Abe reckoned. An old man laughed, *Ki ki ki ki ki*, and whomped a younger man between his broad shoulders, both wearing red calico shirts. Three-four shirt-tail young'uns darted in and out like dollar-fish. One, slinky and sharp-eyed as a weasel, had a kind of yammer-ing woodpecker laugh that reminded Abe of Matt Gentry. His face was the color of autumn oak leaves.

Sephus wasn't at Opelousas Trading. Nor at Cunningham & Raburn. Nor at Tensas River Traders. Abe looked at scores, hun-dreds of people, and looked *pertikler*. LaTour's: a woman who had great round eyes as large and white-less as a deer's. DeCastries: an old man that looked like Reuben Grigsby tarred but no feathers.

Carteret et cie. Grangerfords. A young woman the soft brown of a peccan nut, talking baby-foolish to a baby on her lap that waved its legs and arms like a turned-over turtle. A tall bean-pole of a boy that looked Abe himself in the eye.

It was the shank of the afternoon when he came back to the grand cool arcade of the Bourse Maspero, just across from the Theatre d'Orleans. The tables had been pushed aside and a high auction-eer's pulpit set on the stage in the middle.

"Hey there son, still a-lookin' I see."

It was the farmer from the Opelousas slave-pen. There was nothing to answer but, "Yessir, still a-lookin'."

"Well if you come to look, let's go an' do her!" He put his hard
hand on Abe's back and guided him forwards till they were in front
of the auction stand. Abe saw right away Sephus wasn't in this first
lot. But he had to keep up appearances with Opelousas.

There were two young growed men—one had the water-
smoothed-stone look to his face, one had freckles and a chucklehead grin. There was an old man and woman the same age, small
and gnarly looking. The old man had a carpenter box at his feet.
There was a pert roundish young woman, a growed girl really, her
skin was red-brown like dried apples but was smooth and with a
buttery shine.

A few other men were looking over this lot. A couple looked
to be back-country farmers, like Abe's Opelousas friend. A mild-
looking old gentleman reminded Abe a little of Judge Pate, only
with side-chops and high-top riding boots, the crop jabbed in a
boot-top. There was a little oily-faced Frenchy with twirled-up mus-
tachios, and a lanky gent with a silver-head walking-stick that
somebody called "the General."

Abe thought at first the growed-girl young woman was fat, but
no—she had a small baby wrapped in scarves slung against her
front. She tried to look steady, but she had the kind of bunchy
cheeks that make you look like you're smiling even when you're
not. Her face reminded him of Sary when she was just a girl, before
the Grigsbys got her.

The farmer poked Abe in the ribs. "Might *seem* like a notion, son.
But you got to calc'late five years feedin' afore the sucker pulls a boll
off the stem, eight to do a real day's work. An' *she* won't be worth a
lick while she's calvin' or at the suck." Another farmer leaned in,
shifting the quid in his cheek: " 'Course they's got other *edvantidges*,
haw haw haw." He eased himself of the quid, carefully, into the saw-
dust between his boots. If the woman understood she never let on.

The mild old gentleman who looked like Judge Pate was studying the smooth-stone-face man. The "Judge" curled his top lip off
his teeth like a horse and pointed with his riding crop for stone-face

to do the same. The man just looked off somewhere, letting on he didn't understand. The old chap stabbed the end of the riding crop up one of the negro's flared nostrils and pushed it up, till the man's nose wrinkled and his head tilted back and back and his jaw dropped open. The old gentleman stuck the crop in the black man's mouth, lifting his cheeks and lips to expose his strong yellow teeth and pink gums—"Judge Pate's" own jaw was slack with the closeness of his attention. "Healthy enough," he remarked to the General, "once you work the sulls out of him."

The little Frenchy was looking at the smiling young woman, pursing his lips over and over like he was kissing something that wasn't there, rocking his head side to side like he was having some sort of argument with himself. The young woman's smile slipped out and got hauled back. The Frenchman smiled and said something nice to the baby—the woman's eyes drooped and her mouth wrung up as if her whole face was going to melt. Then she pulled together—like *that*.

Meanwhile the General had walked around in front of the young woman. He took hold of her right breast with his hand—feeling of it with his fingers, and she, the young woman, her eyes went wild but she stood stock-still. The General stepped back, considered a moment. Then he slapped the young woman's leg with his stick, and spun his free hand in rapid circles. The woman's eyes went white with fear. She lifted her feet and began to trot like a pacing horse, the General spinning his hand faster so she lifted her knees higher, pounding her bare feet on the dirt floor of the Bourse at the same time cushioning the scarf-slung infant with her hands to still the shock of bouncing. A flick of the General's hand stopped her. "Hmm," said the General giving nothing away to the other buyers.

The auctioneer rapped for the sale. "Judge Pate" and the Frenchy bid for smooth-stone, the Judge got him for eight hundred. "A thousand if it warn't for the sulls," said Opelousas. *He* bid on freckle-face, if he was a chucklehead so be it, it warn't his *brains* was wanted. Abe had his doubts. He had seen Sephus show out stone-face *and* chucklehead, turn and about as it suited *him*, all those weeks they were working their way downriver. Maybe these men

were chameleons too, smiling on the face and something else, murder even, in the heart.

Then they sent up the young woman. Once she was up there she
cut her smile loose. She looked happy as sin, rocked the baby back
and forth to show him off, pushed out her milk-swole breasts. Her
face shone like a polished apple. She rolled her eyes around and
around.

"Edvantidges" jumped in with a bid, General topped it, Frenchy
topped General—the farmer dropped out. The woman staked
everything on the Frenchy: "Ah voo, m'shay!" she sung out.
"Courri po' voo, m'shay!"—crying out all the things she'd do
for Frenchy. *Buy me buy dis baby, I work for you twice.* General raised,
Frenchy answered. The auctioneer whacked his gavel. Sold to the
Frenchy.

The woman stepped down from the block. *A part to play and a
stage to play it on.* Abe caught a glimpse of the woman's face as she
stepped down: it looked dead.

And after that the old negro carpenter and his old wife, and after
them another lot, and after that another . . .

On into the evening: dozens of negroes, and not one of them was
Sephus.

Abe stumbled out into the street. Empty. He was so hungry his head
spun if he turned it too fast. It was falling dark and the lamps were
being lit. He had forgot to eat since that gombo yesterday. His
busted head was throbbing.

Negroes.

Negroes niggroes niggers. An ugly name put on those people so
you'd think it was *them* that was ugly, and not the Thing that was
made of them.

Which is *slaves.* Slaves and *slavery*—the Thing itself, by its right
name, not just words on the page of some book: "The Institution,"
"The Question," "that remnant of a former age which in the fulness
of time . . ." Pap said he was "ag'in the *Thing.*" But Pap had no idea,
not the shade of one, what it was he was "ag'in." It was big—bigger

than anything. This-here New Orleans, this was the gut middle of it, this was the knot, it was cinched in this clutch of streets and houses a man couldn't see his way out of. But the Thing went out beyond the knot, It stretched further than you could see or guess, out into the woods and bayous and swamps and prairies, through every day of the year and backwards more years than he knew to count and forwards as long as he imagined time could run. It was like the River, you couldn't push against it without a steam engine to drive you. A flatboatman like Abe Lincoln couldn't do more than run with the current.

He'd gone, heedless, with the push of the crowd leaving Maspero's. Now he came to—out of reckoning again. By the look of the houses he was in the back district. He slapped his pocket. Cradok was missing, lost or stole. There was a woman standing in one of those arched garden entries in the golden light of a wall-hung lantern. He thought to ask her what street this was, but she was quicker:

"Bo' swa, Kaintock." She had one of those turbans round her head, open at the top to heap her glossy black curls and let them loop over and fall free to her bare shoulders. Her skin was a softer color than white, and all of her shapes, her shoulders, her eyes nose and lips, were soft and rounded. The woman let a slow smile come over her. She took two pinches of her skirts and lifted them deli-cately: there was her little foot in a smooth satin slipper, her neat small-boned ankle, the glowing supple length of her calf. "Aaah," she breathed, and smiled a sugar-smile, "aaah Kain*tock*!" and her breasts like ripe golden peaches rode up in the cups of her bodice. She looked like comfort, she smelled like sugar-cake. She'd make him feel again like a long strong horse-back-high whup-the-world full-growed man. "How much," he said.

She took her lower lip between her little teeth and bit it a little. She cocked her head, smiled, and licked her thumb slowly with her pink wet tongue. "Fi' dollar, Kaintock."

"Ain't got but three an' some," he answered.

"Fo' you Kaintock"—she shrugged her naked shoulder—"t'ree dollar."

"All right," he said, and reached for his money. But he felt a clutch in his chest, he was scared. He remembered the General squeezing that smiley young colored woman's breast and "Pate" sticking his riding crop up the stony man's nose to force open his mouth so he could inspect his teeth—and something turned inside him, sick and sharp at the same time. "Are you free?" he cried.

The woman startled. "Je n'sais, Kaintock! Qu'as tu dit?"

"Free," he snapped, "can you say *no* to a man if you want to? Can you go off somewheres, away from here if you want to?" *If she was free it was fair trade, just like Offutt said, he'd pay the money and bury himself in her, pole first and brains last and never think twice about it.*

She was alarmed. "What you mean, Kaintock?" she complained. "Why I say *no*? Where I gon' go from here?"

He had no answer to that, no answer at all. A bell bonged in the Cathedral, he turned and wandered stupidly in that direction.

He heard rushing, as if the Old Man had broke the levee and was chuting down the streets towards the swamps behind the city. He rounded the corner: a rush of people filled the street, a great mob flowing away from the River, faces gleaming like riffles where the streetlamps lit them—the street bank-full and no way to ford it. Singing or chanting floated on the drift, a sharp snatch of something Frenchy with handclaps, women flashing their tongues back-and-forth *uloolooloolooloo*—black and brown all of them, a river of negroes niggroes niggers run wild in the streets. The river picked him up and carried him, *why not, there ain't anything else worth doing. Uloolooloolooloo . . .*

The river of negroes broke out of the town where the main street up from the River crossed Rampart, and poured into a broad open grassy field backed by the black wall of the cypress forest. Someone pulled Abe's sleeve: a little man, light-colored with negro hair. He wore a jug in a shoulder-sling. "Oo-eesky, Kaintock? Oo-eesky two sants?" Abe fished up the coppers and held them: "You got anything to eat?" The little man rummaged his own pocket and came up with a hand of sausages tied by the nose. He popped one off, "Two sants," then poured Abe a cup of whiskey. Abe bit the sausage, pepper hot but he was hungry enough to eat fire, and threw back the whiskey to wash it down. It was queer whiskey, sweet and syrupy. "Call that whiskey?" he complained.

"Tafeeya!" the little man grinned. "Oo-eesky memm shows."

The tafeeya left a good warm taste and made Abe feel hellish calm and excited both at once. In the circle tall black men were dancing. Bare to the waist, they wore bands of white cloth around their brows and bunches of grass tied to their necks and ankles. They strutted like cranes, rustled their grass crests, and hooted. Women were singing through their noses a lowdown one-note whine. "Mandeenge," the little man said proudly. He gestured at another group, blue turbans. "Menday," he said contemptuously, as if it was understood these were people of no quality.

A tall man in a striped robe shook the jaw-bone of a horse and raked it with a stick so it rattled, chanting something in words that had no shapes but only ran and bumped and thrummed. The drumming shook Abe's spine and made his joints rattle. The tafeeya sang in his head. "Whoo-hoop!" Abe hollered and jumped into the circle. He stamped and banged his feet, he yelped and kicked the sky and slapped his boots together before he lit, *Abe Lincoln can dance good as ary nigger even Sephus goddamn you Sephus!*

A black man with a white band around his head popped up in Abe's face just as he lit, jolted him with a stiff-arm to the chest and knocked him flat on his ass. "Sal' mulatt'!" he yelled, snatched at the white band on Abe's head and tried to jerk it off. Abe fended him off—got his feet under him and came up in a wrassling crouch. A fight was just what he wanted now! He showed the negro his teeth and . . .

But the tall Mandeenge was distracted—loud screams from back in the crowd, "Courri courri!" The crowd veered like the wind, and in the next breath they were bulling past Abe, running for the streets.

Constables, Abe reckoned, *it's time to git.* He turned and lit out with the rest, black white brown yaller, Menday Mandeenge Mulatt', down the street *pash pash sploop* through the plashy mud-ruts, jostled, stumbling, everybody yelling so Abe hollered too, riding the rush like a chip in a riffle—spank into the man in front of him and they all went down, arms to the elbow in horse-shit-flavored mud.

The splash cooled his head a little. He heaved himself up. The street ahead was blocked with a line of horsemen, crescent badges on their hats flashing and blacking as they passed in and out of the streetlights. They had dammed the crowd's rush and now waded their horses in, whopping left and right with long limber clubs, breaking the crowd into pieces. No going back either: another set of riders closed the hind end of the street short of the intersection.

Abe was in front of a warehouse, big double doors tight shut it might as well have been solid wall, barrels were ranked in two rows along the front. The Mandeenge was there too: a wolf-hunch to his shoulders, ready to jump anyway he could see a hole. But there were no holes.

The lead constable was maybe three rods off. His eyes snagged on Abe and stuck: tallest thing in the street except the light-posts. The constable clucked his horse and plowed forwards, colored people parting reluctantly at the horse's breast, another constable following just off his flank to see he wasn't took from behind. "Nègres goddamn!" the flanker yelled. "We t'row all you in Calabozo!" The Mandeenge spat on the ground.

The constables rode right up on them and backed them against the barrels. "You got it wrong, Cap!" Abe hollered. "I'm white! I'm Kaintock!" The Mandeenge gave him a haughty look and snorted, "Kaintock goddam'."

The captain poked Abe with the nose of his truncheon and said, "Don't talk to no white man 'less you're *bid*." He poked again and Abe flashed angry, snatched at the stick but the captain jerked it through his hands and whopped him right on the sore-spot of his forehead. "Come git this yaller son of a bitch!" the captain yelled. There were cries and shouts in the crowd, a piercing yell. The constables' horses danced and jittered nervously. The captain poked at him with his stick and Abe couldn't stop himself snatching at it, which only made things worse. "Hang it, Captain!" he cried. "Can't you see I'm white?" He ripped his shirt to the waist to show the pale skin below the sun-brown of his face and neck.

The captain pulled back. In the dull yellow glow of the streetlamp the son of a bitch could be either a white man or high yaller. *Ugly as a nigger—light eyes, but you can't go by the eyes in* this *town.*

"Don't let he mek fool, Copt'n," the flanker called out, "I see heem mek danz, mek fight wiz deece-wan," meaning the Mandeenge. "Look heem white bando', hees head!"

It was a damn joke, and he was it. In Indiana a man could dance like a nigger and not be mistook for one.

A sudden bulge in the crowd spooked the constables' horses, they turned and sidled into him as the riders struggled to control them. Abe hopped up onto the barrels to get out of their way.

Up here he was over everything. Below him the captain and his flanker had turned their horses and forced the crowd back. The captain reined his animal round to face Abe again. But the flanker's horse was still jittered by the crowd, and kept backing in a circle while his rider cussed. The Mandeenge spat in the horse's face and the animal snorted and half-reared. The whole street was heaving, faces flashing and darkening as they shifted in the streetlamp lights. The captain pointed his stick at Abe and hollered, "Git down off o' that, you!"

A part to play and a stage to play it on. Abe felt light in the head, like he was still drunk and dreaming a thing that could never happen to him, even though it was happening. The look of the crowd, the size and mass of it gave him a shock of something—fear, also a kind of joy—the faces all turning his way, white brown black yaller.

He jumped straight up, crowed, scissored his legs and banged his heels together, and lit with a great booming thump on the barrel-head. Then he drummed his feet hard and fast like a shirt-tail brat pitching a temper-fit. Then he jumped and lit on a different barrel-head and begun to clog stamp, the rapid battabat*bang* Sephus used to do.

"Oyeh Mandeenge!" someone hollered out of the crowd, and a whole bunch of voices shouted "Oyeh!" all together. He side-jumped left, side-jumped right, and they howled again.

The captain hollered, "I told you you was a nigger you lyin' son of a bitch!" The constable had been forced backwards into the crowd by the constant pull and push. Now he jabbed his heels in and began to work his horse back to Abe.

Up on the barrel and his long hind legs, Abe Lincoln stood a mile and a half above the crowd, every eye looking up at him. "Hey Cap," Abe called, "you ever hear a nigger say Shakespeare?"

The leader gaped at him, stick-hand froze in mid-swipe.

Suiting word to action, action to word, Abe moaned, "Hath not a nigger got eyes?" and pointed fingers at his own eyes, "hath he not hands," and flung his arms wide, "organs, senses, affections, passions like another man? fed with the same food? . . ." There were calls from out the crowd meant for him, he couldn't understand a one of them but he waved and bowed anyway. "If you tickle us do we not bleed? If you poison us do we not laugh? . . ."

"Arrrooooo!" called the crowd. The Frenchy constable was whopping at the crowd, his horse half-rearing, walking backwards with the pressure of bodies building against him. The captain had hauled his riot gun free of the scabbard.

Abe suddenly remembered his money, jammed a hand in his coat pocket, and hauled out the coins. "Hold on, Cap—here's the money to buy me out!" Abe tossed the money at the constable, coins spangling the air. The captain went for them, swatting them off or grabbing at them it was hard to say, but his horse spooked so he dropped the scattergun . . .

As if that was a signal the crowd heaved and surged all in one direction, the flanker's horse went over with a squealing whinny. The captain turned to face the rush but too late, he had time to cuss just once before his horse reared and tried walking backwards on her hind legs till someone jabbed a stick in her belly and she went over shrilling, with the captain under her back.

A gun boomed. Abe jumped down off the barrels and ran with the crowd, they washed out the horse-dam at the end of the street and split left and right into the blackness.

Abe ran three streets before it occurred to him that if he stopped running he had every chance of being mistook for a white man. *Change colors like the chameleon.* He whipped the white cloth off his head. A horseman came charging up the street, but Abe waved and hollered, "Hey! hey there!" He pointed down the street: "Those niggers busted my head and stole my money!"

The man on the horse hollered, "I'll fetch 'em!" and spattered off down the street.

That was the Cathedral just ahead. Abe knew where he was now. He turned and walked, slowly and with deliberate dignity, towards the River.

.

When he got back the sun was just crawling up out of the swamps back of the city, sky a cold clabber-color.

The boat was gone.

The boat was as gone as if it had never been there.

Well, that tears it.

Abe sat down on the levee. He was cold and sore. His head hurt on the inside from the liquor he'd drunk, the wound on his forehead was bumping. As he sat there the awfulness of the night he'd come through and the day before came up like black water like waves of dead pigeons and swarmed him under. Sephus was lost for good and all, and he had nearly got took for a nigger himself. He was alone, illegal, and he'd throwed his last cent at a constable to keep from getting shot.

Bottom of the River. It didn't get lower than this.

"Abe?"

Saved! He grabbed Offutt in both arms and heaved him in the air—"Hey now, Abe! Cut that out!"—and set him down soft on his two feet. All he wanted now was to get shut of this place, and all reminders of the fool he'd made of himself. "Mr. Offutt," he said, "when can we go home?"

Chapter 23: **Homecoming**

New Orleans to Little Pigeon Creek, April–May 1829

There was a steamer leaving for Cairo that morning. She was a twin-stacked sidewheeler beauty, her castellated superstructure slathered all over with carved carlicues, a gorgeous woman dressed in clouds and blowing a long-stemmed trumpet-horn painted on her wheel-boxes and her name in gold-red letters: *Fame*.

Offutt was as proud as if he owned her. "There now! What do you say to *this*?" Abe allowed it was grand, but Offutt saw he didn't rise to the splendor of it. "Don't worry about the fare." He fumbled in his carpet-bag and hauled out a sack that chinked and crinkled with the coins and bills stuffed inside. Offutt grinned as he set it in Abe's hand. "There's two hundred fifty dollars and something over—your share of the sang-roots and Elixir, plus wages."

Abe hefted the sack of money. Two hundred fifty was less than he'd hoped for, but it was still more cash money than Pap cleared in a year. He could have had more if he took his share of the Sephus money, but he'd given the note of hand back to Offutt. Sooner go home with empty pockets than profit by that piece of business. Anyway, two hundred fifty dollars was enough to let Abe crow over Pap if he liked. Some such was what he dreamed to do when he started out. Now it seemed a mean and pitiful thing to want.

Offutt beamed upon him. "*There* now! You can afford the price of a cabin, and sail home in style."

"Maybe I won't," Abe said. When he saw Offutt's disappointment he added: "I reckon I owe Pap my earnings. Already spent more on myself than I ought to done." Nothing Offutt could say would change his mind: he'd take deck passage. The ticket seller said Abe could ride free if he wanted to work it out: they were shorthanded on the black gang—"Engine crew," he explained. Abe said that was just what he wanted.

He didn't see Allen Gentry again till they went aboard. Gentry was surly and shamefaced both. "I hope you ain't goin' to tell tales when we git back. That sale was perfectly legal, and I will see the Donaldsons get their due." But Gentry had no monopoly on bad conscience. Abe said, "I'd as soon forget the whole thing myself."

He couldn't forget. But when he went aboard *Fame*, and set to work among the engines, and felt the vibration of the River through her fabric as she bucked the Old Man's downstream brunt, he began to feel better.

A part to play and a stage . . . Well, engine-deck suited *him*. Work wasn't too hard, though you might be called at any hour to fire up boilers or take on wood. Steam roared in the pipes, pistons pumped, drive-arms heaved and thrusted, paddles churned. One thing leads to another.

They pounded upriver back the way they had come, and the voyage minded itself over in Abe's head, as he re-read it mark after mark. What did all that journey add up to besides the two hundred and fifty dollars? Wasn't any Crusoe adventure, nor Pilgrim's Progress as far as he could tell. Money apart he was no better than when he started—someways worse.

.   .   .

They passed the mouth of Red River in the noonday dark that ran before a Texas thunderhead. But the rain never broke, only thunder, and the darkness stayed with him after the thunderhead blew over eastward. Sephus was bound up Red River, and if Abe knew the man that river must be the death of him. Seasoning and hard labor in the swamps, working for some got-rich skunk-eater like Jones or cold-eyed quality like Cahoon—his pride would get him whupped to death, eat up by bloodhounds if he run, or burnt on a tree if he raised too great a ruckus. Abe had meant to do him good and only helped to get him killed.

This gloom was different from what got hold of him at first, back in New Orleans. He felt ashamed then because he'd put himself forwards, proud of his cleverness, then come up a failure and a fool. But this now was a harder bite than shame. This was *blood* guiltiness. He'd give up his pride, dance like a nigger his own self, shuck and grin if that would buy Sephus off the death they had sold him into. *Hell: I danced like a nigger for less than that, just to keep out of the Calabozo one night.*

But if he was willing to sell his pride, there was no one to buy. The chance to save Sephus, if ever there had been one, was washed away like yesterday's river. *What's done is done. Can't fix history no more than you can raise the dead.*

They laid over at Natchez. Abe didn't go ashore except to help the navvies roll cotton bales up the gangplanks. Irishmen mostly, no negroes: man don't risk a five-hundred-dollar slave *loading* cotton, when he is wanted to *make* cotton. Let the Irishmen bust their backs. *There's more ways of being a nigger in this country than just to be black in the face.*

Offutt came aboard after a jaunt up-Hill. From his look Abe judged he had got his satisfaction of a woman. Abe didn't grudge him. Had the hankering himself, strong as ever. But he wouldn't buy no woman now, not down here.

"What man would *not* wish to have all things as *he* chooses, if it were in his power?" That was Judge Davis's question. First time he heard it, he'd had no better answer than what the Judge expected. *But if it was asked again I'd say, 'I don't want nothing for myself that any other man can't get for the same work.'* Negroes included? *Negroes included. Start turning some people into niggers and you might not be able to stop.*

Offutt stood beside him on the lower deck watching Natchez sail backwards down the River. "City on a Hill," Offutt said admiringly, "just like the Judge said."

" 'Tain't a hill," said Abe. "It's a bluff."

Offutt looked to see if the boy meant anything by that. But Abe had on his poker-face.

They passed Hurricane in the dark, and New Carthage, where Abe had come near killing a man in pure rage and hate. If Starkey was still alive it was no fault of his. There was a wolf inside him, just like the one you saw in Uncle Mordecai's cold white eyes. It had showed its teeth before: with Will Grigsby at muster, with Eph Taylor when they wrassled, way back in Knob Creek with Andy Simms. But he'd cut it loose on Starkey, and then it was all he could do to stop it going for Cahoon and never mind who else it killed, even himself. Rage like that was a sign of darkness in his spirit and nature. If there was justice in the world he'd be called to account.

If there was justice in the world. If Starkey's showing up like he done was something more than just the worst bad luck I ever heard of.

It was soothing to the mind to be amongst the big engines. Their whooshing and ramming and chunking and throbbing drowned all other sounds, and for hours at a time even washed out the words and voices that plagued Abe's thinking. It was work and play to watch how the pistons rose and fell, that turned the wheel that drove the arms that cranked the huge paddles round and round and drove the ship upstream. Frances Wright said one true thing at least:

there was a beautiful system to steam engines, a logic, one thing happens and the next follows, the same every single time—no chance to it, no mistakes, and no providence required only steam and iron arranged just so. As for the American republic: maybe the plan of it was that beautiful, but from what Abe had seen the government wanted improving before you matched it against steam engines.

They passed Greenville. The Indians were gone, all but the scar of their wrecked village below the old Mound. Whether the promised government steamboat finally came to get them, or they starved to death, or were massacred by the Greenville militia Abe never learned. *"Gov'ment that cain't or won't keep its word ain't no gov-'ment at all."* Gov'ment that says men are equal in their rights then lets some make niggers of the rest, sell men women children like they was hogs . . .

But it's all the gov'ment *this* country has got.

Napoleon: *Arkansaw River Fur Comp'y* was gone upriver to the Shining Mountains. A whole new country. *Chance like that don't come twice.* The Old Man rushed and slid and whispered backwards below them.

They chugged to the landing at Helena. There was a solemn ugly look to the waterfront. At the upstream end was a large gallows, four bodies slung by the neck from the beam. They were ripe—you could smell them.

"Them? Them's the niggers that kilt their Master an' wracked his boat behind Cooper's Island two month back. Army snatched these four, lost a couple in the swamps but I don't reckon they got off—high water week after that. We got two wenches, a boy, an' a buck: strung 'em up good an' proper."

Abe snuffed the odor of the negroes' rotting bodies. *So that was the real of Sephus's story after all.* He was sorry they were dead.

The light changed. Abe felt horrible and satisfied both at once.

The hangings proved Donaldson's wrack was no accident. Sephus *had* done it. Planned it, kept dark, then cut his Master's throat and stole his boat. *And when it went wrong and we got hold of him, he played his part for us as good as Booth could have done. Smole his smile, worked his workings, a little luck he might have made them good: might have killed the three of us—or two, anyway, for he throwed me in the River when he could have killed me. But didn't, you see, because he thought he owed me something . . . He had pride and honor enough to risk everything, just to be even with me.*

And if *Sephus* was "Mordecai" enough to take things that far, why shouldn't Abe Lincoln be able to take them that much further, who was Mordecai's own blood-nephew? In a world of Wolves, if you want to help the Lambs you need to be more than a little Wolf yourself. What was the good of knowing the right thing to do, unless you had the power to *do* it? Gov'ment is supposed to do justice, but if it don't, ain't it on people themselves to take it in hand and make it keep its word? He remembered the riot in the street, how he stood higher than the crowd and they all looking up at him, listening, and if he'd known what to do with them . . . the rage rising in him, rage not like a sin but like a blessing, rage that come of knowing in your soul you *deserved* to get justice and meant to have it or die.

A part to play and a stage to play it on.

He'd do better next time.

At Cairo they shifted to an Ohio River boat. Offutt hunted Abe up to say good-bye. He intended to get off in Shawneetown and head up to Springfield. "There's new settlements there I want to prospect around."

Abe couldn't say a word. He owed Denton Offutt more than he could say all at once—and it was all there at once, wanting to be said.

Offutt read the boy's face and patted his arm. "Abe: you're about the best partner I ever had, man or boy. You're smarter than you look, and honest as a man has any right to expect. Why don't you come along? With me to do the thinking and you the heave and haul, I'd bet on us against the world!"

It was there again: a chance. But Abe shook his head. "I can't. I owe Pap these wages. Promised Ma I'd come back. When I leave I want to be square with them both." Abe was still thinking: "But you know—Pap has been talkin' *Elanoy* ever since that muster in Vincennes." He drew his lip up in his horsey smile: "He's heard the land is cheap and the terms is easy. I know he's gone sour on Pigeon Crick."

Offutt broke out in a grin. "Well then: if you come next year, look for me or leave word in Springfield. You'll be of age then, son: you can do as you like." He put out his hand, Abe swallowed it up with his, and they shook on it. Offutt rubbed his hands together. "I'll scout us up a splendid location. Some place with good navigation . . ."

He came back again to the same gate he'd left by, and stood there. It was a surprise to see how small the Lincoln cabin was in its naked clearing poxed with stumps. The cherry over Mam's grave was in leaf again.

As Abe lifted the gate, Pap stepped out the cabin door. Pap looked uncertain, older than Abe remembered him, smaller. Abe thought *I must give him the wages right off and not make him ask. I am too old to play that grudging-game with him.* Tom Lincoln squared up in the doorway. Abe stopped at arm's length and made a smile: "Well, Father." He was a good head taller than the old man. He bounced the money-sack in his hand to sound its substantial crumple and chink, then held it out—set it in the hand Tom Lincoln haltingly extended. Pap started to say something, *Howdy* or *Welcome home* or maybe just his usual *You're back*—but the heft of the sack shut his mouth: he shot Abe a look, puzzled—uneasy.

Before he could grouch John D. busted whooping out the cabin door and jumped Abe's back to ride him home. "John D., you have growed too much for me," Abe complained. But John D. was the only thing that *had* growed: everything else, Pap, the cabin, Pigeon Creek, had shrunk down and thinned out.

Ma came out to stand next to Pap in the door. Her bird-sharp eyes were running tears. "Oh Maw," John D. complained, "what are you cryin' for? Abe's home! Abe's home for good!"

But Sarah Bush Johnston Lincoln had took one look in Abe's eyes, and she knew better.

Little Pigeon Creek, May 1829

Ma sent John D. to fetch Denny, Betsey, and their children, and laid on a feast with four kinds of pie to welcome the Prodigal home. Abe told stories enough to satisfy the family's hankering for sensation, without giving away any secrets. Pap sat silent through it all, chewing some grievance with his vittles, though what there was to be mad at with Abe back safe and a poke full of money was more than Sally could tell.

But Abe read the signs, and reckoned he had more of an accounting to make before he could say he was *home*. No use putting it off. He went looking for Pap early next morning, and found him splitting fire-wood behind the smokehouse.

Pap raised up slow to face him.

"Pap."

"Abe." Tom Lincoln meant to wait his son out, make the boy *ask* something afore he *told* him. But he wasn't sure of himself. The boy had brought home more cash money than Tom Lincoln ever held in his hands at one time. They needed that money bad. He ought to be grateful. Ought to say thanks. But he didn't feel grateful. Felt grudgeful—as if Abe give him that much money just to make him small. He'd show him who was still his father: "I reckon you are *satisfied* with yourself."

"I might have brought more. But I spent some on myself." Not quite the *George Washington* of things, but close as Abe meant to come to it.

Pap went red in the face, and looked away. "What do you tell *me* for? You've gone your own way and done what pleased you since . . ." But he couldn't say how far back it went—a *long* way, so long it scared him to think of it.

Abe smiled: couldn't help it though he knew it would rile Pap worse. He knew what Pap would say before the man himself did. If Pap was a generous man he might have told his son, *Well you earned it, I hope you got some good of it.* A hard man might have said, *Wasn't yours to spend.* But Pap wasn't *hard:* only mean, and scared. Whup a man like that you feel mean your own self. But let such a man boss you? *Not likely.*

The blood rose in Pap's face. "Grin all you like," he snapped. "I mean to sell us out here and go to the Elanoy. It's good land there, terms is . . ." But he remembered how Abe made a joke of his *easy terms.*

Abe said: "I told you about the money because it was wages I was obliged to give you. I will make it up. I've got the right to leave when I turn twenty-one, but I will give you one year . . ."

"*Give* me? *Give* me a year?" Like to say Tom Lincoln was a beggar at the hands of his own begot son!

". . . one year over—to settle you in the Elanoy. I judge that will square things between us."

"You?" Pap spluttered. "Who are you to judge? Who are you to say when we're *square*?"

Abe felt cold and high and sure of himself. "For such a matter as this," he told Pap, "I am all I need to be."

Tom Lincoln hung fire, he was full up with righteous bitter anger and knew he *ought* to let it fly, *ought* to lay into his son, as he was a *man* he ought to.

But couldn't—what would come of it if he did? Abe might flat leave. They couldn't get to Elanoy without him.

Pap squinted his eyes to seem hard: "Well. *I* am done talkin'."

Abe took that in. Nodded. "Yes. I reckon I am too."

Ma was waiting for him in the cabin. She made him set and "tell her everything" while she did her mending. She listened, as she liked to say, with *both ears:* one taking in the stories he was willing to tell, the other listening for the story inside the stories. What had the journey done for her Abe? He was proud of himself, and from where she sat he had right to be. He'd run that flatboat down the River through storm and sun, snags and shoal water, and come home with his pockets full of money. But yet there was some trouble in it, something that set wrong with him. So when he *thought* he was done, she commenced to ask questions, picking away at the threads till she found the right one, then pulling it out.

Abe didn't mind her questions. They felt like *home* to him, as if his boy self was setting on his own growed-up knee blabbing away with Ma, and *himself* just watching and listening, apart. If he held back the Sephus business, it wasn't for mistrust of her keeping the secret. Nor in fear of her judgment: he reckoned she'd say he done the best he could, and more than most other men would have tried. But he knew himself what he'd done, and failed to do, and what his reasons and meanings were. The right and wrong of it were on him. There was no use nor good in trying to share it.

But there was another, different trouble he felt: the kind a man couldn't judge for himself.

So he told her about Starkey: how he let himself be goaded into fighting the man, got throwed in the River; and come back mad enough to beat the man any way he could. "I shammed him, kicked him where it hurt. *Crowed* over him when he was down, to shame him the worst way I could think. Then I kicked him into the River."

It was a hard story for her to hear. Sally didn't like to see meanness come out in Abe. But he was a man, wasn't he? And it was in him, even if he mostly kept it down. "I don't reckon you done any worse to him than he done to you."

But that wasn't the troublesome part, he told her. It was what *come* of that: it was how Starkey turned up again, unaccountable, just when it could do them the most hurt. "So I had to fight him again, and this time there wasn't any way but to hurt him so as . . . so as to *finish* him."

"And you done that, Abe?" No wonder he had trouble at heart, with guilt of blood on him! She weighed it in her mind, holding back her love so as not to cheat the scales. Even so, they come out level. "I wish you hadn't come to it, Abe. But I don't see no fault in you. The man laid for your blood with false witness. And you fought him fair."

No no, he waved that comfort away. "That ain't it, that ain't what bothers me."

It made her sudden cold to think a man's blood didn't bother him. She was afraid for him: "If it ain't that, Abe, then what?"

"It's *how* the thing come. That's what I can't make out." He squinted as if he had to see something miles off, and looked right through her. "I can't make out how sech a thing could happen, and it be nothin' more than jest my luck."

"Your luck?" She nearly called him *fool*. "A thing like that don't come by luck! There's *judgment* in it! There's the plain hand of providence!"

"You think so?" His face lit up, suddenly, with a glow of pure joy—he whooped like an Injun, grabbed her under the elbows, and lifted her right up into the air.

"Put me down, you eejit! I am hanged if I can tell what there is for you to laugh at! It's a *fearsome* thing for the Lord to take notice of a man!"

He looked up at her, held aloft in his out-size beech-oar-driving hands. "Ma," he explained, "it's a lot more fearsome to me if He was to pay me no mind at all."

That summer Pap and Denny sold their claims to Jim Gentry. With the proceeds and Abe's River-money they bought a pair of Conestoga wagons and teams to haul them, and piled their plunder aboard. Last of all Pap prized out the window and lashed it atop the blankets and bedding. The gutted cabin turned its blind eye to them. The door lolled on its hinges like a drunk man's tongue. The empty moved in and took the place, the cabin Abe and Pap and all of Pigeon Creek had squared and raised to keep Mam and Sary snug and safe—back in the days of the War Against the Trees.

The blackcherry over Mam's grave was in full leaf and fruit. *Cheerry-pie, jest wait till I make you some . . .*

Pap hollered "Git-up!" and gave their mules the goad, and they hauled out for the Elanoy.

Some day when I get the money I will come back and put a stone over her. So you won't forget she ever was here, you won't forget her name as if she never was.

"Abe?" said John D. "You know what I want to do when we git to Elanoy? I want to go downriver with you, next time you go. You reckon Pap will let me?"

"I think I can manage it."

"Thanks, Abe!" Then, to show he warn't selfish, John D. asked, "What do *you* want in the Elanoy, Abe?"

Abe kept the answer to himself. *A part to play, and a stage to play it on.*

BOOK VI:

The Republic

Chapter 24: **New Salem**

April 1831

Young Tom Clary was first to see the flatboat. He was laying shakes on the roof of his Uncle Bill's Grocery, which sat on the bluffs at the head of a sharp bend in the Sangamon River. Tom's "Flatboat a-comin' " caused a stir down on the porch of the Grocery (which was what they called a saloon in those parts), where the Clary's Grove Boys had gathered for their weekly toot. They'd been wondering what to do with the time—had about concluded to wait and see what turned up. Which showed judgment: for here something *had*.

Big Jack Armstrong hauled himself to his feet, and the Boys did likewise. Uncle Clary came out of the Grocery, wiping his hands on a calico rag. They saw the flatboat steering cautiously down along the opposite bank. "Didn't stop to scout the turn," said Uncle Clary. "Reckon he knows there is a dam?"

The bend was so sharp—swinging right around from due east to north—you couldn't see the dam till you were round the point. But if a man was running a flatboat down the Sangamon he *ought*

427

to know there was a dam. It hadn't been there long, but it was famous: the water it banked ran the Rutledge and Camron mill, a gristmill and sawmill both, and the mill was the reason there was a Clary's Grocery up on the bluffs, and a town of New Salem back of it.

"Reckon she'll get over?" Pleasant wondered.

Jack judged she was heavy in the water. "Two bits she don't," he challenged. Bully Bob Kirby, being obliged to bet against Jack, said "Done." Pleasant and Buck Armstrong sided their brother, also Tom and Royal Clary, while Bill Greene and Cluff McHenry sided Bully Bob. They settled in to watch.

Down at the mill the schoolteacher, Mentor Graham, and a farmer named Babb McNabb were waiting their turn at the grindstone when McNabb saw the flatboat clear the point. His holler brought Rutledge from his office and Camron out of the mill. Graham saw a flash of brilliant red hair at the upper window of the mill—Rutledge's daughter Annie had heard the holler too. The flatboatmen were bucking their oars and the steersman leaned into his sweep to ride her across the swift of the current. On the cabin roof a little man in a yellow-green plaid suit hopped up and down and waved his arms.

The river poured over the top of the dam in a long shining curve, the crest of the wave maybe two feet over the lowest section of the dam. Any fool could see the flatboat drew more'n that. Anyway, they wouldn't bet against the dam that was New Salem's pride. So they begun hollering at the flatboatman, some wanting him to haul out and portage, some wanting him to run it close in to the mill where they could get a better sight of the wrack. Red-haired Annie called, "I don't want another flatboat, Pa—can't you ketch me a steamboat?" The men laughed, the things Annie said could make a *goat* laugh, and her Ma (who just then come to the window) told her hesh, but give her a hug and stayed to watch.

The steersman was uncommon tall, and when he threw his weight on the steering-oar the boat slanted across the current at speed. He hollered for his oarsmen to pile on the sweeps, too—driving her hard at the spillway. The man in the yellow-green suit hung himself to the for'ard lantern-post, waving his arm like he was some sort of pilot. With the whole push of the Sangamon behind it and the oars driving, the flatboat came surging up—her nose rising to lip the crest but her belly dragging with an awful grating sound on the rocks of the coffer-dam—

"Bung-up, by cracky!"

—she jerk-jumped and stuck, throwing her whole crew flat except the yellow-suit man who swung round his post like a weather-cock. The river jumped into her stern-well as the bow rode up, filled her quick as *that*, and she settled on the dam part-way over.

The Clary's Grove Boys gave a raucous cheer from the top of the bluff, and congratulated themselves on wracking the boat. The citizens on the riverbank laughed, snorted, or nodded sagaciously, according to temperament. The air was rich with advice, not all of it sarcastic.

On board the flatboat the man in the yellow suit stamped his foot and danged it. The tall steersman hauled himself up. Looked round at the folks alongshore, the red-haired girl and her mother hugging and laughing in the upper window of the mill, the rowdies hollering from the bluff—saw more folks gathering up there, drawn by the shouting. He smiled, gave them a little wave of his hand like to say he had grounded his boat just to entertain them, and was glad they enjoyed the performance.

That was the first New Salem saw of Abe Lincoln.

Saw him, but not to notice. It was the man in the yellow suit that caught the eye, and the ear. He began talking while hauling off his boots and kept at it as he waded the dam-top with the water creaming and banking over his knees. "Offutt's the name, Denton T. . . . ," introducing himself to Camron and Rutledge first, which showed he recognized the quality.

And a good townsite, too, when he saw one: "Mister Rutledge, sir, Mister Camron, my congratulations." He hadn't ever seen a better location for commerce, and let him tell you he had done some *looking*, but never the like of this: timber, bottom-land, water power—water power!—to turn the wheels of industry. All she wanted was some river and harbor improvements, a judicious dredging of the channel, and Denton Offutt would be prepared to swear upon a stack of Bibles there'd be steamboats ranked three at a time against the landing. New Salem's Destiny was writ in the shape of the land itself: you couldn't want anything surer than that.

"Well now!" beamed Rutledge. "Mr. Offutt, you are a man of vision." Rutledge had put his money on New Salem, and would back it to the end. Camron here, though he *was* a Preacher, was also a millwright, and a danged fine one begging his pardon. "First we clapped eyes on this spot, we said she was bound to draw the whole trade of the upper Sangamon. And I am glad you agree about river improvements—a man of your experience. I been trying to persuade these folks to send a man up the legislature and get *us* a rivers bill—put that Springfield crowd in their place."

Meantime the long steersman had surveyed the half-sunk flatboat end to end and inside out, not minding the hoots and bellers from Clary's Grove. Babb McNabb called out he ought to unload, but Graham said the boat was full of river and how was he going to pump her out?

Offutt, Rutledge, and the rest adjourned to the mill offices to discuss dikes, dredges, and such. Mrs. Rutledge went downstairs to tend the menfolk, but red Annie sat herself at the window to see how the adventure ended. McNabb and Graham stayed too. Having offered honest advice to the flatboatmen, they felt an obligation to see the matter out.

The long steersman and his two crewmen set to, bucking barrels out of the cabin. The Clary's Grove Boys, from the top of the bluff, recommended Longshanks get hisself a horse and leave boats to boatmen. Longshanks and one other, that he called "John D.," floated the barrels one by one into the water banked up in the stern, and eased them over the fall so they dropped safely into the deepwater trench the water had gouged below the dam. The third man, whose name was Hanks, waited below—waded out, caught the barrels, and swam them to rest in the shallows.

It appeared to Graham the boat was coming up by the stern. The weight of the remaining cargo must all be up front. Yes—the stern was nearly out of the water now, the flatboat tipped forwards. Maybe, McNabb allowed, but not enough to float her with her belly full of river. Take 'em the best part of a day to bail her . . .

Meantime the one called John D. came splashing ashore. " 'Scuse me, sirs. Abe says I'm to ask is there a man here a carpenter? and could we borry the loan of a good-size auger?" Graham kindly told him to go in the mill and ask for Mr. Camron, he was sure to have one.

Longshanks took a rest, sitting on the cabin with his legs dangling, his shins bared by his too-short pants. He didn't seem to mind the Clary's Grove Boys, who were working as hard as ever they had in their lives to come up with useful projects for the steersman, now he had busted his boat on their dam. He could saw the boat into planks and build a shit-house with it. Or set fire to it—and himself, if he liked. Jack Armstrong said he'd a *damn sight* ruther burn up than drown hisself—then Pleasant caught on and hee-hawed, damn sight/dam site, haw haw haw. There was a female holler from inside the mill, and Annie Rutledge disappeared—her Ma didn't want her hearing the Clary's Grove Boys cussing.

Which Longshanks seemingly paid no mind to. So their advice, which was raw to begin with, got downright shameful—enough so there was a decent chance that (once he finished what he'd set his mind to do) the long stranger would feel compelled to go on up and *try* to whup Jack Armstrong in front of his whole clan. It was in hopes of that that McNabb and Graham stayed on, and most of the people up the bluff. Jack Armstrong was well-named. It was said he had killed his man back in Kentucky. It was proven fact he could whup any man in Sangamon County. Still, there was a first time for everything.

John D. waded back out with the auger. Longshanks vanished inside, and they heard him shifting barrels. Then the grinding sound of the auger, barely audible above the rush of water. "Well I'm blessed," said McNabb, "looky there!" Beneath the forequarters of the boat that jutted out over the dam-fall, a line of water rushed out like piss from a cow, from the hole Longshanks had augered in the floor of the flatboat. As they watched, another line of piss erupted next to the first.

"There she goes!" Sure enough: the flatboat, tipped forwards on the dam by the shifting of the cargo, now lightened and lifted as the water rushed out of her. Longshanks and John D. were shoving with their poles. She grated on the coffer-dam rocks, slewed a little—then slid over with a rush, clear of the dam, her blunt nose plowing up water where she dug in at the bottom of the fall, but she bounced up right enough.

The people down at the mill raised a cheer. Up on the bluff the Clary's Grove Boys still hooted derisively—if they couldn't get no satisfaction from the result, there was still some enjoyment in how foolish Longshanks looked riding all that lumber downhill.

But there was a kind of consensus—a silent one, considering Jack Armstrong—that Longshanks come out top dog. He'd done the job, and never give sign he heard the Clary's Grove Boys no more than if they was shitepoke-birds.

By late afternoon, Offutt and Company had reloaded the flatboat and were ready to sail for New Orleans. As Offutt skipped back aboard he told Rutledge he meant to come back to New Salem to invest his capital. The boatmen pushed off, farmers give a cheer, everyone was waving. Annie's red hair flashed again at the upper window, a white handkerchief fluttering in her hand. The tall steersman lifted his slouch hat in salute. Rutledge told Graham he hoped Offut *would* come back: just the sort of man this country needed. Graham wasn't sure: thought Offutt might be like Babb McNabb's rooster, ten-dollar strut but not worth a dime in a cockfight.

Up on the bluff Clary's Grove hollered good riddance to the flatboat, and clapped Jack Armstrong on the back as if he had bullied her off. Jack took that as his due: but he wasn't entirely satisfied. He'd hoped to get Longshanks to come up and fight—but the man paid him no mind at all. And there was something about the *way* he'd paid them no mind that rankled: like they was no-account.

Jack saw the steersman lift his hat in farewell to the folks at the mill and steer into the swift of the current. Being high on the bluff, Jack could see the boat for a ways after she turned the downstream bend. The steersman was still looking back; raised his head a little as if to meet Jack's eye: then suddenly he broke at the waist and flourished his slouch hat in a sweeping bow, which meant *Kiss my ass Jack Armstrong* as clear as if he'd spoke it. Then the boat passed full behind the point, and was out of reach forever.

"Dang him!" said Jack. The son of a bitch had laughed at him and got away clean. Such a thing never happened to Jack Armstrong in his life. He felt cold all of a sudden. The Boys had gone inside the Grocery.

June–December 1831

It was Denton Offutt most people remembered when he came back to New Salem—still wearing that yellow suit. They greeted him by name and give him good welcome. Their *Howdy* included Longshanks, who stalked along in Offutt's wake carrying their baggage, and who (if he was remembered at all) was just that Long Feller that pulled the bung on the flatboat—till Offutt put a name to him: "Lincoln, Abe Lincoln, he's come along to clerk for me at the store."

You'd say *Howdy there, Abe*, he'd say it back and look down kind of sweet and bashful at you from way up top of his neck and shoulders, and your hand would disappear inside his huge warm oversize paw. He was a lot to take in, but not much to look at. Tall as a draft horse, wiry strong and lean as a rake, with a long bony-jawed slab-lipped big-nosed face that looked like it been rough-hewed with an ax and smoothed with a jack-plane. His linsey shirt and worn jeans pants were busted and patched at knees and elbows and came a good deal short of ankles and wrists, as if he'd grown longer since putting on his clothes. He was an extra added attraction to the Denton Offutt show, on the order of a pet monster.

Offutt held court on the porch of his store, on the bluff road just down from Clary's, giving and taking generously of whiskey and sang-root Elixir. It was a treat to hear him discourse on channel dredging and dockage. He was a powerful second to Rutledge, insisting they elect a man to legislature to get their rightful share of the next improvements bill. Of course they wanted a decent survey of the river to support their claims: maps, depth in the channel and on the bar, riverbed samples . . . But that was *child's-play*, a trifling investment of time and labor. Offutt talked so grandly that Rutledge began to worry he was *all* talk. So he was happily surprised one morning to see Offutt's Abe out on the river in a scow, sounding with a hickory pole.

While Offutt entertained, Abe took care of customers. Now and then he'd come out and throw in a remark—which, after you thought it over, might sneak up and tickle you:

Like the time the men were arguing free will and predestiny, and Camron said he didn't see no objection, in principle, to the idea that the Lord had determined from the start who was going to sin, but *still* had right to damn a man to hell for doing it. After a little Abe spoke up, as if a memory just come to him. Said he knew a man once, put his bull to stud on his tarrier-dog to breed him a bull-tarrier. "Spoiled the dog and displeased the bull." Abe scratched his head in puzzlement. "Yet there warn't a thing wrong with the idea—in principle."

The ladies in particular liked to buy at Offutt's. Offutt was a gentleman, not a rough like Clary, and Abe was always agreeable—raising his shag-haired homely head out of some book or other, as queer a sight as if it was a horse trying to read. He wasn't forwards, but in a quiet way would say things to make a woman pleased with him. And if she said something kind or gentle in return, even just to wish him a good day, he'd get a look in his eyes like a good hound that wanted petting. Of course you couldn't pet him—but felt a little sorry you couldn't: and so it was the women that first took to him, talked him up as a *good* young man, an orphan prob'ly. And looked for good turns to do him.

All but Rutledge's Annie, who true to her red hair and freckles was all pepper with him; and whenever she came into the store with her mother was sure to drop a word like "shanks" that would make Abe blush and try to haul his bare ankles up into his pants.

Out on the porch Offutt bowed to the ladies, "the grace and beauty of our city," took up his fiddle, and sung:

" 'Twas here the Queen o' Sheba came, with Solamun
        of old,
    With an ass's load o' spices, pom'granates and fine gold,
    And when she saw this lovely land her heart
        was filled with joy,
    Straightway she said I'd like to be a Queen in Elanoy!"

The men laughed and made their bows to Queen Martha and Princess Annie. Mrs. Rutledge told Offutt, "Get along now!" for modesty's sake. Miss Annie arched her brows and said he might call her *Queen* the day she moved into a castle. "In the meantime, don't sell me no butter till you get yourself a cow." Red-haired girls are *all* pepper.

Abe came out on the porch and leaned against the wall. "Miss Annie might like that other verse, Mister Offutt."

Offutt was puzzled. "What other verse is that?"

Abe cleared his throat and stood up. He gave red-haired Annie a good straight look, and she sent one back. He lifted his chin and sung out in a high scrapy off-note tenor:

> "Oh she's bounded by the Wabash, Ohio, and the Lakes,
>   She's crawfish in the swampy lands, she's Milk-sick
>   and the shakes,
>   But these are light amusements, our leisure to employ,
>   While livin' in this garden land, the State of Elanoy!"

Offutt blushed and threw up his hands, the laugh on him but he knew how to take it. Miss Annie rolled her eyes teasingly at Offutt, and applauded Abe. Her red hair flared off the top of her head in fiery waves.

A wild glee leaped in Abe and shook him: he crinked his nose and curled his top lip to show his teeth and gums like a jackass and *haw haw hawed*, couldn't stop no more than if it was a coughing-fit—and Miss Annie turned red and near busted herself laughing at Long Abe.

People said there was as much fun in him as Jack Armstrong, and a lot less ruckus.

Yes, Offutt's was a popular establishment. If he had got himself some decent merchandise he could have made his fortune. He'd bustle about, full of talk about the high-bred seed-corn he'd took consignment on, be in any day now—only the seed-corn never *did* manage to get there.

It was astonishing to James Rutledge, and to Mentor Graham, that the man could be so businesslike about the river survey, yet neglectful of a simple matter like stocking his shelves. They set the matter before the New Salem Debating Club, which met at Rutledge's twice a month. They proposed that human gifts were particular: a man might have a gift for the grand enterprise and be a fool in more mundane matters. Rutledge, a Deist, took the position that such a division argued the existence of a rational order in Nature. Camron, who was Cumberland Presbyterian, said it was an illustration of the Lord's sovereign power, giving and taking as He will. Kelso the freethinker said the world had no more rules to it than rolling dice: some points being likelier than others, but all combinations possible, however queer.

Graham believed it was one of the best debates they ever had. It raised his admiration for Offutt that he could be the occasion of such a forensic exchange. So next day at noon he hailed Offutt, who (as was his custom) had just breakfasted, congratulated him on starting the river survey, and asked how was it coming?

Offutt blinked stupidly. His sang-root and whiskey regimen made for splendid late afternoons and evenings, but was hard on the hours between breakfast and supper.

. . . and it turned out Offutt had no notion of Abe's sounding and mapping the Sangamon. Must have been Abe's own idea. Heard the talk, never said a word, but set to work.

Rutledge took notice of Abe as well: Graham came into Offutt's to find the two of them poring over Abe's river-map. The shallows were measured and marked, even the odd rocks, for a quarter mile above the milldam. Abe had located his soundings by lining them up between "marks" on opposite shores—dead trees, white rocks, and such. "I reckoned it might come handy when you take the improvements bill up to legislature."

"Handy?" said Rutledge. "Well I should think. It's near as good as a survey." And later Rutledge remarked to Graham: "He's got a long head to go with those long shanks."

Graham hesitated: "I wouldn't want it to get out, for the boy asked me to keep it close: but he's been coming for lessons, grammar and mathematics mostly. He's read a sight more than a body might think, just to look at him."

Rutledge cocked an eye at the schoolmaster. "Graham," he said, "I have a notion . . ."

That winter New Salem was astonished to learn that the town's "Respectables"—the men Bill Clary called "the b'iled-shirt bunch"— had taken Offutt's boy into their debate club. Offutt was stunned, and a little in envy. But after the first shock most people said *good on him!* They reckoned he worked at it, always reading in a book or ciphering over his river-maps—out in the chill of the morning with his shanks bare, ought to buy hisself a growed man's set of trousers though. Truth was, they'd grown fond of him.

March 1832

Along towards the end of winter, word came from Beardstown that the new steamer *Talisman* would try a run up the Sangamon. It was Fourth of July in winter for New Salem. Every man of property thanked the Lord, and began in his mind to lay up treasures for the moth and rust. Offutt crowed like a dunghill rooster, "See now, I said that if you have location on a navigable waterway . . ." as if he had built the steamboat instead of just fiddling and jawing about it till a body lost his rest. (The village had got the measure of Denton Offutt: a windy, gassy sort of man, like Babb McNabb's rooster: plenty *cockadoodle*, but not a lot of *do*.)

But Rutledge and Camron warned it was early in the day to count the coin: *Talisman* had not yet made the trip, nor it wasn't certain the Sangamon had water enough to carry her. They'd be wanting those internal-improvement appropriations—and a canvass for legislature coming up. For token of seriousness, Rutledge was said to be paying Long Abe a wage to push his river survey and set buoys to mark the channel.

Rutledge didn't fool Uncle Bill Clary. The man thought New

Salem was his personal property, didn't mean nobody but himself to run it—not unless that man wore a collar reading, "My dog: James Rutledge." Well, Clary had his own dog, proved best in every fight so far, if only he could get Jack Armstrong's hackles raised. He'd stand on the porch with Jack and watch Longshanks Lincoln stride up the path from the river, his sounding-pole shouldered and his map-board tucked under an arm. "There's a boy gittin' above hisself. Someone ought to take him down a peg."

Jack Armstrong didn't answer. Of course he had took note of the newcomer. But it was a point of honor not to let on he had. Jack Armstrong was the big bull of this lick: the best rider fighter wrassler joker hunter whiskeydrinker in the district. Jack Armstrong could have crushed this Longshanks or whatever he called himself any time he wanted. But it was beneath his dignity to take such notice of a reuben. If Offutt's clerk wanted the honor of a Jack Armstrong whuppin', he'd have to come ask for it—and ask polite.

Yet Jack could not help but take notice when Brother Pleasant came back after working alongside Lincoln over at Kirkpatrick's saw-mill on Spring Creek. "Saw it myself. Man bet him a dollar he couldn't. It was a double-blade ax, long as a man's leg—a reg'lar size man, that is. He took it in his one hand by the endest part o' the haft—lift it straight up without bendin' his arm—an' holt it like that, arm's-length straight out while a man counted a hunderd: arm never shook no more'n a rock."

Jack shrugged. "It don't signify." But when he tried the trick himself, alone in the woods, he found he had to flex his arm to raise the ax; and for the life of him could not have held it out longer than a man might count twenty. It gave Jack Armstrong to think.

But Uncle Clary didn't need to think, didn't want to think. While Jack and the boys stood around scratching fleas, Rutledge and Company was heaping coals of fire on his head, piling outrage upon insult. "Ain't you heard?" he cried to Jack. "Ain't you heard what them sons a bitches gone and done? Appointed Rowan Herndon to pilot that steamboat up from Beardstown."

"So what?" said Jack. "Herndon's the only man in the district ever steered one o' . . ."

"And Longshanks Lincoln to be his Number Two!"

Son of a bitch.

"Huh!" nodded Clary, "now you get it." He poked his finger in Jack's chest. "If Rutledge kin take that scrawny jackass, that ain't been in this town half a year, and make him pilot of the *Talisman*, what d'you reckon they'll make him next? Postmaster? Or: *maybe they'll run him for constable*."

Jack rose to it slow. "But I'm the constable."

"Well! I reckon you see it—now it's got *your* nose in a twist!"

"Constable," said Jack. He glared at Clary. "It ain't right. I won't stand for it."

Clary smiled. He didn't think they *would* run Lincoln against Jack, but what did that matter? It was the fact they *could* that rankled.

In fact, the Respectables had no intention of putting Lincoln up for constable. They didn't show their hand until the day Lincoln and Herndon left for Beardstown to fetch up the *Talisman*. Then Graham and Kelso filed the papers, and the day after, a long letter appeared in the *Sangamon Journal* over the signature *A. Lincoln*. Denton Offutt's clerk had declared himself, all six feet four inches of him, candidate for a Sangamon County seat in the legislature of the State of Illinois:

> Fellow Citizens: Having become a candidate for the honorable office of one of your representatives in the next General Assembly of this state, in accordance with established custom, and the principles of true republicanism, it becomes my duty to make known to you—the people whom I propose to represent—my sentiments in regard to local affairs . . .

He was first and foremost for internal improvements, roads canals and railroads, "for the purpose of facilitating the task of exporting the surplus products of our fertile soil." He'd like to have the railroad, but the cost of the thing was two hundred and ninety thousands of dollars, "the bare statement of which, in my opinion, is sufficient to justify the belief, that the *improvement of the Sangamon river* is an object much better suited to our infant resources." The rest of it was as full of statistics as Genesis is of begats, and it finished:

> Every man is said to have his peculiar ambition. I have no other so great as that of being truly esteemed of my fellow men. I am young and unknown to many of you. I was born and have ever remained in the most humble walks of life. I have no wealthy or popular relations to recommend me. My case is thrown exclusively upon the independent voters of this county, and if elected they will have conferred a favor upon me, for which I shall be unremitting in my labors to compensate. But if the good people in their wisdom shall see fit to keep me in the background, I have been too familiar with disappointments to be very much chagrined. Your friend and fellow-citizen,
> A. Lincoln.

All of which meant that Long Abe Lincoln, Denton Offutt's Abe, was the Rutledge candidate to go to legislature and stand up for Sangamon County before the powers of the land—not six months since he walked out of the woods behind Denton Offutt, taller and leaner than a human man had any business to be, with a name nobody ever heard of, unkempt, uncombed, uneducated, with boots too busted to contain his long dirty toes, and clothes that come short of his bony shanks and knobby wrist-bones.

So when *Talisman* came chugging and hooting up the river from Beardstown, it wasn't just the steamboat the town turned out to look at (on which their hopes and fortunes were riding), but also to get a look at Abe Lincoln in this new light. There he was up in the little pilot-house, you couldn't miss *him*: head and shoulders taller than everyone, conning the steamboat across the current to land

below the dam cool as billy-be-damn, his blue-white eyes flicking
over the marks and buoys. (Which, you will recall, he measured and
set out his own self.) The whole town shouted as he sidled the boat
to waterside and the crewmen hitched her fore and aft.

There wasn't a boy in town wouldn't have sold his chance of
heaven to be Abe Lincoln for that one day. There was a grand cele-
bration, with the town's own pilots Lincoln and Rowan Herndon
seated with the owner and captain of the *Talisman* as guests of
honor. Someone had written a poem in honor of the occasion, which
was published in the *Sangamon Journal*, and read out to the company by Jack Kelso (who, it was guessed, had most likely wrote it
himself):

> ". . . Then what a debt of Fame we owe
> To him who on our Sangamo
> First launched the Steamer's daring prow;
> And sailor-like steered right ahead—
> Nor cared, nor feared the dangers great
> That on his devious course await—
> Past rocks and shoals and sawyers dread,
> To win the Commerce for his town,
> And for himself, deserved renown.
> Hey-ho! I must not fail to tell,
> What great rejoicings then befell,
> Such stuffing—all the pork in town,
> And fowls and such were then crammed down,
> And by next morn Old Ned quite high
> Had ris'n in price, and none to buy.
> Clary's whiskey sold off slick,
> Some for cash, but most on tick—
> For Jackson men will take, with thanks,
> Credit from 'Grocers' instead of banks . . ."

Uncle Bill Clary was about done. "Well Jack. Do you reckon
it has gone far enough?" The Boys watched their hero in eager
expectation.

Jack didn't like how Uncle Clary kept pushing him. "When it does I will know it." The Boys were with him, of course, but they were disappointed. Why didn't Jack just go on over to Offutt's and throw Lincoln on his ass?

It wasn't that Jack Armstrong was afraid. Only, there was something *back of* that Lincoln, a man couldn't say what: like Abe was a thicket in which something was lurking that might or might not be a bear. One minute he's scratching fleas, the next he's piloting *Talisman* and James Rutledge is backing him for legislature. Still waters run deep. You want a read of the current before you jump in.

In fact, the Debate Club were almost as surprised as the rest of the town by their decision to make Abe their candidate.

The Club was constituted by the best-read men in town, without regard to wealth. James Rutledge and his nephew-in-law Camron had money, but Jack Kelso (the hugely fat and florid blacksmith) and Schoolmaster Graham were barely middling. Old John Berry, a veteran of 1812 and a prosperous farmer, was Bible-learned. Rowan Herndon owned a store and (like Kelso) was a freethinker who read Tom Paine and Jeremy Bentham. Dr. Allen had a Dartmouth College degree. The sons of Berry and Rutledge, and the Greene brothers, had attended the Illinois College at Jacksonville.

They adopted Abe as a kind of charity. Rutledge appreciated Abe's cleverness in the informal debates of store and tavern, a rough diamond that wanted polishing. Graham vouched for his earnestness. Fat Jack Kelso chimed in with his own tale of Lincoln coming by to talk Shakespeare and borrow books. "He will speak you a piece out of memory, and not badly—if you could scrub the *Ken*tuck and Hoosier off his tongue."

The Club met in the main room of Rutledge's tavern, which was closed to the public on their sacred evenings. An issue would have been proposed at the previous meeting, and principals and seconds named (either deliberately or by drawing lots). The parties would work up their positions during the week, and come loaded for bear. The debates were various: the good of a strong vs. a cheap currency;

free will vs. predestiny; free trade vs. Henry Clay's American System; whether an act is to be judged by its motives, or its consequences; whether a state can nullify national legislation; female education; that the vices of the rich are of greater benefit to society than those of the poor; which is the surest guide to truth: reason or revelation? A presiding member would state the issue, then each side make an opening statement, followed by an exchange of rebuttals. After which the Club would vote a winner, and the losers treat to a good-night round.

They kindly invited Abe to name a subject and have a go at it. Graham and Kelso exchanged mother-fatherly smiles when he picked "Which has more to complain of against civilization—the Indian or the negro." Straight out of the old *Columbian Orator*, as they both recognized. They gave him Kelso for second, Graham for opposition (who went easy on the boy), and he showed a steady hand with the argument: wasn't content to repeat the ideas set out in the *Orator*, but mixed in bits and pieces from other books plus some observations from his flatboat trips. But *next* time they showed no mercy: Fat Jack Kelso skinned the boy alive arguing the affirmative case that "greatest good for the greatest number" was as safe a guide to morals as the Ten Commandments.

Abe took the lesson well, and three weeks later Lincoln, with Rowan Herndon as second, broke to shards and flinders the book-learned team of Graham and Dr. Allen, arguing the affirmative of the case "That there can be no republic without the equality of man." Dr. Allen was the best educated man in the district, a handsome smooth-faced cleanly man, with wavy auburn hair and always a boiled shirt with a collar. He argued (with Graham's support) from classical precedent the compatibility of republican government with aristocracy and slavery; drew the analogy between the orders of men and the parts of the body; and closed with the government of the family, which is like God's government of nature, benevolent wisdom and power overruling lesser natures for their good.

Lincoln allowed he was impressed by the examples of Athens and Rome—but what become of those people? He'd heard they had gone to pot a thousand years ago. That took them down a bit, in his estimation. Graham and the Doctor were astonished by the boldness of the stroke. Abe lowered his head and went for them: might be those old republics went bust because they *didn't* go for equality. Why should a man stand up for a town that won't give him a fair shake, nor treat him like a man? He supposed there was such a thing as progress: that just as a man learned better ways the older he got, so the human race had learned a thing or two since Rome. He reckoned it was such learning made the Fathers put "All men created equal" at the top of the page. As for parts of the body, he reckoned that by some measures the head *was* more valuable than belly or bowels. But he suspected that if the head was to try the experiment of seceding from the rest, it would come to regret it after a time.

That got a laugh. Young Dr. Allen went red in the cheeks and huffed up his chest. "A figure is no argument!" But Kelso hushed him with, "It was your figure to start with," and Abe went on.

Now as to family government: it was well the child should obey the parent. Son ain't equal to a father in the father's house. But in their natures, they are the same. The son will grow and become a father in his turn. That's equality: and what sort of father was it, who would deny a son the chance to become a man in his own right? He had read somewhere that the first governments out of nature *was* family governments, the patriarch ruling his children. But as families grew, and trade, and warfare, people saw family warn't enough. They had to band families together and make up rules to live by: to let the wisest rule, or the strongest, or yes, even the *tallest* (and he grinned). And as history run on they learned, by trial and error, what was the best arrangement. And in conclusion, the way *he* saw it, the good of a republic was that it *warn't* a family, but another thing altogether. Where sons and fathers stood equal, and could state their case with the same respect, and be judged upon their merits.

They judged Abe on the merits, gave him and Herndon the victory and a cheer in the bargain. Abe's argument left them exhilarated, even a little hilarious. Jack Kelso hailed Abe as a fellow democrat, and treated them to a performance of "that grand poem of equality by the immortal Robert Burns":

"Then let us pray that come it may,
As come it will for a' that,
That sense and worth, o'er a' the earth,
May bear the gree for a' that."

"Say what you will," said Rutledge's son Davey, "the nigger don't stand equal to the white man, and I don't believe Tom Jefferson meant to say so. Why, the notion would have amazed him."

"A childish race," said Dr. Allen, "tickled with a feather and pleased with a straw."

"If you prick us," Abe shot back, "do we not bleed? If you tickle us, do we not laugh?"

"Right for you!" cried Kelso. "The Bard for answer! Hath not a Jew eyes, hands, affections like another man?" He swung his fat red face this way and that, gleeful, challenging them to a duel of quotation.

"Who said anything about Jews?" Herndon was confused.

Old John Berry told Kelso he ought to quoted Scripture. Christ was born to divide sheep from goats, no equality there.

"Judged on the merits," Camron affirmed. "To him that hath, more shall be given. From him that hath not shall be taken away, even that little which he hath."

Kelso chanted in reply,

"For a' that and a' that,
It's coming yet, for a' that,
That man to man the warld o'er
Shall brothers be for a' that."

Dr. Allen lifted his hand, index erect, and intoned, "Cum pare contendere, anceps est; cum superiore, furiosum; cum inferiore, sordidum!" And for their ignorance, "Which I translate thus: 'To strive with an equal is doubtful; with a superior, madness; with an inferior . . . *vulgar*.' " He bowed to applause: "Seneca," he explained, "a classical Roman."

Rutledge gave him the nod. "Doctor, you raise our tone considerable."

Red-faced Kelso offered "the fig of Spain" (whatever that was) for Allen's classical Romans. "Your worm is your only true emperor. Your fat king and your lean beggar is but variable service; two dishes, but to one table. Here's fine revolution an' we had the wit to see it."

Camron waved that away. "More Shakespeare. Just because it sounds like Scripture—I wonder, Kelso, if you remember the difference between . . ."

"All things come alike to all," said Lincoln. "There is one event to the righteous, and to the wicked; to the wise man, and to the fool." He nodded his long, bony head. Then, quietly: "I reckon that is our equality in nature."

"Bard or Scripture." Fat Jack beamed triumphantly from Allen to Camron. "Take your pick!"

As they were leaving Rutledge remarked to Kelso, that if he didn't know better he'd have said Abe got that story of the origin of government—the people picking their tallest man to rule—out of Blackstone's *Commentaries on the Laws of England*. Kelso gave him a look: "I showed him the passage for a joke on *him*. He borrowed the book. It seems he read it."

That gave Rutledge a notion to sleep on. Next morning, when he rode down to the mill he saw Lincoln out on the river in his scow, sounding and dropping marker-floats weighted with blocks of stone. Less than half a year in town and he had taught himself more about the river than Rutledge, Graham, or any of the others, that talked so large about improvements, had bothered to go out and learn in five.

Rutledge chewed over his idea for a day, then put it up to Camron, Kelso, and Graham. Camron took it like a blow on the head. "Run Offutt's Abe for assembly? You can't mean it!"

"Why not?" Rutledge wanted to know. "He knows the river better than any man in the district. He can write and cipher. And he can argue as well as any man in town, as we can testify."

"By heaven!" Kelso was gleeful. "Abe Lincoln for legislature! Well I'm blessed!"

Camron shot Kelso a look that questioned Fat Jack's state of grace, and to Rutledge pleaded, "Why Uncle, it would be a scandal! He . . . he's a store-clerk, poorer than dirt. He hasn't been in town a year, hasn't got a clean shirt nor a decent pair of shoes . . ."

"Shirts can be washed," said Kelso, "shoes can be bought or borrowed."

"He has no schooling worth the mention."

"He's got the *Preceptor* and the *Orator*, Shakespeare enough to face Jack Kelso here, and Scripture enough to answer you."

But Camron was dogged. "The Devil can quote Scripture. We don't know who he is, where he's from, who his people are—if he has any people."

"So he is an orphan," grinned Fat Jack, "all the better. He might be anybody. How do you know he ain't George Washington's left-hand son, or the Lost Dolphin of France?"

Graham was beginning to be persuaded. "He can learn the manners and arguments he will need. When he sets himself to learn a thing, he *takes hold*."

Camron raised his hands in surrender. "But the town will take it for a joke. Denton Offutt's Abe!"

Kelso became thoughtful. "What you want is a way to bring him out, so folks can see him in a different light."

Rutledge already had the answer for that: it was part of his notion from the first. They would get Abe a place as pilot on the *Talisman*, and time his announcement to coincide with the steamboat's arrival.

Kelso spread his arms to embrace the idea. "Rutledge, that is positively *gaudy*!—so long as the boy don't wreck the steamer like he did his flatboat!"

The other members of the Club were more and less enthusiastic about Abe's nomination, according to how they had rated their own chances. Dr. Allen had rated *his* rather high. But Rutledge persuaded and they went along, as he expected they would. It was persuading Abe to accept that concerned him more. The young man was modest to a fault.

His daughter could have told him that that *particular* worry was needless—if she'd been willing to talk.

James Rutledge's daughter Annie had red hair, and you know what they say about red-haired girls. She was rising fifteen, but the head on her shoulders was half again as old as that. She had milk-white skin, a fine small pink mouth, green eyes like a cat, and a way of looking at you like you were her meat. She was smarter than a woman had any need to be, she thought like a cat moved—smooth and quiet, now you see her now you don't, and she had claws, too. She was a temptation and a trial to every man and boy in the district. You couldn't help but notice her, with her red hair and green eyes, the way her dresses swung when she walked or clung when she stood, the way she showed her mouth laughing. If she took notice of *you*, it would be some way that would make your ears burn. The only worse thing was if she never noticed you at all.

The joke about Annie Rutledge was that she was engaged to be married "in a manner of speaking." A fellow named McNeill stopped in town and took a fancy to becoming James Rutledge's son-in-law; asked to pay court to Miss Rutledge; spent part of an evening talking with her in the parlor—then rose early, said he must leave next day on business. Miss Annie said, "I will marry you when you come back," and the young man was never seen or heard from again.

Annie of course knew the story, and told her own version, her eyes green and hot as a catamount's: "What I said was: 'I will marry you *if* you come back.'"

She had an eye of Abe from the start. A male critter of that size, awkwardness, dishevelment, and unseemliness of feature—yaller-skinned, jug-eared, thatch-headed, teeth like a horse and a nose you could plow with—was good game for her. If she didn't devil him too much at first it was because he was an easy mark: bird not worth her shot. When her Pa started taking the boy seriously, talking river improvements with him like he was a regular man, she gave Abe a second look. There were possibilities she'd missed.

When he showed up for the Debate Club she burst out laughing—got hushed and chased to her room, still giggling—and was the toast of New Salem for a week on the strength of her description of Abe among the Respectables, "like a draft mule at choir meeting." But that wasn't satisfactory: she hadn't bested Abe face to face.

She needed to get an edge on him. So she took to spying on him as he worked on the river unconscious he was watched, seeing how careful he was in his work, how slow, how watchful and considering—taking time to look and feel of the water, scrape up bottom sands and palm them and roll them between his fingers. But sometimes he would just cross the river, beach the scow, then disappear into the brush.

She borrowed a canoe, paddled over herself, and tracked him like an Injun. Heard him a ways ahead, talking to someone, so she slipped off sideways through the trees to come up on him unseen. Peeked at him through a screen of brush.

He was having an argument with a hickory tree. It wasn't a particularly intelligent pignut either, as far as she could tell. Her wit sparked like a new flint: she would amble out cool and quiet, and when he noticed her she'd say, "Well I reckon a pignut is someone you *can* win a debate with." She started—then stopped. Maybe it wasn't safe. Maybe he was a crazy man, standing out in the woods, explaining the Ten Commandments to a pignut tree.

Then she saw him stop, pull a book out of his pocket, and take a look in it. "I ain't got it," he said, "I ain't got it yet." He looked helplessly at the tree and spread his arms. "I'm sorry," he said. "It's hard to argue a thing when you ain't got convictions on it one way or t'other. The Commandments is mostly sound, but too particular. 'Greatest good for the greatest number'—I ain't *sure* but what it might not work. As long as the lesser number ended up with lesser good, not something just plain bad." He stood awhile staring. Then he told the pignut, "Well! Maybe that would do the trick! Shall we give her a try?"

She sat in the brush and watched him work and read and talk himself through the debate he would have with Jack Kelso that night. It was as good as reading to listen to him. But that was not a thing for *him* to know about *her*: when he looked at the sun to see the time, she slipped off the way she came.

But sneaked back again whenever she knew he had a debate to get ready for. Just spying him out, you understand. He was deep, and clever, and when she tried him next she wanted to know what surprises he could spring before he sprung 'em. In the meantime, it was a joke on him that he was being watched, and never knowed it.

She enjoyed the joke until the week before *Talisman*. She was watching as he sat on a stump, scratching away with a buzzard-quill pen at a paper pegged to a board. She had just said to herself she wished she knew what he was writing, when he raised up and called: "Miss Rutledge? Annie? Come on down here, won't you, and give me a hand with this?"

Caught! She blushed like a prairie fire as she stepped out of the brush. But he wasn't laughing at her, he spoke serious, "I'd be grateful if you could see your way . . ." as if he had known she was watching him from the start, and took it as a kind of friendship, a way of keeping him company. "It's got to rhyme, you see—poetry."

> "Then what a debt of Fame we owe
>   To him who on our Sangamo
>   First launched the Steamer's daring prow . . ."

It took them the rest of that afternoon. The best of it was trying to rhyme "win the Commerce for his town." They ran through "starry crown" and "falling down," then got silly, "hope he don't drown," and a dozen even funnier than that which they couldn't remember after, till she finally came up with: "And for himself, deserved renown."

He gave her a blazing look out of his white-blue eyes and his sad-horse face turned itself inside out in a pure joyfulness that tickled her under the ribs and made her laugh—and then he rolled his top lip back and crinked his nose and showed his teeth like a horse and whinnied *Hee-hee-hee*, and made her laugh till she couldn't hardly stand it.

She wasn't much use for rhyming after that. But she thought

"Clary's whiskey sold off slick / Some for cash, but most on tick"—thought that was just about the funniest thing she ever heard wrote.

Then it was late. All of a sudden she felt how alone she was with Abe Lincoln, her body aching after all that laughing with him—and how it was late. "I got to go!" she said and jumped up. "Don't come right along with me." Then she blushed again, for his knowing that their meeting was secret with her.

"Course not," he said, as if it was always understood. Then he looked bashful, "*I'd* be obliged if you kept dark about this . . . this poem here."

That gave her back her poise. Now she had a secret of his. The *vanity* of the man: writing a poem to celebrate his own doings, which he hadn't even done yet, and ashamed to let his neighbors see his big head. She smiled: "Well I won't—leastways, I don't *think* I'll tell." There, she thought, that will keep Mr. Lincoln guessing.

Maybe it did—she couldn't be sure. But she never did tell anyone it was Abe wrote the poem about the first man to pilot a steamboat from Beardstown to New Salem.

New Salem, March 1832

The *Talisman* came and went, and after the five days' wonder of it Abe came shambling back to town with his toes muddy and his shoes slung round his neck to spare them. The noted river-pilot and Assembly candidate could be seen thereafter sweeping dust out of Offutt's store and joshing the customers. Camron got another attack of skepticism. "It ain't six months since he came out of the woods with burrs in his hair. He's showed he can clerk store and tell a joke. How do we know he can stand up for us? And you're asking the people to take him on our say-so."

Rutledge saw the point: "It's too bad he has no service to point to, no scalps on his belt." For politics you wanted a man with more than willingness, brains, and good nature. You wanted a man with some iron in him.

"Prince Hal needs a war to fight," said Kelso, "and a Hotspur to whup."

Rutledge shrugged. "He'll have to settle for a steamboat to pilot, and a clean shirt to wear on the stump."

"If you think that's enough," said Camron.

"Well," said Graham, "we've said our prayers for him."

"Careful what you pray for," said Jack, "you might get it."

It was late morning. There was a big crowd in front of Clary's, a keg set out, bets given and took. The Clary's Grove Boys were running foot-races between Clary's Grocery and the gander-pulling tree— racing past Offutt (where he sat on his porch) with a whoop and a holler.

Denton Offutt had found, by scientific experiment, that while sang-roots and whiskey made a lively wit livelier, they were no anti-dote for injustice. He felt a grievance, though he was too big a man to be bitter. Was it not he who had seen what a prime location New Salem was for commerce? Now every jack in the district was setting up for a merchant—Berry, Rutledge, Hill, Herndon—which was an excess of surplusage for a town this size. No wonder he couldn't make a dollar. He could have borne the decline in fortune if New Salem had given him credit for foresight. *But a prophet is without honor—and without profit too, hee-hee, at least I have not lost my ability to take a philosophical view.* He'd given these people too much credit. Pearls before swine. Abe more their style: a jibe, a funny story. Just the sort they'd make a pet of—Debate Club, pilot steamboat, run him for legislature. Who was it found the boy, he wished to know? And taught him everything he knew about boats rivers and internal improvements? Well, he wished them joy of him, and him of them.

Offutt blinked: he was surrounded by Clary's Grove Boys! By some mysterious operation his body had been transposited unawares from his own porch to the front of Clary's Grocery. *The Elixir was more virtuous than he had dared suppose!* But here was Clary looking insolent, asking if he'd come to buy hisself some *decent* goods—maybe some superior high-bred seed-corn, haw haw haw. Or did he want to wager on the next race: Royal Clary, Bill Greene— or Jack Armstrong.

Armstrong: standing there bluff and red-faced, a clutch of cock-feathers in his hatband.

Fiery inspiration came to Denton Offutt: "Oh I'll bet on Jack Armstrong all right—bet on him to *run*."

Uncle Clary's heart leaped for joy, he was so full of gratitude it was almost religious. "Why Mr. Offutt, that sounds like a challenge." He grinned. They all grinned, the whole gang of them, Clarys, Armstrongs, and the rest.

Only Jack Armstrong's face took a hard set. "Bring on your boy whenever you please," he said. "Fightin' or wrasslin', as you like."

The whiskey left Offutt and the fire too, quick as you snuff a candle. *What had he done?* Got Abe into a brawl with the town bully-boy, and him a candidate for legislature! But there was no going back. Offutt wobbled on his legs, but managed to front Armstrong. "Let it be this day next week. Straight wrassling—you have a wife and children to consider." He tipped his hat and turned back to his store, while Clary's Grove hooted—no more than was called for, though: they appreciated the style of Offutt's parting shot.

By the time he confessed to Abe what he'd done, Offutt was feeling like Judas. Abe looked down at him from the top of his height, his heavy lips pursed up most solemn, his blue-white eyes cold under the shag of his brows. "You needn't glare at me that way!" Offutt cried. "After all I done for *you*, paying you wages and dragging this place along while you're off fishing in the creek or jaw-boning the night away with the quality."

Abe's look settled on Offutt consideringly. They both knew what Offutt said was angry nonsense. No need to shame the man by saying as much. Offutt was ashamed of himself though. He said he was sorry again.

Abe shrugged. "It was bound to come. If you hadn't took a hand, I'd have had to find some other way to make him fight."

Chapter 25: **The Candidate**

New Salem, June 1831–March 1832

He had found the stage he was looking for. All he wanted was the part to play on it. He didn't know at first what the part would be— he knew it would have to be big, that's all. *When I was a child I thought there was just two ways for a man to get things done. The story-book way, which an ordinary living man could never do, of Moses and Washington; and the ornery bully-boy way of Pap, and the Grigsbys, and Allen Gentry. But now I'm a man I see different. Between Sephus, Ruby, and the Old Man I have learned a thing or two. There's ways* between *the impossible of Washington and Moses, and the low-down skunk-eating meanness of Grigsby and Jones and Starkey, and Uncle Mordecai. And Pap.*

And it ain't Judge Davis's way neither. I don't want a world of my own making, and every man and woman in it smiles to my face and wishes he could stick a knife in me.

So he didn't care if, at the start, New Salem took him for "Offutt's man." He was himself alone. Nobody, not even himself, knew all of what he was, let alone what he might be. New Salem's laughter just gave him a blind from which to take in the lie of things and make his plans. He would earn the respect of men like Graham, Rutledge, and Kelso; find what they valued and show them he had it, or knew where he could put his hands on it. And he would catch the eye, and whatever else there was to catch, of Annie Rutledge, because she was the finest, cleverest, sharpest, prettiest, most hot-eyed red-headed girl he ever met. And he'd whup Jack Armstrong, have to, because there can't be but the one Big Bull to a lick.

Not a year since he first saw New Salem, and he had got nearly all the things he wished for. Then Offutt went and put him in the way of a brawl with Jack Armstrong.

Rutledge and Graham were very much afraid the scrap would hurt him with respectable folks, the election only six months away. "If you win they will think you are one of the rowdies, and if you lose . . ." Graham beseeched him.

"Why would I lose?" As if the idea was outlandish. Besides, Abe had his own calculation as to the consequences of wrassling Jack Armstrong, and was set on it, pig-headed, no matter *what* the best heads in the county might think.

The best heads had to ask themselves if they hadn't made a mistake after all. And that was the moment Dr. Allen picked to spring his long-laid ambush on the candidate.

New Salem, March 25, 1832

At the end of the evening's debate, the Doctor proposed a subject for their next encounter: "Resolved: that the institution of negro slavery is contrary to the law of nature, and of nature's God."

The subject made Rutledge uneasy. He did not want the Club divided with the election approaching, and this was an issue on which honest men—*these* honest men—differed strongly. Not that any of them had the least interest either in owning negroes or setting them at liberty. But the lack of material interest somehow made their difference more intense: a question of conscience and moral character. Rutledge expected the Club to shun Allen's proposal. But to his surprise, there was a rumble of support for the notion—and from his nephew-in-law Camron too! albeit with a hang-dog look. Graham looked puzzled. Kelso looked grim.

"Well then, gentlemen, since you will have it so," Rutledge said ruefully. "Who will contest the palm?"

There was a silence. Herndon cleared his throat. "How about you, Lincoln?"

"Yes indeed," said Camron—refusing to meet his Uncle's eye. "It would be good practice for our candidate."

Rutledge's lifted eyebrow told Graham his friend was alarmed. Graham smelt conspiracy. Kelso *harumphed*, and lowered like a fat thunderhead. Lincoln looked cool enough. "That suits me." There wasn't anything else a man could say under the circumstances, not without backing down.

"And who to oppose?"

"Well," said the Doctor, "since it was my suggestion, I suppose it is only fair . . ."

Rutledge gave him an empty grin. "Then all that remains is to determine who shall argue the affirmative, and who the negative." It was bad business that would cost Abe votes either way.

"Oh, I don't mind arguing the affirmative," said the Doctor with elaborate off-handedness.

"And Lincoln the negative?"

Abe shrugged carelessly, "I don't mind."

There was a silence while Rutledge, Graham, and Kelso took in the fact that they had been circumvented. The only question was, how deep did the malice go? Were their colleagues just aiming to make Abe sweat a little, for his too-easy winning of the prize? Or did they mean to do him in?

Lincoln seemed neither to notice nor to care. After the meeting broke up, Graham took Abe aside and said he was sorry it turned out so. But Kelso said there was nothing to worry about. "What a man argues in here is secret and sacred. That's our rule. So have no fear, my son, but let her rip!"

Graham and Rutledge exchanged looks: Kelso was too sanguine.

Nothing was secret very long in this town. If you were to switch from a right- to a left-hand hold, taking a piss in your own outhouse, the town would hear of it inside a week.

"I'm not worried," said Abe. "I've argued him down before." He grinned wolfish: "I've seen the institution first-hand. If I can't argue against it, I don't know—"

The three men were took poorly at the same time. "Abe?" said Graham. "Don't you know what 'the negative case' is?"

He got it, sudden: his brownish skin went janders-yellow, his slab-lips bloodless. His eyes winced.

"Resolved: that slavery *is* against the law of nature, and of nature's God," Kelso recited grimly. "You have got to argue that it *ain't*."

Rutledge was stern: "And fight Jack Armstrong the day after that."

New Salem, March 31–April 1, 1832

The day before the debate he went off into the woods, to his secret clearing on the other side of the Sangamon, to puzzle out his argument. He meant to stay all night if he had to: packed a cut of meat and some corn bread, and a flask of Elixir against the night chills and paludals. He took his *Orator* and *Elocution* and his Grimshaw too, but they weren't help enough. What he wanted was a book that did for *thinking* what Cradok's *Western River Pilot* did for the River: something to map the shoals and snags and teach you how to run the bends. This argument had a double-back in it as bad as any the Old Man had ever thrown him.

He ate supper for strength, a sip of Elixir against the chill as evening came down. The Elixir warmed his chest and belly, and made his thoughts squirm more energetically without helping them make more sense. The only thing that got clearer were his wishes and hankerings. He wished he had Ma here: she had a sharp-eyed way of listening at him that woke him up and helped him hone a sharp edge on his thinking. A small bright-eyed blackbird flipped into the pignut tree and perched, looking down at him speculatively. *All right then, you stand up there for Ma and let's see what comes of it.* Konkapot would have liked him talking things out with a blackbird. *But Konkapot is dead.*

The law of nature and of nature's God. Ma would say the same as Mam: *There can't a sparrow fall but the Lord is in it.* The bird bobbed her head, to signify that suited *her* notions.

"I don't like to be the one to say it," he told the bird, "but seems to me the Lord is a little careless when it comes to birds." And not just birds. *Everyone and everything dies, and I'm hanged if I can see the reason or justice in it. Not that it makes a difference what Abe Lincoln thinks.* Abe took another sip and stretched out on his blankets, the Elixir had a kind of softening effect on the knobby ground. "Here lies poor Lincoln 'neath the sod," he said. "Have mercy on his spirit, God. As he would have, if he was . . ."

The blackbird cocked her head at Abe. Abe's campfire made orange points in her bright eyes. While he'd been talking to her the dark had come down. He took another sup of Elixir against the chill. The sang-roots loosened the cramp in his brains and made it easier to talk to the blackbird.

Listen, he told her, *in my experience Providence don't take account of nothing smaller than the United States of America. Don't care for sparrows nor pigeons, don't care if Mam dies of Milk-sick, don't care if Uncle Mordecai kills a million Injuns and their camel and their ass, don't care if you buy dis 'ooman Catrun Massa—don't care if Gentry sells Sephus to be seasoned or whipped or worked to death on Red River. Providence ain't reasonable, nor kind, nor even mean the way a man or a woman would be: if there's any justice in it, it's cold and slow as drip-water wearing at a rock or tree-roots working at a fault in the stone till they pick it apart. Or it gathers blind like the River and drives downstream by its own heedless rule, busting out this levee and flooding the bottoms, raising up that levee for a man to grow sugar and sell niggers behind, drownding babies and floating steamboats with naked women painted on the sides full of actors and merchants, but always driving down and down and down the ways it is bound to go . . .*

. . . and he was adrift on the River, rushing swift and silent towards the rising shadows. A black ball bobbed in the welter alongside, a face—

Sephus! His eyes were white . . .

The River foaming rolled Sephus under and he was gone in the terrible hurl of dark water that still rushed Abe headlong towards the shadows, lifting him sailing him into the . . .

. . . Sunlight?

Sunlight flickering through leaves. There was a tree-root sticking in his back. Ouch.

Abe lifted his head—his brains bulged a little and his eyes watered. The Elixir: it was greased lightning going down, but heavier'n a sack of lead shot waking up next day.

It wasn't till he had gone down to the Sangamon and washed the sleep out of his eyes that he realized the gravity in his brains was more than the dregs of the Elixir. Whether it was the bird, the books, the sang-roots, or something else that gave it to him, his head was full of argument—pretty *heavy* argument too, if he was any judge.

That was a signifying dream that come to him: he reckoned it meant Sephus was dead. And it was on him how Sephus died—maybe not the whole of it, but a good piece of it. It was the dead weight of the man Sephus that give his argument that leaden heft in his mind. It was almost more than he could carry—almost. But it was his best holt, and if it wasn't good enough for the work . . . ? Then he'd take his whupping. And first thing next morning get out of bed and whup Jack Armstrong in front of Clary's Grove and New Salem both. And if he lost that one too . . . ?

Well, he'd done what he could. Whup, die, or go to Texas—he was never more ready for anything in his life.

New Salem, April 2, 1832

The Clary's Grove Boys, hilarious, clad every one in his finery and foofaraw, hailed their champion to the goose-pulling ground. The crowd opened up to make way for the Boys, who bullied up half the wide circle of bodies that framed the wrassling ring. From the opposite side here came Long Abe Lincoln, head and shoulders above the crowd he waded through.

Every man in New Salem district, and every boy who could get away from chores, was in the crowd. The women were supposed to keep away, but most found places at the upstairs windows of the Herndons' house and Onstott's cooper shop, which had a view of the grounds. Of the Club only Fat Jack Kelso stood with Abe and Denton Offutt. Rutledge and Graham took their stand in sight of the ground where a man was free to suppose they had come in the ordinary course of business. If they joined the crowd they would appear to countenance a spectacle that could do their candidate no good. But to stay at home might suggest they did not support Abe. Besides, they were as het up as every other man woman and child in the county to see who would come out on top.

Offutt and Uncle Clary shook hands and gave their wagers (ten dollars silver, each) to Babb McNabb to hold. Ten dollars was the least of it: the wagering had gone on for days, odds running from even-up to Armstrong, five against three.

Jack glowered at Abe. His retainers, Royal Clary and Pleasant Armstrong and Bully Bob Kirby, stripped off his cockfeathered hat, fringed hunting-shirt, and white undershirt. Jack swelled up his chest so the muscles rolled across his breast and back and upper arms. He roared like a bear, bulging his eyes out. The Clary's Grove Boys hollered for Jack to go on and show that Bean-pole who was boss! The whole crowd bellowed its joy, and Armstrong felt his strength swell with it.

Jack stomped up to meet Lincoln and McNabb in the middle. He was shorter than Lincoln by a head, but a good bit wider in the shoulders and hips, heavy-boned, heavy-muscled. At the first look, Abe was just that bean-pole the Boys had called him, lean and narrow throughout his whole extraordinary length, so narrow his head looked oversized. But Armstrong had a closer sight of what Lincoln had hid under his ragged shirt and pants: his chest was solid, lean twists of muscle showed in his neck and shoulders, his arms were like braided cable. Those arms were plenty long too—sort of freak-ish long, as if Lincoln had unfairly spliced on an extra foot of reach. It gave Jack Armstrong to think about that story of the ax held straight out while a man counted one hundred.

Little McNabb was dwarfed by the two wrasslers, but he had the law to lend him dignity. "This here's straight wrasslin', not a scuffle. No kickin' no buttin' no gougin'. No *grabbin'* holts below the belt, but you kin hip-throw an' bang shins all you're a mind to." He looked from one to the other to see he'd been heard. "Shake hands, and git at it."

The Boys hollered for blood. The two men hunched their backs and circled, swiping for a hold first with this arm, then that. The Boys were screaming for Jack to close and whup that son of a mule, but they didn't have to get past that pair of long-handled scythes Lincoln was swinging at him—grinning all the time so goddamn calm and pleasant.

Lincoln let his hands drop. Jack saw his chance and jumped in roaring, charging the center of Lincoln's chest in a bull-rush with arms wide.

He must have blinked, because instead of busting through Abe's ward to slam chests grapple and throw him back, Jack only bumped him—spoiled his own balance—and suddenly found he had run his neck into the crook of Abe's left arm, and Abe was slamming him across the belly with a thigh hard as a log of wood trying to get a hip-throw, and then Abe's other arm like some horrible giant snake come grappling around him, squeezing and scrunching up under the edge of his ribs to drive the wind out of him, to start his feet . . .

Jack felt his ground snatched away, he was horribly light in the air, then the earth slammed him head-to-heels.

"That's a fall!" hollered McNabb, and the Boys groaned jeered and complained. But there was a lot of hollering for Abe now, Fat Jack Kelso howling, "A touch a touch! O think not, Percy, to vie with me in glory any more!"

Abe offered Jack his hand. Jack batted it off and hauled himself up. Offutt was bowing to the crowd as if it was himself had made the throw. Clary was purple with chagrin, crying foul, promising vengeance, the Boys clamoring like wolves over the corpse they would make of Longshanks if he didn't wrassle fair.

Jack stood straight, trying not to show he was sucking wind, flinching the muscles across his back to feel if they were hurt. The hollering of the Boys was like dogs barking at him, *Git 'im Jack Git 'im Jack*, dang if you think it is so easy whyn't *you* come try it and let *me* do the hollerin'? He wished they'd let him alone, but they wouldn't. They barked him back into the center of the ring.

Abe's long ugly face was solemn, and the white-blue eyes met Jack's straight and calm. Jack had the sense Abe knew what he was thinking, and knew Jack knew it too. It was almost funny: the two of them out here. Might have been better if there wasn't nobody around, but only the two of them, man to man.

"If you're ready," said McNabb, "then git at it!"

This time Jack was careful. No bull-rushes. They hunched and circled, reaching and slapping arms away, Jack easing in a little bit each time around, a quarter-step, a half—he banged Abe's forearm aside and closed, his left shoulder digging into Abe's breast. They clinched, freeing an arm to snatch for a hold, quick leg-kicks as they risked their balance to hook a leg behind. Then they gave that over and stood grappled, front to front, legs braced and straining, arms locked. In the crowd the betting swung to Jack, he looked heavy and solid against Offutt's whip-lean boy, and you had to like his weight and low position in a straight grapple.

Only Jack couldn't budge him. It wasn't reasonable. The Clary's Grove Boys were howling, Uncle Clary beside himself with rage. But Jack couldn't budge him. He was straining every muscle in his body full out, his toes clawed in the ground, pushing with his legs, spine stiff as a musket, the muscles of his neck swole with the force of his pressure, arms bulging, hands going numb. But inside his head he was nothing, he was light as air, wondering as if it was happening to someone else, *I can't budge him no more than if he was a rooted tree.* It wasn't reasonable.

Lincoln's brown skin was nearly black with straining: but his white eyes looked very cool and steady. Jack felt Lincoln gather himself a little—then felt Lincoln begin to bear down slow and steady, felt himself begin to bend down under it, to bend back . . . *I am going to lose,* Jack's thought blew around inside his head, *and there ain't a goddamn thing I can do about it.* He wished the Boys would quit their yapping and leave him alone. *Get mad,* he told himself, *get mad get strong.* He was losing the match, losing Uncle Clary's bet, he'd have to eat his brags and the brags of all his friends and kinfolk too, the Boys piling it on his head even now with their goddamn yapping and bellering, Uncle Clary yelling: *"For Christ's sake, Jack, throw the son of a bitch any way you can!"*

Done by God! Jack loosed his right arm, dropped, and slammed his hand between Lincoln's legs, *crutch-hold goddamn you!* heaved him off his feet, then throwed him sideways and down. *"Got you you son of bitch!"* he roared blind mad, next thing he would knee-drop and bust his ribs . . .

But hands were grabbing him, Kelso, McNabb, his brother Pleasant . . . The crowd was hooting, cries of "Foul!" popping off like scattered shots. The crowd was mad enough for some hardy souls to push against the Boys—and the Boys abashed enough so they didn't push back.

It came down hard on Jack Armstrong right then and there, in the middle of that crowd, standing over Abe Lincoln with every eye in New Salem on him. He had showed out shameful. Fouled a man he couldn't whup fair. He knew it, so did Abe, and all the people there—even the Boys knew it. His eyes pinched, he shook his head, he couldn't make out what to do, what a man was supposed to do in such a fix. He looked down at the man he had throwed.

Lincoln met his eye: not mad, not jeering, just earnest. He reached out his hand. Jack got the idea. He reached down and hauled Abe back up onto his legs. Abe nodded thanks, but it was Jack that was grateful. Lincoln turned and lowered his head at Uncle Clary. "If you want a scuffle, Clary, why don't you come get one *yourself.*"

Clary turned red. The Boys eased away from him. Lincoln wouldn't let him off: stood there staring him straight in the eye. He had to answer. "Naw," he said, trying to wave off his shame with a swipe of his hand, "go on an' wrassle."

A sigh ran through the crowd. Some no doubt sorry there would not be a grand riot, Abe Lincoln versus the Clary's Grove Boys. Some satisfied to see Clary put in his place.

McNabb took his stand in the center and beckoned Abe and Jack to him. "Let's go ag'in, boys. Whenever you're ready."

Abe and Jack stood looking at each other, as if each waited for the other to hunch his back and start to circle. Abe grinned. "Jack, if we keep on we are liable to find out who is the best wrassler in Sangamon County." Jack nodded. Abe lifted his eyebrows like a pleasant notion just come to him: "On the other hand, if we stop now New Salem can boast she is home to the *two* best wrasslers in Sangamon County."

Jack Armstrong considered. Then he smiled. He felt as light and clean and peaceful as ever he felt in his life. He stuck out his paw, and when Lincoln took it clapped him round the shoulder and give him a bear hug—a tight one, to show his strength. Then he rounded on his Uncle, pointed a finger at him and cried, "Drinks on Uncle Clary!" The Boys mobbed them, whopping Abe and Jack and themselves on the back, and swept off to the Grocery shouting victory.

McNabb, Offutt, and Kelso were left like flotsam in the backwash. McNabb took the twenty dollars out of his pocket and gave them to Offutt. "One fall for Abe, the second a foul. I reckon you win the bet."

Offutt hefted the coin. "That's my boy Abe," he said.

"Not for long," said Kelso.

McNabb looked after the mob. "By Josaphat," he said, "I can't believe he done it. That was the coolest thing I *ever* see."

Kelso said, "Maybe. But I have seen one to match it."

New Salem, April 1, 1832

What Kelso had in mind was the debate the night before, "Resolved: that the institution of negro slavery is contrary to the law of nature, and of nature's God," Dr. Allen arguing the affirmative and Abe Lincoln the negative.

James Rutledge regretted the necessity of going through with the debate, which could only harm Lincoln's prospects. Even Mentor Graham—who held slavery was a providential institution, given to bring the benighted heathen of darkest Africa into the Gospel light—Graham felt a grievance with Dr. Allen. "It was a trick, and a mean one at that, to put the boy where he must defend a principle obnoxious to him."

Oddly, Jack Kelso, who held views opposite to Graham, was willing, even eager, to see how Abe would handle himself. "It don't signify what the boy says, or even thinks, about the question. If a man is to get on in politics, and serve his people, he must argue for things that aren't near to his heart—maybe even for that which his soul abominates, if his constituents adore it."

So be it then. Abe put on a clean shirt for the evening, and had worked upon the pitifulness of some good woman to such an extent as to get her to darn up his elbows and patch his knees. Dr. Allen's face was buffed to a cleanly pink shine, his collar and shirt-front crisp and white, he wore a soft woven coat of gray wool.

The Doctor rose up, and spoke for the half of an hour by the glass. He reviewed the Scriptures on the question of Christian holding Christian in bonds, and Graham (with sinking heart) heard him anticipate Abe's possible citation of "servants obey your masters." Then reviewed the Natural Law, showing its consistency with the Moral Law, a thing evil in the one producing with mathematical certainty evil in the other. And wound up with a grand review that took in manufacturing and shipping statistics, fluctuations in the price of the staple, the British Empire, the soaring flight of Freedom's Bird, and the Declaration of Independence. He even managed to condemn slavery without conceding an inch to the superstition of negro equality. Graham judged the arguments sound enough that John C. Calhoun himself might have "nullified," but could not have answered them.

Then Abe got up on his legs. His shoes were a misfortune, and he had destroyed by nervous rumpling whatever hope of decency he had combed into his hair. He had a paper in one out-size fist, clinched hard enough to fuse it in a crumpled mass. He never even tried to look at it. He looked off over the head of every man, into the far unlit corner of the Rutledge tavern's main room. What he said was spoke in an ordinary conversational way—except he was talking past them, to those shadows in the corner. He said: "Well, I ain't got all that much to say. I was taught, when a boy, that the natural world is in the Lord's keeping. It is writ so in Scripture, I believe. My understanding of what is meant by 'the law of nature and of nature's God,' is that the Lord made the world; and being good He made it good, and meant it to be kept so. I was taught, and read it in Scripture too, that there can't a sparrow fall in the wilderness but the Lord will see—and take keer of it—make good the evil done to it."

He paused, and pressed his lips into a grim line. He looked sad, his white eyes burned off into the shadows.

"But when I 'came a man," he said quietly, "and come to look at the world, what did I see? Weasel eats the sparrow, wolf eats the weasel, man kills 'em all—I can see the sense of that, I can see the *nature* of it: what I can't see is the *providence*, or the justice, or the law of it. They say a sparrow can't fall—but I've seen pigeons fall out of the trees in their thousands, shot, knocked down with poles, busted on the ground with clubs, more killed than we could have et in a year—listened hard all through it, and never heard a word spoke for their sakes. I seen Milk-sick . . . I seen . . . I've seen Milk-sick take off the best and kindest woman ever breathed a Christian breath, and leave a mean selfish squint-eyed bully to track his boots across the world. I don't see the justice in that; I don't see the providence.

"I see one man lord it over another, by his strength or riches. I see one man make another crawl, and *smile* crawling. I see one man buy another, buy a woman away from her child, and sell them like they was hogs—and I see men and women beg for a kind man to come buy them, to save them being worked or seasoned to death on the Red River. If you was to ask, every one of those men—the proud and mean and the crawling poor and shameful, the buyers and the boughten—every one would say he was a Christian—say it was the Lord's providence he should be who he was, where he was, doing what he's doing. I can't deny that that is nature. That is the world as it is give to us."

He stopped. He lowered his eyes, and leveled them at Dr. Allen, then Rutledge, then Graham, then Kelso. "I can't deny that that is nature. But I don't see the providence in it. Nor the *law*: leastways, not no law that takes account of sparrows—or poor men—or women—or niggers."

He looked off into the corner, and nodded to his shadowy interlocutor. Looked down at the crumpled unread paper in his hand. Then he took his seat.

There was a horrified stunned silence.

Dr. Allen rose, hesitantly, unsure whether to begin rebuttal. "I'm sorry," he offered, ". . . is that all? I mean, is that your argument?"

Abe signified it was.

Allen cleared his throat, and glanced uneasily around. There was some trick, he was certain, but for the life of him could not tell what it might be. Perhaps Kelso . . . but no—the fat blacksmith was wringing his hands, Graham looked nauseated, Rutledge bereft. Camron gave the Doctor a grim nod. "Well then," said the Doctor, "I'm afraid, my boy, you've made my rebuttal rather difficult"—he laughed a little—"or rather easy, I'm not sure which! You haven't offered a single argument in favor of the proposition that slavery is consistent with the law of nature, and of nature's God. All you have done—and I cannot believe this was your intent—all you have done is offer evidences that the moral law, and the providence and justice of God, have no relation to nature—none whatever."

"Yes," said Abe, "you have understood me about right."

"By thunder!" cried Camron. "That is blasphemy!"

Dr. Allen reached out a hand as if to snatch Camron back, the outburst had broken the thread of his rebuttal. But it was no use, they were all hollering and shushing each other at once, Camron castigating Fat Jack for filling the boy's head full of Bad Tom Paine, Kelso denying he had but defending his right to do so if ever he . . . Rutledge was a Deist when feeling respectable and an Epicurean when feeling his oats—but Abe had just about took *his* breath away. But he recovered himself, pounded his stick on the floor-boards, and demanded they hush and let Abe and the Doctor finish.

Dr. Allen was sweating now. He was either about to win the debate and show up Rutledge for his choice of a buckskin as candidate, or he was about to fall through the smartest trap one debater ever laid for another. "Then Lincoln," he demanded, "you admit all you have offered in argument is a denial that nature is governed by the law of God?"

Lincoln was cool. "If by *law of God* you mean justice for the critter and the man—yes, I have said I don't see evidence such a law exists."

"Why man," said the Doctor, "that isn't an argument! It is simply blasphemy."

"Yes," said Lincoln. "The root of any law has got to be justice. So if slavery *ain't* against the law of nature and God, that can only be because there *ain't* any justice in nature—and so there can't be no God, neither."

Camron rose in outrage, all he could hear ringing over and over again was Abe Lincoln denying the existence of the Lord! Rutledge and Graham jumped between, hauled Camron off, trying to get him to see it. He *wouldn't* see it.

Meanwhile Dr. Allen slumped in his chair, stunned. Kelso loomed over him: "Play it square after this, won't you? If you want to hurt him, you can spread this around."

Allen met Kelso's eye. "I'm honor-bound by our rules—what's said here is for argument only."

"Damn the rules and you too," Kelso growled. "You know, don't you, it wasn't any blasphemy."

The Doctor looked like he needed a dose of something. "No, you're right. It wasn't meant for blasphemy."

But it took a lot longer than that to convince Camron, long after the others had left, and Abe too—Kelso giving him a comforting pat on the shoulder and a promise to make it good with Camron. The persuasion was complicated by the fact that one of the persuaders, Graham, thought what Abe said *was* blasphemy—only spoken thoughtless, and not out of heathenism. That mollified Camron, and Rutledge would have settled for that.

But not Jack Kelso. "You don't see it, do you? Not any of you." He shook his head wonderingly. "Young Abraham went and found the only way there was to win that debate, without arguing against his own principles." The others objected, but Jack overrode them: "Of course he won. He won on *rebuttal*. He tricked Doc Allen into asking him that question, so *he* could answer: The only way slavery *ain't* against the law of nature and nature's God, is if there ain't neither law nor God."

The light dawned, but slowly. Rutledge saw it first: "So if there *is* a law of God . . ."

"If!" cried his nephew-in-law.

"My word," said Graham, "he argued the negative, while maintaining the truth of the positive." The joke suddenly dawned on the schoolmaster: "He turned Allen's rebut into his own summation! Hee hee hee!"

"He won the debate without compromising his principles," said Kelso, "and risked all his prospects with us to do it—and you know danged well he ain't got anything *but* those prospects. Now you tell me: have you ever seen anything *cooler* than that?" Kelso shook his head, and gave Rutledge a look. "Remind me in future: if young Mister Lincoln ever raises my bet, I will call or fold my hand."

Rutledge mused, "You're right, Jack. He has got *some* iron in him, anyways. Too bad this ain't the kind of thing you can set before the people."

"No," said Kelso, "people prefer Jack Armstrong's sort of iron. I hope Abe whups him tomorrow—whups him as good as he whupped Allen tonight."

Rutledge shrugged, "I'd rather it was something more honorable than a brawl."

"Pray for war," said Kelso.

Camron sniffed. Graham had a notion, and said: "Mind what you pray for."

New Salem, April 18–20, 1832

The mounted courier, two days out of Vandalia, spatterdashed into town on the puddled track from Springfield just before noon. He called James Rutledge out of his tavern and handed him the Governor's call to arms: "Fellow Citizens! Your country requires your services. Black Hawk and his Indians have assumed a hostile attitude, and have invaded the State . . ." Then he rented a fresh horse on the Governor's credit and pounded off westward to Beardstown. Rutledge clanged the iron triangle that hung by the door, summoning all in earshot to assemble and pay heed:

"The militia of New Salem is hereby called out. All able men will meet here—mounted, with arms, accooterments, and five days' rations—day after tomorrow, as near first-light as may be. They will march for Richland, where the Sangamon County troops will assemble and elect officers. They will then proceed to Beardstown, for swearing-in. Any man who does not come to muster will be fined one dollar, cash money."

The day of the muster Abe was up before first-light. Offutt snored in his room off the store. Abe had a good buckskin hunting-shirt to wear, decent pants (an old pair of Jack Armstrong's, repaired for him by Jack's wife, Hannah), and boots refurbished gratis by the cobbler. New Salem would not send a soldier off looking discreditable. The new rifle he shouldered was only half his—he was partners in the piece with Offutt. Abe had all the other accooterments for service but the horse. The animal he shared with Offutt was spavined, so Jack Kelso had said Abe might borrow one of his.

Jack had the animal ready in his stable, a stumpy brown mare with hairy hocks and ears like a jackass. They talked horse while the street outside got loud with militiamen, and dozens of men women and children who came to send each of them off. "War fever," said Kelso, "the whole district is down with it. Symptoms plain enough: patriotism, with whiskey complications. I'm hoping you ain't caught it."

Abe grinned: "Well I'm goin', ain't I?"

"Oh, you don't want that fever to be a soldier. Can't tell what fever will make you do: whup the world, run away, or do bloody massacre." He gave Abe a shrewd look. "So keep a cool head. We don't want a hero, what we want is a man for legislature. 'The paths of glory lead but to the grave.'"

Abe gave him a straight look: "What paths don't?"

. . .

"Here he comes!" hollered Jack Armstrong, and waved Abe to join him at the head of the column. The other troopers were already mounted. The chosen twelve were, most of them, sons of the town fathers—the new generation off to fight the Indian as their fathers had done in their day, and their grandfathers before them. They yipped and waved Abe up to the head of the column, glad he was with them—as if his being with them was a guarantee of good luck and a good time for all.

Annie Rutledge's pale face flashed in the crowd, framed in a blaze of hair. From the height of Kelso's horse Abe gave her a straight look and touched off a blush that took her like fire in dry brush.

Then with Abe and Jack at the head the New Salem contingent of Mounted Rifles went clop-jouncing out Main Street. Miss Warburton remarked to Miss Potter that Mr. Lincoln could use shorter legs or a taller animal: his feet hung so low it looked like he was riding a six-legged horse. Miss Potter wished to know, What did Miss Rutledge think?

Miss Rutledge had never took no notice of Abe Lincoln in the first place.

Misses Warburton and Potter rolled their eyes, they knew what *that* signified.

Once they cleared the town the company slowed to a lazy horseback amble. It was a fine, sweet-aired spring day. Abe felt himself *growing*, expanding. The broad reaches of the sky were about his limit. He was on the road to History at last, armed and friended and hot on Black Hawk's trail. Tonight they would join up with the rest of the County and elect officers. *With Jack and Clary's Grove to politick the other towns, I will bet Jack Kelso's horse I can get myself elected captain.* This was how all of them started: Columbus and Boone and Washington, Mordecai and Moses, they all went out after Injuns, or in the case of Moses *Egyptians*, which was nearly the same thing.

The sun drew a moist haze out of the tall prairie grasses through which they rode. Saddles squeaked, canteens sloshed, tin pans panked and ponked. Usil Meeker rattapanked his drum, Royal Clary's Jew's-harp boynged and boybadadded, and the New Salem troop sang,

> "Old Black Hawk may be bold as brass,
>   But we're the boys to chop his ass—
> You Injuns *git*—and start to-*day*!
>   O'er the hills and far away.

> "O'er the hills and crost the plain,
>   Through burnin' sun and pourin' rain,
> Our country calls and we obey,
>   O'er the hills and far away."

Abe was happy—as happy as ever he had been since Mam. He wasn't afraid of the war, not a bit. It come to him, like prophecy, that it would be easy, much easier than the River had been. He wasn't but a boy when he took on the River. Now he was a man growed. A man respected. A man followed by the strongest and roughest, the finest in New Salem. He'd lead his people to the war and through it, and when he came back he'd ride his horse right up to that stump on the edge of the goose-pulling grounds where the candidates gathered to address the people.

I will look out over New Salem, and they will be watching and waiting on me, all of them: James Rutledge the best man in town, and dour Camron, and Doc Allen that used to think he was the smartest man in New Salem but now he knows different. Jack Kelso with his wise grin: will he think I have come back a hero? Well Jack, a man's a man for a' that. Maybe Denton Offutt will still be there, I hope so, he's the only one knows how far I've come. And Jack Armstrong that used to be the Big Bull of Sangamon County? He'll be there, and Clary's Grove with him, to whoop for me and see I don't lack parade.

And she'll be there: Miss Annie Rutledge, her clever head her quick tongue her cat-green eyes, red-haired girls is randy girls and I am her hankering or if I ain't yet I will be soon enough—the same as she is mine. All it needs is her to see me standing up there on the stump, New Salem's favorite son. And when she hears what I will say she will rise to me and shine love in her green eyes, and open me her secret self like a book of a thousand and one stories . . .

This was dreams of course. He knew that when he did stand up on that stump what he said would be the same he had agreed with Rutledge Graham and Kelso, the same as in the letter they put in the *Sangamon Journal:* River improvements. Steamboats. Relief of debtors. "That every man be enabled by education to read the histories of his own and other countries, by which he may duly appreciate the value of our free institutions." And the laws of estray. "I am young and unknown, have no wealthy or popular relations . . ."

Oh, but in his heart and spirit he would be speaking a different speech altogether, suiting the word to the action the action to the word, and he wondered and he hoped, and under that huge open sky and grass-billowing prairie his heart rose to a certainty: that She would hear the speech underneath his speech, and see behind his ugly face and candidate's smile the truth of what he was:

I am Abraham Lincoln—the Bull of the Lick from Pigeon Crick! Half-horse, half-alligator, and blood-nephew to the meanest son of a bitch west of the mountains. The universal sky is my shake roof and I stake my claim to the whole American republic.

I've been mothered twice and not fathered even once. I pass for quality with the b'iled shirts and a rowdy with the coon-hats. I have seen the elephant and heard the owl hoot. I can track like an Injun, dance like a negro, shoot like a Kaintock, lie like a drummer, and cipher past the Rule of Three. I can out-chop out-wrassle out-talk and out-think any man in this district. I can shoot or hold fire, according to my need. I have wrassled the Old Man, rode his back, and made him tote my goods. I've measured rivers with a stick and made their currents run to rule. Sparrows may fall, but if they fall in my district I will see it don't happen regardless. I've read the books, now I'm fit to have the books read me.

I've been to the bottom of the River and come back to tell the tale. I ain't afeared of Nothing. I can smile and murder whiles I smile, change colors with the chameleon and set the murd'rous MacIvell to school. Can I do all this and cannot get elected to the General Assembly of the sovereign state of Elanoy, that earthly Eden garden-spot of the West? that paradise of speculators rattlesnakes Milk-sick patriots and sang-root whiskey?

The blue sky stood high and spread creation wide around him. Islands of trees misted with haze stood like tow-heads in the rippling flow of the tallgrass prairie. Abe stood tall in his stirrups, balancing tipsy and waving his hat like a daredevil on a fence-rail.

"Whoo-hoo!" he hollered at the open sky. *"Whoo-hoop!"*

Afterword

Abe is a novel based on the early life of Abraham Lincoln. It draws deeply on historical scholarship, but it is not a biography. Rather, it is an imaginative re-creation of life as a young Abe Lincoln might have lived it, and of the people, scenes, and influences that helped produce his character and shape his conscience.

My account of Lincoln's family life, of the books he read, and of conditions and customs in the frontier settlements of that time are based on extensive research. His townsmen in Kentucky, Little Pigeon, and New Salem are generally given their proper names and roles, as far as research can establish them. However, I had to imagine or invent most of the personal quirks and incidents that develop them as characters and establish their significance for Abe.

Lincoln actually made two flatboat trips to New Orleans: in 1828–29 with Allen Gentry, and in 1831 with Denton Offutt, John D. Johnston, and John Hanks. I merged the two journeys into one (in 1828–29) to dramatize their effect as a turning point in Abe's development. My accounts of river navigation, of life in the towns, cities, and plantations along the river, of the ecology of various regions and their agricultural methods are as accurate as research can make them. The episode in which the flatboat passes safely through a levee break is based on the passage of Federal gunboats through a break at Yazoo Pass, during Grant's 1863 Vicksburg campaign.

My portrayal of slavery and nineteenth-century racism derives from forty years of reading and research. Cahoon's interrogation of Octavius is based on an actual incident, and the main events of the Regulators' campaign on Roundaway Bayou are based on the outbreak of civil violence in Madison County, Mississippi, in 1835. Sephus's story was suggested by the autobiography of Josiah Henson, an escaped slave who was a model for Harriet Beecher Stowe's Uncle Tom.

Junius Brutus Booth, Frances Wright, and Joseph Davis are historical figures who were active in the Mississippi valley in 1828–31. My versions of their ideas, character traits, and personal relationships are based on standard biographies. There is no evidence Abe met any of them—though Booth was performing in New Orleans in February 1829. What I have done is to transform indirect or "reading" relationships into face-to-face encounters, dramatizing some of the influences that played upon Lincoln's developing intelligence.

Joseph Davis was indeed a friend and follower of Wright and Owen. He offered Wright "expert advice" on managing negroes, and in 1828 counseled her to exile a recalcitrant slave woman named Dilly to his own plantation.

$14.00
$21.95/Canada
FICTION

A *New York Times* Notable Book

One of 10 Best Books of 2000—Salon.com

"*Abe* is such a rich and beautiful portrait of Abraham Lincoln that I barely know where to begin. So I'll just say this: read this book." —*Raleigh News & Observer*

A stunning work of historical imagination, *Abe* immerses the reader in the pas Abraham Lincoln kept hidden: the isolating poverty and frontier violence that shaped his character. Marked by the death of his beloved mother and the struggle to keep reading and learning in the face of his father's fierce disapproval, Ab perseveres, growing into the man who changed the course of American history.

Abe comes of age in the course of a dramatic flatboat journey down the Ohio an Mississippi Rivers to New Orleans. Along the way, Abe and his companions encounter slavery firsthand and experience the violence—and the pleasures—of rough rive towns, plantations, and the cities of Natchez and New Orleans. Numerous historica figures make appearances alongside the colorful characters of the Mississippi: preach ers and vigilantes, planters and thieves, prostitutes and lady reformers. Transformed by what he has seen and done, Abe returns to make his final break with his father and to step out of the wilderness into New Salem—and history.

"Lively conversation, colorful characters, memorable scenes, and inviting prose . . . substantial achievement."
—*The Wall Street Journal*

"An entrancing, highly imaginative yet historically rigorous account."
—*Chicago Tribune*

© ART RICH PHOTOGRAPHY

RICHARD SLOTKIN is the Olin Professor and the former director o American Studies at Wesleyan University. His previous title include *Gunfighter Nation* (a National Book Award Finalist) *Regeneration through Violence* (also a National Book Award Finalist and a winner of the Albert J. Beveridge Prize), and *The Crater*.

ISBN 0-8050-6639-X

51400

9 780805 066395

Cover design by Raquel Jaramillo

www.henryholt.com